House of Fire & Magic

Myths & Outlaws

SHERRILYN KENYON

OLIVERHEBERBOOKS

HOUSE OF FIRE & MAGIC Woodward McQueen, LLC © 2024

Cover Design Copyright © Dar Albert Wicked Smart Designs

Page edge design by Painted Wings Publishing Service

Printed in the United States of America

Published by Oliver-Heber Books

0 9 8 7 6 5 4 3 2 1

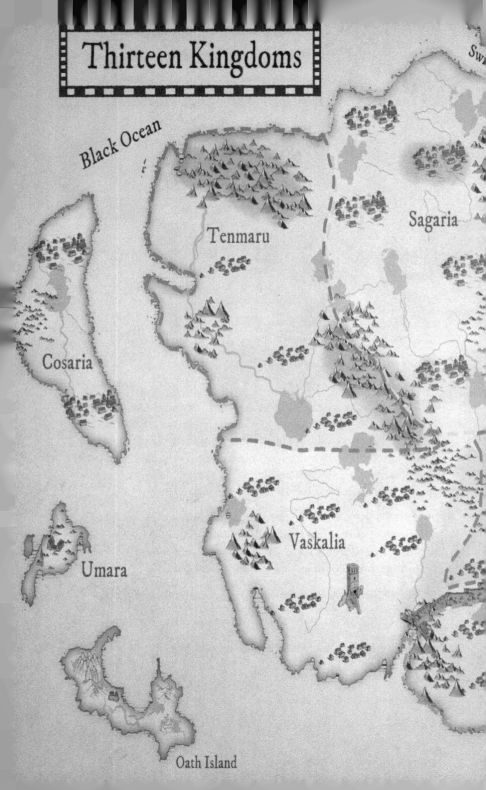

SherrilynKenvon.com

If you control magick, you control the world.

CHAPTER 1

"I need your help to kill a man." Tanis watched as the black unicorn she'd captured stopped struggling against the net that had caught it mid-run.

She had a bit of guilt over that. When she'd set the trap, she hadn't realized how hard the unicorn would hit it. Nor did she think it'd cause the poor thing to spin and land so hard on its side.

That had to hurt.

I'm so sorry.

She'd fallen into traps herself and knew firsthand how awful it was to be snared unawares, but she was desperate.

And, unlike the ones who'd trapped her, she'd meant no harm to the beautiful, majestic creature. Not really.

With a jet-black coat that shimmered blue in the fading light, the unicorn's silken mane begged to be stroked and brushed. Its eyes were an unholy shade of green that glowed with fury and told her just how much it wanted to pierce her heart with the deadly, black, spiral horn that jutted from the center of its forehead.

Unicorns were known to be every bit as lethal as dragons.

Even more vindictive and savage. They took no prisoners and never negotiated.

Yes, the unicorn High King had brought peace to the Thirteen Kingdoms. But he'd done so by slaughtering any and everyone who'd challenged him. It was said that the unicorn king was evil incarnate.

Worst of the worst. The very beast who had single-handedly hunted her species, and others, to the brink of extinction.

He reigned by exterminating anyone who questioned him. And not just that one person, either. Their family. Their friends. Their pets.

Anyone they were even remotely fond of.

So why are you trying to negotiate with one?

Because I'm a desperate idiot.

This was the dumbest idea she'd ever conceived in her life, but desperation rode her with spurs. She had no choice. Not if she was to claim the revenge that burned through her soul like lava.

As bad as she hated the unicorn race that had once preyed on hers, she hated one particular human even more. And nothing would stop her from feeling his blood on her claws.

Tasting his heart on her lips.

And this unicorn was the key to her greatest wish. So, if she had to trip him and bruise his ego a bit... small price to pay for what she needed.

If he killed her for it, that, too, was a price she was willing to pay.

Blinking slowly, the unicorn pinned a viciously cold stare on her. "You want *what*?"

Stunned he would deign speak to her, she crept closer while still keeping a respectable distance. "I need your help to kill a man."

His laughter filled the air. "You're a dragon. Is that not what you do for fun?"

Well... some of her brethren did. But there was a big difference between killing for survival and committing wholesale homicide. Being a unicorn, he might not understand that, but she certainly did.

"I refuse to kill an entire village of innocent people because I want one man dead. It seems rather harsh, if you ask me." Maybe not to the unicorn, given what she knew of them.

But the equity of that just didn't sit right with her.

"Why?"

Confused by his angry question, she stepped closer to the net that held him. "Why what?"

"Why do you want this one man dead so badly that you'd risk your life to trap me?"

That was easy enough to answer. "He killed my brother... while my brother slept. Coward snuck in as if my brother were a monster and not the best brother who'd ever lived. Best father and husband, too. Then, the real monster took my brother's head. I want him to pay for his crime!"

The unicorn tried to untangle its horn from the loop that held it. "Dragon slayer, you say?"

"Aye. A putrid, vile beast I have to find. I know you have

the magick to make me human. And I need that." Unicorns were born of magick the likes of which no other species could match, except for one, and it wasn't hers.

It was said they could do anything they wanted, even live forever. And there was only one thing she craved. "I want to look him in the eyes when I take his life and reclaim my brother's head from him. Please. Help me save my brother's honor."

Dash eyed the vengeful dragon curiously. With ombre scales of red to orange, she held a pair of dark-brown eyes that smoldered from her passion for vengeance.

Hell, she could blast him with fire right now. While it wouldn't kill him, it would take him centuries to heal.

Ruin his day most definitely.

Piss him off to absolutely no end.

Yet she refrained, and that restraint impressed him. And impressing him was a hard feat for any creature to accomplish.

He also understood her hatred for a human. They were treacherous, cutthroat bastards, first and foremost. Especially since he had one in particular he needed to spear with his horn. But then, dragons weren't much better than a human. Most days, they weren't better than maggots. Dragons, too, were known for their treachery.

And their treasure hunting. Before peace had been brokered between the reigning monarchs of the Thirteen Kingdoms, dragons had laid waste to entire nations for no other reason than to take their gold and jewels. No one knew exactly how wealthy the dragons were, but they were said to be richer than all the other Twelve Kingdoms combined.

Given his own experience with them, he could easily believe their riches were beyond measure.

Not to mention dragons and unicorns were natural enemies. Back in the day, dragons had helped wizards enslave his kind. Until unicorns had learned to command the same power those wizards had...

His horn itched as a reminder of what he had to lose.

And what he was desperate to find.

It'd been why he was rushing in such a state that he'd missed the lure the dragon had used to snare him. In his normal frame of mind, he'd have never fallen for such a trick.

Damn me.

And damn her as well.

"If I say no?"

She let out a tired sigh. "I don't like to hurt things."

Weird comment for a dragon, especially given their natural tendency to set things that annoyed them on fire. Not to mention, she'd be hard-pressed to harm him, given his powers. "But?"

"I need this. And I'm willing to do whatever it takes to get to the man who killed my brother. Please don't make me into something I'd rather not be. I just want justice."

How simple she made it sound. But life was never easy. Nor was it that simple. "If you kill this man, you'll become a killer, Madam Dragon."

"I know. But this is one life to appease my soul that craves equity for the life he took. And to keep that... that... *murderer,*" she spat the word as if she could taste it like bitter fruit, "from killing more innocents. If I don't stop him, his future killings are on me. I won't have that, either. Someone has to stop him from taking someone else's father from them."

That made perfect sense. He'd done worse to protect those he cared about.

And he intended to make his past sins look petty once he caught up to the man he was currently seeking.

As he looked into her clear, dark eyes and saw the depth of her grief and determination, it touched him. How could he deny her the very thing he was out to claim for himself? No one should lose a loved one. Not needlessly.

Especially not to cruelty.

And he wasn't hypocrite enough to deny her the very thing he wanted most in his life. The very thing he was out here, trying to claim.

Maybe if the death of his beloved sister wasn't so fresh, he would be hardened against the dragon's request. But Renata's loss was too recent.

Too painful.

And if there was anything in life he understood, it was justice. He'd dedicated his entire life to establishing law and order. To making sure that those who preyed on innocent lives paid for it.

The time of warlords and brutality had ended.

She would have her vengeance. It was her right to claim it.

"Very well. Free me and I'll grant you this favor." He would free himself, but he didn't want to expose his powers to her or risk her learning his real identity. The less anyone knew about him, the better.

She hesitated. "How do I know this isn't a trick?"

"I've given you my word. And, because I'm not human." Or a centaur or dragon.

"I've heard unicorns can be even trickier."

Well, that was true. His brethren had their moments as much as anyone else, he supposed. "Do you have a choice?"

Tanis cringed at his honest question. No, she didn't. She'd been lucky to trap one unicorn. Who knew if or when she'd be lucky enough to capture another. Her sisters had called her all kinds of stupid for even thinking of going after her brother's killer, and Ragna had forbidden it.

Never mind the fact that the next unicorn might not be so agreeable.

Given what she knew about their abilities, she was really at *his* mercy. Most likely, he could turn her into a toad or some other poor creature. She was lucky he hadn't already done so.

All she could do was hope he was a unicorn of his word.

"Very well." She used her powers to dissolve the net.

He shook himself free and snorted as he came to his feet.

Wow... he truly was a magnificent beast. While he was small compared to her dragon form, he was still powerful, and it was evident. His muscles rippled beneath that shiny coat. And though his shiny hooves weren't pointed or sharp, she was quite sure they were just as capable of doing as much damage as her black claws.

When he pawed at the ground and shook his head, Tanis tensed, expecting him to run for the trees or turn her into anything other than what she'd requested.

He didn't.

Instead, he stood steady as he eyed her with those piercing, vivid eyes. That horn in the center of his forehead held her attention... black as pitch, it looked even sharper than before. Longer. Deadlier.

"So, little dragon, what will you give me for this favor you ask?"

She blinked. "What?"

"Magick has a price. As such, it's seldom freely given. The spell you're asking for isn't easy to do. How badly do you want to become human?"

She hadn't thought of that. But he was right. Magick always took something from the one who commanded it. The wrong or right spell could even take the spellcaster's life. It was what made spellcasters so sought after.

And rich.

Every wizard she knew wanted to be reimbursed for the pain of the spell. For the mental and physical toll it took. That price was either paid by the one asking for it or the one the spell was being cast upon. Most of the time, they were one and the same person.

Sometimes, as she knew better than she wanted to, they weren't the same person–the victim had no idea they were being enchanted until it was too late. Sometimes, they were just hapless and at the mercy of the wizard and the one who'd paid them for their services.

Thankfully, that wasn't her case today.

"Whatever you want, I'll pay it."

He snorted at her answer. "You don't have a lot of experience negotiating, do you?"

Not really. As the youngest female born into the noble court of her Dragomir ancestors, she'd been surrounded by those out to build their reputations by tearing hers down. Backbiting sisters who lied about her to their father and mother. Courtiers who were jealous and out to rip her to shreds.

Opponents who wanted her dead and gone for no real reason. There was no negotiating with any of them as they wouldn't be deterred from their goals. They were too determined to destroy her for their own petty greed and wants.

As a dragon, she didn't require much and wanted even less. Most of the time, she just wanted to be left alone.

Because of all that, she didn't like others as a rule. The handful she'd put her faith in had betrayed her, thinking to advance themselves with her family or other nobles.

Or they'd actively plotted against her for no reason, other than entertainment. Only her brother and his wife had ever been kind to her. Davin had done his best to protect her and shelter her from their father's wrath, and their sisters' viciousness.

She didn't like the games that others played with dragons' lives. So she'd avoided those snares and the dramatics that went with them. "I've never had to negotiate before."

"It shows. I should warn you before you traipse through the human world, humans will not play fairly with you. They'll destroy your innocence. Think long and hard before you agree to this, because the knowledge of being human cannot be undone. Not even by magick."

Tanis knew he was right. Humans preyed on weakness and innocence, even more so than unicorns. She'd only been in their world once and it still fed her nightmares.

She loathed them all and had vowed to never go near their world again. Not for anything.

But that old grudge no longer mattered. She had to see this through.

For Davin.

No matter what her father said or what punishment he'd deal to her later, she couldn't allow Davin's head to be some man's trophy. To be paraded around and mocked. It sickened her all the way to her soul every time she thought about how they were treating Davin's remains.

When she'd fought her way back home after she'd been taken and abused, and her father had wanted to banish her again, Davin, alone, had made sure that she wasn't a complete outcast.

Now, it was time for her to return that favor. She just wished he was alive to see it.

Pushing down memories she'd give anything to purge, she forced herself to do what was right. "I don't care so long as I kill that human beast. Painfully. With relish. Lots and lots of relish. And even more bloodshed."

"Are you sure you don't care? Because the price for magick of this magnitude is always the one thing you value most."

There was a note in his voice that warned her against this. One that told her to run as far away as she could. But she was set on her course.

Besides, what could he demand from her that hadn't already been taken? Brutally.

At least this time, she had a choice.

There was nothing left in her life that she valued. Davin had been it.

"Name your price, Unicorn."

The unicorn stared into her eyes for a moment as if he could see all the way into her battered and weary soul. "Then the price is your freedom."

You've got to be kidding me...

Tears caught in her throat as she realized that there had been one last shred of something she valued. One last semblance she'd managed to hold on to, even though they'd taken it from her for a while.

Of course, he wanted to own her. What had she been thinking? He was a unicorn. They were soulless animals, just like the humans they worked with and sheltered.

Why would this one be any different?

Just set fire to him and to the village. Kill them all and be done with it.

That was the sanest course of action. Safest, too. And why not?

Haven't I suffered enough?

But Davin deserved honor. He'd been a true hero, and he'd taught her better. She would *never* shame his memory. He deserved to be buried whole. To have a sanctified funeral, surrounded by those who'd loved him, and placed in the catacombs with their noble ancestors.

His children deserved to bury their father with that honor. How could she deprive them of that?

Davin had been a royal prince who'd given mercy even when it'd cost him to give it. Shown her love even when he'd been mocked for that kindness. He would be with their ancestors where he belonged if it was the last thing she did. Not in the hands of those who thought him an animal.

Besides, she couldn't kill innocent children in the village, no matter how much she might hate humans. They didn't deserve to die because their parents were horrible people without conscience. Granted, those kids would most likely grow up to be the same awful, horrible monsters their parents were. But she wanted to believe some of them might be better. That they might do better.

I will not pass judgement on all of them because one of their kind did my brother wrong. Or me wrong.

Most of all, she deserved to have her one moment of vengeance in this world. In a life marked by misery, she wanted that pure second of bliss where she accomplished the one thing she wanted most.

Kill the bastard. Bathe in his blood. Devour his heart.

I could die happy with that.

After all, she wasn't just a princess. Thanks to an unconscionable beast, she'd been trained as a warrior. One who'd been forced to fight for food.

For her life.

No one would ever defeat her. Just like she'd done as a scared teen, she would find a way out of captivity. No matter what it took.

At least this time, she wasn't a scared child with no knowledge of their world. She knew how to survive among humans.

How to kill, if needed.

"Fine. Your terms are acceptable."

Her answer seemed to surprise him. "You understand what I'm saying. Your life will belong to me once you kill your dragon slayer. You won't be able to go home again to your family."

"I understand." Without Davin, she had no home or family to return to. No one there would welcome her.

He turned his head to give her a haunted stare. "Make sure you think this through. Being a human woman isn't an easy thing in this world, and once you're a dragon again, I will own you and you will live in Licordia, not Indara."

"I'm willing to risk it."

Dash inclined his head to her. If that didn't dissuade her, nothing he could think of would.

Damn. Being human was hard for those who were used to it. He couldn't imagine being a dragon turned human. Worse was being forced to live among others you didn't understand. His own memories of that nightmare were never far away.

But she was determined, and as such, he knew she wouldn't give this up. The next unicorn or wizard she trapped might not be so accommodating.

Or forgiving.

There was no telling what the wrong one might do to her.

How he wished he could make her reconsider, but far be it from him to deny her, her stupidity.

"Very well." There were worse things in the world than a pet dragon, he supposed. To his deepest chagrin, he actually knew a number of them.

Closing his eyes, he felt his horn heat up. This wasn't an easy spell, nor was it the first time he'd performed it.

For whatever reason, magickal creatures wanted to be human and humans wanted to be wizards. None of it had ever made any real sense to him. He loved being what he was and had no wish to be anything else.

Sadly, others weren't so content.

And the last time he'd cast this spell hadn't turned out so well for the man who'd craved a similar vengeance.

He was sure there was still a bitter old man in the world

who wanted to gut him. But as with the dragon, Dash had done his best to talk Thomas Drake out of his folly. Just like her, the gryphon had refused, swearing he couldn't live without having his revenge, even if it meant being human.

Desperate beings do desperate things.

He should know, given all he'd done in his wretched life.

"Brace yourself, Dragon."

CHAPTER 2

Dash waited until the dragon was centered, then he unleashed the spell she needed. Fire shot from his horn, toward the heavens, and it rained sparks over them.

The sparks turned to ash and, as they did so, her body began to transform. Her scales rippled and bubbled as they turned from their shimmering incandescent beauty to pale, opaque human skin.

She cried out from the pain.

He hated that for her, but birth was never an easy thing, and transformation was particularly nasty. It was to be expected.

What he didn't expect was the exquisite form she'd take.

Vibrant red hair cascaded over the face of an elfish beauty that came complete with pointed ears. Perfect lips and luscious curves the likes of which most only saw in their dreams.

She held her dainty hand up so that she could examine it. "I don't remember humans having claws."

He laughed at her earnest words. "They're fingernails, my lady. And they will break if you're not careful."

She didn't comment as she tried to push herself to her feet, then fell back down.

He smiled at the consternation on her face. "It takes a moment to adjust to being on two legs when you're used to four."

Lying flat on her back, she let out an exasperated breath. "Two legs are just not steady. What a stupid evolutionary thing. No wonder humans are only good for food or torching. I hate this!"

Dash smirked at her mini rant. "Two legs are weak, but you'll get used to them. I have all faith in you."

And to help protect her, he gave her the knowledge to instantly balance and run fast. Especially the latter as she would definitely need it in the human world.

Then again...

He took in her beauty and slight form and added the ability to defend herself with the strength of a male. She'd definitely need that to deal with the vermin who might be tempted to overtake her. While unicorns and dragons were mortal enemies, he had no wish to see her preyed upon.

No one deserved that and it was the last thing he wanted for anyone, especially a dragon he'd made vulnerable by granting her strange desire.

"Try standing now."

She let out a long, annoyed sigh, then rolled to her side so she could stand. Thankfully, she came easily to her feet and lifted her head with pride.

Until she tried to take a step. Then she wobbled and reached out to steady herself.

Dash shivered at the sensation of her dainty hand sinking into his dark coat. It'd been a while since he'd allowed anyone to touch him. Given his past, he wasn't keen on contact of any kind, especially when it came to females who were normally scheming ways to tie him to them forever.

Females who would do anything to seduce him because of his station and titles. Everyone was conniving and out for themselves—a hard, bitter lesson he'd learned far too young in his life. They saw him as a mark to be manipulated and used. A friend only so long as he gave them what they wanted. And the moment he didn't, he was an enemy to be eliminated. They flattered him to his face and lied about him the moment they were out of his earshot.

Or worse, they saw him as an enemy they wanted to assassinate.

And many had tried.

That was the sole thing he'd admired about his father. At least the old bastard had insulted and abused him in his presence.

But the dragon meant nothing by it. She knew nothing of him and that seemed to make it mean more than it should.

"Are you all right?" he asked.

Biting her lip, she slowly stepped away from him, then tripped on her skirt and fell back to the ground. "Ugh!" She slapped at the gathered material. "What is this thing?"

"It's called a dress. Women wear them."

"I don't like it. Why is it so heavy?"

Then it probably wasn't a good idea to leave her swathed in so much fabric. Even now, he could hear his sister complaining about wearing them for formal events. Renata much preferred hunting clothes for daily wear.

I don't see you standing in line for restriction, brother. When was the last time you wore a counselor's or king's robe,

hmm? And I'd pay good, hard coin to lace you into a tight corset. Just once. Let's see how you like it.

Shaking his head at the memory of his sister's repetitive rant, he traded the gown for an outfit more akin to what Renata normally donned. A light-green leather, loose corset covered by a short-sleeved brown jacket that was short in front but went to her ankles in back, and a matching pair of leather leggings and black boots.

Aye, that was vintage Renata. Right down to the ornate gold embroidery around the collar and sleeves. All that was missing was his sister's statement jewelry and preferred small tiara that had shone almost as much as her mischievous smile.

"You wear that well."

Tanis scowled at the unicorn's comment. "How do you mean?"

"The garb of a female archer and huntress. It looks good on you."

Her stomach wrenched at that word. "Huntress?"

"Not of dragons. Most female hunters seek smaller game such as birds or deer... or other men."

Ah. She could live with that. And honestly, she was grateful her breasts weren't hanging out of this outfit.

Nor was her rear. She actually liked it. If she couldn't

have her scales, this was a nice alternative. "I suppose I am hunting, aren't I?"

He inclined his head. "Indeed. One stupid, cowardly dragon slayer."

She straightened the hooded jacket with a quick jerk. Unexpectedly, a sack appeared at her feet.

Along with a sword.

With a frown, she toed the sack. "What's this?"

"Supplies. The sack, you drape over your shoulders. The sword—"

"I know what the sword is for." She'd seen enough of them used on her brethren, and had been stabbed too many times herself by overzealous morons.

Damn them all.

The last thing she wanted was to ever touch one. But given the fact that she no longer had talons or fire, she'd need some way to protect herself.

While his kind and humans often thought of dragons as mindless animals, dragons were no such thing. They were a peaceful race who preferred to live in herds, in their own mountainous kingdom, far away from everyone else.

That was why she wanted the heart of the man who'd invaded their kingdom and snuck up on her gentle brother. She still had no idea how the dragon slayer had managed it. How he'd been able to traverse into their lands, never mind her brother's home unseen, kill him, and then leave their island kingdom without anyone else knowing it.

Indara was isolated from the other kingdoms by intention. While gryphons, hippocampi and wyverns were welcome to settle and visit there, her father didn't tolerate other species or races. Visitors were required to register and only allowed to stay briefly. Their activities in Indara were heavily monitored, and she had no idea how anyone could breach their border without one of their visguard seeing it.

Because of their past grievances with dragon slayers and trophy hunters, a human would have stood out in Indara, and wouldn't have been allowed freedom in their realm.

Davin's death made no sense. No human should have been able to get near her brother.

And yet, that rat bastard had absolutely butchered him while Davin's hatchlings had hidden in horror. They would never be the same.

Even when her sister-in-law had returned to find them while they were hiding, they had refused to come out or speak a word of what they'd seen. It'd taken Marla more than a day before her little ones would leave their hiding spots.

Indeed, they'd screamed in terror the moment Tanis tried to see them and help her.

All because they were terrified their father's killer would return and kill them, too. Their fear was so bad, that Marla had taken them to her father's lands in the north of Indara, hoping to soothe them and let them know they were safe.

Tanis swallowed hard against the tears that misted her eyes. No hatchling should ever know such horror that it drove them from their home.

Why had she not been there that day?

Any other time, she'd have at least stopped by to chat with Davin for a little while. Instead, she'd spent that fateful day by the lake, reading.

If it's the last thing I do, I will avenge you, brother. I swear I'll see your enemy in pieces.

The unicorn is your enemy, too.

No. The unicorn race was an enemy to hers. As was the bastard unicorn who'd kidnapped her as a girl.

This particular unicorn had given her a chance to right a wrong. Granted his payment was harsh, but she had made the choice. Unlike Baracus, he hadn't kidnapped her and forced her to serve him against her will.

She'd sold her freedom for her brother's dignity. And she was grateful for the unicorn's assistance. Without him, she wouldn't have this chance.

"Thank you for helping me."

Dash was astonished by her sincerity. Honestly, he'd hoped his bargain would have awakened her common sense and kept her from her foolish quest.

Sadly, she was too similar to him. He would have made the same deal to get back at the mongrel who'd killed Renata.

I should have chosen something else for payment other than her freedom. He regretted it already. No one should ever be bound to another.

Having been forced into captivity himself, he couldn't bear the thought of it for anyone. It was why he'd vowed to never marry. End of the day, he couldn't stand the idea of anyone having any kind of sway over him, no matter how innocuous.

But the deal was cast. He'd forgotten that others weren't as fiercely protective of their freedom as he was. There was nothing they could do now except see it through. "I just hope you don't hold this against me. Remember, you wanted to be human, lady dragon."

She actually laughed. "Indeed. And, since you now own me, might I ask your name?"

"Dash."

She pressed her lips together with a determination he was sure would get her into even more trouble. "Regardless of what happens, I will always be grateful to you, Dash."

A part of him wanted her name as well, but names held power. They made the bearer real. Personable.

And since he had no doubt that they would become enemies once she killed the human she was after and came to regret this bargain, he had no intention of learning hers.

He was certain he would be her next target for execution. And he couldn't blame her. He wouldn't want anyone to have any authority over him, either.

When she eventually came for him, he needed to have no reservation in taking whatever steps required to protect himself.

He who hesitates dies. It was the one lesson he'd learned most in life.

Dash wanted nothing to put that hesitation in his attack. And he wondered if that had been what had killed Renata.

Had she hesitated when she should have struck?

Flinching, he wanted to bury that memory so deep inside that he *never* saw it again.

If only he could.

Every time he closed his eyes, he imagined her death. Her panic and pain when they'd driven her aground and then cut her horn from her forehead. The guilt that he hadn't been there to protect his sister was overwhelming. How could he have let this happen?

Just how much had she suffered? It was said that having a horn removed before death was the most excruciating pain a unicorn could endure.

No one survived it.

While he'd failed to protect her, he wouldn't fail to avenge her.

With that thought in mind, he fully intended to leave this dragon to complete her quest.

Until he noticed she was walking in circles.

"What are you doing?"

She paused at his question and gave him an adorable smirk. "How do humans and unicorns know which direction they're going?" She looked up at the sky, then around at the trees. "Everything looks the same from down here. Is there some special means you use to get your bearings? A magick homing beacon? Some inner compass? Is that what you have your horn for?"

He bit back a laugh at the frustration in her voice. In this form, she was as helpless as a child. "Where are you heading?"

"Auderley."

Odd... that was his destination as well.

Leave her to her vengeance. She's no concern of yours. You have a lot more to deal with and a lot more to worry about.

Dragons had declared war on unicorns to such an extent that they had once been virtually extinct. It was only now that his people were regaining their numbers.

And that was only thanks to him and the treaties he'd put in place.

Granted, but you swore you'd protect all *your people. Including dragons.*

His horn itched, reminding him again of Renata and what he owed to his sister and people.

True. The dragon was nothing to him. Yet his mind merged her current human form with that of his sister and he couldn't stand the thought of anything happening to the dragon because he'd made a bargain with her and left her without her innate abilities and powers.

You swore you would protect all your people...

It always came back to that, didn't it? He couldn't forsake his oath. No matter what, the dragons were one of the Thirteen Kingdoms.

Fuck me.

He would respect her quest and help her with it as that was his duty, too. Not to mention, it was ultimately his responsibility to find the culprit who'd taken her brother's head and make sure he didn't do that to anyone else.

You could assign someone else to help her run the bastard down.

It was why he had stewards and others. Ryper came to mind. Be a good use of his talents, for once. That ruthless little bastard might even enjoy it.

But his quest was personal, and he knew hers was, too. Since they were headed the same way...

What would it really cost him other than some time?

Using his powers, he created a saddle for her. "Climb on my back, and I'll take you there."

By her expression, he could tell his offer surprised her as much as it irritated him. "Why are you being nice to me after our bargain?"

"I have no idea." And he didn't. It really wasn't in his nature to be kind.

He was more likely to rip someone's throat out than he was to speak with them. Even Renata had called him 'jackass' more than 'brother.'

In truth, he prided himself on his surly nature. It tended to keep users and courtiers at bay.

Still, the dragon didn't move to accept his offer. Rather, she stood by his side with a frown. "Can you not just wish me there?"

He let out an irritated sigh. "My powers don't work that way. Again, all magick has a cost. Your clothes, the saddle and small such things are easy for me to pay. Magick is a hungry beast that always wants more and more to feed her. To teleport you that distance would require a much greater sacrifice. I can't afford to weaken myself, and you have nothing else to give to make it worth my while."

"Oh... then, thank you."

Yeah... thank you, he mocked her silently, hiding just how truly aggravated he was. He didn't need this distraction. He had so many other things to deal with.

Why did this have to happen when he needed to find his sister's horn? Not like time was of the essence or anything.

Every second he was gone was precious and dangerous.

He needed to get this done and return home as quickly as possible. Last thing he needed was a bit of chatty baggage that wouldn't cooperate. He had other irritants he was dodging for that.

Grinding his teeth, Dash lowered himself so that she could easily reach the saddle. "By all means, take your time."

She let out a deep growl at him as she took a few more seconds to try and figure out how to mount him.

Then again, he instantly regretted this decision, given

the way she wiggled all over his back as she slowly situated herself. Grimacing, he tried not to think about what she was doing. But it was hard while she slid her long, slender legs over his body. Then, wrapped them around his rib cage and straddled him.

Oh dear God.

Now he was grinding his teeth for an entirely different reason and cursing his rash decision to help her.

This was going to be a long, hard ride.

Emphasis on both.

My father was right. I am an idiot, and he should have gelded me at birth...

Tanis bit her lip as Dash stood up under her. She grabbed at the saddle horn and held on as tightly as she could. Every muscle in his body flexed between her thighs as he righted himself.

With a frown, she realized he didn't have reins for her to hold on to. *Well, that's annoying.* How was she supposed to ride like this? "Where are the reins?"

Without thinking, she sank her hands into his thick, silken mane.

"Saddle!" he snapped instantly. "Hold on to the saddle! Not my hair."

Well, that was certainly a rude tone. Offended, she moved her hands to the ivory horn and stuck her tongue out at him. 'Course had he seen her, he would have probably bucked her off his back. But he deserved it for being so testy when all she'd been trying to do was not fall off.

After all, it was a long way to the ground. He was an extremely tall beast from this perspective, and she had no wish to break her neck before she had a chance to kill the human she was after.

And as she adjusted herself, Tanis realized why he was so put out by her grabbing his mane. "You don't like anyone having control over you, do you?"

"Do you?" There was definite challenge in that tone.

"You know I don't. Is that not why you chose the price you did for my conversion?"

He didn't respond.

Which suited her well enough. She didn't want to speak to him, either. Contrary beast.

Fine then, she'd complete this journey in silence. Complete and utter silence.

"My God, Halla. What have you done?"

Halla jumped at the sharp bark that came from the shadows behind her. Trembling and afraid, she turned to see a tall, dark assassin that made everyone quake in fear... or wet their pants.

Everyone except King Dash.

Mostly because this was the only creature alive Dash trusted. If he trusted at all. The two of them had been friends since they'd been boys, trapped together in a hostile court that had done its best to break them both.

"Keep your voice down, Ryper."

He slammed the door behind him shut with powers that were terrifying in magnitude. Lifting his hand, he used those same powers to pull her to him. "What did you do?"

"Not me!" She choked and coughed. "Not me! Not me! Let me go!"

He released her so suddenly that had she not been winged, she'd have fallen against the floor.

Without speaking to her, he walked slowly toward the body on the floor that she'd been weeping over on his arrival. A beautiful blue roan with a star that had once high-lighted a bright golden horn.

Only now that beautiful spiral horn was gone.

And so was her life.

It'd taken almost all of Halla's powers to get Renata here on her own, without being seen by anyone. Now, she was so tired that all she could do was weep for the loss.

Reverently, Ryper sank to his knees and put his hand on the princess's lifeless body. "What happened?"

"Someone killed her for her horn. She ran away last night, and His Majesty went after her. By the time he found her..." She choked on another sob as she gestured toward the body. "I promised him that I'd bring her home while he went after the one who killed her."

Ryper cursed under his breath. "This is bad, Halla."

"I know."

"No, you don't." Balling his hand in Renata's mane, he sucked his breath in as if something shocked him. There was only one reason to take a horn... someone knew it could be used as a magick wand. And no wand would be more powerful than Renata's. "Does anyone else know that she's dead?"

"No. King Dash told Kronnel at dawn that he was going to fetch his sister home and to let no one know that he'd left the palace. After we found her, he told me to bring her body here and make sure no one knew until his return."

"Thank God he still has half a brain."

She didn't comment on something that only Ryper could get away with saying.

He looked up and pinned her with that scalding blue-eyed stare. "We need that horn, Halla. It must be found."

"That's what King Dash said, and it's what he's off doing."

Ryper shook his head. "I know him. He's not thinking clearly while he's grieving her. Where's he headed?"

"The brownie said that her killer was going to Auderley."

He scowled. "What brownie?"

Halla scratched at her neck as she remembered the tiny creature sitting beside the princess's body. "She was with Princess Renata when we found her. Said she saw the human man what killed the princess for her horn."

Ryper's eyes began to glow in the dim light. "Are you sure it was a brownie?"

Oh no! She widened her eyes as she realized what she might have done. "It looked like a brownie."

He gave her an agitated stare. "Of all beings, you should know that things aren't always what they appear."

Halla cursed the fact he was right. As a shape-shifter herself, she was more than aware of how many forms she could take. Hobgoblins seldom appeared in their natural bodies to others. "Well, it wasn't a hobgoblin. That I would have known."

Ryper counted to ten in his head. He wouldn't fault Halla for not being more suspicious. Unlike them, she'd been lucky enough to have a life that afforded her that luxury. She didn't have to doubt everyone who came near her.

To her, a brownie was a brownie.

To them, a brownie might be a brownie, a traitor or an assassin, or anything else they hadn't thought of. While none of them liked living the way they did, life had taught them to be on high alert at all times for the most unexpected catastrophe.

Too bad Renata hadn't been more cautious as well. It would have saved them all endless grief.

And regrets.

Rising, he let out a tired breath. "Get to Dash as fast as you can."

"And?"

"Watch his back."

Halla nodded. "Where are you going?"

"Where I'm needed."

Arms akimbo, she stared at him in a pique. "You don't really expect me to tell him that, do you?"

"You're his court jester. Make it humorous."

"Humorous? He's likely to spear me for it."

Ryper winked at her. "Better you than me."

She mocked him under her breath as she skittered toward the nearest window.

Ryper waited for Halla to leave then used his powers to preserve Renata's body and seal the room closed so that no one could enter it and find out what had happened to the princess.

Damn me. He'd known something was wrong. Had felt it the moment he woke up, which was why he'd been searching the palace when he happened upon Halla.

Ever since he'd first met Dash when they were boys in Meara's court, they'd had an unholy, natural connection. He always knew whenever Dash was in trouble or needed him. It was a connection that had concerned some and pissed off others.

Not that it mattered. As a bastard halfling, Ryper had done his best to avoid being around others. The last thing he wanted was Dash's throne and the headache that came with it. Watching out for those who wanted to kill you for your crown. The ones scheming against you at every moment.

Life was too short for that kind of drama. Ryper preferred keeping his head low. Killing whatever annoyed him and having no responsibilities for vassals or others.

His father had never wanted him, and he was fine with that. His mother had only wanted to stifle and suffocate him. If she had her way, she'd still be breast-feeding him her venom.

While he appreciated her love, Dash was all the family he needed. It was why he'd kill or die for his High King, and why he'd mostly killed for him.

No one else held his loyalty, and never would.

No one else was worth it.

Clutching at his baldric that held the two swords he was famous for wielding, Ryper headed for the crow's nest in the upper west wing of the palace. He hated to wake Chrysis this early in the morning.

As much as she despised the daylight, she should have been an owl instead of a crow.

Set on the farthest western tower of the palace, her elaborate nest was designed to stay shaded throughout the daytime hours. A courtesy Dash had afforded his longtime friend who often carried messages for him to other kingdoms and their representatives and monarchs.

And just as expected, Ryper found Chrysis curled up, asleep, with her beak tucked beneath an ebony wing.

"Chrys?"

She didn't so much as flinch. "Go away."

He poked at her head. "Can't do that."

"Hate you, Ryper. Go away."

"C'mon, Chrys. I need you."

She opened one black eye to glare at him. "I need you to go away."

Snorting, he jostled her nest.

Ruffling her feathers, she squawked and rose up, then spread her wings wide. "You are aware that crows hold grudges better than anyone, are you not?"

"Very much so. But you hate me already. Nothing to lose."

She actually growled at him. "Why are you here?"

"I need you to summon the Outlaws."

Chrys lifted her rather large black head to pin him with an eerie stare. Outlaw was a slur that unicorns used for those who were unmanageable, vicious or bastards. Or someone who'd survived a traumatic event.

In this case, it was a specific group of friends who'd come through hell together and barely survived. They were vicious, unmanageable and bastards...

The name they'd embraced was more than apropos.

"Are you out of your mind? Dash will kill you after what happened the last time they were all together." Again, they were a vicious lot who didn't bend to the will of anyone else.

"Dash will thank me."

She scoffed. "Don't know about that. I seem to recall a whole lot of damage. Angry villagers. Missing livestock. Fire. *Lots* of fire and swearing. I'm not sure if Mischief ever learned to walk straight again."

Ryper stifled a smile. She wasn't wrong. Mischief was more than aptly named, too. That woman was forever getting herself into all kinds of trouble.

Chrys tucked her wings down. "May I ask why you wish to anger your High King?"

He wanted to tell her about Renata but couldn't risk it. "Safer this way. We need to protect Dash and I need backup. There's something really wrong here."

She made an odd choking sound. "You're an assassin. You always think something's wrong."

That was true.

However...

"This time I'm right." He pulled a handful of seeds from his pocket and piled them on the post beside her nest. "Brought you breakfast."

"And a problem. Food doesn't make that better."

"Not what you told me last time."

She pecked at the seed. "Last time I was an idiot and don't think that handsome smile gets you out of trouble."

It normally did, especially with women. "Get flapping, crow. I need you. Dash needs you more."

She made a noise that sounded suspiciously like a raspberry. "You want all of the Outlaws or just a few?"

That was a loaded question. Especially if he was wrong. They'd probably hang him with his entrails for dragging them here if they weren't needed.

But if he was right...

I'm always right. Which meant Dash needed his only friends at his back. No one else could be trusted.

"All of them." It might cause an interkingdom war to bring them all together, but it could also avert one.

Speaking of problems... "On second thought, let's leave Xaydin out of this, for now. And I'll go after Dove." As a half-elfin bastard, Dove was a handful. No tolerance for much of anything, especially being summoned from the home Dove loathed.

Yeah, that was an errand Ryper wouldn't ask anyone else to undertake. He'd grab Dove himself.

Chrys nodded. "Good. I'm not in the mood to dodge any arrows or daggers."

Dove did have a bit of a temper, but that wasn't why Ryper wanted to seek him out. Dove was the only one Ryper knew who had access to a higher magick that might be able to find Renata's horn, and if he was lucky, that was where Dash was heading.

He turned his attention back to Chrys. "Have them meet me here at the lodge. I'll be there as soon as I can."

She took one last bite of food before she flew off.

Ryper watched after her as he considered everything that had happened.

Someone had taken Renata's horn. There were only two reasons for that.

Trophy hunting. Though it'd been popular at one time, it'd been outlawed ever since Dash took the throne. Cutting off a unicorn horn from a living target had always carried a severe risk as unicorn magick was some of the most powerful in the world. But a gold horn was priceless.

Especially given the one power it held above all others.

It could assassinate Dash.

Then the one who held it could seize power and rule. Or throw the Thirteen Kingdoms back into chaos and war.

Ryper winced at memories he'd give anything not to have. All too well, he remembered the wars. That unending vying for power.

Peace came at a cost and was a fragile flower that needed to be nourished.

Whoever had done this...

They wanted war. He could feel it with every part of himself.

And if they wanted war, they were about to meet the Outlaws. The deadliest bastards ever spawned by the Thirteen Kingdoms that had begrudged them all every breath they'd ever taken, and that had done its best to break them and bring them to their knees.

Yet they still stood in spite of every degradation and blow.

Determined. Steadfast.

And ready to kill to protect each other.

"You want war. Saddle up." The Outlaws had been through hell, and they were more than willing to go there again to protect each other.

CHAPTER 3

The more Tanis considered her bargain with Dash, the more it chafed. Why not ask for her soul instead of her freedom?

You don't value that.

Well, that was true. But did it really have to be her freedom? She'd already lost it once, and it'd been more than enough for one lifetime.

She hated for anyone to have control over her. It'd been bad enough when she'd been a girl in her father's court. But her slavery had been unbearable. Every day in captivity had been an eternity. She still bore those scars, inside and out. She'd fought hard for her freedom.

And she'd promised herself that no one would ever have sovereignty over her again.

Now here she was. Captive once more.

By her own stupid choice.

Tears filled her eyes as she remembered the past. Everything she'd been put through for greed and selfishness.

Human and unicorn cruelty that enjoyed watching others suffer. Even their own kind.

She knew nothing of this unicorn she'd bargained with. He could be wanted. A doctor. Banker. Anything really.

Now, she was part of his life.

Why did he want *her*? "What are you planning to do with me, beast?"

"What?"

"After I kill the dragon slayer... what are you going to do with me once I go to your kingdom?"

He snorted. "Little late to be asking that now, isn't it?"

Yes. But she still had to know what he was thinking. Why he'd chosen such a repugnant thing for her payment. "Are you going to sell me?"

Dash heard the underlying panic in her tone. If he were as sadistic as his father had been, he'd draw this out and make her sweat her poor decision. It might actually be good for her and keep her from being so hasty in the future.

But lucky for her, he didn't enjoy seeing others suffer. He'd had his fill of that when he'd been a colt. "That's been outlawed."

"True, but some still practice it, anyway."

"And they are gutted by the High King when he finds them. He has no tolerance for such savagery."

"Doesn't mean they won't risk it. For all I know, you could be one of them."

She was right, and he had no patience with those bastards, either. He took a lot of pleasure in seeing them caught and gutted. "Rest your mind, Dragon. I'm not a slaver or trader of flesh. I'd never do such a thing to anyone. Not even my enemies."

The dragon instantly relaxed. "Good. And you should know that I won't be your plaything."

He scoffed at where her mind had gone to next. Though it was probably a fair concern for her, given her beauty and form. "Trust me, Dragon. I've no shortage of offers when it comes to lovers wanting a place in my bed."

That made her instantly go stiff again. "Well, you don't have to be so nasty about it. I'm not a pox-ridden nag."

Wow... the ire in her tone was incredible as was the unconscious kick she'd given his ribs. "Now you're offended that I don't want you in my bed? Should I make a score card so that I can keep up with your mood swings?"

She shifted on his back in such a way that he suspected she might actually be making a face at him. It was very much something his sister would have done whenever he displeased her. Which was quite a lot.

Renata was one of only a tiny few in his life who had the temerity to stand up to him after he'd gutted his powerful father in a fit of rage.

Mostly because everyone had assumed his father was immortal and invincible.

And he had been... until the day he wasn't.

Bully bastard.

No one had ever believed that someone could kill his father. Especially his father. Too used to shoving everyone around as if they were rag dolls, the last thing Cratus the Conqueror had expected was for his bastard son to return home with a vengeance.

And a vicious craving that had demanded blood appeasement.

It'd been a welcomed bonus that by killing his father, he'd quelled everyone else in the process.

To this day, Dash regretted nothing about his homecoming. Especially the bloodshed.

The dragon cleared her throat. "You still haven't answered my question, Unicorn. What are you going to do with me?"

"I don't quite know."

"That's not comforting," she said wistfully.

"Neither is life. Sooner you accept that, you're doing better than most."

She scoffed. "Trust me, Dash. I learned that a long, long time ago."

Something in her voice resonated with him. A kindred soul who'd been kicked enough to know that life wasn't the prized cherry bowl bards had promised them in their nursery rhymes. It was hard and it was brutal. More times than not, it sought to bring everyone to their knees and laughed in their faces while it kicked them in their tenderest places.

He hated that she knew that pain.

"If it makes you feel better, Dragon, I promise I won't make you do anything too grisly. No dungeon dwelling. Or maiden eating. Perhaps I'll find a nice treasure for you to guard."

She smacked her lips as if he'd struck a nerve with her. "That's a stereotype, you know. Like saying unicorns kidnap maidens."

"Who says we don't?"

"Do you?"

"Been known to... with their permission." He glanced

over his shoulder at her. "Imagine what someone would think if they saw us right now? Would it not appear as if I'd kidnapped you?"

An attractive blush covered her cheeks. "They'd be stupid."

"Would they be wrong?"

"You didn't kidnap me. I kidnapped you. Sort of." Still, a deep sadness haunted her eyes. "But your point is well made."

"What's wrong, Dragon?" Not that he cared. At least that was what he told himself.

She blinked quickly and swallowed hard as if she were fighting back tears. "Nothing."

It wasn't nothing. He saw the horrors she was trying to hide. Something dark in her past that she didn't want to talk about, and he regretted that he'd pricked whatever memory was there. Of all people, he knew the demon that lurked just below the surface that never gave him peace.

Sometimes it was well caged.

Other times...

It emerged with the slightest provocation.

A smell. A whisper. Any little thing could unleash that demon until it raged against the world, and mostly against him.

I am a bastard.

From birth to the end. Like father like son. And so, he vowed to say nothing more. Least he could do for her.

Tanis sighed as she tried to think of something else to focus on. Right now, she was seriously starting to panic.

Just what had she gotten herself into?

Davin had always chastised her for not thinking ahead. For being too rash and emotional.

He was right.

She'd been so focused on the result of avenging him that she hadn't thought through the steps to get there. Impetuosity would always be her downfall.

And trust.

Though she'd gotten much better about the last one over the years.

Well, not really. Rather than mistrust everyone else, she'd merely learned to withdraw. It was easier to avoid others than to let them take advantage of her because she refused to assume they were going to use her. She didn't want to be hateful like her sisters.

Vicious like the monster who'd taken her.

If that was what it took to live in this world, she'd rather not. She just didn't want to be like them. To hurt and take advantage of others. Why did everyone have to be so mean? It had never made sense to her.

What pleasure could they really take from their cruelty? And if they did find pleasure in such meanness, then she pitied them for it. She found her happiness whenever she caused someone else to smile. She liked helping others, even when it caused her father to chastise her.

Why was that wrong? She'd never understood it.

As they continued through the forest, she saw a shadow in the trees that seemed to be keeping pace with them. "Is that a human?" she whispered.

Glancing over at the shadow, Dash let out a very heavy sigh before he responded. "No. Something much more sinister."

Dread filled her at his heavy tone. Was it an ogre? Troll? Oni?

"What's worse than a human?"

"A beast it seems I can never escape."

Tanis swallowed at the anger in his voice. What awful thing was after them? "Should we run?"

"Won't do any good. It would only catch us." He slowed down so that the shadow could rush toward them.

She frowned as she saw...

"Is that a hobgoblin?"

The second she asked the question, it transformed into a lovely blond woman in the prime of her youth. She strode toward them with a cocky swagger.

Dash let out another long, exaggerated sigh. "Thought I left you behind to take care of things. What are you doing here, Halla?"

"Following you and your new passenger. Should I ask where you found your lady?"

"She's as much a lady as you are."

Halla opened her mouth to speak, but Dash cut her off. "She's a dragon I ran into after I left you with orders to stay put. And to keep an eye on things."

She stopped dead in her tracks to stare at them. "Dragon, you say?"

"Fire-breathing. Scaly... dragon."

Tanis frowned at his unflattering description of her. "Not sure I like the scaly part."

He glanced at her over his shoulder. "Do you not have scales?"

"Not at the moment, and they're not scaly scales." They were quite lovely, in her opinion. Almost identical to her mother's. Though not quite as pretty as her mother's had been.

"But they *are* scales," Dash said decisively.

Well, yes. Technically.

Tanis rolled her eyes at him. Which felt entirely different as a human than a dragon. She felt like she was wearing an ill-fitting suit. Too tight and restrictive.

"I like my scales," she said under her breath.

"Well, since she's not human..." Wings sprang out of the hobgoblin's back as she shrank in size. "No need in wearing out me legs. I'm getting too old for this, and you need to stop traveling so fast. You're making it bloody hard to keep up with you and find you every time you give us the slip."

"Told you to stay home, didn't I?"

"Bah!" Halla flew so that she hovered beside Tanis's arm. "Why would I do that? Other than to bring you tales about how incompetent Kronnel is in your stead. Which he is, just so you know. Bloody boring, too."

"You should have stayed home," he repeated yet again. "Keeping an eye on Kronnel while I'm gone might be helpful."

Halla made a rude noise. "When have I ever been helpful to you? Me job's to harass and make you think twice."

"Point taken. I think twice about killing you every time you're near."

This time the hobgoblin laughed at Dash's surly tone. "That's what your father used to say."

"And here I thought all of his animus was saved up for me alone."

Tanis didn't speak as she realized the unicorn had said

something she was rather sure he hadn't meant to in front of her.

Something confirmed by the clearing of Halla's throat to catch Dash's attention. "Methinks you've forgotten the bit of baggage on your back, me lord."

Dash groaned. "'Course I did. She weighs nothing. Make some noise, Dragon."

"Didn't want to interrupt you, Lord Unicorn."

Was he really unicorn nobility? What was his rank? Was he important? Given his bearing, she wouldn't be surprised if he was high ranking. Not that it mattered. She was just curious. She'd never met a unicorn noble.

Before he could comment or she could ask about it, Tanis heard the sound of men approaching. This time, there was no mistaking it.

It was a group of them.

Dash quickly moved them from the road, deeper into the woods so the humans wouldn't see them. Halla shrank herself to the size of a butterfly while Tanis slid from Dash's back to lower herself to the ground so she could hide in the underbrush.

As the riders came closer, she saw that there were eight men of warrior age, though two were still relatively young. All were covered in furs and appeared gruff. Smelly, in her opinion. Not that she wanted to get close enough to smell them. This was quite close enough. She already had bile in her throat. Any closer and she might actually yield to the urge to unload the contents of her stomach.

The one who rode behind the leader scratched at his hairy chest. "How much further is it?"

"Least two more days... maybe three. Less if we ride through the nights," the leader said.

The one who'd spoken first growled low in his throat. "My arse is tired of this journey."

"Yea, but we're going to see the dragon skull," a young one in the back said. "Imagine the luck it'll bring us if we touch it."

The leader shook his head. "You keep saying that, but all I can think is that it wasn't so lucky for the dragon what lost its head."

Fury rushed through her that they'd dare make light of her brother's tragedy. Tanis started to rise, but Dash lightly placed a hoof over her rump.

"Don't move." His voice was loud and clear in her mind.

She knew he was right. Still, it was hard to lie here while they bantered so over her brother. As if his life meant nothing.

How dare they!

Thankfully, they passed quickly. Even so, she wanted to run them down and thrash them for being so callous.

If only she were still a dragon, they'd be on fire...

But you're not a dragon.

True. Still, she wasn't without skills. And she did have a sword. She was sure she could have taken them. Or at least a few of them, and make them bleed.

Most of all, she wanted to scream out in frustration.

Damn me.

Dash waited until the humans were completely out of sight before he lifted his hoof from her rear.

She glared at him as she pushed herself up from the ground. "Was that necessary?"

"Were you planning to run at them?"

Sort of. "Wasn't really a plan. More like a reaction."

"A bad one. Need I remind you, Dragon, you're currently human, with no powers?"

No, he didn't. And that irritated her as much as his calm demeanor and tone. "*You* have powers," she reminded him.

"I do, indeed."

She arched a brow at his agreeable tone. "Would you not have helped?"

"Probably not."

She gaped at that. "Seriously? You'd have done nothing to them?"

"Not over words."

"Not even when they're insulting you?" she asked incredulously.

It was his turn to lift a brow at her. "Do dragons always attack when they're being insulted?"

She sputtered.

"I believe they do, me lord." Halla made herself the size of a large rodent while she floated in the air between them. "It's a matter of honor for them."

Nodding at the hobgoblin, she brushed debris from her clothes. "Halla's correct. We do."

"Is that why you destroy so many villages whenever you're off on a furious bender?"

Anger rose inside her at Dash's question. "I've never destroyed any village. I know no one who has ever done such. Have you ever speared a human with your horn?"

Dash didn't respond, but Halla began to whistle and look uncomfortable.

She arched a brow at his lack of response. "You've speared a human?"

Halla cupped her hand around her mouth and whispered loudly, "He's speared many things, Lady Dragon."

Dash spoke in that calm, emotionless tone. "Plan to do so again. But I'm not rash enough to run headlong into a group of trained and armed warriors who may or may not be wizards or shape-shifters when my backup is a hobgoblin, whose sole choice of weapon is sarcasm, and a defenseless dragon in the body of a human woman who would have been at their mercy had I failed to kill them all."

The way he said that made her want to run from him. There was a lot of darkness inside him that she must not forget. Just like the one who'd stolen her innocence. Unicorns were dangerous.

Cold-blooded.

Merciless.

As a human, she was no match for his speed.

And he might spear her, too.

He's my enemy.

She couldn't afford to forget that important fact. They weren't the same. Unicorns weren't dragons. They were an entirely different species, who valued entirely different things.

At least that was what she'd been told. Truthfully, she didn't know what they valued. And at the moment, she didn't care.

Dash shook his head, causing his mane to flow eerily. "Are you ready to continue your journey?"

She wanted desperately to say no. That she could find

her own way. But as a human woman, that would take forever on foot.

And those men and others would continue to mock her beloved brother while she dawdled.

No. If the unicorn could get her there without devouring her, she'd be that much closer to finishing this and returning to her own body.

Then she could flash fry the unicorn and return to her kingdom.

I will see this through. No matter what it takes.

And then she'd free herself from this terrifying unicorn. One way or another.

CHAPTER 4

S he's gone!"

Ragna growled as her sister, Reva, swept into her bedroom without preamble.

Her lover, Trexton, jumped away from her instantly, and began looking for...

Who knew? His dignity or an escape. Probably his brain as she hadn't chosen him for his intellect as much as another piece of anatomy that had definitely not been disappointing her before her bitchy sister had intruded.

Furious over the interruption, Ragna glared at Reva, who didn't seem to care in the least that she'd walked in on them. "Don't you knock?"

Reva drew up short as she realized what she'd interrupted. Completely unabashed, she let out an irritated sigh. "Seriously? Can't you go an hour? How many males has it been today so far?"

Trexton gaped. "What?"

Ragna rose up at her sister. "Don't you dare!"

Using her tail, Reva pushed him toward the door. "You need to leave now. I'm sure she'll be horny again in ten minutes. Come back when the grownups are through talking."

As soon as she forced him through the door, she used her tail to slam it shut.

With a furious sigh, Ragna ruffled her wings. "That was rude, sister."

"Don't care." Reva turned back to face her.

With orange and brown scales, Reva was a beautiful dragon, if not a large one. Ragna had always been grateful she hadn't inherited their father's wider girth. Her slender form was much more graceful, especially for flight.

"Why are you here?"

Reva sat back on her haunches. When she spoke again, she enunciated each word slowly. "I told you. *She's* gone."

"If you mean Marla, I already know. She packed the hatchlings up and headed to her father before I had a chance to get to them."

Reva sneered at her. "Not Marla, you idiot. *Tanis.* She's nowhere to be found."

That wasn't good. Tanis was a stubborn little bitch who listened to no one. For days now, she'd been demanding justice and driving everyone to madness. So much so, that they'd both been tempted to throw her skull to the same dragon slayer and imp.

"What do you mean, she's gone?" Ragna asked.

"You heard what I said. No one has seen her. The last anyone heard of her was Marla. Tanis told her that she was going to avenge Davin and reclaim his skull so that Marla could bury him properly."

Ragna cursed. "When was that?"

"A day or so ago. I don't know. I thought you told her to forget it."

"Of course I did. Since when does Tanis listen to anyone?"

Reva belched fire and fluttered her wings. "What are we going to do?"

Ragna pressed her claws to her snout as she tried to think through this. Leave it to Tanis to screw up all their plans. "Where's the idiot?"

"I just told you, I don't know."

"Not our sister idiot. The other idiot!"

Reva gave her a droll stare. "Which other idiot? Really, Ragna, you need to find other insults. It's rather tedious and extremely confusing."

"Fine. Imbecile. Moron. *Human*!"

"That was uncalled for. I'm not human, you bitch."

Ragna hissed at her sister. "You deserve it, and I didn't mean *you*. That dragon slayer moron you found who pissed himself when he saw you the first time. Where did he and that imp of his go?"

"Oh…" Reva paused to consider it. "I don't know. I suppose they headed home? If they'd stayed here, they would have been eaten. If not by one of us, then a gryphon or wyvern."

"You're useless! Why didn't you keep an eye on the human and imp until they left?"

"Don't take that tone with me, Ragna. You didn't tell me to keep an eye on them. How was I supposed to know you'd want them later?"

Ragna let out an angry burst of flames. "Fine. You go

after that idiot dragon slayer and his companion. See if you can find Davin's skull so that we can get in tight with Marla again and finish this, and I'll go find Tanis."

"What are you going to do with her when you find her?"

"Depends."

"On?"

Ragna examined her dew claw and how sharp it was. "How much trouble she gives me."

Reva understood that threat and was glad she wasn't the one Ragna was angry at. "What about Father? What do we tell him?"

Ragna paused as if to consider options. "Leave him to me. I'll deal with it. You worry about the human and imp."

"If I can't find them?"

Ragna gave her a cold, piercing glare. "Then don't come home."

Just after the sun had set, Dash found them a comfortable spot to camp for the night. Tanis slid from his saddle in a way that left him cursing everything, especially his life and, in particular, the stupidity of making deals with dragons.

She laughed at the latter one as he groused about it.

He conjured her a bedroll and a few supplies before he headed off into the woods alone.

"Is he all right?" Tanis asked Halla.

"I'm sure he just needs a few minutes to attend his needs." Halla wagged her brows to convey a meaning Tanis didn't want to think about.

The hobgoblin was incorrigible.

"You didn't have to go there, you know." Tanis set about laying her bedding on the ground while Halla piled up rocks to make a circle. She scowled as she watched the hobgoblin. "What are you doing?"

"Getting ready for the fire."

Tanis was very confused by that. "Why would you have to get ready for a fire?"

Halla gave her a droll stare. "Not a dragon. We don't just belch flames. We have to make one and contain it."

Oh. She hadn't thought of that. As Halla had noted, dragons didn't concern themselves with such things. When they wanted a fire, it was an easy thing to burp.

Tanis gazed off into the woods as she considered her two companions. They were very different from one another. Dash was as quiet as Halla was chatty. Huge as she was small. Terrifying as she was friendly.

Halla stood back from the fire pit to survey her handiwork. With a satisfied nod, she wiped her hands together. "You wait here, Lady Tanis, and I'll gather more wood."

"Wouldn't it make more sense for me to help?"

"Ever gather firewood?"

Tanis paused. "Well, no. Part of being a dragon. We don't need it."

"Then you won't be very helpful, will you? Because the one thing you don't want to do is gather the wrong kind or the wood that something's making a home in. Especially the kinds of things that bite."

Tanis shivered at the thought. Definitely not something dragons had to worry over.

Halla patted her gently on the arm to take the sting out

of those words. "Don't worry. I won't be long. Just rest a few and I'll be back."

"Try not to get bitten."

Laughing, Halla ventured off in the direction Dash had vanished.

Tanis was tempted to follow, but truthfully, she was too tired to bother. It was nice to have a little reprieve by herself. Not that they were bad company. Halla was very pleasant.

Dash...

He was intense. Dangerous. Not in a bad way. It was just... There were no real words for it. He lured her like no one ever had before.

The more they traveled, the more she wanted to know why he was so quiet and mysterious. She felt as if Dash and Halla had a secret they were keeping from her. Not that it was any of her business. But a part of her would like to know what was behind some of the side glances they exchanged.

Didn't matter. She had a mission. And she intended to finish it as quickly as possible.

Then, she'd work on regaining her freedom.

DASH FROZE at the sound of someone rustling in the brush in front of him. "Better be Halla."

"You better be dressed."

He snorted at her irritable tone as she broke through the clearing where he was stretched out on the grass. "Where's the dragon?"

"I left her at the campsite. You should try being nicer to her."

"Nicer how? I haven't yelled at her, and I've been carrying her on my back all day."

Standing over him while he lay in the grass, staring up at the sky, she gave him a peeved stare and crossed her arms over her chest. "You know, you could fly with her."

He smirked. "I could do a lot of things with her."

She threw an acorn at him. "Get your mind out of the gutter. You know what I mean. It'd be a lot faster if we flew."

"She doesn't need to know I can do that anymore than she needs to know I can be human."

Halla cocked her head as she raked a look over his human form. "I'm assuming that's why you're not in camp at the moment, too?"

"It is." He just needed a moment to stretch out and relax in his human body.

"Then why is she with us if she's slowing you down?"

He had no idea and no real answer. Except for one thing. "I'd like to think that if I was the one who was dead, Renata would be as determined to avenge me."

"Why don't I believe you?"

Because it wasn't the entire truth. There was something about the dragon that compelled him, and he had no idea what or why. Only that she haunted him.

It made no sense, but all he could think about right now was heading to their camp, scooping that dragon up in his arms and shocking Halla right back into her hobgoblin hill.

You need a woman.

Perhaps that was all it was.

He'd been alone far too long, and he knew it. But lovers

came with all kinds of complications he didn't need or want. He'd learned a long time ago that he was better off on his own.

And still, his thoughts kept drifting back to that auburn-haired temptation. To those searing dark–brown eyes that were filled with intelligence and fire.

Stop.

He had so much more he needed to focus on. Someone had his sister's horn and with it, they could do all manner of damage. Not the least of which was kill him.

If he died...

The dragon would have a lot more to worry about than just her brother's skull. All he'd fought and bled for...

It would be for nothing. Chaos would return and it would own the world once more.

Maybe that was the only point of his life. To hold chaos off for just one more day.

Do not fail.

The price of failure was too high for all of them. But particularly for the innocents like their dragon.

He glanced back at Halla. "Did anyone follow you when you left the palace?"

"Not that I know."

Not that she knew. Lovely. "You haven't seen *him* following you?"

She laughed. "Does anyone ever see Ryper?"

Not unless he wanted them to. Damn it. He should have been named Shadow with the way he blended into the darkness and traveled without sound. Although, given the fact he'd been an assassin for most of his life, Ryper was probably the most fitting name for him, and Dash had always wondered if it was the name his mother had bestowed on the boy or one he'd chosen.

The one time he'd asked that question, Ryper had just stared at him and said nothing.

He was good at that, too.

Noncommittal to the bitter end.

"Besides, Ryper told me to keep me eyes on you, Sire."

Of course, he did. Ryper worried as much as a nursemaid.

"He also told me that he was going where he was most needed."

Dash scowled as he tried to figure out where that might be. "What does that mean?"

She shrugged. "It's Ryper. Could mean anything. But he was insistent that I watch your back, Sire, as he was sure something bad was coming."

That sounded about right. And it sounded like Ryper's normal paranoia. Which tragically had a way of coming true.

Dash let out a tired sigh. He'd acted rashly and he knew it. Leaving his lands had been a bad idea, and Ryper would be the first to lecture him on the stupidity of it. But this was something he dared not trust to anyone else. No one could know about his sister.

Most of all, they couldn't know about her missing wand.

Just a few more days and they'd be in Auderley. He'd have Renata's wand back. The dragon would get her skull.

And he'd put the darkness to rest before it devoured them all.

CHAPTER 5

"Are you sure this is a good idea?"

Bink cast a disgusted smirk toward the human he was beginning to wish he'd never met. "You're supposed to be a dragon slayer, Fort. Act like you have a set of balls between your legs."

Instead, the whiny, shriveled human rubbed nervously at the back of his neck. Just under average height for a male, he had a bloated face and boorish features more akin to an ogre than human. Bink had known the moment Fort had shown up with a dragon's head that he hadn't won it by honest means.

His first thought had been that Fort had stolen it from some drunken knight who'd put it outside his room while he was whoring or taken it from the dragon catacombs. That had made the most sense, especially given the fact that Fort was a thief.

Besides, no one in their right mind would ever believe Fort was capable of taking a dragon's head in a fight.

Then Fort had explained he'd done it while the dragon had been drugged and was sleeping in its bed. After a few cups of ale, he'd then confessed that he hadn't even been there when it happened. That another dragon had killed it and then given the head to Fort so that it'd look like a dragon slayer had slain the beast.

Hadn't even been there...

Coward.

Bink had no respect for such repellent creatures, but he did have uses for them, and Fort had been an above-average flunkey, most days. Especially after he'd introduced him to the dragon who'd given him the skull.

Right now, they were here to see a centaur rebel prince to negotiate for another conspirator of Bink's.

He curled his lip at the human. "Stop arguing, Fort, and do what you're told." After all, thinking wasn't Fort's forte. That was where Bink came in.

Hopefully, they wouldn't have to flee here in the middle of the night as they'd been forced to do after Fort had stolen a knight's sword two months ago.

Or after Fort had accepted the dragon's skull. They'd barely made it out of Indara with their lives. Not an experience he wanted to relive anytime soon.

Patting the top of his head to make sure all his spindles were down, Bink then smoothed his jacket. They were meeting a prince, after all. No need in looking like the street trash they were.

"How do I look?"

Fort shrugged. "Like an imp?"

Troglodyte. Why did he bother? He needed to find a better class of accomplices.

Which was why they were here. He wanted to hobnob with the rich and noble. To be with the class he should have been born to, not run around with the wannabe riffraff.

Grimacing at the oaf he could barely stand, Bink turned about and snapped his fingers for Fort to follow after him, like the dutiful dog he was.

The majordomo opened the heavy wooden door that led into a posh office where the centaur prince sat on a brocade cushion behind a low-to-the-floor, ornate, gilded desk. Royalty bled from every pore of the prince's body. He moved with grace and dignity that Bink envied. Wealth clung to him like a second skin. It wasn't just evident in his mannerisms, but in the stylish cut of his navy-blue jacket and the gold thread and trim.

Yet it was the desk and gold gryphon quills that held his attention the most.

Bink could just imagine how much he could sell those for in a market, then caught himself. He wasn't here to steal. He was here to strike a deal.

Make a bargain to end all bargains.

Forcing himself to bow, he hoped it looked like he was posh, too, and not a groveling beggar from the street. "Your Highness."

Bink glanced under his arm to see that Fort continued to stand behind him, looking around the paneled room like an unsophisticated goon. Clearing his throat, he used his eyes to convey to the moron that he needed to bow as well.

"Oh." Fort finally caught on and duplicated Bink's actions.

Oh dear God...

He prayed he didn't look like *that*. Fear that he did so

made him straighten up immediately and tug at his coat again. "May we approach, Highness?"

With dark hair and beady eyes, Prince Lorens cast a speculative look at him, then to Fort. "Depends. Do you have what you promised?"

"Why else would we be here?"

That caused a weaselly smile to curve his lips as the greedy centaur rubbed his hands together in glee. "Then show me my army."

Bink pulled a piece of parchment from his pocket and approached the desk slowly. He set it down in front of the prince who looked it over and then scowled.

"What's this?"

Was Lorens illiterate? It was obvious. "It's a wanted poster."

The prince shoved it back toward him. "This isn't what I wanted. I wanted a unicorn alliance with soldiers!"

"This is better."

Lorens looked at him as if he were daft. "How so?"

"This is a bigger alliance. One that will help you to over-throw your sister with the backing of six other kingdoms."

"Why would they help me overthrow my sister?"

"To rid themselves of the High King they hate so much."

Tapping his finger on the desk, Lorens considered the matter for several minutes.

Too long actually. It became rather tedious and uncom-fortable as that finger tapping became like a second, drum-ming heartbeat. Had he broken the prince with his new plan?

Carefully, Bink cleared his throat to get the prince's attention. "Highness?"

"Are you sure about this alliance?" Lorens asked. "They'll send me the forces I need when I need them?"

Sort of. Those kingdoms hated Dash and had said they'd pay anything to be rid of him. He was relatively sure they'd reward him for helping them get rid of their nuisance, and with that money they could hire an army. But he knew better than to let his uncertainty show. "Yes, Highness."

He nodded slowly. "Get me those backers. I have a revolt to lead. I need soldiers and coin!"

Bink bowed low and walked backwards from the room, making sure to grab Fort on his way out and haul him with him.

He didn't dare speak again until they were outside the manor hall. "Collect your skull, Fort."

"Are we going to auction it off now, like you said?"

Bink shook his head. "We have to cover our tracks."

"What do you mean?"

"I think I might have miscalculated." He needed to get back to his partner, Keryna, in Licordia, and find out just how entrenched she was with Lorens and his rebellion. He knew those two had been plotting together for months now. And that Keryna had been using her influence with Renata to make promises with the centaur rebels to back them with Dash's army.

What he didn't know was exactly everything Keryna had promised the rebels. But he was grateful Keryna had put one thing in his hands...

He opened his pouch to touch the golden horn he'd sliced off the princess's head. Stupid, trusting bitch. The princess had thought Bink was going to take her to rendezvous with Lorens so they could negotiate for her to provide unicorn soldiers for his rebellion.

That would have been all kinds of stupid. The last thing Bink had wanted was to fight in a war of any kind. Better to let the lot of them tear each other down.

Last creature standing would be the one to wear the crown. Rule of survival.

Everyone hated the High King. He would be easy to remove, given all his enemies. Lorens would take care of Queen Meara. The dragons would take care of themselves.

With his wiles, he'd be able to stir dissension and mistrust among the other kingdoms so that they'd never turn their eyes toward Licordia. They would be too busy fighting amongst themselves to mount a war with him.

All he had to do was take care of Keryna.

Simple.

She'd already delivered Princess Renata to him. Only one more task, and Bink would have what he wanted.

While he wasn't a unicorn, he had the magick to control the unicorn race. To rule over their kingdom and unleash his homeless brethren who were currently enslaved to the Sagarians.

It hadn't been that long ago that the unicorns had been on the brink of extinction. With a little whispering here and there, they would tear each other apart again.

Then, he would be king, and they would all bow down to him. Licordia would no longer be the homeland of the unicorns. It would belong to the imps. And then all the other kingdoms would bow down before *them*.

CHAPTER 6
AUDERLEY, DYTHNAL

THREE DAYS LATER

Tanis bit her lip as she found herself alone on the edge of the human town she'd been so desperate to find. How she despised being here.

Years ago, she'd sworn to never venture near a human village again. To never even fly over one of their settlements.

Over and over, she could hear them cheering for her defeat. Or worse, cheering whenever she'd been forced to kill another so that she could live.

Those who'd made bets on her life.

Bets on her death.

How I hate you all.

For some unknown reason, fate had brought her back to them. Why? She couldn't imagine. Had she not suffered enough in her life? What more would they take from her?

They'd already taken everything that mattered.

Her dignity.

Her honor.

Davin's life.

Having suffered at their hands, she refused to allow her brother to know her degradations. Even in death, he deserved better.

I promise, I'll take care of you. His words echoed in her head. He'd always kept that promise. In a royal court filled with those out to betray her family, it'd always been the two of them against the world. She had her brother's back, and he had hers.

Until she hadn't.

I'm so sorry I failed you.

Davin should have died at a ripe old age with hatchlings and great-great-great-grand-hatchlings by his side. This was not how it was supposed to end for one so kind-hearted.

I will make this right.

If it was the last thing she ever did, she would return his skull to their kingdom.

Dash and Halla had gone on ahead of her after she'd told them that she needed a few minutes to gather herself together. Her panic attack had been absolute. Even now, she still wasn't completely recovered.

She wanted to return to her island home.

No, she *needed* to go home and hide.

But it was too late. Even if she was still in her dragon's body, her father wouldn't welcome her back—he hadn't wanted her to begin with. He'd ordered her not to do this.

Her sisters would most likely kill her for leaving. Definitely kill her for being human.

You would endanger us for a fool's quest? If Davin allowed a human to kill him even while sleeping, then he should be dead for his weakness!

Dragons were completely unforgiving. It was why she'd been shunned on her return after she'd been kidnapped.

You're a dragon, Tanis. I don't care what kind of magick he had. You let a unicorn capture you when you should have fought him with everything you had. If that's as strong as you are, then you should have died in their world rather than come slinking back here, begging for mercy! For once in your life, have dignity. Go kill yourself!

And she'd been so tempted. Only Davin and Marla's charity had kept her alive when she had absolutely no reason to live.

Her sisters' cruelty still cut her all the way to her battered soul.Lucky them that no one had ever snuck up on them when they were distracted hatchlings, playing in a meadow. It was easy to be a sanctimonious asshole when fate hadn't shit all over you, for no reason. But Tanis knew the horror and humiliation of being caught unawares. Not because she was stupid or careless. Not because she was weak.

Because she'd had no concept of evil back then.

What that wretched unicorn had done to her could have happened to anyone.

Anyone. Even her sisters.

She had just been the unfortunate soul playing in the valley that afternoon.

It should have been her sister, Ragna, or her father, who suffered in her stead. Then maybe they would have had some compassion for others.

They needed the lesson in humility.

Not her.

She would never understand why fate or the gods or whatever it was that had dealt this to her had chosen her that day. Because she had never been callous toward others. Unlike them, she'd always tried to be fair and kind.

Yet she was the one who had been punished for trusting a stranger. The one her clan had branded pariah.

But not Davin.

He and Marla had welcomed her home after her captivity. They, alone, had helped her to heal and had given her shelter when no one else would even look at her because they'd labeled her tainted.

Now Davin was gone.

How was that fair or right?

Damn you, universe! Damn you straight to hell!

Tears choked her, but she refused to let them fall. No one would ever see her cry.

Taking a breath for courage, she forced herself to head toward the gate where two very stout men stood guard to watch over the steady stream of people who were going and coming through their town.

Her legs shook so badly that she wasn't even sure how she could walk. How did humans handle this? Emotions were horrible as a dragon, but as a human...

They were so much worse. She couldn't remember her body wobbling like this before. Her heart pounding so ferociously. Truly, it was terrifying.

She was even sweating in places she'd forgotten people could sweat. Ew! How did they stand it?

It made her entire body itchy.

"Halt!"

She froze at the fierce bellow. Had she done something wrong? Her hand wanted to pull her sword, but that didn't seem like a wise idea. Not in a crowd of this size.

Aggression bred aggression. That was the one thing she remembered most from being human before. Stay calm or they'd hurt her.

One of the burly men came storming in her direction.

Her stomach tightened to the point of pain as she rested her hand on the sword hilt. *Wait for it...*

She was sure he was going to grab her and yank her with him.

If he dared...

She'd slit him from gullet to beard.

Instead of grabbing her, he brushed rudely past her with a sneer on his face. Following him with her gaze, she saw that he was glaring at a group behind her.

Oh, thank the gods.

She let out a relieved breath as he began yelling at them for reasons she didn't understand. Using that distraction, she quickly swept into town before someone else stopped her for real.

That was the easy part.

The hard? She had no idea where to go. There were people everywhere.

Literally everywhere.

They swarmed through the streets like a colony of ants, heading in all directions with no rhyme or reason. There were buildings all around, but she didn't know what they were. Some had signs, but the pictures on them made no sense to her.

Where in the world had Halla and Dash gone? The stables? A barn?

Why hadn't she asked them where they'd be?

Because I'm an idiot.

No, she'd been panicking and not thinking clearly.

"Move, girl!"

A man brushed past her, with his arms full of bloody hides.

Bile rose in her throat. She felt terrible for those poor, butchered animals. Humans were monsters! Did they respect nothing? Why kill so indiscriminately and so many? Had there been a purpose for it?

Were the animals rabid?

Suddenly, she wished she'd stayed in her dragon body and had just torched this entire place. It would have been a courtesy to the world to rid it of the vermin rustling around her.

Horrible memories flooded her of her days in captivity, and she didn't want to be here, especially not alone.

Worse, she felt as if she were being watched. But she didn't see anyone in the crowd that was paying her any heed. Still, that feeling persisted. It made her skin crawl...

"Where are you, Dash?" she breathed.

She silently kicked herself for letting them go on ahead. As bad as the panic attack had been, she should have forced herself to stay with them.

The one she had now was making the old one look like a hiccup.

"Are you a huntress?"

She turned around with a frown, expecting to see one of the nasty men.

Instead, it was a young boy who barely reached her hip. The sight of him there, with a bruise on his cheek and tears in his pale eyes caught her off guard. "Pardon?"

He gestured at her sword and bag that she wore across her back. "Are you a huntress, my lady?"

"Uh..." Tanis wanted to say no, but technically, that was what she was and how Dash had dressed her. The only question was why this boy asked her that. "Yes?"

The boy hesitated, then swallowed audibly. "Have you any meat I can buy?"

She scowled at his odd question. "What?"

He held his grimy hand out to her to show her a small silver coin there. "Me pa's passed out again from his drink, but he said for me to fetch some meat. He said that huntresses usually give more meat for the coin, and if I don't have meat when he comes to, he'll beat me. Do you have any meat I can buy from you?"

Those words infuriated her. Even if the child was human, he didn't deserve to be hit.

Especially not by the man who was supposed to love and protect him.

A strange tenderness rose up inside her, making her want to keep the boy safe. "Sorry, little one. I don't have any."

With one grimy fist, he wiped away the tears in his eyes as he turned to leave.

It's none of your business...

No doubt that little human would grow into a man who would one day hunt down her kind for sport or trophy.

Yet as she watched him wander through the crowd, all she saw was a lost little boy who needed help.

Like her brother's hatchlings.

Hating herself for the weakness, she went after him. "Boy?"

He turned to show her the tears that were streaking down his cheeks again.

That succeeded in breaking her. Kneeling down, she lifted his shirt to wipe his cheeks. "I'm new to this place. Where do you normally go to buy meat?"

"There's a market, but me pa said that they'd rob me there. He told me to look in the crowd for a huntress or to seek a cart with carcasses."

"Where's this market?"

He pointed toward the huge tower in the center of town.

Tanis considered her options. There weren't many, and she wasn't about to chase down the man with those hides. Not unless she could legally beat him.

Which was probably a bad idea. The last thing she wanted was to be arrested or beaten, or whatever it was that humans did to punish those who broke their laws.

So, she focused on the little boy's needs. "Let's try your market and see if I have better luck negotiating for meat."

What she knew about people was that they liked to prey on those who were weaker. If she was with the boy, maybe she could keep him from being victimized.

And if they were really lucky, she might run into Dash and Halla there. They would definitely help them.

He hesitated, then took her hand. She allowed him to lead her through the crowd until they came to an area where merchants gathered.

It seemed harmless enough. Until she saw two thieves steal a man's purse. Laughing, the one who cut the strings tossed the small bag to his companion, who pocketed it and then dodged madly into the crowd.

The man they'd robbed shouted, then took off running after them.

Humans...

Things such as that *never* happened in Indara. Her father's watch would have a thief roasted alive. It explained why humans weren't allowed in their kingdom without an escort. And even then, only for a limited time.

"You'd best clutch your coin tight, boy."

He let go of her to hold his coin in both hands, under his chin. "Me name's Arthur."

She smiled at him. "I like your name. It's very regal, Arthur. My name's Tanis."

That made him smile back at her. He was rather pleasant. Very sweet. She'd had no idea that human children could be so adorable. Or cute.

"Wart!"

The boy cringed at the loud shout. "Me father calls me Wart 'cause he says I'm a useless wart on his arse."

Tanis saw the stout, angry man storming in their direction. She could tell by the anger lines that were permanently seared into his skin that this was a man who seldom smiled. Scowling was his natural state. And he rubbed her the wrong way completely.

Without a word, he grabbed Arthur and backhanded him. "Where's the meat I told you to get?"

"P-p-please, Father." Arthur tried to break free.

"I'm not your father, brat! I'm just the one who got stuck raising you."

When he moved to strike the boy again, Tanis caught his arm. "Enough!"

He turned on her with a sneer. "You need a slap, too?" he snarled at her.

A deep, resonant voice spoke before she had a chance. "Not if you want to keep your arm attached to your body."

Only one creature growled like that.

Dash.

Her gaze went past the bitter man to...

Whoa. She couldn't breathe or move as she beheld the handsomest, most splendid male she'd ever seen. With long, wavy, black hair that reached to his shoulders, he towered over Arthur's father. Power and lethal strength bled from every pore of his body.

He was fierce and massive. A natural predator.

The dragon in her recognized his kind. This one was a true dragon slayer. A warrior of unparalleled skill and cunning.

That was her thought, until she met his eyes.

A vibrant, unholy green, filled with fury. A most unusual color she'd seen only one other time...

Her unicorn.

So... dragons weren't the only ones unicorns could turn human. And it explained so much. It made her wonder if that was why her father had always been opposed to their kind.

Did all dragons know the unicorns could shift, or was she the only one ignorant of it?

"Who do you think you are?" the human sneered at Dash.

A wicked smile spread across the unicorn's sharp, chiseled human features. "The one who will rip your arm off and beat you with it if you don't find another place to assault with your stench."

Arthur's father bristled. It was obvious he wanted to argue. But his common sense prevailed. He was no match for the unicorn, and they all knew it.

When he started away with Arthur in tow, Dash stopped him. "You won't be needing *that*."

"He's me boy."

"You said he wasn't," Dash reminded him.

That sneer returned as he flung Arthur away from him. "Fine. Take him. He's useless, anyway."

Dash caught the befuddled boy and waited until the old man had vanished in the crowd.

Tears streaked down Arthur's face. "What am I to do now?"

"Live." Dash ruffled his hair. "I know someone who'll care for you and not beat you."

Arthur looked up with hopeful eyes. "Really?"

With a tender smile, Dash nodded. "You shouldn't have to pay for your life with pain, little one. Never let anyone make you feel that you're less." He set the boy on his feet. "Hally?" Tanis smiled at the nickname Dash used for Halla whenever he asked her to do something for him. He always said it like an endearment.

Once again in human form, the hobgoblin stepped forward. "Aye, lord?"

"Take the boy to Ector and ask him to squire him for me."

Halla arched a pale brow. "You certain? Last time we

were there, Ector wasn't so kind. He rather took issue with you, as I recall."

Dash snorted. "Ector will get over it. Besides, this one has a destiny. Ector will be grateful to have him in his household. Trust me. And if he gives you grief, remind the surly old bastard that he owes me a favor. Tell him to take care of our Arthur. Otherwise, he'll answer to me."

With a curt nod, Halla took Arthur and left.

Tanis glanced around to make sure no one else was paying attention to them. "So... I'm not the only one you can make human, I see."

Dash started to lie to her, but what was the use? Lies weren't a unicorn trait. And he had much more important things to do.

"It's not something we talk about."

"Understood... and thank you for helping Arthur."

Her gratitude embarrassed him. He wasn't used to people showing appreciation where he was concerned. Only anger, resentment and demands.

Even Halla.

No, especially Halla.

Her smile turned speculative. "So... my lord, thought you didn't want to get involved with others. Why the sudden change for the boy?"

"No change. I didn't want the boy hurt."

"Or me?"

He sensed that she was teasing him. "That, too, would have been unfortunate. Especially before you've had a chance to wreak your vengeance."

"Indeed. But may I ask why you care?"

Dash wished he had an answer for her. It wasn't like him

to care at all. He just didn't like to see others suffering. Not after what they'd done to him when he'd been a colt.

And while she was beautiful, it was a façade. This wasn't her real body.

You know better.

The magick that allowed them to shape-shift didn't naturally make someone beautiful. Like a unicorn horn, it echoed what was on the inside.

An ugly soul manifested as a hideous beast.

No one could hide their true nature from his spell. So, for the dragon to be so fair...

She was as naive inside as his sister had been.

And that naivete had killed Renata. She'd refused to see the ugliness that others hid so carefully. To believe darkness could devour all light. And that the goodness in her soul could become the ultimate weapon that an enemy would use against her.

Or him.

"You've yet to answer my question, Lord Unicorn."

"What do you want me to say, Dragon? That I care for you?"

She burst out laughing.

He arched a brow.

"You were joking, were you not?" she asked.

In truth, he didn't know. The last three days with her had been... he didn't know how to describe it. He wanted to strangle her more times than not. She teased him when she shouldn't and even took delight in it. Even more stunning, he'd teased her back.

And yet...

There was something about her that he found...

He had no words. Interesting didn't explain it.

Quirky? No.

Beguiling? Definitely not.

She was under his skin in a way that was both chafing and pleasant. How that was possible, he didn't know.

The dragon challenged him. Made him think of things he didn't normally consider. Most of all, she wasn't afraid of him, and he found that refreshing.

That's because she has no idea who you are.

Probably. Those who knew him were terrified of his wrath. Well, most who knew him. Halla didn't fear him because she'd been his father's court jester. She foolishly believed her position protected her.

As for Ryper...

No one knew his mind. Ryper had a death wish and feared nothing and no one.

As for the other Outlaws, most of them were like Ryper and didn't care if they lived or died. Therefore, they feared nothing.

Not even him.

But that wasn't what drew him to the dragon. It had to be something else. Not that it mattered. Whatever it was, he was in a state of constant arousal around her, and it wasn't just sexual.

Yes, he was physically attracted to her, but she stimulated much more than just his cock. She kept him on edge and sharp.

No one had ever done that before.

And he strangely liked it.

She was a unique creature and while he didn't know what these feelings were that he had for her, they were unlike any he'd ever felt for anyone else. "Do you really value yourself so little, Dragon?"

Tanis paused at his peculiar question. "We don't know each other. At all. It's far more likely that my magick you took is playing havoc with you."

That intrigued him. "How so?"

"Dragons are made of fire and venom. Unicorns are made of... well, unicorn magick, whatever that is... fluff and glitter."

"Fluff and glitter?" Offended, he quirked one handsome brow at her. "You think I can't handle your fire?"

"I would think it a burden, yes."

He snorted. "As I said earlier, you don't weigh enough to be a burden to me."

She gave him a goofy look as she held her hands up to indicate her body. "Only in this form. If I were a dragon, my weight would crush you... and it would have been my foot on your rump to hold *you* down."

"As long as you were keeping me from foolishness, I'd welcome it."

His confession surprised her. "Truly?"

"Why do you think I haven't speared Halla over her incessant digs and impudence?"

Tanis paused at that. "I hadn't given it any thought."

"Perhaps you should. I value prudence and intelligence, even when it's not my own. And sometimes, especially because it's not my own. And for the record, unicorns are *not* fluff and effing glitter. Contrary to popular opinion, we don't fart or piss rainbows." He actually shuddered.

Dumbfounded, she watched as he headed off into the crowd. How strange that she'd taken him as arrogant.

Now that she thought about it, he wasn't. He did actually listen to Halla's advice a great deal. And unlike her, he watched and weighed matters before he acted. He was very thoughtful. Circumspect.

There was something deeper inside him. Something...

He was vanishing! Oh, he was leaving!

Her heart skipped as she realized that fact.

Not wanting to be left alone again in this world that she really didn't understand, she ran after him. It wasn't weakness that made her follow. Just confusion. She hadn't tried to live among human people, only to escape them.

Dash seemed to know a good deal about the human realm... like his friend he'd told Halla to take Arthur to. Unlike her, he wasn't a stranger in these lands.

Prudence dictated that she at least remain friendly with Dash until she found her dragon slayer fraud.

So, she headed after him.

And as she followed, she noticed how much attention he drew from others. Men and women. Especially the women.

It wasn't just that he was handsome and well-dressed in his black leather armor and cloak. It was how he carried himself. With the confident swagger of a beast well accustomed to respect and victory. To command.

By that cocky swagger, it was obvious his conquests weren't just on the battlefield.

Yet he paid no attention to any of the people he passed. He strode forward with a determined stride that made her very curious about him. All the time she'd been held captive by her last unicorn master, she'd never cared to learn anything about unicorns or anyone else. She'd hated them all and wanted them dead.

This time, she was curious.

Baracus had never shifted forms around her. He'd been a gray, filthy horse with an equally gray horn. While he'd spoken to others, he'd never once deigned to speak to her.

Not even when she'd killed him for her freedom.

There had been nothing remotely appealing about him.

Unlike Dash, who bled sex appeal from every molecule of his body.

For the first time in her life, she felt attraction for someone, and it terrified her. It was so unexpected. Because of what Baracus had done to her, she'd never, ever looked at another male of any species and found them attractive.

Never looked at anyone.

She'd expected to live out the rest of her life alone and chaste.

But as she watched Dash, she wanted to touch his hair and see if it was as soft as his mane had been.

Don't you dare!

Men were cruel and hateful. She knew that better than anyone. So were women. Sometimes even more so. No one could be trusted. Not for anything.

Her heart had been shattered and she would never trust anyone again.

They were enemies and they must remain so. She was nothing to Dash other than a servant he'd bargained for, and that was all she'd ever be. There was no need to ever delude herself with stupidity. Her days of dreaming and believing that the world was a kind and decent place were over.

He thought of her the same way he did Halla. A burden that followed him around.

She was no longer that little dragon in the valley who believed in fairytales. In the kindness of strangers. That one day she might find someone she could share her life with. A wonderful life partner who would value her and treasure her. Treat her with respect... like Davin did with Marla.

That would never be her life. And thinking about it would only lead to more heartbreak and sorrow.

Dash was here for the same reason she was.

Vengeance.

Her father had always called her an impetuous daydreamer. It was why he'd blamed her for running into the snare that had cost her two years of her life.

Get your head out of your ass, Tanis. Just because you can fly doesn't mean you can keep your head in the clouds. You need to pay attention to what's right in front of you!

But there had been nothing to pay attention to.

To this day, her father blamed her for everything that had happened. Blamed her for being taken against her will.

Don't think about it.

And don't think about Dash. He was definitely off limits.He slowed his pace as they neared a building with a white shield hanging outside. It had a red hand holding a gold cup painted on it.

To her surprise, he opened the door and allowed her to enter first.

Then, he took her arm.

"What are you doing?" she asked.

"Keeping you safe."

Her first instinct was to be offended and to tell him that she could take care of herself. But as she noticed the attention on her from the building's occupants, she was very grateful for his consideration. "Thank you."

This was a den of thieves and cutthroats who made their living preying on others. There was no mistaking the nasty, barbaric clientele. As a fellow predator, she easily recognized their breed, and she wasn't really looking for a bar fight with them.

They would have gladly challenged her, thinking they could overpower her and prove themselves at her expense. Some she could have taken in a fight.

Several, she'd have to work for.

But there were a number of them that would be very iffy and some she'd definitely lose to.

And that wasn't counting the two in back who could quash her like a bug.

That being said, Dash was easily the deadliest creature here, and they all knew it, too. So, they stepped aside as he walked through them and gave him space, and her deference because she was with him.

He headed to the bar where the keeper stood with a nasty glower on his face. Even when they approached, he offered no greeting. Just a grim sneer that acknowledged their presence.

Dash pulled out a gold coin and placed it on the counter. "I'm looking for a man with a distinct spiral gold wand. I was told he was heading this way, and I'm hoping he came in here to run his mouth and brag."

The keeper took the coin and examined it before he slid it into the pocket of his tunic. "Not a man. You're looking for the Imp Peddler."

Dash narrowed his gaze. "Pardon?"

"That's the name he goes by. He was in here saying he was planning to auction off all kinds of items in a sennight. Wanted us to know where to go if we were interested. Told me to let my clients know about the auction. More the merrier, he said. He's hoping to get enough money to be richer than a dragon in a gold mine."

Tanis felt her heart race at something she hadn't considered before. It sickened her to think about someone holding an auction to bid for her brother. "Did he have a dragon's skull, too?"

He pointed to a hand-drawn poster on the wall beside the bar that had information written on it. "The so-called dragon slayer with him said he had one. But if you ask me, the boy looked more like a peasant farmer."

The keeper wiped at his nose. "'Course, I think it's all fake shite they either made or found. But if you want to waste your fool money on what they're selling, be my guest. They're holding their auction at the Sester castle in Pagos."

There was a strange light in Dash's emerald eyes as he looked at the list on the poster. Tanis moved closer to read it while the keeper kept talking.

"I don't remember everything the drunkard was rambling on about. Golden wand stood out 'cause the imp was showing it off, threatening to use it. Said he could turn us into crickets or maggots. The boy braggart said he'd cleaved the skull from a dragon prince in a fierce battle when he'd gone to Indara to visit. As if anyone with sense would ever venture there." He paused to think for a moment. "Seems like the imp said he had red fairy tears, supposedly from a queen what was in love with one of them. Penis from a virgin troll. Twelve feathers from a gray battle gryphon. Flayed skin of a murderer what was hanged on a rainy night. Crazy shite such as that. Other than the magic wand, I have no idea why anyone would want any of the rest of it."

A man to the right of her started laughing. "I do. The imp swore you could combine the lot of them into a spell that he was selling with it."

"Spell for what?" Tanis asked.

He took a deep swig from his mug before he answered. "They're all the ingredients you'd need to kill the vilest bastard in this world."

She still had no idea who that was.

Not until a man on her left spat on the floor and sneered. "Wish it was true. If I thought for one minute you could cast a spell to kill the unicorn king and take his place, I'd be the first to outbid them all for it."

"Unicorn king?" she repeated.

The keeper looked at her wryly as if she was as daft as she felt. "Deciel Coeur de Noir. The bastard what rules all Thirteen Kingdoms. Who wouldn't want to kill him?"

Tanis gasped as that name went through her head like a clap of thunder, and she turned to stare at the man who wasn't really a man standing right beside her.

The black unicorn.

Deciel Coeur de Noir. *Dashell*... Blackheart.

Dash.

Fuck me.

CHAPTER 7

S*ay nothing, Lady Dragon.*" Dash's voice was loud and clear in her thoughts.

Tanis considered how much she wanted to out him to the ruffians in the tavern. But he held her dragon powers, and she would definitely need those back. Along with her dragon body.

And given who he was...

He would gut her long before they gutted him.

Not to mention, she was no longer sure killing him would return her to her dragon form. He wasn't just *a* unicorn.

He was the most lethal creature in existence.

The High King of all kingdoms.

What have I done?

Of all the beasts she could have captured...

The High King of the Thirteen Kingdoms. Deciel Coeur de Noir.

How? Why?

Oh dear gods...

She was so lucky she was alive. No wonder he appeared dangerous.

He *was* dangerous.

No. He was danger personified.

This was a unicorn who literally impaled others for entertainment. He wore body parts as statement pieces.

The stories about him were legendary and terrible.

Honestly, she wanted to run. No, she wanted to run screaming. Screaming and rending her hair.

What do I do?

Dash smirked at the keeper. "Well, as you said, I'm sure it's all bullshit. If a mere spell could kill Coeur de Noir, he'd have been dead ten times over." He inclined his head to the man. "Thank you for the information."

Then, he gestured at the poster. "Mind if I take this?"

"Go ahead. Not sure if anyone else here is even literate."

With a gruff snort, Dash took the poster down, folded it up and tucked it into the pouch at his waist.

Taking her arm, he headed for the door.

Don't act suspicious, she told herself as they walked across the room.

But how did one not act suspicious? She was no longer sure because she felt like everyone was staring at them.

Were they?

They'd been before. How could they not know who he was? It was so obvious.

You didn't know till they told you.

'Cause I'm an idiot!

No wonder her father had always called her one. He'd

been right and she'd been lying to herself when she'd thought herself smart.

I'm going to die. Slowly. Painfully. Most likely impaled on a black unicorn horn. With her soul sucked out of her for good measure.

Her ears were buzzing. She was sweating and shivering at the same time. Damn this human body.

"Breathe, little dragon," he whispered.

Easy for him to say. He was the most feared monster of all time. Forget being a dragon. They had nothing on him when it came to brutality. They might breathe fire and fly, but he had quelled the mightiest of her people.

Even her father paid tribute to him. Not out of respect. Balls out, holy terror.

They weren't even allowed to say his name in her father's court for fear that he might somehow know it and wipe them out. Every kingdom lived in terror of this king's wrath.

Not of his army.

Fear that he'd show up, personally, and slaughter them all. Just for entertainment.

Not even in their sleep, either. No. He made an example in how he executed those he declared his enemies. Bloody. Gory. There was no mistaking when someone crossed him.

He had stabbed his own father in the heart, in front of their court and his father's bodyguards.

Not even bards wrote songs about him.

They were too afraid to lest it offend him, and he used their lute strings to cut off their heads and fingers.

His deeds were spoken of in terrified whispers. Or by

mothers who wanted to frighten their children into good behavior. *Don't do that or the Unicorn King will come for you!*

And she had just spent three nights camping with him. Three days riding on his back.

I captured him in a freaking net!

Oh my God...

How was she still alive?

By the time they were outside, she could barely stand.

And she was angry. Furious, actually.

So much so that she couldn't contain herself. Without thinking, she shoved him. "Why didn't you tell me who you were?!"

Dash froze in complete shock at her attack. No one had dared to strike him since he'd killed his father after his father had backhanded him.

Not even Ryper.

To this day, he could see the shocked look on his father's face when he'd finally fought back.

On that fateful day when his horn had turned black, he'd promised himself that no one would ever again lay a hand to him without paying for it with blood.

And no one had.

Until now.

But Dash could never harm someone so much smaller than him. Ever. It wasn't in him to do such.

Besides, she wasn't out to hurt him. She was merely upset and had no idea how close she was to being splintered into a thousand pieces.

Calming himself, he cleared his throat. "Probably for the same reason you didn't tell me you were the daughter of King Iagan."

That took some of the anger from her as she stepped back and looked around nervously. "How do you know that?" she whispered.

Was she serious? "He just said the dragon's skull was royal. There's only one royal dragon family. If that's your brother's skull... he was Prince Davin Dragomir."

The king's only son. Was she not aware of how many times Dash had met with her father? Or the fact that he'd known her brother? The only surprise here was that he hadn't met *her* when he'd been to their court.

She bit her lip. "Oh."

"Oh? Is that really all you have to say?"

"You're a villain?"

He blinked slowly. Mostly because he was strangely amused by the insult that should have pissed him off. He wasn't a villain. He'd done what he had to, to ensure peace for his people. To protect *all* kingdoms.

Yes, he'd been vicious. Ruthless, even. But when he'd come to power, the kingdoms had been in a constant state of war.

No one had been safe, and millions had been needlessly slaughtered.

His father had made countless treaties and allowed others to walk all over their people. Just as the other kings and queens had done. No one's throne had been safe.

Dash made no apologies for what he'd done to restore law and order to the lands. And he *never* would. He'd brought about an unprecedented time of peace. If that made him a villain, then he relished the title.

"Tell me something, princess. When you left your island

kingdom and crossed my border to set the trap in my land for a unicorn, were you afraid?"

She frowned at him. "What?"

"You heard my question. Even though unicorns and dragons have been enemies for generations, when you entered Licordian lands, were you afraid of being caught in our territory?"

"Well... no."

"What did you think would happen if a unicorn found you visiting in our lands?"

Tanis wasn't sure why this was important. "Nothing."

"That's right. No one would have bothered you for being there. They damn sure wouldn't have butchered you. Have you any idea what would have happened twenty years ago had you been caught in Licordia?"

"I'd have been slaughtered."

Yes, she would have. Brutally. They would have sent her back to her father in pieces. And no one would have been punished for it.

"Now, after more than a decade of peace, someone is killing my people and yours while they sleep. I want to know who."

Tanis paused as she remembered his questions when they'd met. "Is that why you asked me why I didn't burn down the village?"

He nodded. "You wanted justice against a single person for your brother's murder. My job is to make sure you get it."

For a monster, he seemed remarkably reasonable. But one thing concerned her. "Had I wanted to burn down the village?"

"I think you know what I would have done to you."

Kill her. Without any hesitation or reservation whatsoever.

She swallowed hard as her fear returned. He had no remorse for all the lives he'd taken. "How do you sleep at night?"

"With my head on a pillow."

That was not comforting at all. Nor was the cold look in his eyes. His beauty made that brutality all the more obscene and shocking.

Kill him.

For the sake of all the kingdoms, she needed to. No one had ever been able to get this close to him. Over and over, she'd heard her father and uncles talking about it.

Someone needs to stop that psycho. He has spies everywhere and an assassin at his side. Always demanding lives when they breach the laws he passes. If only we could get our own assassin inside his castle and end his reign.

But every time someone had tried, they'd failed and died for their attempt.

His laws were brutal, and he made no exceptions. If found guilty, he made an example of the guilty party as a warning to others.

Obey me or die begging for a mercy I will not give.

Granted it was something she planned to do to the man who'd killed her brother, but that was different. Hers was personal.

His wasn't.

She'd heard the tales. He'd gutted people for doing nothing more than stealing bread to feed their starving family. That was unforgivable. Heartless.

"Why aren't you killing me?" she asked him.

"I believe in justice, Dragon." He paused in the street and jerked his chin toward a group of children who were playing nearby. "You see them?"

"Yes."

"When I first inherited my father's crown, mothers kept their children hidden in their homes. They were too afraid to let them outside for fear of what would happen to them if they dared leave their homes for even a few minutes. Men hid their daughters and wives for the same reasons. Innocents were kidnapped and sold for brutal games, slavery and brothels. I fought constantly with my sister, because I knew what someone could do to her, and she hated me for it."

Tanis swallowed as she remembered having those fights with her own father.

Worse was the fact that she'd been one of the innocents who'd been taken.

"I did what I had to, to make sure my kingdom was safe for her and all the other children who deserved to grow up without fear. And once Licordia was secure, I did whatever it took for the innocents in the other kingdoms to sleep in peace and security. I am the monster they all fear, and I will remain so until the day I die. Because as long as I'm here, those children will play in the streets and know no harm. I will never apologize for that. If the world wants to hate me for it, so be it. Better they fear one monster in a distant palace far away from them, than thousands of monsters lurking in every dark corner and alley they pass, seeking to do them harm. Or worse, monsters who break into their homes to hurt them whenever they lay their weary heads down to sleep."

The sincerity in his voice sent a chill down her spine.

What had made him like this? Had he been harmed, too? He spoke with the same determined fury inside him that she held. That inconsolable rage that burned so deep and hot that it often frightened her because it never dulled. Nothing quenched it. While she might be able to set it to simmer at times, it was always there, waiting to bubble up at the worst moments.

If he had suffered as she had, it would make sense and explain his need to control the world. She'd felt the same way once she returned home.

Only she'd lacked his power to make everything better.

And if what she suspected was true, it made him all the deadlier. Because that rage was eternal.

Without another word, he took off through the crowd.

"Where are we going, beast?" she asked.

"I have a man to kill and so do you."

"You mean an imp, don't you?"

Dash snorted. "Imp, man, irritant. All the same."

To him, probably, but she didn't think of them that way. "Did the imp steal the magick wand from you?"

"What?"

She had to struggle to keep up with Dash's long strides. "The golden wand you asked about. Is that what you were after when I captured you?"

Dash slowed as he realized what he'd let slip. Over the last three days, he'd said much of nothing to the dragon.

Halla had done most of the talking, and the two of them had chatted about nothing of any consequence. Halla was good at that. So was the dragon.

Damn it. It wasn't like him to talk about personal

matters. He'd learned long ago that such things could and would be weaponized against him.

Never let anyone see any kind of vulnerability.

Never let anyone know what bleeds.

How could he forget that?

So, he quickly switched the subject. "You didn't capture me."

"You ran into my net."

"A technicality."

"You landed on your arse, beast. I saw it."

He growled low in his throat at her reminder. Why did he tolerate her insubordination? Not even Halla would have dared such with him.

Renata would have. She'd have laughed, to boot.

But she was an exception. His sister had nerves of steel honed by the knowledge that she could get away with murder where he was concerned. That was only because she'd won his heart the moment she'd been born.

God, he could still see her laughing at him while she yanked at his hair.

No one else had ever loved him. Ever accepted him without judgement.

Not his father, nor his mother who forever let him know that he was a disappointment.

And he'd failed his sister...

Never had he hated himself more than he did right now. All he'd done to make this world safe for Renata and it hadn't been enough.

You're worthless, boy! They should have cut your throat when you were born instead of your cord!

His father had been right, after all. They should have

strangled him with his umbilical cord and saved them all the misery of his life. He hadn't been worth the cost of raising him.

Or the trouble.

He sighed heavily as he stared at the dragon. "Is your sole purpose to torment me?"

"Not my *sole* purpose. Just a happy bonus."

"Lovely." He headed toward the village gates.

She kept pace beside him. "You didn't answer my question, beast."

"Because I didn't want to."

"But I want to know. Were you after all the ingredients to destroy them so that they couldn't be used against you? You only asked about the wand, at first. Did you know about the others? Or was the wand the only thing you were after?"

"Oh dear gods..."

"You know, if you turned me back into a dragon, we could get there faster. I could fly."

"Is everyone in Indara so loquacious?"

She blinked at his question. "There's a word you don't hear every day. Loquacious. It's kind of fun to say, isn't it? Loquacious."

"Is it your sole intent to drive me to madness? Or do you just want to piss me off?"

Tanis stopped as she realized that he was getting irritated, and that really wasn't her intent. She wanted him to answer her. "No. Definitely don't want to upset the bogey man. I just forgot again who you were, and I did want to know about the wand. I'll shut up now."

Dash stopped as she pressed her lips together to stop her

insane rambling. And it was only then that he fully realized why he'd tolerated her impertinence.

Over the last three days, it really had been because she'd had no idea who he was.

To her, he'd been a random unicorn. Granted, he'd been the unicorn who owned her, but she'd had no knowledge that he was the scourge of their lands.

For the whole of his life, he'd either been the crown prince or the High King.

Those around him had either hated him for it. Or kissed his ass.

How he'd love to say his title had been a blessing, but it had brought him nothing save absolute misery. His parents were a prime example of that, too.

Because of their highborn positions, they'd been unable to marry. Unable to tell anyone of their relationship for fear of the political consequences. So, his mother had left Licordia, an embittered woman who got along with no one.

Not even Dash.

She'd birthed him far away from Licordia, then sent him to his father to raise in a home with a stepmother who had no use for a bastard heir, or anything that reminded her of the fact her royal husband had cheated on her.

And because his father had been the fourth born son who'd only inherited the throne after his brothers had died without issue, he'd resented the fact that Dash was a constant reminder of a love he could never claim due to a responsibility he resented just as much.

You won't be like my brothers.

According to his father, even though they'd been the highest born princes, they'd been wastrels. Bullies who'd expected everyone to wait on them and do as they commanded. He'd wanted his son to understand what being a king meant. To never take for granted a position his father felt he didn't deserve.

Fucking bastard.

Till the day Dash had ended his father's life, Dash had expected him to leave the throne to his legitimate daughter, Renata. It was, after all, his father's favorite threat.

Honestly, he wouldn't have cared. She'd have been the better monarch.

At least Renata had a heart. As was proven by the fact that her horn had been golden. A gold horn on a unicorn was one of the rarest of all. It'd been over three hundred years since any unicorn had grown one.

The only other horn almost as rare was his.

A black one.

Not that it was better. Indeed, a black horn came from the darkest magick. Soulless magick. No one was more powerful. Not even a gold horn.

And only a gold horn could kill him.

Or the spell the imp was trying to sell.

The two of them combined... Dash didn't stand a chance. Now it wasn't a question of just finding Renata's wand, he had to find and destroy that spell, too.

If he could manage to destroy both the horn and spell, he'd be invincible.

At least technically. While in human form, he was still vulnerable to a degree. As a human, he could fall victim to another spell. And if someone found his own horn while he was in human form, they could use it to kill him.

But it would be a lot harder to find his wand and use it against him, than it would be to kill him with Renata's.

Which was why he had to recover Renata's horn at any cost. Not just because it held the ability to kill him, but because it was all he had left of her. The thought of any part of her being in the hands of her killer...

It disgusted him.

She had been the purest, kindest creature ever born. If he could get to her horn in time, he had the powers inherited from his mother that might allow him to reawaken her spirit enough to say goodbye.

To ask forgiveness for the harsh words he'd said that last time he'd seen her.

That was all he wanted. He just needed to make peace with the only person in his life who'd loved him.

"I didn't mean to hurt your feelings, Dragon."

Tanis scowled at the odd note in his voice. She wasn't sure which of them was the most shocked by his apology. "You didn't hurt them. I know I'm irritating. My father and sisters are always telling me to shut up and go away."

"You're not really irritating. I'm often impatient with others. My sister and Halla have often told me it's one of my greater flaws."

Those words caught her off guard, too. Wrinkling her nose, she playfully nudged him. "I won't say you're not impatient. But it's easy to be impatient when others try your patience."

He actually smiled.

And that made her breath catch in her throat. As handsome as he'd been before, he was truly spectacular when his eyes sparkled with humor. She'd never seen anything so incredible.

It sent a wave of desire through her so fierce that it was shocking, and for a moment, she couldn't breathe.

How in the name of the Thirteen Kingdoms had the High King remained unmarried? Were the unicorn princesses insane?

Or completely cold-blooded?

Her brother had been nowhere near so gorgeous, and she-dragons had hunted him relentlessly from the moment he'd hit puberty until Marla had dragged him to the altar, kicking and screaming.

Well, not entirely screaming.

But Davin had done his best to delay marriage as long as possible. He'd wanted to keep his options open. Their father, however, had wanted to secure their throne.

Which had really infuriated her sisters who'd wanted to be named heirs instead of their brother.

Iagan Dragomir hadn't cared what they wanted. His goal had been to incorporate their northern lands that were ruled by Prince Dagur, and Dagur only had daughters, which meant Davin was forced to marry Marla or risk being disinherited forever.

Davin had quickly seen the wisdom of his father's wishes. And Marla had been more than pleased to marry him in turn. Who wouldn't want to be a future queen and the leader of her own lands in her own right? Something neither of their fathers knew about because Davin had promised Marla in private that he would never exert his control over her father's land. Her brother had promised to make her queen in her own right once he inherited their father's crown.

That was what had made her brother so incredible.

But what in the world would have kept a king of Dash's magnitude from marrying? How was it possible that she-unicorns weren't lined up the street, after him?

And before she could say anything more, excitement broke out all around them.

Tanis frowned as she tried to figure out what was happening.

Dash pulled her close to his side. It took her a second to realize that he was doing so in order to protect her from the rushing crowd that would have trampled her easily in their excitement.

"Is it true?"

"Have you heard?"

"I want that money!"

"Give me the poster!"

Voices ran together, sharing news. But she couldn't quite tell what the news was that they were passing.

Dash grabbed a man as he rushed past. "What's going on?"

The man handed him a poster. "The High King's left his palace without his army. His guard's hunting him. There's a bounty being offered for his life!"

CHAPTER 8

Tanis froze as she saw the amount being offered for Dash's life. One million gold sovereigns. It hung there like a tangible, taunting beast.

Never had she seen a bounty so high. Not for even the worst criminals.

"Who's offering *that*?" she whispered

Dash handed her the poster. "Seven kingdoms are providing a portion of it. Doesn't name which seven. But it's to be paid to whomever delivers my head to my palace... so I would assume the ringleader is already sitting on my throne."

Her jaw went slack.

Until she saw the drawing, then she almost laughed. Luckily, she caught herself before she did so. "Well... good news. It's not an exact likeness." She turned the picture toward him. "Your cheeks aren't quite that sharp. Nor is the cleft in your chin so pronounced. You do have whiskers, but not that thick, and your ears aren't freakishly small. You only have a slight widow's peak, not that deep V thing they drew that makes you look like a vampire caricature. And while they did do a good job on your lips, they totally messed up your eyes. Thank the gods they didn't get a better artist."

He didn't appear the least bit amused or flattered by her attempt to make him feel better.

Folding it up, she held it out toward him. "Look on the bright side, it's not enchanted. Imagine if they'd hired an elf or wizard to draw it. Those are terrifyingly accurate and animated, to boot."

He gave her droll stare.

"Well, they are. Besides, all you have to do is change back into a unicorn and who'll be able to identify you, then? I mean, really. A solid black unicorn? No one would ever know it's you."

He smacked his lips at her and the black unicorn on the poster. "We don't all look alike."

"Don't you?"

He glared at her as he snatched the poster from her hand. "No."

She gestured at the horses around her to prove her point. "Really? You can tell them apart?"

"I promise you, another unicorn or centaur would know the difference immediately. Just as a dragon would know you in your dragon body."

"Fair point." Biting her lip, she glanced at the crowd that had yet to recognize him. "So, what do we do?"

"Get out of here as quickly as possible."

That was a sound idea. Survival was normally a good thing. "You lead. I follow."

Taking her arm, he gently pulled her through the crowd that thankfully wasn't paying any attention to them. Yet. Even so, she kept waiting for them to realize who they were and pounce.

Then again, they were looking for a lone black unicorn. Or a handsome king. Not an inconspicuous traveler with a woman by his side.

Well, he wasn't exactly inconspicuous.

Okay, he wasn't inconspicuous at all. He was an ominously handsome traveler.

However, they were a couple. No one expected the hated High King of the Thirteen Kingdoms to be dragging a bumpkin like her around with him. And why would he, given his lethal reputation? He should have been traveling with an armed escort or a noble snobby lady.

"Should we ride out of town?" she asked.

"No. That could draw too much attention." Dash said those words to her, but he really wanted a horse, or to use his magick to get them out of here as quickly as possible. He just couldn't risk it.

Changing into a unicorn would definitely draw unwanted attention. Sadly, there was only one unicorn with a black horn in existence.

And he was it. They were already lucky no one had remembered seeing him come into town as a unicorn with Halla. That had been an act of utter stupidity, and he wouldn't make it again.

Although... he could use his powers to disguise the horn or remove it while he was in equine form, but that would cost him in terms of his powers and physical strength, and if he had to fight his way out of here, he couldn't afford to be weakened. If he bought two horses, that could raise questions from a nosy stable attendant who could become a witness later for someone to question.

Or a body they'd have to hide.

No, best to walk out of town nonchalantly with the crowd and pray no one noticed them.

But the real question was who had placed that bounty on his head? Only Ryper and two unicorns, Kronnel and Keryna, knew he'd left his palace to go after Renata. He hadn't mentioned it to anyone else.

Which meant one of them must have betrayed him with that poster.

He knew for a fact it wasn't Ryper. If Ryper had wanted the throne, he would have cut his throat long ago and taken it. For that matter, Ryper had his own throne he was entitled to that he could take.

But the man held no interest in power.

Not to mention, Ryper didn't play games, and he had no ambition to rule anyone other than himself. In truth, he didn't know what Ryper valued. It wasn't money. Wasn't power.

Ryper was a mystery to everyone.

Which left only two others. His second-in-command or Renata's best friend. Or the two of them working together.

Why was he even surprised that they'd done this? Betrayal always came from within, otherwise it wouldn't be betrayal.

Fucking, power-hungry roaches, making a play for his throne the minute his back was turned. As if they could keep the peace he'd maintained this last decade. The only reason he could sustain it was because he was immortal and powerful.

Even so...

Look what happened the first time he left his throne room. One of his advisors or Renata's had called out the dogs on him, thinking they could bring him down and take his place.

They might. If he didn't get back to his army and quell this uprising, they could succeed.

But it wouldn't last. The other kingdoms would go back to warring, and everything he'd accomplished could end.

Damn it all.

And where was Ryper in all this? He knew to stay behind and keep Dash's absence from the others. Obviously, he was as reliable as Halla.

Never trust an assassin.

They had a nasty tendency to vanish when they were needed.

Dash sighed as he tried to figure all this out, and a bad feeling went through him.

The dragon patted him on his back.

Dash scowled at her. What was she doing?

"You look like you could use a hug. But since I'm not sure you'd appreciate a hug, I thought a friendly pat might be welcomed."

She was such an odd creature. "You're trying to comfort me?"

"Of course. It's what you do when someone's upset. And you definitely look upset."

Not in his experience. If he'd ever cried over anything,

he'd been beaten until he stopped. *You want to cry? I'll give you something to cry over.*

She duplicated his scowl. "You know, Dash. The old *there, there.*"

He bit back a smile at her conciliatory words. "I'm fine, Dragon."

"If you say so. But really, you need to tell that to your face, because your expression says that you're about to gut whatever or whoever comes into your path... or you ate something that didn't agree with you. Either way, you're starting to scare small children and one dragon in human form."

He snorted at her peculiar humor that somehow made him feel better. It didn't make sense. And he had no idea how it worked, but she had cheered him. "Really, I'm fine."

He offered her a smile.

"That is even more terrifying, beast. You should go back to brooding." She held her hands up like claws to her chest and screwed her face up. "You know, errr! Errr!"

Shaking his head, he laughed. She was... he had no words. He'd never met anyone else like her.

Without thinking, he pulled her close and gave her a light squeeze. "Thank you, Dragon."

Tanis couldn't breathe as she felt his arms around her. No one had given her a hug like this. It was sweet and heartfelt.

Most of all, it was warm. And it pulled her against a body that was rock hard and incredible. One that sent an unexpected wave of desire through her that was so strong, it left her breathless. Shaking.

The scent of leather and unicorn was unlike anything

she'd ever experienced. Worse? She wanted to bury her nose against him and just inhale it until she was drunk from it.

Oh my God...

What was wrong with her? He'd be horrified if he had any idea what she was thinking.

She was horrified by what she was thinking. Swallowing hard, she put a little more distance between them. Because right then, the thoughts in her mind brought a heated blush to her cheeks. And this wasn't like her. She *never* had these thoughts.

He's a unicorn, Tanis!

More than that, he was the unicorn High King. But her body didn't care. It suddenly had a mind of its own. And a hunger unlike anything she'd ever known.

One that was getting worse and not better.

What am I going to do?

She knew what she *wanted* to do. But that was even worse. He was being hunted and they didn't have time to even think about *that*.

Why did he have to look so damn masculine and handsome in those clothes?

Which made her wonder how much more masculine and handsome he'd be without them.

Stop it! Stop it! Stop it!

He's a unicorn!

Tanis wanted to plug her ears. But it was the images in her mind that were betraying her. Over and over, she saw herself peeling that armor off him, piece by piece like a present she savored unwrapping.

Look to your right, Tanis! To the right!

There was an older man over there, riding a white horse. Average looking. Yes. That was what she needed. Normal.

Average.

But her gaze really wanted to travel to the mountainous beast on her left who was all masculine grace and beauty. She could feel his presence there even though she wasn't looking at him. He was feral and unpredictable.

"Are you all right, Dragon?"

Don't look at him.

"Fine."

He scoffed. "That's *never* true."

"What?"

"Whenever a woman says she's fine in that tone of voice... it's never true and it never bodes well."

She scowled at him. "Excuse me?"

"And there it is. That underlying anger that says I'm right and you're not fine."

He wasn't right. "I wasn't angry until you said that. It's the same thing as when you ask a man what he's thinking about, and he says *nothing*. It's never nothing."

"Exactly."

She stopped walking at his unexpected honesty. "What?"

"I'm admitting you're right. Men say nothing to avoid a fight the same way a woman says *fine* to avoid fighting. So, why are you so flushed?"

She'd walked right into that one. "Let's stay with this current discussion."

That caused one of his eyebrows to lift. "What? Why? Were you thinking of me naked?"

Aside from the fact it was true, it irritated her that he

was able to guess what had caused her discomfort. "Excuse me?"

The grin he gave her only increased her heart rate. "You were, weren't you? I know that look. Those dilated pupils. Those flushed cheeks."

Now her face was flushing for a whole new reason. "Ugh. You are *so* arrogant! Why would I *ever* think of you naked, beast?"

"Am I wrong?" He let out a deep, rumbling laugh. Why did he have to be so adorable?

Dash leaned down toward her, causing her breath to catch. His green eyes glowed with mischief and gave him a boyish appearance. "You still haven't answered my question, Lady Dragon. Was it my arrogance or were you picturing me naked?"

Folding her arms over her chest, she continued forward. "I will not feed your gargantuan ego, beast. I'm sure you have courtiers enough for that."

Dash grinned as he watched her head through the town's gate. He had no idea why he was teasing her so. Never in his life had he acted like this or teased about this particular topic. Ryper and Halla would have died of shock if they'd witnessed it.

He was always a surly, brooding asshole who thought of teasing playfulness as something to be left to children and drunken fools. Something he hadn't done even as a child. His life had been too brutal for such.

But he loved to watch the way her cheeks darkened from embarrassment. To match wits with her.

She was funny and quick.

Delightful.

What the hell was wrong with him? His entire world was on fire, and he was teasing a dragon about sex. It made no sense.

Coeur de Noir was an epitaph given to him because he was morose personified. Humorless.

Brutal.

Single minded about war and determined to keep order.

You should learn to smile, big brother. It won't break your face, and who knows? It might even let others see the wonderful unicorn I know you to be. I promise it won't hurt you. You might even find that you like it.

How many times had Renata said those words to him?

God, how he missed her. Yes, she was aggravating as hell. Almost as challenging as his dragon.

But she'd been his little sister. Pissing him off was just part of her role. At times, he'd been convinced it was her raison d'être.

They were supposed to clash from time to time. And they had, in that way that only siblings could.

Dash sighed as he remembered their last night together. The harsh words they'd exchanged.

Why did their last encounter have to be a fight? Until Keryna had come into Renata's life, they'd seldom ever clashed over anything. And then, only over the fact that he'd been overprotective. Which he admitted freely. He was an overprotective asshole where his sister was concerned. He had stifled her. That was very much true.

Because he'd been so afraid of something happening to her. Of having to live out the rest of his life knowing that he'd failed to keep her safe.

And as they walked, Dash kept seeing his sister's body in

his mind. The way Renata had been left by the old ruins from the Unicorn-Dragon Wars as if she was nothing when she'd been everything to him.

How could anyone destroy such a beautiful soul?

"Was this why she died?"

"What?"

He hadn't realized he'd spoken out loud. He started to ignore the dragon, but he was too upset. "The wand I'm after belonged to my sister. She ran away to join Lorencian rebels against Queen Meara after I refused to allow her any troops to donate to their cause. She wanted to be a commander and I didn't want her to see the ugliness of battle. I just wanted to protect her."

Tanis sucked her breath in sharply as she realized who he was talking about. "Princess Renata."

He inclined his head to her.

"I'm so sorry." While everyone called him a monster, Renata was said to be the noblest of creatures. Kind-hearted and generous, she was celebrated for her beauty and charity. "She was planning to fight with rebels?"

He let out a bitter laugh. "Exactly. It wasn't like her. But she'd been talked into it by her puerile advisor who convinced her what a great idea suicide would be." Then he screwed up his face as he mimicked Keryna's words and voice. "*Your brother won't let you have any fun... You're grown... You can do what you want... I wouldn't let him dictate my life.* Fucking idiot bitch."

His eyes flared. "Why couldn't my sister see through her? I will never understand it. She was a jealous dart donkey, who wanted what Renata had. All she did was insult Renata and try to move in on her life. She was always wearing her dresses and jewelry. Trying to be Renata. It was nauseating."

Tanis understood that a lot better than she wanted to. There were plenty of courtiers in her father's court who'd done similar things. Or worse, if they couldn't have what they wanted, then they sought to tear it all down.

Anything to destroy the life of the person they envied and wanted to be.

It was terrible, and it was why she'd happily withdrawn from court life.

But the one thing that didn't make sense..."Why did either of them want you to fight with centaurian rebels?"

He shrugged. "No idea. I had no intention of getting involved in centaur politics."

She couldn't blame him for that. The Thassalians and Licordians had been at war for even longer than her race and his. Had Dash not forged a treaty with Queen Meara when he took the throne, they'd probably still be fighting it.

The only other time in their history that she knew of a truce had been years ago, when Dash's father had sent hostages to Meara as a guarantee his army would stop fighting hers.

Tanis had been a hatchling at the time. But she remembered the horror stories of the battles and wars. Several kingdoms, including her own, had sent noble hostages, mostly children to Meara as an assurance that there would be no more attacks on Thassalia. In turn, Meara had sent her own children and other hostages to them as a guarantee that she'd abide by the ceasefire.

What they hadn't counted on was that Meara would use the hostages sent to her as a way to thin the heirs and nobles of her enemies. She hadn't cared what they'd done to her own children or relatives. All that mattered was her ego and ambition.

Meara had abused, then slaughtered her hostages. And after she'd done her damage and lulled the kingdoms into a false sense of peace, she'd attacked, intending to destroy them and become High Queen.

Only a tiny handful of hostages had survived to make it home. No one knew how they'd done it, either.

Tanis didn't even know who those hostages were or if any were still alive today.

Whatever had happened to them had been so brutal that no one spoke of it, except to remind each other never to trust the centaur queen.

To never trust another kingdom with what they loved. It was terrible.

And it made her think of Renata and Dash. "Do you know how your sister died?"

Profound grief darkened his green eyes. "They took her horn. After she ran away, I found her body in a meadow, with her horn missing. I was on my way to find her killer when a certain dragon slowed me down."

She placed her hand over her face as guilt consumed her. "Again, I am so sorry, Dash. I had no idea you were after her killer when I captured you."

"We're all sorry for something, princess. I let my temper get the better of me, and now my sister's dead because of it. Your brother's dead for reasons unknown, and our kingdoms are on the verge of war again."

Tanis walked by his side as they left the main road to head off into the forest. "So, what's our strategy, then?"

"There's no *our*, little dragon. You know where your brother's skull is located. Go to the castle in Pagos and claim your vengeance. Then you can go home and live out your life with all the hatchlings you want. I wish I could return your dragon's body to you sooner, but sadly we made terms, so I can't. Maybe if they succeed in killing me, your body will revert before you kill your dragon slayer."

That was it?

"Seriously?"

"Yes." He placed a leather band on her wrist. Cupping his hands around it, he whispered something that caused it to glow. Then, he met her gaze. "I release you from my service. You will never be a servant to me, now or in the future. The band will help protect you in Pagos. Tell the king there that you're a friend of mine, and he should help you regain your brother's skull from the one who took it."

Her heart fluttered at those words. She couldn't believe he was releasing her. The kindness was as overwhelming as it was unexpected. Other than her brother, no one had ever shown her such.

And in that moment, she knew she couldn't leave him. Not alone like this to face the nightmare that was coming.

"What about you?"

He shrugged. "I have an enemy to deal with. If I don't stop this..." He didn't finish that thought.

Tanis was still dumbfounded. "You're really going to let me go?"

He stepped away from her. "Of course, I am. Besides, I have much larger problems at the moment."

Yes, he did. And they were armed for unicorn and intent on mounting his head to their wall.

Worse? He had no one at his side or at his back. Not even Halla. While their people might be enemies, she couldn't abandon him. "Then you know I can't leave you."

Dash wasn't sure he heard those words correctly. "What?"

"You are out here alone, Dash. I don't know where you sent Halla or when she'll be back. We both know you're not the most well-liked monarch. I mean, face it, no one is going to nominate you for a popularity contest... *If* you get to your army, they may or may not follow you right now. I don't know how many enemies you have, but I know it's enough that you can't fight them all by yourself. They will slaughter you if they find you. For a million gold sovereigns, you're lucky I'm not taking aim at you, beast."

All of that was true. But it didn't explain one basic thing. "Why do you care?"

She smiled at him. "Because I was once left alone with my enemies to fight by myself. And I won't do that to someone who was willing to help me save my brother's memory. I know how awful it feels to fight alone, and no one should ever feel that way. Besides, I am one of your sovereign subjects. Consider me loyal to the bitter end." Her eyes glistened with unshed tears, and that sight touched a part of his soul that he'd closed off from everyone except his sister.

A place so vulnerable that he didn't want it exposed.

Yet it was undeniably there, and it suddenly softened even more where she was concerned.

And he hated that she'd ever experienced such pain in her past. She was right. No one should feel like this. No one should be betrayed and left alone.

Before he could stop himself, he pulled her close and held her. She was so small against him. So frail.

He could crush her, and yet he was the one who trembled. The one who felt weak in this moment. She had a power over him that he hated.

But in this moment, he needed to feel her against him. As she said, to know that he wasn't alone.

Because she was right. He didn't want to be by himself through this. He was so fucking tired of fighting by himself. Of looking around and seeing nothing more than his shadow. In the past, the only thing that had kept him going was the knowledge that Renata had needed him. That if he failed, she'd have no one to protect her. He was her strength and her guardian.

With her gone...

He had absolutely no reason to keep fighting.

Let the world burn. It wasn't as if it had ever done him any favors. Hell, most of the time he didn't even want to be here. Didn't want another day of drudgery.

No one cared if he lived or died, and most wanted him dead. No one mattered.

Except one little dragon who made him crazy.

Closing his eyes, he felt her hand in his hair as she held him and comforted him. No one had ever held him like this. Like he mattered. And definitely not when he felt so vulnerable. Not when he needed strength.

She had no idea how much he needed this, and he could never let her know that, either. His world was brutal. It devoured creatures like her. It had shattered him and forged a monster so feral that even he was scared of the demon inside him.

Because even he wasn't sure what he was capable of. All he knew was how much horror he'd done in his past.

Why his horn had turned as black as his soul. Renata hadn't been wrong in her accusation that last night when they'd fought.

He was the very thing that made the darkness weep. His mistress had been brutality, and he'd claimed her fully, without regret. And he would do it all again to get here.

His enemies had no idea what they were facing.

But they would learn why he was called Coeur de Noir. Why Meara had signed an *apaswere* truce with him and abided by it when no one else had ever been able to cow that bitch.

Suddenly, a bright flash went off several feet away from them.

Dash stepped around to protect her.

Tanis wasn't sure what to expect as a herd of unicorns appeared in front of them.

Well, maybe *herd* was ambitious. It was seven total. A brown unicorn, two grays, two white, and two that were a bluish sort of color. All of them had red horns that were covered by silver armored face plates. Which made her wonder if the color of the horns was some kind of uniform or family designation.

Were they? It would explain why they were all one color.

Again, she wished she'd bothered to learn something about unicorns.

Dash immediately shifted into his unicorn form that was larger and more muscled than theirs. He was at least two hands taller.

"Who's the human?" the brown unicorn asked. He was slightly larger than the others with him.

Dash didn't hesitate with his answer. "A girl I was asking for directions."

"Town's that way," Tanis said, pointing toward Auderley with both her hands. "Thinking I should be heading back to it before anyone misses me."

"Yes, you should." One of the grays moved aside for her to pass.

Holding her hands up over her head as if she were surrendering, she moved slowly through the group of unicorns. The tension in the air was so thick she felt as if she were moving through a sea of heavy foam.

No one else moved. It was very creepy and unnerving. Not even a tail swished or jerked.

She was about halfway through the herd when Dash finally spoke. "You're the Unicorn Head Guild I signed an order for."

The brown one nodded. "We are."

Dash seemed pleased by that. "Veterans of my army. You fought by my side."

"We did," a blue one said.

She paused at that as relief swept through her. They weren't enemies. They were his soldiers who'd come to help him.

Thank the gods.

Smiling, she turned toward him.

Until the brown leader spoke again. "And we hate you, you worthless fuck. Kill him!"

Tanis gasped as they rushed in unison toward Dash. Wait. What? Why? What was wrong with them?

Fury consumed her as she did the only thing she could think of, she unsheathed her sword and ran back to join the fray.

"Here, horsey, horsey." She used the sword to spank the flanks of the first one she reached.

She probably should have stabbed him, she realized, as the smaller blue unicorn turned on her with fury in his dark eyes. Growling, he tried to pierce her heart with his horn.

Tanis quickly parried the horn.

But what she didn't expect was for him to turn human and swing a sword at her throat. She barely caught that stroke before it decapitated her.

Stunned, she realized that unicorns didn't fight the way anyone else did.

Oh, I'm in serious trouble.

They had unique fighting skills. No wonder other species had fallen so easily to their ranks. They fought with magick fire and ice balls and shifted constantly between their unicorn and human bodies.

Whoa...

Impressive and terrifying. You never knew what was going to be thrown at you or which form you'd be engaging.

Cursing, she jumped at the gray's back and would have landed on him had he not vanished and left her to sprawl on the ground. *Very* undignified.

Dash ran over to her side to give her cover. "I regret taking your powers right now."

"Not as much as I do." She pushed herself up and grabbed the sword. "Any advice?"

"Run."

"Not happening. How do I kill them?"

"If they're human, same as any man or woman. If they're unicorns... best to wait until they're human."

Beautiful.

A shield appeared on her arm.

"That will keep their magick from harming you. It will also shield you from their magick weapons."

Nice.

Dash grabbed her with his arms and threw her in the air as he turned into a unicorn. She landed in a saddle on his back. They ran at three of the unicorns. Thankfully, this time he'd given her a bridle to hold onto.

Tanis's heart pounded in time to his hoof beats, especially when her sword changed to a lance and the tip began to glow.

"Aim for the horn. Slice it off and they're dead."

Good to know. And that explained why they wore the armored face plates as unicorns to guard them.

"If you can find their horn on them when they're human and claim it, you have total power over them and can kill them or control them."

Really good to know.

"Your shield will draw their magick attacks to it. You don't have to catch the blasts."

In that case... she threw the shield over her back. "I need you to return my sword to me."

"You sure?"

"Positive. Elfin short sword. Extra sharp."

The lance shrank down to her exact specification. Tanis drew her legs up until she was squatting on the saddle.

Dash wanted to ask her what she was doing, but he was too close to the others now. All he could do was grind his teeth against the bit and do the hardest thing he could in battle.

Trust her.

He rammed his shoulder against the bastard on his left and drove his horn into his rear flank. Tanis grabbed the mane of the horse on his right and rolled over his back, using her sword to slice at the horn before landing on her feet to meet Dash behind them while Dash flipped, turned human and stabbed the third unicorn with his sword, making a clean cut through his torso. He dropped the sword, sent three blasts at two more unicorns before he returned to his equine form.

The dragon gracefully swung herself into the saddle and laid low across his back. It was strange to him to have her there. While it wasn't unheard of for unicorns to have riders in battle, he'd never had a partner before.

In his youth, they'd tried to break him for it... hence the first time Outlaw had been applied to him and his temperament. But he'd refused a bridle. As he'd told her when they met, he would not be controlled. Not by anyone. And especially not when his life depended on it.

But someone else had trained her for war. This wasn't just a result of the powers he'd given her when he made her human. She knew how to fight in a human body as if she'd spent time doing so.

Aye, she had been trained in this form and had a lot of experience. She instinctively knew how to protect her battle partner.

He ran fast toward the last four who were rushing at them.

"Use my fire."

Dash scowled at her words. "What?"

"My dragon fire. Unleash it on them."

Surely, she wasn't serious. "We're in the middle of a forest."

"I know. Scorch them."

"It'll scorch us, too." And burn down the forest.

Tanis growled at him. "No. It won't."

"Yes. It will."

"Trust me, beast. I know what I'm doing."

Was she insane?

He literally had one split second to decide.

"I'm a dragon, Dash. Trust me."

I'm going to regret this. In spite of his doubts, he opened his mouth and let fly the powers he'd taken from her.

One moment the unicorns were on top of them, and the next, they were screaming, then silent. He watched as her dragon fire instantly vaporized them into ash.

The fire also destroyed his bridle. Dash spat it out as his rig dissolved. Coming to a halt, he turned around to survey the landscape behind them. The only trace of the four remaining unicorns were tiny bits of smoldering ash that floated in the breeze.

The dragon sat up in the saddle, then slid to the ground. "Aren't you glad you never fought in the Unicorn-Dragon Wars?"

Yes, he was.

"Did you?" he asked her.

"Nope. Wasn't born. But I heard the stories of how awful it was."

Now, he understood better why his father had been

insistent on those treaties with her people. Why Cratus had never wanted to go to war against the dragons.

Holy shit...

Because of the power of his black horn, he'd never known what dragon fire could do to the average red horn. He'd been extremely careless with the lives of his people.

No, he'd been as reckless as his sister. A lot more so than he'd ever known.

But then he'd come into his black horn young. Too young in retrospect. Not to mention the powers he'd inherited from his mother. Dragon fire would burn him, but not like this. He could withstand it. Granted it would leave him mangled and blistered. Still, he would survive. Just not happily.

His stomach tight, he headed back toward the first three they'd attacked.

While they weren't barbecued into oblivion, they were just as dead.

Damn. He'd hoped they could interrogate one of them.

They?

Dash paused as he realized what he'd just thought. When had he started thinking of them as a team?

What was even more terrifying? The idea of being part of a team wasn't as scary to him as it should be.

The dragon knelt beside their leader so she could examine him.

Sighing, Dash returned to his human form. He took a moment to his conceal his wand so that she wouldn't see it before he searched the others for theirs.

Tanis watched as Dash cut the horns, that had since turned white, from the bodies of their attackers. Weird given how vibrant and red they'd been before. "Is there a significance to the color?"

"Yes. These are warriors."

"Black for a king?"

"No."

She waited for him to elaborate. When he didn't, she cleared her throat to get his attention. "Then what is black?"

"The color of mine."

"Wow..." She was astonished at his tone. "You're really not going there?"

When he spoke, his voice was flat and crisp. "Really not going there."

Now, she had to know what he was hiding. "Is it embarrassing?"

"No."

"Then why not tell me?"

"It's personal."

What in the world could be personal about the color of their horns?

Oh...

Yeah, that made sense.

"So, what? Black horns are the unicorn equivalent of a small penis?"

His jaw went slack as he stared at her as if he couldn't believe what she'd just said. "What?"

She snorted. "Well, why else wouldn't you tell me?"

He was aghast. "What in the name of the Thirteen Kingdoms would make you think that?"

Did he really have to ask? "Why else won't you tell me?" she repeated.

"Because it's personal."

"So you said. But what else could be more personal than *that*, that you wouldn't tell me?"

Dash sputtered indignantly. They had dead bodies to contend with. Probably more bounty hunters coming for them. A death warrant and she wanted to distract him with *this*?

Really?

Frustrated, he did what he rarely did... he explained himself. "It lets unicorns know how much power we hold."

"Why not just say that, then?" She scowled at him. "What about *that* could possibly embarrass you? Unless... you have, what? Baby unicorn powers?"

"No! Wait. What? Have you not seen how much power I have, dragon?"

"Well, yeah, but I don't know how much they," she gestured at the bodies, "have in comparison. How would I know? I'm a dragon. So, on the grand unicorn power scale what does black mean?"

He glared at her. "I have no soul."

Tanis froze at that unexpected, growled comment. "Huh?"

"You wanted an answer. There you go. A black horn means I have no soul."

She scoffed at his words. "Well, that's just ridiculous. Everyone has a soul. Who told you that?"

Shaking his head, he closed the distance between them so she could see the evil in his eyes. Evil she was sure that had quelled so many and made them flinch. Even well-seasoned warriors. "No, Lady Dragon. Truth. You want to know why everyone fears me. That's why. When I was a youth, I killed my own father in a fit of rage. The moment I did, it turned my horn black to show the world that I have no soul or remorse. That my power is absolute, and that I am capable of anything. It is my mark of shame, and my greatest badge of honor."

Tanis swallowed hard at his ominous tone. Well, that explained a lot. She should probably be terrified of him, too, and yet she wasn't.

But she did have one burning question. "Why'd you kill him?"

A tic started in his jaw. "For talking too much and asking intrusive questions."

She snorted at his sarcasm.

"Look, we need to get out of here. The tracking spell those unicorns used isn't unique. If they found us, someone else can, too."

He handed the bloody horns to her. "Put those in your bag."

She looked at them in distaste. Did he really want her to touch them? They looked so disgusting. "Ew. This is so revolting. Unicorn cooties."

He actually chuckled. "Why do I find that funny?"

"I'm adorable."

"No," he said, dryly, "you're not."

"Sure, I am. It's what my brother always told me. Besides, I wouldn't worry about the others. You have Tanis dragon fire."

"What's Tanis dragon fire?"

"I'm Tanis and you have my fire. Pretty powerful stuff as you saw. It stops evil unicorns dead in their tracks."

Dash paused then cursed as he realized what was

happening. She was becoming real to him. Worse, she was charming him in a dangerous way.

He was starting to care about her. The last thing he wanted to do.

Liabilities were a danger to him. Because when he put one life above others, he made mistakes.

Like with Renata.

But he owed this particular dragon his life. She'd stayed with him when she should have run.

No, she'd stayed with him when anyone else would have run.

"Thank you, Tanis."

"For what?"

"Standing by me."

"It's all good, Dash." She took the white horns gingerly and put them in the bag, trying her best not to get the blood or tissue on her hand. "Why are we keeping these, anyway?"

"So that trophy hunters can't sell them, or a sorcerer use them for nefarious purposes."

That made sense, until she thought of something. "You know, you can use my flames to completely incinerate their bodies and the horns, right?"

Dash winced as she reminded him of something he should have thought of himself. Damn it. But then, those weren't his powers, so he wasn't used to thinking about them.

You just incinerated them. How could you forget?

'Cause his mind was on other things. Now, he looked like a complete, fucking idiot to her. So much for being the intelligent, suave leader of the Thirteen Kingdoms.

Smiling, Tanis leaned into him. "This is the part where

you say, 'Oh crap. I didn't think of that.' Then you apologize for making me handle unicorn cooties. Yeah?"

He didn't want to laugh. He really didn't want to and yet found himself bursting out into laughter at her playfulness. Thank God, Halla or Ryper wasn't here. They'd never believe he could laugh like this.

"Sorry I made you handle unicorn cooties."

The look on her face was so adorable that he snickered again.

What is wrong with me?

He *never* behaved like this. Not even when he'd been a colt.

She handed him the bag. "You can pull them out yourself. I've handled enough unicorn for one day, beast." She shivered in an exaggerated manner.

Trying his best to not let her charm him anymore, he took the horns to the bodies and then incinerated them.

Then, he turned back to her. "We do need to get going."

"Waiting on you, beast." She pulled her sack over her shoulders. "And can I let you in on a secret?"

"Sure."

"Get my brother's skull back to my sister-in-law, and she'll help solidify your kingdom."

Now that was interesting. "How so?"

"Her father rules the Pyrigian Lands... our northern borders. My father may be king, but her father holds the most territory and commands the largest part of our army. He will do whatever Marla wants. As his youngest, she is his heart and soul. And while my father may not think much of me, Marla likes me, and she loved and adored my brother more than her life. Her gratitude at having her husband's remains restored for proper burial cannot be understated."

Her words impressed him. "You know politics?"

"I listen to things."

Dash didn't miss the note of sadness in her voice that reminded him of something else. "How did you learn to fight so well?"

Shame filled her eyes. "Which way is that castle, again? Don't we need to get going?"

So, he wasn't the only one who changed subjects when it struck a bitter memory. "Now you're the one who's avoiding a subject."

She drew a ragged breath as she avoided his gaze. "Remember those kids playing in the street that you spoke of? I was one of them. Taken from home by a unicorn bastard and sold for bitter entertainment." Her eyes held the shadows of her past horrors. "Let's just leave it at that, shall we?"

Those unexpected words struck him like a fist to his gullet. It was a blow so staggering that Dash couldn't catch his breath.

He knew her pain so much deeper than he wanted to, and it broke his heart that he hadn't been able to spare her the past that haunted him.

"Tanis..."

"Don't, Dash." She held her hands up and moved away from him. "I don't want to hear that you're sorry or anything. You don't get it. No one does. And I don't want empty sympathy. The past is the past, and there's nothing to be done about it."

He caught her arm as she started away from him and

pulled her to a stop. His anger, pain and grief churned inside him. When he spoke, his voice was a full octave deeper. "My father traded me for peace to the Thassalians when I was a colt and barely able to defend myself."

Recognition hit her dark eyes as she understood instantly what he was saying. Centaurs and unicorns were natural enemies. Since the dawn of history, they'd fought for dominance. Because they were half-human, centaurs had always believed themselves to be the superior equine species.

And once unicorns developed the ability to shape-shift, it'd only fueled their hatred of each other. Because the unicorns no longer tolerated centaur arrogance, they set out to destroy it and the entire centaur species. And because unicorns could turn fully human, the centaurs hated them all the more and became determined to wipe them out.

"I know your pain, Dragon. And I am sorry no one was there to protect you."

Tanis's heart pounded as she realized that he was one of the mysterious handful of survivors who'd returned home against all odds. Those who'd been given up for dead.

No, one of those who'd been turned over to his father's enemies and left for dead.

"You were one of the hostages sent to Queen Meara's court to maintain peace?"

His gaze hollow, he nodded.

She sucked her breath in sharply as she felt for him. "How old were you when you were sent?"

"Seven."

Tanis couldn't imagine the horror of her father sending

her out to die. At least she'd been a teenager when she'd been captured. Mostly grown.

And she'd been the fool who'd refused to listen to her father and others who'd warned her about venturing off on her own. She'd always thought they were being stupid and paranoid. What did they know?

Back then, her father would have done anything to protect her.

She couldn't imagine him offering her up to their enemies. "I'm—"

He placed a finger over her lips. "No apologies. I do understand *exactly* how you feel."

Yes, he did. For the first time in her life, she was standing in front of someone who knew her nightmare. Who'd walked through the same hell... no, a worse hell... and who bore scars she could relate to.

"Then you know why I can't leave you, beast."

"And you know how grateful I am."

Yes, she did. Because nothing sucked more than being left alone to face a nightmare. To have no one to rely on.

Nodding, she held her arm out to him. "Friends?"

Dash hesitated. In all his life, he'd only had one friend he could truly rely on. And even that had been out of necessity. Mostly because he'd seen too many people betrayed by those they'd called friends and family.

Trust for creatures like them was very hard won.

Tanis smiled at him as she wiggled her fingers of her outstretched hand. "It won't bite you, beast. My arm has no teeth."

Laughing, he shook her arm. Then, he pulled her close

and kissed the top of her head as he used to do his sister. "You are certainly a unique creature, Dragon."

"It's okay to call me a major burr in your arse. It's what Davin always did."

"More like a barnacle. You're growing on me." Dash returned to his unicorn body.

Tanis gasped as she saw that he had wings on his side. "You can fly?"

"When it suits me."

She sputtered. "Why weren't you flying when I captured you?"

"You didn't capture me, and I was trying not to draw attention to myself. I didn't want anyone in my kingdom to know I was leaving. Again, I'm the only unicorn with a black horn. I tend to stick out among my kind."

Made sense.

She swung up into the saddle and saw that, once more, he wore a bridle for her. Without a word, she gently held it, taking care not to tighten it. Instead, she held mostly to the saddle horn so as not to trip on that scar. "Ready when you are, beast."

He shot off at a gallop, then leapt into the air.

Tanis actually gasped as they left the ground. Until now, she hadn't realized how scary it was to fly when she wasn't the one in control of it. She clung to Dash's back, terrified she was going to fall.

"Are you all right, Lady Dragon?"

"Not really. I think I might be afraid of heights."

He laughed. "I'll catch you if you fall."

"Please do." Because it was a long, long way down to the

ground. Funny how it'd never seemed so when she was a dragon. Perhaps because she was so much larger?

She wasn't sure. But this was absolutely terrifying. It required a level of trust she wasn't comfortable with giving someone else. Not even her adorable beast.

Closing her eyes, she tried to think of other things.

Happy things. Like not falling to her death.

Normally, it would be images of her as a girl, learning to fly with her brother. For some reason that had always been her most comforting memory.

Today, it was an image of her unicorn laughing as she teased him. Of those bright green eyes shining with humor.

Weird. Even stranger? She wanted to lay herself over his back for comfort. And before she could think better of it, she did exactly that.

Instead of holding on to the saddle or reins, she held on to his mane and let the heat of his body soothe her fear.

This close to him, she could feel his calm heartbeat, and it quieted the frantic beating of hers. With every ripple of his muscles as he flapped his wings to keep them in the air, she felt calmer. It was just the two of them with the winds sweeping over their bodies.

And for the first time in a very long time, she felt peace. It made no sense at all. She didn't really know him. They were being hunted, and she could fall to her death at any second.

Yet she was at peace here.

More than that, she felt secure.

I am not right.

But there was no denying this. If she could stay here with him forever, she would. She hadn't felt like this since she was a little hatchling, tucked in her nest. That feeling that nothing could reach her. That all was right in the world.

Then the ugly had come and shown her the hidden, horrible side of things. She had seen the bitter truth of others who only sought to use and abuse those they had power over. Those who wanted to profit from the misery they caused others.

This moment wasn't reality, and she hated the demons that gave her no peace. No calm.

And she wondered about the beast inside Dash that had caused his horn to turn black. She knew exactly how hungry it must be. She had her own to contend with. That frightful need to lash out whenever she felt threatened or cornered. Those who had never been abused didn't understand.

They couldn't.

It was a rage so fierce that words didn't do it justice. If there was a way to calm it, she'd never found it. All she could do was avoid things that caused it to boil over. Certain places... words.

Sometimes it could be something as simple as a smell.

Then all those memories would come rushing back, and the rage would escape with a fury so raw that she'd want blood vengeance against those who'd harmed her.

That was when she'd retreat. When she'd find her comfort in solitude and scrolls. Anything to avoid thinking about the past or the pain. She'd become good at hiding.

Smiling and even jesting through the pain that was ever present or just lurking under her carefully crafted façade.

Like Dash.

I should be scared.

Yet he comforted her. Because she understood him and knew his pain.

And right now, she needed him and his comfort more than she wanted to admit.

How odd that in the midst of her nightmare, she'd found him.

But how long could this last? He was being hunted and by now, her father would have discovered her absence. He would know that she'd defied him. While he might not have searched for her after she'd been kidnapped, he would send out trackers to hunt her for disregarding his orders.

One thing about her father, he never suffered insubordination. He would have her hauled back in chains for punishment.

Another reason why she'd wanted to be human to do this. It was the only way to complete her quest before her father's spies or trackers found her.

What are you thinking, Tanis? Given everything that had happened over the last few days, there was no way this would end well.

You know better than to believe in happy endings.

Those were for fools and children. This was the real world and here everyone suffered.

Their enemies were going to find them. That was a given. The only question was if she'd avenge Davin before they killed her.

Or Dash.

CHAPTER 9

Ronan grabbed the bow from Mischief's hands as she took aim for Chrysis. "Don't shoot the crow." His voice was laden with aggravation and impatience.

Mischief pouted, then stamped her booted foot. "Please... it's a moral imperative."

Flying to the top of a post where she was partially hidden from Mischief's range, Chrysis glared at them. "Kill the messenger crow, the High King kills you."

Swaying in the doorway of the stable, Cadoc laughed. "Who wants to place odds on that?"

Leaning his head back, Ronan let out a deep, guttural groan. What had he done to be named the leader of these imbeciles?

Well to be fair, they were drunk.

Still...

He held Mischief's hand-carved, dark wooden bow in his fist. "I'm confiscating this, Missy."

"I hate when you call me that." With her gold eyes flashing her ire, she sat down hard on the ground, then ran her hand through the straw. "Why are we in a stable? I thought we were in a brothel."

Cadoc lifted his hand to point in Ronan's general direction. "His fault. I think. What were we talking about? I thought I was taking bets in a card game. Or a wizard game. Or something."

Ronan shook his head. Only for Dash would he suffer this. Otherwise, he'd have left these two to sleep off their ale in the comfort of the whorehouse he'd found them in.

Humans...

They were a special breed. Though to be fair, it took a lot of ale to knock Mischief into oblivion. Marauders didn't normally get quite so *happy*. Her people were known for their sword skill, ferocity and ability to cut the throats of anyone who got in their way—even when they were knee deep in their cups. Honestly, he hadn't seen her this drunk since they were kids, and Dove had dared her into a drinking contest that had ended with her dinner on Dove's boots.

And it'd been a while since he'd last seen her. She was still beautiful. Even with her face paint smeared over her dark skin, and her braids tangled with straw.

Of course, it helped that for once she wasn't stern and frowning.

Nor was she cooperating.

Ronan grabbed her before she headed back to the whorehouse he'd just dragged her out of. "No, you don't."

"Stop being a kill flint... joy flint... a—"

"Fun sucker," Cadoc supplied.

"That's it! I paid good coin for that hard cock, and I'd like to have it."

Losing patience, Ronan looked up to where Chrysis was still hiding. "Could you take human form and help me out, Chrys?"

"Could. Rather not."

Why was she always so impossible? "Please?"

She shook her crow head. "You know how I feel about that."

He glared at her and her ever insistence to remain as a crow no matter what. "We're the same species."

"Don't insult me. You might be a Vairloche, but—"

"What? Just because you choose to live solely as a crow doesn't make you a different species. You can shape-lock all you want, but you're still a shifter, same as me."

That literally ruffled her feathers. With a shrill caw, she refused to turn human. "I hate you, Ronan."

"That line forms to the left and wraps around the countryside. Now give us a hand, love."

Grimacing, she flew toward Mischief. "Why are they drunk anyway?"

Mischief laughed as Chrysis landed in the straw next to her. "We're celebrating. It's my birthday."

"It's not your birthday." Chrysis scowled at Ronan. "Is she so drunk she doesn't know?"

"Probably."

"I know." Cadoc held up his arm. Then he lowered it and frowned. "No, I don't. What were we talking about again?"

Chrysis let out a long, exasperated sigh. "How are we supposed to get them back to Licordia like this?"

"Put her on horseback and she'll sober."

Chrys gave him a look that said she thought he was as out of his mind as they were. "That's impossible. Even if I changed into a human, I wouldn't be able to lift her. She's twice my size."

Ronan wanted to beat her. Crow or not.

Flying to another post, Chrysis rolled her eyes as Mischief struggled to get into the saddle of her horse. Sadly, she kept sliding off and falling back to the ground.

Ronan let out a fierce growl. "You're right, Chrys. You're not helpful at all."

He lifted Mischief from the ground, but not before he took a moment to glare at Chrys who was resting on a post near the horse. Nose to nose. Then he hoisted Mischief up into the saddle.

True to his words, Mischief came out of her stupor, grabbed the leather reins and placed her feet into the stirrups. "Is there a battle?"

"Not yet," Ronan said.

Chrysis gaped in awe. Completely stunned, she watched as he went to Cadoc and repeated the process.

As with Mischief, Cadoc sobered almost instantly.

"How is that possible?"

Ronan shrugged. "They're still not completely sober. It's a holdover from our shitty youths. Put them on a horse and they fall in line."

Chrysis hated to admit it, but she was impressed. When they'd first arrived to find them drunk and sprawling in the middle of an orgy, she'd been ready to go home and forget this stupid errand.

At least Ronan had been alone when she'd found him hunting in the woods. But to be honest, she'd forgotten just how massive he was in size and how attractive she'd always found him. No wonder Ryper had wanted him for this venture.

He stood head and shoulders over almost all human males. With long, dark-brown hair that held golden highlights and stormy gray eyes, he was a fearsome beast, even for a shifter.

And Cadoc. Even though she normally didn't find humans or particularly red-headed humans attractive, she made an exception for him. Ruggedly handsome and as dangerous as Dash or Ryper, Cadoc was lethally charismatic with a sharp sense of humor that could be registered as a weapon in most kingdoms. He didn't need a sword. His tongue could cut to the bone.

Worse?

The more biting his comments, the funnier they usually were. As Dash liked to say, Cadoc was akin to someone bumping their head. It was hilarious so long as it wasn't happening to you.

As much she hated to admit it, she'd missed them.

Ronan began saddling a black stallion.

"Are we stealing a horse?"

He didn't pause. "I can't fly with them drunk. Someone has to lead them. Otherwise, they'll end up who knows where. Our luck, inside Meara's palace with a battle axe aimed at her throat."

Chrysis scowled at the restrained fury in his tone. "All of you hate her, don't you?"

"You have *no* idea. Be grateful for that."

She was. From the handful of stories she'd overheard over the years, she was more than delighted to have been spared the nightmare they'd endured. She had her own demons to battle, but they were paltry compared to the ones that gave the Outlaws no rest.

Ronan left a stack of sovereigns in the stall to cover the cost of the horse before he swung himself up into the saddle. He took Cadoc's and Mischief's reins. "We'll head to Licordia to get Aderyn, then wait for you and the others to join us at the lodge."

"What about Xaydin?"

Ronan paused to think before he answered. "He's off on his own quest. Best we leave him to it. Besides, we can handle this without him."

That was probably true. Xaydin was an irritable one, and he had a price on his head that was staggering. Granted not as staggering as the one currently on Dash's head, but impressive, nonetheless.

When Ryper and Dash had proclaimed their group Outlaws, it'd been in the unicorn sense of the word. Someone who wouldn't be broken or tamed.

Xaydin had taken the word as a personal challenge. Out of their entire clan of miscreants and malcontents, he was the one who'd actually gone off and decided laws would no longer apply to him. He'd become a vigilante who made Ryper's body count insignificant.

Yeah, they should leave him out of this.

"Be careful." She watched as they left.

Chrysis had no real idea where Ryper had gone, but if he was after Dove, they'd most likely be in Alarium. While Dove had a lot of hard feelings for his elfin brethren, he still tended to stay in their lands.

Maybe I should be a wolf.

It'd be a lot easier to track them that way. But unlike others of her kind, she didn't like moving from one form to another. She much preferred to stick to one shape.

Shape-lock. Their people considered it an unforgivable sin to remain in one form. So much so that she'd been banished from her home because she refused to leave her crow body.

Yet King Dash had never minded or thought less of her for it. He'd welcomed her into his service and had built her an unbelievable nest.

For that, she'd always be loyal to him. Others could insult him if they wanted, but she knew the truth. He was a good unicorn with a kind heart. He took care of those who were under his protection.

And she would do whatever she could to keep him safe. She just hoped they weren't too late to save him.

CHAPTER 10

W hy do you think they picked Sester for their auction?" Tanis carefully dismounted Dash's back and rubbed her arms.

Dash returned to being human. He looked around from the shadows where they were hidden on an icy shelf from the small city that rested atop a hill. "Neutral territory, I guess. The revenants don't usually involve themselves in politics. Pagos is the one kingdom I've never had to worry about scheming against me."

"How do you mean?"

"They don't care. They can't have children and they're immortal. All they do is sit around, debate, have contests, and play chess, or some such. Those who join them with ambitions of conquest are usually culled before they can gather an army."

She gaped at his bleak description of their existence. "You're kidding?"

"Not really. They don't want anyone to disturb their

hard-won peace." He gestured toward the castle that appeared to be made of solid ice. "King Ambrose has been the ruler here since he was brought back by a necromancer almost a thousand years ago. No one has ever challenged him for his throne because most of the dead have no ambition. They're content with what they have, and they don't want the stress that comes with wanting more. Their lands are virtually inhospitable for the living. That's why I gave you the band when I sent you here to get your brother's skull. It'll help you breathe as a human in their atmosphere that's not as rich in oxygen as what you're used to."

She blew her breath against her freezing hands to warm them, wishing he'd also given her heat. "Why was Ambrose brought back?"

Dash created a thicker fur coat and gloves for her, along with fur boots and a hat. He held them out to her. "Land dispute."

She paused while pulling them on. "Wait. What?"

He wrapped a thick wool scarf around his head and neck. "As stupid and unbelievable as it sounds, it's true. Centuries ago, there was a simple land dispute between Ambrose's heirs. When they couldn't settle it, the judge wanted to be fair, so he had a necromancer raise Ambrose from the dead to tell him how he wanted his lands divided. Problem was, no one knew how to send Ambrose back to the dead once it was settled."

"Seriously?"

"Seriously. How do you kill a dead man?"

He had a point. She braided her hair and put it under her fur hat. "No one ever figured it out?"

"Not for Ambrose's kind." Dash pulled on his own

gloves. "Worse. Other necromancers kept bringing the dead back for all manner of reasons until Queen Morvana finally had the good sense to outlaw zombies, liches and the like, eight hundred or so years ago in her kingdom, and it caught on in the rest. Since no one knew what to do with a walking, talking corpse, they carved out a kingdom for them here so they could live in peace."

She laughed nervously. "I thought that was just a myth. Are all the Pagosians really dead?"

"Absolutely."

"But don't they rot or decompose?"

"I honestly don't know. What I'm told is that the climate here is unlike any other climate in the world, and they have their own magick system they've developed that isn't anything we know or that they share with outsiders. Some of them are exceptionally powerful."

"Meaning?"

"I'm glad they stay isolated and don't come off their ice island. Why they're allowing this auction to be held here, I have no idea. But I plan to find out."

And she was definitely glad she wasn't in her dragon body. She'd never experienced cold like this. As a dragon, she'd be inert from the freezing temperature. No wonder her people had never even thought of coming this far north. Or fighting with them.

Brr...

She had no idea anyone could shiver this much and continue living. Every part of her body felt brittle and stiff.

"Are you all right, Dragon?"

"No." She let out a puff of breath to marvel at the cloud it formed around her face. "Have you ever seen cold like this?"

"Not quite this cold, but close to it."

"Why?"

He laughed. "Our winter months can get rather nippy."

"Again, why?"

"We're born with fur coats, not scales. Although, I'd think you'd be more tolerant of the cold given the degree of fire you can make with a single belch."

"I'd like to be burping that heat right about now, too. Especially, feeling it in my belly."

He paused on the narrow trail. "Here." He took her hands in his.

Tanis gasped as she felt warmth spread from his touch to every inch of her body. "What are you doing?"

"Tiny bit of magick to warm you."

It was doing a bit more than that as she met his gaze. Really, she didn't need his magick when he looked at her like that. His presence made her feel rather hot all over.

"Why are you always so nice to me?" she asked.

"I'm not nice."

She arched a brow. "What would you call it, then?"

He shrugged. "Nice is when you derive pleasure from something."

"Nice is when you show kindness to someone, beast."

He scoffed. "There's nothing kind about me."

She reached up and cupped his whiskered cheek in her hand. "Dash... You've been nothing save kind since I met you. Please tell me that you know that."

Dash didn't know what to say. He'd been called every type of name he could think of. Insulted with a great deal of creativity.

But kind...

That was one epitaph no one had attached to his name.

Not even Renata.

He didn't know how to respond.

And before he realized it, she was pulling his lips to hers. Dash closed his eyes as he tasted the most amazing thing in his life. But what amazed him most was the innocence of it. This wasn't a demanding kiss.

It was sweet. Hesitant. And delicious.

He could tell that she'd never had a real kiss before. Never known real passion. That she was afraid of her own emotions and of his reaction.

And that made him furious at the ones who'd hurt her. Even madder at the ones who should have protected her and failed. This was why he couldn't afford to lose his throne. Why he had to keep fighting. Because of those like her who had no one else to stand for them.

They deserved better.

Her heroes had let her down. And here he was, a demon life had done its best to destroy, and he only wanted to keep her safe. It made no sense.

But then life seldom did.

Tanis fisted her hand in Dash's soft hair. She still couldn't believe she was doing this. She'd never in her life been so forward. Never even wanted to kiss someone.

But there had just been something inside him that reached out to her. That shadow of inner loathing that she understood more than she wanted to.

She just wanted to comfort him and let him know that while she wasn't much, she was here.

Embarrassed, she pulled back from his lips. "Sorry. I slipped."

He smiled down at her. "Feel free to slip and fall against my lips anytime you want." Leaning down, he gave her another quick kiss before he stepped back.

Oddly enough, that warmed her more than his magick had.

As they started forward, up the narrow pass, Dash kept her by his side. Both to shield her from the harsh winds and to help her with the climb up the icy path to the castle.

"Wouldn't it be easier to fly in?" she asked.

"We don't know who's there or how friendly they'll be. I'd rather not draw attention until we see if we have allies."

That made a lot of sense. "You're right. There I go again, not thinking ahead."

He tightened his hand on hers. "Don't fret about it. What you said is correct. It would be a lot easier."

"Again, you're being kind, Lord Unicorn. Very charitable."

"Then perhaps our flaws are not as bad as we both perceive them to be."

Tanis liked that thought. Maybe he was right. Or maybe they didn't judge each other as harshly as others did because of what they'd been through. Either way, it was nice to be around someone who didn't snap at her for her shortcomings constantly. She wasn't nearly as nervous or uncomfortable around him as she was other beings because of it.

Unfathomable, given who he was and his reputation for cruelty. But she didn't know that side of him. She only saw a friend who watched out for her.

Another stiff wind blew past them. "Is it possible to freeze to death before we reach the castle?"

"It is... but..." He stopped and knocked on the side of the hill.

"What are you doing?"

Before he could answer, a huge, blue eye slid open to stare at them.

Tanis gasped.

"Who are you and why do you come?" The voice was loud and thunderous.

Dash winked at her. "A pilgrim to pay homage to King Ambrose. Tell him it's the boy who sent him a pigeon rope."

"Pigeon rope?" The eye squinted at him. "What kind of foolishness is that?"

"He'll know."

The eye blinked slowly. "Might order me to throw you down the hill."

"He might," Dash said. "Or he might let me in."

"Hmph. Wait there." The eye went away and the door turned to solid ice.

Tanis cocked her head as she tried to make sense of what he'd said. "Pigeon rope?"

"It's a game we play in Licordia. The rope is long and tied in complicated knots that you have to figure out how to unknot."

"Is it hard?"

"Can be."

She thought about that. "How do you know you're the only one who ever sent one to the king?"

"When I sent it to him, it had the head of the necromancer lich who'd awakened him attached to it."

Tanis made a sound of extreme displeasure. "Tell me you're joking."

He shook his head.

And the door opened.

She was still squealing at the thought of a living head being gifted to the king when a frost giant led them inside the huge palace courtyard. Pressing her lips together, she suppressed the noise, but on the inside, she was still making it.

Not just over the severed head. No. Now it was because everywhere she looked there was something rather grisly.

This was definitely the land of the eternal corpses. All in various stages of rot and decay. Not to mention, it rather stank. Musty. Moldy. Like a nest that had been left out in the rain far too long. She was trying desperately not to curl her lip.

Don't offend them. She assumed they still had feelings.

But it was really hard not to be offensive or to show her distaste.

"Good day," a lady said as she passed by in a tattered red gown.

Dash politely returned the greeting while Tanis smiled and nodded as she swallowed bile. While the woman seemed nice enough, her flesh was mostly rotted off. Some of it still clung to the bone.

"Are they all human?" she asked him.

"No. Other species are here as well."

Interesting.

Although once she became acclimated to their condition and smell, she supposed it wasn't so bad. They all seemed happy to be here. They were all going about their business as if this was normal and to them, she supposed it was. Some strolled about with friends. Most sat about in groups, talking. Some played games while others groomed their undead pets.

All in all, they did appear happier than any inhabitants of any city or town she'd ever visited or known.

Friendlier, too.

Even though it was obvious she and Dash were strangers to this land... and still living... everyone they passed waved and said hello to them as if they were old friends, or family who'd returned to visit.

So much so that she began to feel self-conscious. "Are they always so friendly?"

"They are. I think it might actually have something to do with being dead."

Interesting thought. Perhaps because they were dead, they didn't have to worry about betrayal? It made her wonder. "Have you visited here often?"

"Just a handful of times to speak to Ambrose."

"To negotiate?" she asked.

"Mostly for wisdom."

That surprised her. "Really?"

"He's lived a long time, and he's watched other kingdoms rise and fall. I value his insights and knowledge. He's been invaluable to me over the years."

Tanis slowed her steps as they neared the huge palace. It shimmered in the light and had ornate carvings of figures and scenes all along the walls. Some were of battles, and some seemed to be peaceful. "Does it tell a story?"

"It does. If you start at the bottom, it begins with Ambrose's family in Alarium when they forged an alliance with Elves and continues on until his reanimation."

"Incredible."

"Stop!"

Tanis froze instantly as a she-centaur came rushing toward them. It wasn't until the she-centaur was close that Tanis could tell she was dead as she hadn't decomposed very much at all. She held a small ceramic pot out to Tanis. "You need this. Keep putting it on your skin, and in particular your lips."

Tanis sniffed at the odd concoction. "Why?"

Dash took it from the centaur's hand and thanked her. "It'll keep them from cracking and bleeding. The air here is incredibly dry. It literally sucks the moisture out of your body."

"It's one of the reasons why we don't have to use magick to keep from decaying." The centaur smiled. "And why you can't stay too long."

"She's right. Our time for being here started counting down the moment we arrived."

"Oh." Tanis took a second small container, removed her gloves, then duplicated Dash's actions of smearing the cream across her face and hands.

As they entered the inside of the castle, she saw that it was every bit as impressive as the outside. The carved ice here reflected an eerie green similar to Dash's eyes. It seemed alive and vibrant.

Yet what impressed her most was that fire didn't burn in the chandeliers, it was a bouncing wizard's light, unlike anything she'd ever seen before. Nor did they have fires burning for warmth.

It was then she realized something.

"They don't feel the cold, do they?"

Dash shook his head. "They're dead. They don't feel

anything physically, that I know of."

Very interesting.

They entered a huge ballroom. Lively music played while couples danced all around. It was then she realized how many species lived here in harmony. There were dragrs and liches, along with every kind of revenant imaginable.

"Are we in the right place?" she asked.

Dash nodded. "Ambrose always holds court here."

"Why?"

"Why not?"

Because it was hard to concentrate with all the noise and movement. But it was interesting to watch all the corpses as they swept past. Especially since there was no rhyme or reason to how they danced. They really didn't care what anyone thought. How refreshing it had to be.

The giant led them around the edge of the dance floor until they reached a dais on the far side of the room where a throne of carved ice was set.

And true to Dash's words, there was a well-preserved head hanging from a rope next to the throne. Her unicorn companion definitely had a dark side to him.

But the worst part was that it seemed Ambrose had his final revenge on the necromancer who'd brought him back to life.

The head was alive and alert and singing to the song that was playing.

Shivering at the very thought, Tanis wasn't sure what she was expecting for the king of this land, but this wasn't it. For one thing, Ambrose was very tiny. Probably no more than five feet or so. And exceptionally skinny. He had a long, thin, white beard that trailed to his knees and a gaunt, pointed face. He reminded her of a gnome. A well-dressed gnome, but a gnome nonetheless.

And his bony face lit up the moment he saw Dash. "My boy," he said excitedly as he pushed himself off his seat in a way that reminded her more of a child than a respected king.

No one seemed to notice.

Giddy as he could be, he moved to embrace Dash who welcomed him like family. "Long time, Sire."

"Indeed. Too long and not long enough." Ambrose looked toward her with an interested arch to his brow. "And who is your most lovely guest?"

"Princess Tanis Dragomir."

Instant recognition widened the king's eyes. Clearing his throat, he motioned for them to follow him.

She exchanged a frown with Dash before they allowed the king to lead them to an antechamber behind the dais. Once they were alone, Ambrose turned to face them, and his entire demeanor changed. He actually seemed angry now.

"Are you out of your mind?" he asked Dash.

"Most of the time, but to what are you referring?"

Ambrose gestured to Tanis. "You kidnapped Iagan's daughter and turned her human? What were you thinking?"

Tanis smiled at his assumption. "Forgive me, Sire. But I kidnapped Dash and asked him to make me human."

Ambrose's jaw worked like a fish out of water.

"She actually did. Not so much a kidnapping as a trapping. But she did ask me to make her human."

The king rolled his light-gray eyes, then cursed. "You're both insane."

"I won't argue that." Dash gave the king a charming grin.

Ambrose pressed two fingers to his temple as if he were having a migraine. "Tell me what's happened."

"I need my sister's horn and Tanis wants her brother's skull. We saw a poster that said the ones who'd taken them would be here to auction them off."

Ambrose gaped. "Wait... here, you say?"

Dash pulled the poster from his pouch and handed it to the king. "You don't know about it?"

Unfolding the paper, Ambrose scowled as he read it. "No. No one's said a word about this. You know I would *never* allow such a thing in my kingdom, and I would have killed anyone who came here with Renata's wand. Dear God, she's really dead?"

Tanis saw the pain in Dash's eyes. "She is."

Sadness darkened the pale gray of Ambrose's eyes as he looked up at Tanis. "And your brother, too?"

"He is."

"I'm so sorry for both of you. And for your father, Tanis, please give him my condolences. It's an awful thing to lose a child."

"Thank you, Sire. I will tell him."

He handed the poster back to Dash. "This makes no sense. You two are the only livings in Pagos. No one's visited us in almost a year. And even when they do, no one stays long. Mostly because certain citizens want to start using the livings for sacrifices. And even if they didn't, livings can't survive here for long."

"Then you haven't heard about the revolt?" Dash asked.

Ambrose scowled. "What revolt?"

"There are actually two of them. One against Queen Meara in Thassalia, and since word went out that I left Licordia, seven kingdoms are trying to overthrow me."

The Pagosian king laughed. "Well, that's just stupid. Who thinks they can hold your throne?"

"I'm sure it's the same line-up as always. Someone close to me that I don't suspect. Plus six greedy idiots they recruited."

Ambrose made a sound of supreme disgust. "Morons! Peace isn't a simple thing. Never has been. Never will be." He clapped Dash on his arm. "Have no fear of us. Pagos will always back you. If you need soldiers, I will send them. We have some of the best, and I know they'd be willing to fight for you."

"Thank you. I just need to find out if I still have an army."

"Why would you doubt that?"

"We met a group of my veterans on the way here, and they were definitely not willing to fight for me." Dash let out a tired sigh. "It occurs to me that I've asked a lot of 'corns to die and bleed for me. Perhaps I didn't show as much gratitude as I should have."

Ambrose winced. "That's the hardest part of leadership. Too many focus so much on the goal that they forget the means and the cost. By the time they get what they want, they feel like they've earned it, or that they're even owed it. They forget that they didn't do it on their own. That there are many they relied on. Many they need to thank. And some they need to thank a lot. But I've never seen you forget those around you. It's how you picked your advisors."

Dash shook his head. "Maybe. But you didn't see the hatred in those unicorns when they attacked us."

"Was it something you actually did... or was it something someone fostered in them?"

"How so?" Dash asked.

Ambrose let out a long sigh. "Hatred grows one of two ways. It's something you do that is either deserved or not, or a well-planted lie that's cultivated by an enemy known or unknown."

Tanis frowned as she considered his words. "What do you mean deserved or not?"

Ambrose passed a sad look to her. "Sometimes our actions or intentions cause us to be hated for a reason that is justified." He glanced to Dash. "Such as cutting the head off an enemy who might have family members that take issue with such actions. Or chopping down certain trees."

Tanis understood that.

He turned back toward her. "Other times, our actions are misconstrued by others. If it's by accident, we can rectify it by explaining to another that we didn't mean to cause them harm or that we didn't intend malice. In those cases, all can be forgiven."

Ambrose's tone turned dark. "But then there are times when others are seeking any justification to hate us for reasons only they know. They crave that hatred. They want that hatred, and they will twist and manipulate anything we say or do as a reason to justify it. It's sad but true. It's nothing we do, just something they want, and they will feed their hatred, regardless of how much we try to heal it. No amount of apology will ever be enough to cure it. And nothing will appease them. They are after the life of the ones they feel did them wrong or the ones they hate for jealous reasons, and until the ones they hate are all dead, they will not rest or be placated. You cannot bargain with them. They are beyond all compassion and rational thought."

That she understood. "Like me with my brother's killer. I will never forgive them for what they took."

"Exactly, my lady. Except you have a concrete, justifiable reason for wanting that killer dead. He did you and your family wrong, personally. It's not imaginary and it left a scar in your heart that will never heal." Ambrose turned to Dash. "You, on the other hand... well, it's you. You might have actually done something wrong to the one who hates you."

"Thanks."

Ambrose chuckled. "But it's just as likely that you are the High King. You have what your enemy covets and cannot have so long as you live. Jealousy is a wicked, terrible thing. It is the root of all evil. The best way to take what they want is to knock down the one who holds it. If they don't have the skills to achieve their goal on their own, then they spread lies about the one who holds it. Turn others against them and build a jealous, hate-filled army to topple them. Who cares about the truth? Words are far more powerful than spears and travel twice as far, twice as fast. Many times, they're even deadlier. Words are sharpened weapons, and they can and do kill. Either by suicide from the one who cannot endure them, or from murder by one who is influenced having heard them. Wordfare can be far more destructive than warfare and have even longer—lasting consequences."

Tanis was awed by Ambrose. No wonder Dash listened to him. He was extremely wise.

Dash snorted at Ambrose. "They'll have a hard time toppling me. I didn't get to the top simply by killing my father... which wasn't as easy as it sounds. Bastard did fight back, and I had ten armies trying to lay me low and enemies clawing at my back and going for my throat every single step of the way. It took me years to get to where I am. And while they might think I'm down for the moment, never, ever underestimate someone who learned to fight in the streets. We don't go down without a vicious body count."

"True," Ambrose agreed. "But while you were busy running your kingdom, Lord Dash, you weren't paying attention to the ones you trusted. Those standing at your back, or at your side. One of them was spreading lies and betraying your trust. Who among your advisors feels that he or she is the most capable to take your place? The one who feels you should be most indebted to them?"

He scowled as he considered it. "I don't know. Kronnel leads my army. Yasha oversees the workers. Serran and Anyana manage the nobles. Dersha handles the navy. Renata was the one I leaned on the most, and sadly, I know it's not her."

"What of Ryper?" Ambrose asked.

He shook his head. "Ryper is an entity unto himself."

"But an advisor, nonetheless."

And one who didn't hesitate to kill at his command. "I trust him implicitly. If he wanted a throne, he could have one from another kingdom. Yet he chooses to stay with me." Dash couldn't imagine his advisors daring to turn on him, especially given the fact that Ryper would cut their throats just on principle. It was why he'd put them in their positions. Anytime anyone had shown the least bit of disloyalty, he'd booted them.

More to the point, Ryper had gutted them, which tended to cut down on mutiny.

One hint. One whisper.

Ryper had never taken that chance. Dash's was the one court where no one played political games or vied for power. They knew better. It wouldn't get them anywhere except a shallow grave. He didn't play favorites.

Well, except for Ryper. But he wasn't a favorite. He was family. More than than, Ryper had proven himself loyal when no one else had.

His advisors were competent and when they weren't, they were replaced or killed.

Hmmm...

Maybe Halla had been right. Maybe fear had been the wrong way to lead.

"What are you thinking?" Tanis asked.

"That they were all so afraid of my killing them that the moment I left, they pulled together to get rid of me."

Tanis's jaw dropped.

Ambrose laughed. "When was the last time you gutted an advisor?"

"I don't know. One... maybe two years ago."

"And tell the princess why."

"He annoyed me."

"Dash," Ambrose said, chidingly.

He let out an irritated sigh. "He was embezzling funds and trafficking."

"Trafficking?" she asked. "What's that?"

Ambrose cleared his throat. "Kidnapping and selling children for untoward things."

And it still infuriated Dash. He wished he could dig him up and stab his corpse again. And again, just for good measure. "I slit him wide open the moment I found out and dragged his carcass to the high wall by his entrails for the buzzards to feast on. In retrospect, I should have prolonged his death by a few more days. Wish I'd impaled him. Maybe gelded him first."

She sucked her breath in sharply. "Little more detail than I needed... or wanted, beast."

Ambrose nodded in agreement. "But it made a powerful statement to others, and it cut down on anyone else thinking of doing it. Basically, stopped it cold."

Dash glanced at Tanis. "Someone has to stand up for those who can't fight for themselves."

Ambrose nodded. "That is why you are High King. And why those of us with a brain and who are not corrupt, support you and will always do so." He patted him on the arm. "In spite of what you think, Dash, we know you're a fair king. You don't ride into our kingdoms and demand tribute. You don't tell us how to run our kingdoms so long as we treat our citizens well and they're thriving. The only ones who are unhappy with your reign are the ones who want to abuse others, those who want to be in charge of everyone else, and those who are afraid of what will happen if the day comes when you are no longer in charge. We're aware of the power vacuum your death will cause and the wars that will follow. No one else has the ability to rule the Thirteen Kingdoms. You're the only one in history who has ever held your title for more than a few months without major wars striking up between kingdoms."

True.

And Dash knew which kingdoms wanted to rule in his stead. Dythnal where the humans congregated and where Auderley was located. The centaurs in Thassalia. Elves in Alarium. Indara with her dragons, wyverns and gryphons. Kernan, Vaskalia, Umara, Sagaria, and lastly Cosaria where the Marauders made their home. All powerful. All technically capable of overthrowing him.

If they could only get their shit together.

But none of them would ever tolerate the other kingdoms to exist, unless they fell under their rule.

And those kingdoms included Pagos, Ningyo, and Tenmaru. Tenmaru would never, ever submit to anyone other than Dash as the High King. Makkuro Naomi who led the Tenmaruns had a vast army that was made up of oni, yokai, and renegade demons... and other species the rest of the kingdoms didn't even know existed. She had almost wiped out his father.

Until they made a truce that stood to this day.

Naomi would never make the same truce with anyone else, and Dash knew that for an absolute fact. If anyone overthrew him, Naomi wouldn't rest until she'd enslaved or annihilated all the other kingdoms.

She would fight them to the bitter end.

The same went for Meara.

That was the one lesson he'd learned in Meara's court. Just how deep her intolerance ran for the other Thirteen Kingdoms.

It wasn't just hatred centaurs bore unicorns. They

wanted them exterminated. He and those who'd been sent with him had been punished for their mere existence. There was no negotiation possible with Meara.

With Naomi, it was about power. She wanted to subjugate and rule the others.

With Meara, it was about hatred and annihilation.

All the years he'd spent with the centaurs, he still couldn't understand their mindset where unicorns were concerned. Their unrelenting hatred. Granted their two races had fought wars against each other for centuries, but this went beyond that.

It was systemic, unreasoning and unfounded, and it terrified him. They were both equine and had more in common than not, but it wasn't enough. The centaurs didn't think the unicorns were fit to live. All they focused on was the fact that centaurs had human torsos, and therefore human hearts which somehow made them better.

Meara had gleefully starved or worked to death more than half the hostages his father had sent with him to her kingdom. Dash still wasn't sure how he'd made it through. Other than Ryper and the other members of the Outlaws. Somehow, they had leaned on each other and forged a bond so tight that it had allowed them to survive that nightmare.

Sometimes those years seemed like a faint dream from long ago.

Most of the time, they were a vivid nightmare that still didn't let him sleep through the night.

The only thing he knew for sure, he hadn't emerged sane from it. None of them had.

And it wasn't just centaur against unicorn. It was the dragons against his people and gryphons. Nereids against the mermaids. Stonemen against trolls. Everyone against humanity and humans against them all. On and on it went into madness.

The only ones who didn't seem to hold grudges were the Pagosians. Anyone who could survive in their inhospitable climate was welcomed. They didn't care about species.

Why everyone couldn't take a lesson from Ambrose and his kingdom and just live in peace, he'd never understand.

But the others couldn't seem to let those old grudges go.

All Dash could do was help maintain borders and keep as much civility between the kingdoms as he could.

And pray a war didn't break out between everyone before he stopped it.

That was where their fear of him came in handy. Because he was psychotic, no one tested his temper. They were too afraid to do so as they had no idea how he'd unleash his fury against them. A lesson he'd learned from his mother.

Make them terrified.

Once you kill your own father for power, they realize that you have no value for their lives.

So, none of them had wanted to test his temper.

Granted he had no great love of dragons, but after he'd become king, he'd never sought to wipe them out or fight with them. He'd come to terms with Iagan and left them alone.

Same with Meara. As much as he hated that bitter, intolerant bitch, and had very personal reasons for wanting to wipe every centaur out of existence and have her head planted on a pole beside his throne, he'd set their terms for coexistence and tolerated her kingdom, even though it galled him.

So long as she abided by the terms they'd set, he allowed her to reign in peace for the sake of his people and hers. Better to grind his teeth in aggravation than watch the children of their races suffer and die in an endless cycle of hate and war.

But if he didn't get home with Renata's horn, no one would have peace again. All he'd worked for would end.

"How do I find my sister's horn and her brother's skull?"

Ambrose sighed heavily. "That is the question, Lord Dash. All we know is that they didn't bring them here, but they wanted you to think that. The question is why?"

He had no idea.

Tanis screwed her face up. "I don't know what either of you is thinking, but the dragons wouldn't have turned on you, Dash. Granted, my father didn't want me to search for my brother's skull, but I know he would never have sacrificed Davin. Not for anything. Even to end your life. While he's been no friend to your reign, he would never give up his heir to challenge you. I know he wasn't part of this."

Dash believed her. Granted, his own father would have gladly slit his throat, he knew others weren't like that. And he'd seen for himself the love Iagan bore his son.

No, this was something else.

Something he was missing...

And as he was thinking, sudden clarity slammed into him like a fist to his jaw. It was staggering and it took him a moment to accept the only truth it could be.

How had he missed it?

The traitor wasn't the snake in *his* garden that he'd been looking for.

It was the one who'd been whispering hatred in Renata's ears... The one vile unicorn who had kept pitting her against him. *I am blinder than a Stoneman...*

And dumber than the boots on his feet.

Because he'd been so distracted by his duties, he'd ignored those off-hand comments that should have made him send the bitch at his sister's righthand packing.

"Keryna," he growled the name with all the fury flowing through him.

Tanis exchanged a confused scowl with Ambrose. "What?"

"A friend of Renata's. She showed up out of nowhere a couple of years ago and ingratiated herself to my sister. She wasn't one of *my* advisors. She was Renata's. Keryna had to be the one who started all this."

Tanis cocked her head and looked completely baffled. "If she's your sister's friend, how could she lead a rebellion against you?"

Dash rubbed his forehead as he saw everything so clearly now. "She was always running her mouth and stirring dissention between my staff and advisors. She even tried to turn Ryper with her maliciousness. Thankfully, he was smarter than that and knew me better."

Even now, he could hear Ryper laughing about her malignant lies as he told Dash about one of his encounters with her. *She actually tried to make me think that you control and manipulate me. That you gaslight me, brother.*

As ludicrous an accusation as had ever been made. *What did you tell her?*

What else? Go fuck herself.

Ryper wasn't one who held back his thoughts or emotions. Which was why he was invaluable to Dash. Everyone knew where they stood with Ryper.

Shaking his head, he met Tanis's dark gaze. "I told Renata to get rid of her. Repeatedly. Instead, my sister attacked me for being heartless and unkind where Keryna was concerned."

You don't understand, Dash. She has no one else in this world. She was run out of the last three homes she's had. They were so cruel to her. She's known nothing save abuse. You need to show her kindness. Of all people, you know what it's like to be hated.

He'd been so furious at his sister and her unfounded support of that trouble-making unicorn no one else could stand. *Thrown out for a reason, Ren. Listen to her. She treats everyone around her like shit. She's a nasty dart donkey.*

Renata had just glared at him. *That's not fair. You hate everyone.*

I hate assholes. I can't help it if she's the reigning queen of them.

And so had gone almost every conversation they'd had about Keryna. From the moment he'd first met her, he'd disliked her to such an extent that he'd gone out of his way to avoid her. Just the way she smirked instead of smiled. The way she curled her lip as if she were forever smelling something foul.

She talked down to their servants and his sister and had tried to do the same with him until she realized he had a tongue that could let more blood than his dagger. Not to mention her backhanded compliments that had set his teeth on edge.

The only thing about Keryna that he'd liked was her absence.

In fact, one of the last conversations they'd had, Renata had sworn to him that she'd send Keryna packing.

She'll be gone by morning, Dash. I'll take care of it.

Instead of leaving, Keryna had come to his study to tell him that Renata had runaway after their fight.

But what if the fight they'd had over the centaur rebellion hadn't caused Renata to leave? What if Renata had told Keryna to get out and that bitch had murdered Renata instead?

No...

She wouldn't have dared.

Would she?

As much as he wanted to believe otherwise, it was entirely possible. Keryna had been one ballsy nag. She had convinced his sister that they were the best of friends. "Soul sisters." Closer than blood.

You can trust me with anything. I'm here for you, princess. Whatever you need. I can do it all.

And unlike him, Renata had believed those kinds of lies. Because she'd always been so sheltered and pampered, Renata had no idea just how brutal, conniving and backbiting others could be.

I don't want to live my life like you, Dash. Mistrusting everyone around me. It must be awful to live in your skin and be so paranoid all the time. Just give them a chance and you'll see how beautiful they are.

He'd never been able to make Renata understand the brutality he'd seen.

And if his sister had ever mentioned her powers to Keryna or that spell...

Damn it.

Surely, she wouldn't have been so stupid as to tell Keryna about them. Would she?

Then again, Renata had foolishly believed every lie Keryna had ever told her. Even when they'd been preposterous and he'd pointed them out, Renata had swallowed them whole.

Keryna would never hurt me, Dash. You don't know what you're talking about. Stop being so suspicious all the time. She's a sister to me and I've always wanted a sister.

Why hadn't he sent that trouble-making troll packing?

Because Renata had loved her.

I need her, Dash. I rely on her. She does so much for me. You have your people and I have her. Why can't you ever trust me, brother? I'm not a child. I know what I'm doing. Just please, have some faith in me.

And so, he'd allowed Keryna to stay. Even against his common sense and his own intuition.

I'm such a fool.

Of course, Renata, in her innocence, would have told Keryna everything. His sister had never kept a secret. Because of her innocence, she couldn't imagine anyone using something like that against her or anyone she loved.

Why would she?

Keryna was still in his palace. No doubt still making mischief and turning his people against him.

Damn me!

This had her name written all over it. Who else would have dared something like this?

He met Ambrose's gaze. "She had access to everything, courtesy of my sister. I even caught her sending missives in my name."

"And you let her live?"

"Not by choice. She told Renata it was a mistake, and Renata's tears weakened me. This is why I don't believe in mercy. The one time I showed it, you see what happened? My sister's dead and my kingdom's under fire. I should have choked the life out of Keryna the day I met her."

Tanis cleared her throat. "I really think we need to work on your relationship skills, beast. Just a little."

He arched a brow at her. "I think they're fine."

"Sure. Sure." She coughed and nodded. Then, she shrugged at Ambrose who laughed.

"I like your princess, Dash. I think she's good for you."

Honestly? He did, too. More than he should. But was she another Keryna?

Would she lull him into trust only so that she could betray him, too? That thought haunted him.

The door behind Ambrose opened to admit the older king's senior advisor. Only slightly taller than Ambrose, the human held a sloping pot-belly and one sunken eye. "My lord? I'm sorry to disturb you, but there's a beautiful sunset you don't want to miss. We all know how much you enjoy sitting in your garden with your friends. We'd hate for you to miss it."

"I'll be along, Sam. Thank you for the reminder."

As Sam left them, Ambrose turned to face them. "I don't envy you what's ahead. But I know you can overcome this small hill. You've traversed much larger mountains. Just remember that Pagos is with you. Always." He removed a ring from his finger and held it out to Dash. "This is enchanted. Use it to contact me should you need my army. We will come."

Dash took the ring and inclined his head to the much smaller king. "Thank you for all your help."

Ambrose patted his arm then left them.

Turning toward Tanis, Dash handed the ring to her.

She arched a brow at him. "You're trusting me with this?"

"Not by choice. Unicorns don't have pockets."

"Ah. The real reason you gave me that sack."

Even though he knew she was teasing, he quirked a brow at her. "You know, I do carry you on my back, Dragon."

"Teamwork. I like it." She slid the ring on her finger. "So where to now? Your kingdom?"

"No. First we need to see a wizard."

CHAPTER 11

Tanis wasn't quite prepared for how much warmer it would be when Dash landed on a green, grassy knoll. This was much more like it, and it reminded her of home. "Where are we?"

"Alarium."

The Elfin kingdom? Bold, given that the Elves weren't friendly to either of their races. From what she knew, they were likely to be one of the kingdoms that had put up money to murder Dash. "Your wizard lives here?"

"He used to. I'm hoping he still does." Dash tucked his wings in, and they vanished into his sides so seamlessly that she wanted to touch him and see how. But it might annoy him if she did.

Or worse, give her fantasies she didn't want to have.

So instead, Tanis began peeling off the thick outer layers of her clothing. She'd barely finished when the tree next to her moved in her direction.

"Dryad! Dryad! Dryad! Oh, good Lord. It's a dryad!" She

danced away from the tree as such creatures normally didn't get along with dragons. Mostly because they held grudges over dragons setting them on fire by accident.

Or sometimes on purpose.

Either way, they didn't like her species.

"What do we do?" she asked.

"Try saying hi." Dash held his hand out toward the nymph. "Good day, my lady."

The tree sneezed then extended a branch toward him so that he could shake her leaves. "Good day, my king. Are you looking for Marthen?"

"I am. Is he here?"

"He was, until he wasn't."

Tanis had to bite her tongue. Wasn't that always the case with everyone? But the dryad seemed sincere with her response, and for all his normal impatience with everyone else, Dash didn't seem to mind the odd comment.

"Any idea which way he might have traveled?" Dash asked.

The dryad sneezed again. "Backwards."

"Sounds like him to me. Thank you, my lady."

The tree bowed to him. "Any time, my liege."

Tanis closed the distance between them. "Was that helpful?"

"It wasn't unhelpful."

Now he was speaking in the same riddles as the dryad. Was it contagious?

The dryad sneezed again.

She frowned at the tree. "Do they always do that?"

"What? Sneeze?"

"Yes."

"Only when they're allergic to pollen."

Tanis's jaw dropped at his unexpected response. "A tree is allergic to pollen?"

He nodded. "Some of them, yes."

Well, who knew? "Isn't that a little counterproductive?"

"I don't make the rules, Dragon. I'm just here to see the wizard."

And she was just following along behind a unicorn. Therefore, all must be right in the world.

Irritated, she looked about the forest that didn't seem any different than all the others she'd visited. She'd always thought the elfin lands would be more...

Colorful? Magical? Something other than so basically, boringly normal. In truth, it was rather disappointing. Didn't they have portals or enchanted gates? Something that would make them stand out more?

Where were all the elfin things she'd heard about?

"So, who is this wizard we're after? Is he an elf?"

Dash shook his head as he led her toward a copse of trees on the right. "He's the son of an incubus yokai. His mother was human, and he has a bit of an attitude."

"Worse than yours?"

"Always worse than his, love."

She gasped at the voice that intruded on their conversation.

Out of the shadows, a tall, leanly muscled man approached. His white hair was cut short to frame a handsome, patrician face. Even so, she could see the demon in him. It flashed in his stormy eyes that took in a lot more than just her physical appearance. There was something about him that was absolutely compelling. Intoxicating.

While he wasn't handsome in the traditional sense, he possessed an aura that lured you toward him. She'd heard of charisma all her life, but until now, she'd never fully understood it.

But the wizard had his share of it, and his share's best friend's share, too.

With a wicked grin, he stepped forward and bowed low over her hand. "Greetings, lovely lady. To what do I owe this unexpected pleasure?"

Dash's staff appeared out of nowhere to fall between them. He pushed the wizard back from her so that he could step between her and the older man. "Bad luck, hidden enemies, death, and a reminder that I have a nasty temper."

Marthen laughed. "But this beauty's not yours. You released her. Like a fool, Dash. I would never let something so precious go."

"We're not here to talk about you or my stupidity. We're here to ask you what you know about my sister and the lady's brother... and the imp who's carrying around pieces of them both."

Marthen tsked. "Poor King Dash. Always seeking treasure and always finding pyrite. All the lessons you've learned and you've yet to learn the most important one."

"And that is?"

"Sometimes what we seek most is already in our palm, and we're too stupid to open our hand and see it."

Dash let out a bitter laugh at Marthen's typical babbling riddles. "While I always love these pearls of wisdom you enjoy pelting me with, could you please answer the question I need answered?"

"No."

Dash was aghast at his flat-out refusal. "No?"

"No."

"Why?"

The wizard grinned. "Because that's not the question you need answered."

Was he serious? "It's not?"

"No."

Dash looked at Tanis with a peeved, hopeless stare. "Why did I come here?" He turned back to Marthen. "Every time I have a discussion with you, I end up feeling like a dog chasing its tail."

"Better than one licking his balls. Because sometimes the one chasing the tail actually catches his target."

Dash smirked at her. "See what I mean?"

She decided to try her hand with the wizard. "Good Marthen, could you point us in the direction of where my brother's skull might be, and tell us how to reclaim it?"

The wizard's dark eyes sharpened. "Again, that's not the right question. Even if I tell you, it'll do you no good."

"Why?" she asked desperately.

He didn't even hesitate with his response. "Why is information ever useless?"

Tanis could only think of one reason. "When it serves no purpose."

"Exactly."

At least she was correct, but it made her want to groan out loud. Dash was right. This was extremely frustrating. She looked back at her unicorn. "Is this a wizard thing?"

"It's a Marthen thing. He lives his life backwards, so he already knows what we need and whether or not we get it. It's his whim as to whether or not he reveals it to us."

Marthen winked at Dash. "And you know the future, too, Your Majesty."

"No," Dash said, irritably. "I have glimpses. I haven't lived it like you have. My visions aren't the same thing as knowing history. Not to mention, my premonitions don't always come true. Sometimes they're just warnings that can be averted."

"How frustrating for you to not know the difference." Marthen tweaked him on the nose.

Tanis gaped, amazed Dash didn't slug him for the audacity.

Instead, Dash glared at the wizard. "Not as frustrating as you are at the moment."

Marthen clicked his tongue. "Then ask me the right question. The one you really want to know. The only one that *really* matters to you."

Dash ground his teeth at the game Marthen was playing with him. Why would Marthen do this when the old beast knew exactly what was on the line?

What stunk the most was that if he didn't ask exactly what the wizard wanted him to, Marthen would continue to play this game until he grew bored and vanished. Then, Dash would never have an answer.

If he asked what he really wanted to know...

It terrified him.

Worse, it would leave him vulnerable. He hated that thought even more.

Choose.

That was the real game Marthen was playing, and they both knew it. If he didn't give the wizard what he wanted, Dash would lose and learn nothing at all.

Of course, he could possibly learn what he needed to without Marthen's help, but time was running out. With or without Renata's wand, that spell would kill him. And the time to cast it was within the hour of when the next full moon began to wane. If it wasn't cast then, he'd have nothing to worry about where the spell was concerned.

But he wasn't that lucky, and he knew it. They had everything they needed to kill him. That poster had been his warning.

Time was ticking.

If that spell was cast, he was finished.

And even if it wasn't cast, he was still in danger. So long as Renata's wand was out there.

Just ask the damn question.

He glanced at Tanis and drew a deep breath. Fine. "If I fail in this, will Tanis be all right?"

"That's the right question, King. And deep in that dark place where your magick lives, you already know the answer. No one in the Thirteen Kingdoms will be all right if you fail. But the question you should be asking both of you is what will happen to her if you win?"

CHAPTER 12

Keryna stood in Renata's wardrobe antechamber, admiring herself in her rival's ornate court gown that she'd squeezed herself into by lacing a corset way too tight. Honestly, it was biting into her so badly, she was surprised she hadn't broken a rib. Even so, it was much prettier on her than it'd ever been on Renata, in her opinion.

As a human, Renata had been painfully skinny with dark hair and eyes. The blood red gown had never really flattered the younger unicorn's coloring the way it did hers.

I'm the one who looks like royalty.

She picked up one of Renata's ornate crowns from the shelf to her right and started to put it on her head, then frowned at her image. "I don't have mousy hair." Her sisters had just been mean and jealous of her when they'd said that. While it wasn't the golden blond of her sisters' hair, it wasn't really brown either. Definitely not the color of a mouse. Or the texture of one.

Maybe a little. But only because it was coarse and wiry.

"What are you doing?"

Keryna dropped the crown in her hands as the imp's voice intruded on her thoughts. "Don't do that!"

The imp scoffed at her. "Should you be playing with jewels that don't belong to you?"

"Mind your own business, Bink!" Keryna picked up the ornate crown from the ground and put it back before one of the king's advisors caught her. They still weren't on her side. Not completely. And if they caught her in Renata's room, they'd be furious at her.

She'd already had a fight with Kronnel this morning. Last thing she needed was another skirmish with the old bastard who kept threatening to throw her out of the palace. If she murdered him, too, others might begin getting suspicious.

Her only saving grace was that Kronnel didn't know Renata was dead or that Dash had already banished her. Thankfully, she'd been able to assure Halla that she would tell Kronnel about Renata's death before the hobgoblin had reached the old bastard.

Halla had been more worried about catching up to Dash than anything else. That was the beauty about trust.

No one asked the right questions. They just assumed things they shouldn't.

And speaking of...

"What are you doing here?" she snarled at the imp. She was still furious that he and his accomplice had returned to the palace. He'd promised her that he'd drop Renata's horn in her room and then vanish into another kingdom and never be seen again.

That had lasted all of a few days. Next thing she'd

known, they'd returned, telling her about their ploy to kill Dash by using the other kingdoms to provide a bounty on his head.

It was stupid and dangerous.

The imp flashed a grin at her. "You told me to let you know when Lorens arrived with his group. He's here."

That was good news.

She clapped her hands together in glee. Finally! Reinforcements. She'd been waiting for the centaurs to arrive and push Dash's advisors out of their positions so that she could take over.

For months now, she'd been in talks with the centaur rebels and their leader, Prince Lorens. She'd been assuring Lorens that Dash would back his cause to overthrow his queen sister, even though she knew he wouldn't. For whatever reason, Dash wanted nothing to do with Thassalia.

Every time she'd brought it up, he'd furiously shouted her down.

Do not meddle in things you don't understand!

His dismissals had infuriated her. She knew politics every bit as well as he did. Probably even better because she hadn't been born into it. She'd had to learn it. He might be king because of a lucky birth, but she wasn't stupid. Hence how she'd risen to be so close to the crown.

Her original plan had been for Renata to provide the soldiers they needed, and then kill Renata in battle after her brother was gone.

Everything had been going along perfectly.

Until Renata had decided to listen to her brother. Or more to the point, until Dash had put his foot down and refused to let his sister have the soldiers Renata commanded for his calvary. The soldiers Keryna needed to keep Lorens on her side.

Then, Dash had told Renata to toss her out.

That had been the final act.

If he'd just allowed Renata to have those soldiers...

Stupid bastard.

But this was better. Now they wouldn't have to worry about King Dash, and she wouldn't have to tolerate any more of Renata's whining stupidity.

It was perfect.

Being crowned queen was much better than being a simple advisor to Queen Renata. She'd even let Lorens be High King so long as he allowed her to rule over the unicorns.

All those idiots who'd mocked her would rue the day. She planned to torture them just for fun.

Licordia would be *her* kingdom.

Rubbing her hands together, she let out a squee of pleasure, then remembered that she still had a witness in the room.

"Stay hidden," she told the imp.

"What have I been doing?"

Annoying her, if the truth were told. He was a threat and, as soon as this was over, she'd see to it that he was a dead one.

She cast the imp a sneer before she left him and headed to the main hall where Kronnel was waiting with Anyana for the centaurs to be shown in.

"What are centaurs doing here?" Anyana asked the general who shrugged in confusion.

Keryna cast a royal, haughty stare over them as she

swept into the room. "Didn't you know?" Keryna asked as she moved to stand beside Anyana who was there as a brown unicorn with an orange horn. "His Majesty is planning on sending troops to help Lorens with his rebellion against their queen."

In human form, Kronnel scowled at her. "No, he's not."

"Is to. Renata told me so. She's going to be their commander."

Even though he was human, Kronnel made a very horse-like snort. "You're insane. King Dash would never involve himself in centaur politics. Nor would he allow his sister to fight with rebels against Meara. I know his policies on such matters. He would never have changed them without telling me."

Keryna smirked at the old horse as she picked a piece of lint from her ornate bodice. "Apparently, you don't know him as well as you think you do."

"Apparently, you don't know him at all."

Anyana cocked her unicorn head. "Are you wearing Princess Renata's official state dress?"

Before she could answer, the steward announced the arrival of a royal centaur procession.

When the palace doors opened, Keryna expected to see Lorens, the spoiled illegitimate brother of the centaur queen.

It wasn't him.

Instead, the queen and her imperial guard spilled through the doors and took up post all around the room, surrounding them. Meara's equine half was a resplendent bay with stocking. She wore a dark blue jacket that was embroidered with heavy gold threads and encrusted with jewels. Her black hair was intricately braided with even more jewels and coiled around a golden crown that rested perfectly atop her head.

Never had she seen a more beautiful or regal creature.

Awed by the graceful queen, Keryna stepped back with a gasp so that she could curtsey.

Kronnel moved forward to cut the queen off. "What's going on here?"

Meara raked him with an impressive sneer that said she equated him with something that marred the bottom of her favorite pair of shoes. "Stand aside, unicorn. I want to talk to who's in charge."

"That would be me." Keryna forced herself to rise and step forward.

"She's not in charge," Kronnel said. "I'm the one in command whenever King Deciel isn't present."

Keryna pulled out the document she'd forged from the pocket of her gown. She held it out to the centaur queen. "As you can see, King Deciel put me in charge until his return."

The queen blinked slowly but made no move to touch the paper. Rather, she quirked one brow in what had to be the most imperious gesture Keryna had ever beheld. She would definitely practice that in front of a mirror later.

Meara narrowed her gaze on Keryna. "Then I can assume that you're the one who knows where he went? And how to contact him?"

"Of course."

She smiled coldly. It actually sent a shiver up Keryna's spine. The queen turned her head to speak to the male centaur behind her. "Seize that wretch."

Keryna started to run, but the centaurs circled her

immediately and took her by the arms so that she couldn't escape them.

Worse, one of them placed a collar around her neck that prevented her from using magick or switching to her unicorn form. A third came forward and snatched the piece of paper from her hand.

Without a word, he offered it to the queen.

"Now see here..." Kronnel tried to intervene.

More soldiers surrounded him and Anyana and angled spears with glowing tips at the two of them.

"There's nothing to see." Taking the document from her man, Meara gestured for the others to back Kronnel and Anyana away from Keryna. "The king has left his throne. And apparently, *someone* has the princess's horn." Meara approached Keryna slowly. "Since you seem to be in charge, how about you tell me what *you* know, hmmm?"

Real fear turned her throat dry. She was no longer in charge of anything, and she knew it. This had definitely not been her plan. She'd never dreamed that Meara would dare invade Dash's lands while he was gone.

What was she supposed to do now?

Admit nothing. Act stupid. "I don't know what you're talking about."

"I think you're lying." She cupped Keryna's chin in her icy, well-manicured hand, then she squeezed Keryna's cheek tightly until her nails dug into Keryna's flesh. "I can see it in your beady, little, conniving eyes. You have a great hunger like my brother used to have for things that aren't yours." She released her. "Adsel?"

A handsome, blond centaur stepped forward wearing the uniform of her guard. "My queen?"

"Letter?"

He handed her a piece of paper.

She took it and compared it to the document Keryna had tried to give her. After a few minutes, she returned the two of them to the centaur she'd called Adsel. "What do you think of the signatures?"

He examined them carefully. "Looks the same to me."

"Does, doesn't it?" The queen walked up to Keryna again, and tsked. "You did such an admirable job forging Dash's signature... except for one thing."

Keryna's heart stopped.

No, there was no way she knew she'd forged them.

Wasn't possible.

Was it?

Didn't matter. She knew better than to admit to what she'd done. "What are you talking about? I have no idea what you mean."

"Don't play stupid, girl. It's unbecoming of you and insulting to me." Meara held the papers up to Keryna's face. "I will give you credit. You did an excellent job. To most, it would pass. But you forgot that Dash spent years in my court. I knew him intimately, and the one thing I know is that he's decidedly left-handed when he's human."

She slapped the papers against Keryna's cheeks. "The person who wrote these left ink smudges to the right where they rested their hand while composing them. So, I know it wasn't Dash writing to my traitor, promising him troops to fight against me, or signing an order to say you would be left in charge." She lowered the papers. "Oh, and Lorens is dead, by the way. I took care of him as I do anyone who threatens my crown."

She smiled coldly, tightened the papers into a roll and slapped Keryna on the cheek with them so hard that she saw stars. "But you, girl... are another matter. Talk to me about this gold unicorn horn you claim to have?"

Outright terror seized her as she realized just how much trouble she was in. "I know nothing of any horn."

Meara snapped her fingers and held her hand out.

Adsel exchanged the two letters she'd been holding for a poster.

Meara held it up for Keryna so that she could see the document. It was an advertisement for an auction.

Her stomach sank as she read it and saw that it listed literally everything she'd gathered for the spell to kill Dash. *Everything!*

More than that, it was going to be auctioned off? That had never been the plan.

At least not hers. She was the one who'd learned about the spell from Renata late one night when they'd been talking and drinking. She'd made the offhand comment that Dash was invincible.

Laughing, Renata had shaken her head. *That's what everyone thinks, but I know a secret. There is a way to kill a black horn. But you can never tell anyone. Shh!*

That was the same night Keryna had begun to formulate her plan to overthrow Dash and take her place among the nobility. It'd never dawned on her then to take Renata's horn. Only to use the spell against the king and then manipulate Renata after Dash's death.

The imp would never have known about the spell had she not ingratiated herself to Renata. How dare he go behind her back with that slimy friend of his and do this!

Fools, both of them.

She was furious. Which one of them had betrayed her with this scheme? The idiot imp or the useless dragon slayer?

They were nothing without her.

Nothing!

How could I have been so stupid? Of all creatures, she knew better than to trust anyone.

Now...

Meara smirked at her. "So, you didn't know about this auction." She considered that for a moment. "Imbecile partner? Or a traitor in *your* midst?" The queen laughed. "How perfectly divine." She held her hand out again.

Once more, Adsel provided her with some mysterious paper.

"And *this*?"

Forcing herself to show no reaction, Keryna saw the bounty sheet that she'd commissioned to disseminate throughout all the kingdoms except Licordia and Pagos.

That had been her plan. Keep Dash on the run outside of Licordia, chasing after Renata's wand that was in her possession. She was hoping he wouldn't return before she cast the spell.

Or if he did return before it was cast, she wanted him to be weak.

Then, she'd be able to kill him with Renata's horn.

When he least expected it. If someone else had killed him before he returned home, that would have worked, too. Either way, she would have been regent or queen, depending on what Lorens had wanted.

She'd hoped to keep the news of Dash's absence from

the unicorns since she didn't want them to be aware of the fact that their king had left. Had it reached them, though, she'd had a few concocted lies. She'd just needed a couple of weeks to put it all into action.

Just a few days more. That was all that stood between her and her dreams.

Why couldn't the imp have followed her well-thought out plan?

And why did Lorens have to get himself killed? Moron!

"So..." Meara leaned closer to her. "You knew about this one."

Keryna clenched her teeth. So much for thinking she could keep her features unreadable. Meara had an uncanny knack for seeing through her façade and knowing the thoughts in her head. It was truly eerie. No wonder Dash had feared her so.

The queen handed the wanted poster to Kronnel. "Did *you* know about this, general?"

Kronnel read it and as he did so, he turned red in the face. "*What!* Who would dare put up such money for our High King? Tell me the kingdoms!"

Meara smirked. "So, no. The general wasn't part of the coup." Laughing, she turned a small circle. "Well, isn't this delicious? I always thought I'd have to sacrifice at least three quarters of my army to kill off the *apaswere* who bore our treaty. Turns out, I just had to wait for his idiot sister to die and then I'd be invited to invade his court. I should have murdered Renata years ago. How wonderful that you found the loophole I've always wanted."

"No one invited you," Kronnel growled.

She tsked at the old unicorn. "Technically, you're right."

She jerked her chin at Keryna. "The invitation was for my horrid half-brother and his centaur forces to come take this throne. I'm just accepting on his behalf. Hence my loophole. How beautiful that I didn't have to breach my contract with Dash." This time, she clapped her hands up in the air.

Two members of her guard came forward to lay a decapitated head on the floor at Keryna's feet.

Her stomach lurched, especially at the expression of pain and horror that was permanently etched into Lorens's face.

"Don't worry, dear. Your death will be much slower and much, much more painful. Because there's a lot more I need to know from *you*."

Adsel jerked his chin toward Kronnel and Anyana. "What about these two, my queen?"

Pursing her lips, she turned toward them. "I don't know yet. Round up all the advisors and put them someplace relatively safe and miserable until I decide what their fates will be."

CHAPTER 13

Dash sighed wearily as he sat before a blazing fire. While it'd been warm earlier, there was a chill in the air now that night had fallen.

What really sickened him was the knowledge as to why his sister had been killed.

Not because she was mad at him and had run away in a fit of rage after their fight and was overtaken by some random trophy hunter or bandit. She'd been killed for her horn because of a greedy piece of shit who wanted to sell the ability to assassinate him.

Pain washed through him anew. Gods, if he could just take back that one last moment.

The things he'd said to her...

He hadn't meant them. He'd just been so mad at her for not listening to him. And he was desperate to believe that the harsh words she'd spoken to him had been just as meaningless.

You're a heartless bastard, Dash. No wonder Father sent you away from us. You don't care about anyone except yourself, and you never will!

Nothing in his life had ever cut him as deeply as her words that night. Never in their lives had she spoken to him that way. Because they weren't her words.

They were Keryna's. He'd heard that bitch many times whispering in Renata's ear that he was heartless and didn't care about anyone. Not even Renata. That he'd been sent to the centaurs because their father knew he was incapable of compassion.

Renata had still been a colt at the time he'd been sent to Meara's. She had no knowledge of why it'd happened. Especially since no one dared speak of that time once Dash had returned home and confronted his father.

Nor did Renata understand the contract the kingdoms had signed for peace. It was one that couldn't be broken. Signed in blood on the flesh of an *apaswere* demon.

So long as the *apaswere* lived, Meara could only enter his kingdom by invitation.

But Dash hadn't thought about that or the cause behind the words when they'd left Renata's lips during their fight. His fury and pain had been too great. *I will not allow you to lead my army for Lorens and his rebels. We are not Thassalian and I will not get involved in their politics. I'm not going to allow you to kill our warriors in a conflict that has nothing to with us or any unicorn. Nor will I invade another country because my fool-hearted sister thinks she knows better than a queen who's ruled longer than you've been alive. You're an idiot, Ren. Not a politician.*

He'd known how sensitive she was to being called an idiot. It'd been their father's favorite insult for her. All their lives, Dash had refrained from using it in any regard in her presence.

But she'd hit him below his belt, and he'd retaliated in kind.

And that insult had only fueled her more. *You're a coward, brother.* The fury in her eyes would haunt him for eternity. *They broke you in Meara's court, and you're too afraid to even cross her borders.*

Those words had unlocked a door inside him that no one should have ever touched. When he'd returned home, it'd taken him years to calm down.

Not because he was broken. Rather Meara had awakened the demon inside him that he had yet to fully quell.

After Renata had spoken those hate-filled words, his rage had been such that he'd actually drawn his hand back to slap her for them. It was the only time in his life that he'd done such a thing, and it'd startled them both. But she'd plucked a nerve so raw that he still didn't know how he'd found the strength not to strike her out of the feral rage she'd unleashed.

There was no cowardice in him from his time in Queen Meara's court. Only a nightmare so brutal and lasting that, to this day, he couldn't sleep through an entire night.

Couldn't trust anyone at his back.

And his only fear came from that demon they'd freed and stoked deep inside his soul that he now kept caged. Fear of the times when something unleashed it... such as Renata's hateful words.

Fear of whenever his control slipped because the demon side of him was so lethal, even he didn't know exactly what it was capable of.

He'd lowered his arm and glared at her. *Get out of my sight, Ren. And stay away from me until you learn to show me the respect I've earned. I have done nothing but shelter and protect you. And if that's not enough for you, you know where the door is.*

That had been the last time he'd seen her.

The last words spoken between them.

Just hours later, Keryna had come to him to tell him that Renata had left to join the centaur rebels. He'd been so pissed off that he hadn't even thought to gather his army or even an escort before he went after her. Hadn't even thought to tell Ryper or Chrysis.

His only thought had been to get to Renata before something bad happened to her.

Instead of finding his sister so that he could verbally throttle her, he'd found her body, along with a tiny brownie who'd been watching over her remains.

Sobbing, the small, frail, winged creature had been sitting on the ground, tangled in her mane. Had it not been for the tears, with her brown hair and eyes, he'd have mistaken her for a butterfly or moth.

She'd cringed away from him when his shadow had fallen over her.

"I mean you no harm." It'd been obvious that she hadn't killed his sister. She was far too tiny to cut off a horn. "What happened?"

"T-t-t-they killed her." She blew her nose into the gauze of her sleeve, then wiped her nose on the back of her tiny hand.

"Who?"

"H-h-h-humans." She'd been so upset that all she could do was gesture at Renata's head. "Said her h-horn was invaluable. Th-th-that they needed it. Why would they kill something so beautiful?"

"I don't know." He'd choked on his own tears. Changing into his own human body, he'd knelt beside his sister so that he could lay his head against her soft neck and hold her close.

"I-I tried to slow them down. I-I was too small. They didn't even see me."

Fury had blinded him as he fisted his hand in Renata's bloodied mane. "Did they say where they were going?"

"Auderley."

Dash had heard Halla's gasp as she'd caught up to him. Infuriated and desperate, he'd entrusted his sister's body to her and then he'd been on his way to find her killer.

Until a dragon had slowed him down.

At that time, he'd assumed Renata had been overtaken by trophy hunters, enemies or wizards.

Now he knew it was a planned coup against him. Even if he'd given his sister permission to take his army, she wouldn't have come back alive.

Keryna had other plans.

This was all his fault.

There had been no saving Renata. It both sickened and comforted him to know that. Most of all, it just pissed him off. Because the one thing he could have changed was that last night with her. He should never have lost his temper.

Not with his baby sister.

A sudden shadow fell over him.

"What are you thinking?" Tanis knelt down by his side.

Sighing heavily, he tossed a piece of wood into the fire.

"That I played into hands I shouldn't have. Of all creatures, I should have known better."

She leaned against his side to offer him comfort. "Don't beat yourself up, beast."

"You're right. I shouldn't. There are so many others who want to do it for me. I probably wouldn't have to walk three feet to find one."

She laughed. "You need to get some sleep while you're able."

"Probably. Tomorrow is sure to be an even longer, more fun-filled day than today was."

They were safe for the moment, but it wouldn't last. Marthen's shield would allow them protection for the night. Yet they were still in the middle of enemy territory.

If an elf found them here...

Tanis should be fine even as a human. He doubted they'd harm her.

Dash would be recognized and dealt with. While he could hold them off for a bit, they would ultimately win and his would be a nice hide they'd use for shoe leather. Or a decoration in the hall of one of their three ruling monarchs.

He glanced over to Tanis. "I'm also thinking I should have been kinder to the elves as a king."

Her eyes widened. "What did you do to the elves?"

He tossed another stick into the fire as he remembered it as if it were yesterday. "I sent them a giant wooden statue of myself as a unicorn."

She scowled at him. "Well, that's not so bad. I mean, it is a little egotistical. But not too awful."

He gave her a flat, droll stare. "It was carved from their sacred mother tree."

She gasped as the full horror of what he'd done dawned on her. "Oh, that *is* terrible, Dash! Why in the Thirteen Kingdoms would you do something like that?"

He shrugged nonchalantly. He should probably regret it, but he didn't. Other than the fact that the blowback now would be extreme when he needed their support.

"Don't you dare shrug at me, beast. Tell me what you were thinking."

He let out a tired breath before he explained his actions. "One of their princes raided a fairy distillery, drank a bit much of their ale and ended up setting fire to a grove of dryads in his drunken stupor. Thirty-five of them were severely injured, but thankfully none of them died. When I demanded he be punished, his father refused. Said they were noble elves. It was an accident and that the dryads weren't as important as his legacy. Since none of the dryads had died, he didn't understand my anger over it. After all, he argued, trees were just trees. They were nowhere near as valuable as an elf. So, I decided to make a point. Especially given that the elves are supposed to be protectors of the forest."

If a tree was just a tree...

Sighing, she pressed her forehead against his shoulder. "You clearly made your point, beast."

"I did. As well as an enemy I'm sure still wants to gut me."

Tanis shook her head at him. "What am I going to do with you?"

"If you were smart, you'd run back to your father and keep your head down till all of this blows over."

Tanis paused at the sincerity she heard in his voice. She

probably should. It was the smart thing to do. And she had no idea why she was still here.

He'd set her free. She could seek her brother's head on her own.

Just days ago, finding her brother's killer had been the most important thing in the world to her. So important that she'd made an unbelievable bargain.

With a unicorn—a hated creature that two weeks ago she wouldn't have spit on had he been on fire.

Then she'd met this enigmatic one with searing green eyes that haunted her. Strange that she'd only known him for these handful of days, and yet it seemed like a lifetime had passed since they'd joined forces.

The last thing anyone who knew her would call her was a romantic. She didn't believe in love or romance of any kind. Didn't believe in much of anything other than misery and cruelty.

But her unicorn made her want to believe in impossible things.

What scared her now was the fact that he most likely wouldn't survive this.

That he'd leave her life as quickly as he'd entered it.

"You really have pissed off everyone, haven't you?" she asked.

He sighed heavily. "I've done my best."

"Was that really the only way to have peace?"

Dash shrugged. "I tried to be nice when I was young. I swear I did. They took it as an invitation to walk all over me. They mistook kindness for weakness. My policy was to ask, then kick their ass. Sadly, ass kicking accomplished a lot more than asking nicely."

"You sound like my father."

But she saw the weariness in his eyes. The sadness. "Can I let you in on a secret, Dragon?"

"Sure."

"Having lived through hell, I'd rather have not."

That, she well understood as she struggled with the same feelings every day of her life. Sometimes it wasn't so bad, then others...

It was hard to make through a single hour. "Me, too, Dash. Me, too."

He put his arm around her and held her close.

Tanis listened to his strong heart beating beneath her cheek. Last week, her worst fear had been living without her brother.

Now it was losing a unicorn she barely knew.

It was so weird. How had he come to mean so much to her so quickly?

Was it because Davin was gone, and she didn't want to be alone? Or because Dash saw her when others didn't? That he knew the same pain that haunted her?

She had no idea.

It wasn't like she hadn't been alone before. She had. She'd long ago reconciled herself to the fact that she would never have anyone in her life.

That her only family would be Davin, Marla and their hatchlings.

Tanis knew she could survive it. She just didn't want to. Because she knew exactly how cold and lonely it was. How brutally awful.

This could be the only night we have together.

It could be the last chance *she* had. That was what scared

215

her most. In all these years, she'd lived completely closed off from everyone else. Lived in a shell where she'd never thought she'd ever be attracted to anyone at all. A part of her had been fine with that, but deep down in a place she'd closed off from the entire world she didn't really want to be alone.

She wanted to have what others did. To have someone she cared about, who cared about her, too.

And there was no denying what she felt for Dash. Even if he was a *dreaded* unicorn. The awful, feared High King.

For all his bluster and his horrible reputation, he'd been decent to her.

Even now, he was gentle.

This could be the only chance in her life that she'd have to be with a male. And if it was, she didn't want to let it go without taking a chance.

I don't want to have any more regrets.

"Would you make love to me, Dash?" The words were out of her mouth before she could stop them.

And she wasn't sure which of them was the most shocked when they betrayed her.

She clapped both of her hands over her mouth, then she began to sputter helplessly. "I... uh... um... What was that? I don't know, Dash? Moon lunacy. Fire drunk. I'll go with that. Fire drunk. That sounds reasonable. I've lost my mind. Have you seen it?"

Dash chuckled at the rush of color that stained her cheeks as she quickly sought to cover her slip. He'd never met anyone like her. She never hesitated to speak her mind. Even when it was completely insane.

Never played any games with him. So, when she said that, he knew it was without guile or malicious intent.

It was from her heart.

Even though he had no idea why.

"Have you any idea what you're asking me, Dragon?"

She peeked at him from between the fingers she had covering her eyes. "The mechanics of it, yes. Part A goes into Part B."

Now, he understood why she'd asked him what she had.

She'd never had anyone love her. He knew that from the kiss they'd shared. She might have been taken, but she'd never been held as if she mattered. Never been held with tenderness as she should have.

Tanis was still as innocent as a virgin.

And that pissed him off for her. No one should be abused like that.

"Do you not have a dragon at home waiting for you, Tanis?"

Shadows haunted her dark eyes as she lowered her hands and shook her head. "I'm stained by my past. No dragon will ever have me."

Defiled by another species or clan was what she meant. Dragons were very particular about their mates, and they only had one partner for the whole of their lives that was usually picked for them by their families when they were adolescents. While they might have some lovers before marriage, those lovers were all dragons, and usually chosen from within their clan. There was no such thing as cheating in their culture once they were promised to another, as it was met with a swift death penalty were they caught.

"During your captivity?" he asked.

She started away from him.

Dash gently caught her arm. "You don't have to tell me. I just wanted to understand."

A single tear fell down her cheek. "It wasn't by my choice. Yet my family acted as if it was."

And because of that, she was damned to an eternity of solitude. It was so unfair to her. No one should be degraded like that. Denied a future or any prospect of love or partnership because of some random asshole who'd taken what he had no right to.

He'd seen far too much of it when he'd lived among the centaurs. They gleefully used rape as a way to break their captives.

Used it to break their own.

Sex should never be weaponized.

He would never understand how anyone could do that to another, and it sickened him that someone could have done it to a female as precious as his dragon.

"I would never hurt you, Tanis."

"I know."

Brushing the dark red hair back from her cheek, he smiled at her, then pressed his lips against the hollow of her throat so that he could inhale the sweet rose scent that was his dragon.

She had seen him in ways no one ever had. When he looked into her kind, dark eyes he didn't see the bastard unicorn king who was hated by all, he saw himself as he wanted to be. Kind. Heroic. Noble.

Most of all lovable.

The one thing he'd never been...

Accepted.

Lifting his head, he touched her lips with his fingertips. "Thank you," he breathed.

"For what?"

"For seeing the best inside of me instead of the demon."

She smiled at him. "I only see what's there."

Not believing that for a minute, he leaned forward and kissed her.

Tanis surrendered herself to him with a gentle moan of pleasure. He tasted of warmth and wine while his whiskers prickled her skin.

Nibbling her lips, he toyed with her top. "I've never seen anything more incredible or frustrating than you, Dragon. Except for the laces of your corset."

She laughed at him as he used his magick to remove it and leave her bare to his gaze. That sobered her as she felt completely naked.

Not just physically. She couldn't explain it. He made her feel exposed in ways that defied logic. As if he could read her soul.

As if sensing her discomfort, he quickly conjured a fur blanket for her to wrap around her shoulders. Then more pelts for the ground.

And that was why she wanted to be with him. He was forever considerate.

As if he knew her thoughts, he enveloped her with his arms and held her close to the heat of his body.

Tanis trembled. For some reason, she felt as though she'd come home after a long absence. Something about being with her unicorn just felt so very right.

She looked up to see if he felt it as well. She didn't know, but his emerald gaze burned into hers.

He dipped his head toward her lips, and she welcomed his kiss. Tanis growled deep in her throat as their lips met. This was what she'd been aching for, and she hadn't even known it. Someone in her arms who treated as if she mattered.

With a boldness that astounded her, she took his lips between her teeth and tugged gently. She wanted to devour this beast, to feel every inch of him against her and to never, ever let him go.

His clothes vanished beneath her hands, and his powers should frighten her, but she was getting as used to them as she was to him.

Dash's head swam as he tasted the sweetness of his dragon's mouth. She clutched at his back, pulling him so close to her that he feared he might actually hurt her.

In her innocence, she rubbed her breasts against his chest, searing him with heat. He growled as she shifted her weight in his arms and her hip brushed his swollen groin.

For a moment, he swore he saw stars. Damn... how long had it been since he'd last been with someone?

He really couldn't remember.

Too damn long, honestly. Because of his position, he'd avoided lovers and the complications they brought to his already complicated life. He didn't want their demands or their tantrums.

He'd had a little sister for that.

Nor had he wanted anyone trying to control him. Or pretending to act on his behalf.

Again, he'd learned much in Meara's court over the years he'd spent there, and her consorts had been a nightmare for the queen.

He could have married, but he'd never found anyone who had appealed to him. No one he'd wanted to spend more than five minutes around.

Until now.

Tanis was unlike any female he'd ever met. *She's a dragon, idiot.* True. But she was more than that. She was unexpected.

Beguiling.

And right now, she owned him in a way no one ever had.

Not even his sister.

Leaning forward, she captured his lips with her own.

His will shredded by her touch, Dash was past the point of rational thought. All he could focus on was the manifestation of his dreams. The pleasure of her smell, the feel of her hip grinding against the part of him he longed to give her.

"Make love to me, Dash, for the rest of the night." Tanis felt his hands sliding along the bared flesh of her buttocks as he kissed her fiercely.

She reveled in the feel of him. In the knowledge that she would never want anyone else the way she wanted her unicorn.

Never.

Bliss tore through her as chills erupted the length of her body. She wasn't sure what thrilled her more, the feel of his tongue stroking her neck or the strong hands that touched her in places no one else had ever touched her with such kindness.

Dash cupped her face in his hands and kissed her deeply.

She closed her eyes as she savored ever last bit of it. If she died in this moment, she would be perfectly happy.

And she wanted to please him as much as he was pleasing her. Even though it scared her, she slowly slid her hand down the tight, hard muscles of his chest, over his abdomen through the tangled curls between his legs to touch the hard flesh of him with her hand.

Sucking his breath in sharply between his teeth, he shook all over. Tanis smiled in satisfaction at the thought of the power she had over this powerful beast who claimed he needed no one.

Yes, he was still ferocious and feral, but he was purring for her and her alone.

His green eyes glowing with warmth, he laid her down against the fur pelts, and pulled the fur away from her breasts. Exposed to his gaze, she trembled in uncertainty. Her face warmed as his gaze ran over her.

"My dragon," he whispered. "I want to see you, to touch you."

He dipped his head to her breast. Tanis arched her back at the sensation of his tongue playing across the taut peak. Moaning, she cupped his head in her hands and held him close as his hot breath scorched her skin.

He ran his hand down her stomach and over her hip. Her entire body ached with need. Bittersweet pleasure tore through her.

And then, he trailed his hand around her thigh and touched the center of her body. Tanis gasped as spindles of pleasure whipped through her, while his fingers caressed the tender folds of her body.

Dash took care to make sure he didn't harm her. He couldn't help what had happened to her in the past. But he wanted to make damn sure that this night brought her nothing save the best memory that he could make it.

And if it was his last night in this life, then he wanted to make it count.

Let my last deed be a good one.

Over and over, he stroked her, teasing her with a promise of more pleasure, until he pulled away.

She whimpered in disappointment.

"Don't worry, my dragon. I'm far from finished." Dash placed a kiss on the back of her neck.

She shivered.

He lay behind her to pull her back against his chest and ran his hands over her breasts, down her waist, and then to her hips.

Reaching up, over her head to bury her hands in his thick black hair, Tanis arched her back against him.

He wrapped one arm about her waist, then trailed his hand back to the juncture of her thighs. She growled in pleasure.

"That's it," he breathed against her neck. He rained kisses over her shoulders. She could feel the tip of his shaft pressing against her buttocks.

Dash sucked his breath in sharply between his teeth, then lifted his head. His fingers returned to torture her with pleasure.

Tanis couldn't stand it. She writhed in his arms as his fingers slid in and out of her.

And as the ache in her built, he nudged her thighs wider apart and plunged himself deep into her body.

She cried out in ecstasy as she lowered her hips to draw him deeper.

Dash closed his eyes, savoring her sighs as he buried himself up to his hilt. Never had he felt anything more incredible than the tightness of her heat surrounding him as he thrust himself deeper into her.

Heaven help him for what he was doing. But this was all he had ever wanted in his life. Someone who could accept him and not judge him.

She was a part of him he hadn't realized was missing until she'd stumbled into his life.

Or more to the point, captured him.

Tanis clenched her teeth as exquisite torture wracked her body. Her head spun as he drove himself into her again and again, deeper than before. It was incredible, this feeling of him behind her and in her.

His fingers quickened to a rhythm to match the strokes of his hips. Her body became possessed of its own free will as it met him stroke for stroke, building her pleasure until she could barely stand it.

Never in her life had she known this kind of bliss could exist.

No wonder dragons were willing to risk their lives for this. She clutched at his hair, growling deep in her throat as she craved more of him.

He moved faster as if he knew what she needed. His breathing grew more ragged in her ear.

And then she exploded into ribbons of sheer, unadulterated ecstasy.

Throwing her head back, Tanis cried out as a sheer pleasure, more profound than anything she had ever imagined, tore through her. She tightened her hand in his hair.

Dash closed his eyes as he felt her shuddering in his arms, and then he filled her with his own release.

Sated to a depth he had never known existed, Dash rolled to his back, pulling her with him.

Her head spinning, Tanis turned over on his chest so that she could lay her body over him.

He pulled her lips to his for a deep and possessive kiss. "You are incredible, Lady Dragon."

She ran her hand over his brow, then through his hair as she stared at those brilliant eyes. "I had no idea it could be like that," she said in awe.

"Neither did I."

Tanis moved to kiss his chest, then felt her smile fade as she saw all the scars that covered his flesh. While she'd seen warrior dragons scarred, she'd never seen anything like this. There were claw marks. Sword wounds. Lash marks. And some she couldn't name.

Never in her life had she seen so much damage.

"Dash? What happened?"

Then, she saw the light fade from his eyes. "Sorry. I forgot." He reached for his shirt to put it on.

Tanis stopped him. "They don't bother me. I mean, they bother me only in that I hurt for you. Who did this?"

For the first time, she didn't see the nefarious High King who was always in control. She saw the vulnerable boy he must have once been. One who had been tortured by the looks of it.

Cupping his face, she met his gaze. "I know. We don't talk about the past. We kill things."

A sly smile curved his lips. "Burn the motherfuckers to the ground."

"All of them."

Nodding, Dash pulled her into his arms and held her.

Tanis lay against him in the quiet darkness with the sound of the fire crackling and the wind rustling through the trees. This had been a *very* strange day.

Two enemies had found common ground. But the problem was, she wasn't sure where she stood anymore.

I still need to get my brother's skull. That hadn't changed. And they definitely had to get Renata's wand before his enemies used it to kill him.

CHAPTER 14

Dash woke up just before dawn to the sweetest moment of his life. His body was nestled against soft furs and entwined with the luscious limbs of his dragon.

Every inch of Tanis's body lay against his. Her warm breath fell against his chest as her hair tickled the flesh of his arm. Closing his eyes again, he savored this one perfect moment of being with her.

He'd never known peace like this. All these years past, he'd fought to protect Renata because that had been the only thing he'd known.

His sister and people were his responsibility. Keep them safe no matter the cost.

He'd never thought that he could have anything for himself. Why should he?

No one could be trusted. Most were users. Others were incompetent. The rest just disappointed him.

Even his sister.

As much as he'd loved her, Renata had fought him every step of the way. Hoof and tooth.

Stop trying to control me, Dash!

But it had never been about control. Only fear. Because he'd seen the horror this world had to offer, he'd only wanted to protect her from it.

Now he had someone else he wanted to keep safe. Someone like him who knew the horrors that lurked in the shadows.

Opening his eyes, he toyed with the ring on her finger that Ambrose had given them. And he remembered how hard it'd been to build his kingdom the first time.

All the rebellions he'd been forced to quell. The enemies he'd had to defeat, who'd come after him in droves. Assassins. Traitors who'd buried so many daggers in his back that Halla had joked she should rename him Stegosaurus.

Only it hadn't been a joking matter.

Hard lessons learned. Everyone had been intent on laying him in a gutter and standing on his grave. Yet he had risen in spite of them all.

He still didn't know how.

Or even why. A part of it had been just sheer stubbornness. A need to prove himself to his father even after his father was dead. To prove that he wasn't as worthless as they'd all said. That he could do better. Be better.

And he had.

But did he have it in him to do it all again?

He wasn't sure. Because he knew exactly what it'd taken to build it before. Back when he was young and stupid. Back when he had the youth and energy for it. When he was blind to just how much it would cost his soul to do what had to be done.

Now...

He was tired. Sickened by what he'd seen. Worn down by the blows and battles.

If you give up, what will become of the Tanises in this world?

Someone else would rise up in his stead. They always did.

Yes, but would they be a protector?

Or a predator?

The eternal question.

And he knew the truth. Others were innately selfish and cruel. Even if they meant well, would another be able to endure the hell he'd traversed for the sake of someone else? How long would it take them before they gave in to the stress and quit?

Or before they were defeated by another?

That was if the eternal conflict didn't turn them violent. It was hard not to give in to it. Not to have the soul turn as black as his horn.

That façade was the only real question. Power was hard to deal with. Not so much that it corrupted the one wielding it, but the fact that everyone surrounding you wanted a piece of it.

Wanted a piece of your very soul, and they salivated to take it from you.

But would it matter if he failed? It wasn't all up to him. There was a lot he couldn't control. If someone cast that spell, they could kill him. He wouldn't be here to stop anything.

And that was what really scared him.

He pressed his cheek against Tanis's head. *I will protect you. To my dying breath.*

Using his powers, he carefully removed himself from beneath her without waking her from her sleep and dressed. He went to the cold stream and bathed before seeking Marthen.

He didn't go far before a stalk of grass rose up to block his path. That wasn't the strange part. The fact that the grass had long eyelashes and yellow eyes was the peculiar aspect of it. It blinked at him. "Don't wake the wizard, King. He doesn't like that."

Dash looked about but saw no sign of the wizard's body. "Is there a way for me to have a word with him while he sleeps?" While that might seem like an odd request to most, it wasn't when dealing with Marthen. The wizard's consciousness often roamed around outside his body while he slumbered.

Swaying in the early morning breeze, the stalk considered his request. "Wisp?"

A tiny will o' the wisp flew near them at the call. "Yes?"

"Where's the wizard's consciousness? Is it on the bank of the creek?"

"Was. Shall I look?"

"Yes. Please."

The wisp floated away into the darkness.

"If you'll wait a moment, Majesty. We'll check and see if he feels up to a consultation."

Most would find that strange, but Marthen wasn't like a normal anything. Especially given the fact that Marthen was sired by a yokai. That gave him all kinds of unique abilities.

He easily traversed the land of dreams and could leave his physical body behind whenever he needed to.

To this day, Dash remembered the first time he'd met Marthen. It'd been on the night after one of his nastier punishments at the hands of Meara's goons. He'd been lying mired in mud, staring up at the moon, wishing himself dead from the pain when he heard a faint gasp, followed by an annoying question. "Aren't you a little young for a red horn?"

Dash had sighed wearily at something he'd answered more times than he'd cared to. "I was born with one."

"Impossible."

Even though he trembled from the pain, Dash had forced himself to stand and confront the source of his irritation.

To his surprise, it wasn't a centaur.

At that time, he'd mistaken Marthen for some human servant. Meara's court was full of them. "According to what I've been told, I've been angry since the moment I kicked my way from my mother's womb and my hooves hit the ground."

"Then you must be Prince Dash."

He'd held his head high. "I am."

Marthen had approached him slowly. "I was there at your birth, young prince. Your horn *was* white at the time. I saw it firsthand."

Then, the old wizard had reached through the pen to place a kind hand to his forehead, just below his red horn.

Dash had gasped as his pain subsided. It felt like Marthen was pulling it out through his hand.

With a tender smile, he'd ruffled his mane. "Tell me,

prince... what do you want to do with all this pent-up rage you have inside you?"

"I don't understand your question."

"If you were made king today, what would you do? Would you kill Queen Meara? Take a piss? Roll in your gold? Name me three things you'd do."

Dash had scowled at the old man. "Just three?"

"Yes."

He'd considered that for only a second. "First thing I'd do is take a bath."

Marthen had actually laughed. "Good answer. What's the next thing you'd do?"

There had been a lot of things he'd wanted, including kill Meara. But if he was limited to only three... "I would free the others who are being held with me and take them home."

"And your third... if you had all the power of a king?"

"It's selfish."

"How selfish?"

"I would have a necromancer or lich bring my sister's mother back from the dead."

That seemed to catch the old man off-guard. "Why?"

"Because I don't know how to take care of her like her mother did. No one does. It hurts whenever I hear her crying because I know I can't fix it."

Marthen had fisted his hand in Dash's mane. "All the power in the kingdom and that's the most selfish thing you want?"

It was. Although, at that moment, there had been one other thing Dash had been near desperate for. "Dinner would be nice. But I'd rather Renata not cry." Even if he did hate her mother who'd never had a kind word for him.

"Are you hungry?"

"Starving."

Marthen had pulled an apple from the bag he carried and held it out to him.

Nothing had ever tasted better than that apple. And Marthen had never really disclosed why he'd ventured there that night, nor why he'd returned after their first meeting.

Though Dash had often wondered if he'd been sent there by Dash's mother to check up on him.

Whatever the reason, the old wizard had returned night after night to teach Dash how to use and develop his magick. Schooled him on philosophy, war strategy and politics.

To this day, he was grateful to Marthen for teaching him during the wee hours of the night while others slept. It'd been the only thing that had kept him sane.

As weird as it sounded, that had been the most "normal" part of his captivity. The only time when he'd been treated as anything other than a caged, mindless animal. Honestly, Marthen had been more of a father to him than the unicorn who'd thoughtlessly sired him.

To this day, Dash had no idea why his mother had him delivered to his father within hours of his birth. Other than his mother had wanted a tie to the Licordian throne.

A fact his father had reminded him of constantly. *Not even your own mother wanted anything to do with you, you worthless by-blow. I should never have allowed you to live. You're a blight on my blood and heritage.*

It was also something Renata's mother had held against him every hour of his life until her death. *Don't touch me! You're no son of mine! You're disgusting! I wish you'd died at birth!*

How sad that when his father had first told him he was going to Meara's court as a hostage, he'd been delighted by the prospect. Stupid and young, Dash had thought his life there would be infinitely better than his treatment at his father's palace.

The gods had a sick sense of humor.

As bad as his childhood in Licordia had been, it'd paled in comparison to the cruelty he'd learned under Meara's merciless hooves.

Looking back on it now, Dash suspected the reason Marthen had trained him had something to do with another riddle the old wizard had once posed to him and with another fact he'd learned from Meara.

Those who seek me for their own pleasure are far more likely to inflict pain in my name. Who am I?

Ironically, it'd been the one thing Dash had been born into and never wanted or sought.

Power.

While he was known for his cruelty, he didn't revel in it the way Meara did.

And right now, he would gladly surrender his mantel of authority if he could find another who would rule justly.

After a few minutes, the wisp returned. "He'll speak with you, Majesty. Please follow me."

Dash conjured himself a woolen cloak as he realized just how cold the temperature was here.

He followed the glowing wisp through the trees until

they came to a whispering creek that flowed backwards toward the snow-capped mountains.

Marthen wasn't alone. There was a woman walking with him. One in a gown of pale-yellow, shimmering samite. Her white hair didn't come from old age. She was young and exceptionally beautiful, with light blue skin that glimmered in the low light. It'd been a while since he'd last seen a nereid. They normally kept to the seas in Dash's kingdom.

He'd forgotten that in Alarium, they also lived in smaller bodies of water.

"Rivana... meet Dash."

He bowed before her. "Pleasure, my lady."

"And you, Your Majesty." She turned toward Marthen. "I'll speak with you again soon." With a kind smile, she stepped over to the water and quickly swam away.

"I didn't mean to interrupt you."

Marthen shrugged. "It's fine. We speak often, she and I. Usually when I'm sleeping."

"Should I ask?"

"Probably not."

Dash laughed at Marthen's way of telling him she was none of his business. Fine, he'd respect the wizard's privacy.

And as he started to change the subject, the woods around them lit up as if they were on fire. Yet they weren't burning. Only fey light shined brightly like this. And usually only when an elfin army was on the march.

Dash immediately turned into his unicorn form and suited up in full battle armor, ready to fight whatever was coming for him.

Marthen cursed.

Obviously, the elves had learned he was here. The question was, which clan? The Drakalf, Myrkalf, or Nagalf?

Drakalfs were the most barbaric of the three. Cannibal elves, they had once hunted their brethren for food, believing that if they consumed their enemies, they would inherit their powers and wisdom. As a rule, they tended to be a bit shorter and much leaner than the Myrkalfs or Nagalfs.

Even though they had stopped preying on other elves as their primary food source, their brethren still didn't trust them. And Dash couldn't blame them for it. He wouldn't want to sit down at dinner with someone who might be serving him up elf stew, either.

Rumors still abounded that some of them continued the rituals of their ancestors. He knew from experience that old habits were a little hard to break.

The Myrkalfs were farmers and tricksters. They were the ones who liked to make deals with humans and other species that usually backfired on the ones dumb enough to barter with them. They also traded out their errant children with well-behaving youngsters of other species so that they could use them for farm work or experiment on them.

They were never to be trusted.

Nagalfs were the aristocrats who ruled over all the clans. Warriors, nobles, diplomats and priests, they were sadly the ones he'd pissed off the most in the past.

He really hoped the Nagalfs weren't the ones approaching as they were less likely to be friendly with his intrusion into their territory. Indeed, they'd happily hand him over to Meara and were probably one of the seven kingdoms willing to pay the bounty for his head.

As the small army came closer and he was able to identify them, he cursed.

They had representatives from all three groups. Each one wore the distinct armor and styles that designated their individual clans.

Beautiful. They meant business and he was sure that they were out to skin a unicorn.

He glanced to Marthen. "You awake yet?"

"Thinking I should sleep this one out."

Fine time for the wizard to turn craven. "Thanks."

"Any time, my king."

Dressed in green armor that glimmered in the dawning sun, the king of the Nagalfs approached Marthen with a look of censure. "He's not your king, Marthen. I am."

"Not true, Lord Baldur. He's *everyone's* king."

The sneer on Baldur's handsome face let Dash know he didn't appreciate the reminder or being referred to as a mere lord. Though Baldur wasn't as tall as Dash was in human form, he was still no slacker in height.

His pale-blond hair that he wore braided down his back made him appear almost ghostly. But not nearly as much as those sharp, angular features. Baldur glanced around at the others, then gave Dash a dry, meaningful stare. "I see you're not bearing any gifts for me this time. Guess I should count my blessings you didn't swing by the sacred grove on your way in."

Dash was really grateful he'd switched forms. Otherwise, he'd be hard-pressed to counsel his facial expression. Or keep from smiling snidely. "Should I conjure an olive branch?" He sprouted one from his horn.

Unamused, Baldur blinked slowly.

Marthen, on the other hand, laughed out loud.

"Oh, lighten up, Baldur, that's funny." Hinrik, the leader of the Myrkalfs, slapped Baldur on the back, then stepped around him to approach Dash. His armor was brown, like his hair and darker features. A few inches shorter than Baldur, Hinrik was known for being a tad light-hearted for most things.

The Drakalf leader, Tova, ignored Baldur and followed Hinrik as he approached Dash. She carried her engraved bronze axe over her shoulder which made Dash a bit nervous, especially given the way she eyed him.

Until she stopped in front of him and smiled brightly.

Her brown hair was worn in intricate braids to show off her ornate, pointed ear covers. She'd laced her red leather armor tight to accentuate her curves and was famous for the spiked heels of her boots that she was known for driving into the eyes of her enemies before she killed them.

"A million sovereign bounty, King Deciel..." She tsked. "Makes me axe, Radgar, ache to taste unicorn blood. If only I knew who would pay that for your sorry arse, Majesty."

Dash sucked his breath in between his teeth. "According to the wanted poster, seven of my kingdoms. I assumed Alarium was one of them."

Hinrik snorted before he looked at Baldur. "Is that what you're wasting our taxes on? Trying to break our contract with the High King?"

Baldur looked offended at the thought. "Hardly. I get enough attitude from the lot of you already for the necessary expenditures I make. As if I could ever get the lot of you to agree to pay it for the head of a measly unicorn." He jerked his chin at Dash. "Especially one as worthless as he is."

Hinrik stroked his chin thoughtfully. "Centaurs might pay it. Think we should send a missive to Queen Bitchitis? See if she's the one offering that payout? I've heard she hates him for some particular reason no one can name."

Tova nodded slowly as if she were considering it. "We could definitely use the money to reseed the mother tree some thoughtless unicorn bastard cut down."

Hinrik looked over to Baldur. "I could use a summer palace in my lands. Something facing the north. Pretty picture windows facing the portal..."

Totally confused by their odd discussion, Dash scowled. While they seemed serious, they didn't. Not really. He just wasn't sure. "Are we fighting?" Because it didn't quite seem like they were.

His expression cold and calculating, Baldur closed the distance between them. He stepped between the other two elfin rulers to face off in front of Dash.

"Step away from the High King."

Dash looked past the elves to see his beautiful dragon entering the fray. Dressed in nothing more than her hunter's leather, she held her sword, ready to go to war to protect him.

She was outnumbered in the middle of his enemies. No magick. No way to do anything more than bleed on their elfin army while he escaped.

Yet she was offering herself up as a sacrifice.

Nothing had ever touched him more. But really, he wanted to curse her for it.

Baldur turned back to face him with an arch stare. "She with you?"

"She is." Clearing his throat, Dash slid past them to approach her. He changed back into a human body so that he could place his hand on hers and lower her sword before one of the archers around them decided to get frisky with an arrow and earn hero points with their own king or queen.

Tanis stared at him with an earnestness that was as touching as it was foolish. "I won't let them take you, Dash."

He smiled tenderly. "Appreciate that, love. We can talk about this later."

Tova scowled at them. "Who's the woman?"

A thousand possible lies went through his head. But the truth was the one that would give her the greatest protection. While they might hate him and would probably kill him before this was over, Tanis wasn't their enemy.

And neither was her father.

"Princess Tanis Dragomir of Indara."

That took the piss out of all three of them. Until fury darkened Baldur's eyes. "You turned her human? What did they do to you?"

He rushed toward Dash as if he intended to beat him on behalf of Tanis's father.

Tanis cut him off and once more angled the sword at him. "You *never* approach your king in anger."

Shock stopped Baldur dead in his tracks. Instantly, he held his hands up.

Dash reached around her again and gently pushed her arm and the sword toward the ground. "Really, love, you must stop threatening the elfin king in his own territory. I'm sure his soldiers are taking issue with it."

"They should take greater issue with their High King being threatened and defend *you*." Tanis looked around at the gathered elves. Then she glared at Baldur. "Is that not the treaty you made? It's the one my father holds. The Thirteen Kingdoms owe fealty to their High King to defend him. Soldiers for his command in time of need. If any kingdom or ruler rises to threaten his life or command, the others are to defend his reign, his life, and secure his power. Is this not the oath you signed?"

She had a point. That *was* the bargain.

Tova and Hinrik laughed. Baldur seethed.

"Hell of a defender you've found there, Sire." Tova approached them more respectfully. She inclined her head to Tanis. "I'm Princess Tova of the Drakalf."

Tanis's eyes widened. "You lead the cannibal elves?"

Dash cringed at Tanis's bold question.

Thankfully, Tova wasn't insulted. Again, she laughed. "We only eat the bad ones. And then, only to make a point. It tends to keep everyone else on their toes. You should try it sometime. They tell me dragon meat is quite healthy, and elfin meat is low in calories and good for your heart."

Marthen burst out laughing. "I should write down recipes for an exchange."

Dash shook his head. "Please don't encourage this."

Tanis looked at them and then to Dash. "They weren't trying to kill you?"

"To be honest, I'm not real sure what was going on when you arrived."

Baldur rubbed his thumb over his bottom lip. "I wanted to kill you, Majesty. Make no mistake about that. When word reached me yesterday that you'd left your lands, and someone was offering to pay handsomely for your head... I considered sending my best after you to collect that bounty."

Tova smirked. "Until I reminded our king why he still sits on his high and mighty throne unchallenged because of your reign."

Baldur ignored her. "You don't play favorites, Sire. You could have demanded my son's life for his actions, and you didn't. You could have even demanded my own head when I refused to hand him over to you for punishment. Another king might have used my heir's actions as an excuse to remove my lineage from power. While I'm still angry about what you did to the Mother Tree, you made a valid point with no bloodshed." He looked at the other two leaders. "We've enjoyed these years of peace and have prospered greatly. Alarium has no desire to return to chaos."

Hinrik nodded in agreement. "As the princess said, we're here to uphold our oaths. Tell us what you need, and we'll provide it."

Dash was stunned. Honestly, he'd expected them to side against him.

Tanis smiled.

Tova held her free hand up and waved. Two elves came forward from the army surrounding them. It wasn't until they were close, that Dash saw they looked similar enough to be siblings.

One male. One female. Both were dressed in red Drakalf armor.

Tova smiled proudly. "Me son and daughter. Tora and Viggo. Two of me finest warriors. It's me honor to offer them to be your personal guard until you're safely back on your throne in Licordia."

"Tora and Viggo," he repeated. Thunder and lightning. He had to bite his tongue to keep from commenting on the naming choice.

Making an uncomfortable face, Hinrik scratched at his ear. "They are aptly named, Sire."

"How so?"

"Viggo moves silently and fast. By the time he's struck, his target's dead. Tora... when you hear her battle cry, your head's already severed."

"Then I'd be honored to have their protection. Thank you, Tova."

She inclined her head to him.

Tanis arched a brow. "We're not having to fight anyone?"

"Apparently not," he whispered to her. "A new experience for me, too."

She sheathed her sword. "I could have slept longer? What do you elves have against sleep?"

Tova laughed. "Come. Me fortress isn't far. Let's get some food. A bed for the princess and we can discuss how best to deal with this situation."

As the others went to their horses, Dash returned to unicorn form and manifested a saddle on his back for Tanis. He thought nothing of it until she pulled herself up and the others took notice.

Utter silence filled the air.

Shit.

Marthen's spirit drifted over to him. "You might want to think of something to tell them," he whispered.

The problem was that Dash had no idea how to explain their relationship to anyone. Not even to himself.

You're High King.

He didn't have to explain anything. That was the only advantage of his position. Fuck them.

Let them speculate.

Holding his head high, he headed for Tova's keep and did his best to ignore their curiosity.

Tanis noticed that Dash traveled behind the others. "You don't trust them, do you?"

"Do you?"

She thought about it. "I want to."

"But?"

"I probably have the same issues you do. I'm cautious of anyone wanting to help, especially those who have a reason not to, and given the amount of money being offered for your head... why would they help? Doesn't feel right, does it?"

"Right?" he asked. "I hate being so jaded all the time. But my life has taught me that when given the opportunity to stab someone, even a friend, most will take it."

She reached down and patted him on the neck, agreeing completely. She'd witnessed the same thing.

Dash savored that comfort. It was nice to have someone who understood him. His sister had always chided him for his mistrust. *You're so judgmental! Must you always see evil in everyone, Dash? Give them a chance and they might surprise you.*

While Renata had always made him feel terrible for being so wary, Tanis made him feel normal. But then, she knew the same world he did. Not the safe one Renata had been sheltered in.

"Sorry I wasn't there when you woke up," he said to her.

"It's fine. I'm glad you weren't under attack or dead. But I have to admit, beast, I was a bit scared when I found you in what was an awful situation, from my vantage point."

He smiled at the memory. "Yet you ran to my defense even though you were terribly outnumbered. Thank you."

"You're welcome."

Dash paused and turned his head so that he could look back at her. "Seriously, Tanis. Thank you. It was reckless and suicidal. And a part of me would like to beat you for it. But I'm truly grateful that you were reckless and suicidal."

She leaned forward in the saddle to hug him. "Again, you're most welcome. Just next time, pick better odds for us."

He laughed and started forward. "I'll do my best."

Us. Dash didn't comment on that one word even though it rang out inside him. He'd never really been an *us* before. It felt...

Terrifying.

But good. She had no reason to stand at his back. Yet she hadn't hesitated.

No female had ever done that for him. All he could remember were the times when he'd been flung into an arena, alone, and left to battle on his own.

Prove your worth!

No matter how much he'd won, he'd still felt worthless. Undeserving. That had been the rage that had turned his horn red when he'd been far too young to remember it.

And that was the thing about horns, they could change color at any time. For any reason. To a unicorn, it reeked to have your soul on display for the entire world to see.

Or at least those who knew what the colors meant.

White were the ones who were untainted and pure. Those untouched by the cruelty of life. His sister's had been white for most of hers.

Purple horns belonged to their priests and counselors. Those who'd developed a deep intuition or spirituality. Yellow horns belonged to unicorns who were driven and creative. They were the risk-takers and artisans of all kinds. Green held the stronger magick abilities—the healers and wizards. Blue horns emerged for those with diplomatic traits. Those who didn't like conflict and who were slow to anger. The ones best able to think through complicated matters. His general, Kronnel, was a blue horn.

Sometimes those blue horns would turn silver if the bearer developed a greater level of wisdom or showed exceptional leadership qualities, such as his father's. Although, silver could also manifest from other colors, too. It just wasn't as common for silver to manifest from another source, but it did happen.

Orange horns were natural teachers. They were the ones who encouraged others and helped whenever they could. Then the red which was the normal color for most adolescents and a large number of their soldiers. Many of the unicorns outgrew their red horns. But acts of violence or trauma could turn any color to red at any time.

Then, there was the exceedingly rare gold horns that only Renata had managed to attain. It came from possessing a pure heart that was willing to sacrifice oneself for another. The one thing about his sister that had driven him to utter madness.

Her innocence. Her inability to see danger. Or any kind

of ulterior motives in someone else. He was always suspicious, but never her.

She would defend anyone. Even Keryna.

He'd envied his sister the luxury of her horn. Of being able to trust like that.

While his horn was technically one of protection, it came at a dire cost. It let other unicorns know that he had no restraint when it came to protecting those around him. He was capable of anything.

That was why a black horn was so feared.

There was only one other color that gave unicorns almost as much pause. A gray horn. Not because they were more powerful. Far from it.

Gray horns were the ones who were indecisive and unsure. Tricksters. Dubious, and usually troublemakers.

Keryna.

A dangerous thing to befriend a gold horn who would never believe they were capable of deceit because a gold horn would only see their insecurity and indecisiveness. Never their treachery.

You always see conspiracy, Dash. You have to stop that.

And he was still seeing it. He just couldn't quite believe the elves were helping him because they wanted peace.

Horned or not, he intended to keep his eyes open and watch them closely.

CHAPTER 15

Tanis was impressed by Tova's palace. Like her father's, it was set into the mountainside for protection. But that was where the similarities ended. Blue and gold, it appeared more like a jewel box than a place where someone lived. Spires twisted upward, toward the sky. She half expected to see dragons circling it, yet it was more majestic than their homes.

The road up to it was narrow for defense and there were slits all along the mountain where archers could site victims or others could pour flaming oil on an invading army.

Smart.

Huge battle gryphons lined the drawbridge that led to an outer bailey where there were a group of homes she assumed were for the palace servants and their families.

The gryphons were a surprise for her as she hadn't realized that they lived anywhere other than Indara. Because they had such a large population of gryphons and wyverns in their kingdom, she'd assumed that they were like dragons and didn't intermingle with other species.

But they seemed happy in their guardian roles. "Are there many gryphons here?" she asked Dash.

"A fair amount. Why?"

"I just had no idea any lived here."

"Don't worry. They're not prisoners. The elves use them in battle against us... or they used to. We have our own small population of them, too."

"Do you?"

"We do, but ours are strictly civilian. Since we fly, we don't need them in our military."

That seemed odd to her, given that Indara was a neighboring kingdom with a large gryphon population. "Then why do they choose to live in Licordia?"

"Like the elves, they're paid better to live among us than they are in Indara. And the humans and other species in our lands use them to fly between the kingdoms."

"Why not use a unicorn?"

He paused to pass an annoyed look at her over his shoulder. "We're not passenger unicorns."

"Really?" she asked sarcastically, holding her hands up to remind him that she was his passenger.

"You're an exception. We normally only allow riders for battle."

Smiling, she patted him on the neck. "Glad to know I'm an exception."

The very thought warmed her all the way through. And she had an odd feeling that it embarrassed him as he immediately started forward and didn't speak anymore.

She was still smiling when they went through another

set of bridges that led to an inner bailey and finally to the courtyard for the palace.

Intricate and scary, yet beautiful.

And speaking of beautiful...

An exceptionally tall man waited at the steps with a large crow perched on his muscular shoulder. He leaned against a long, twisted staff that held a crystal at one end and wore the red garb of an alchemist or shaman. His long black hair was pulled back from his face with a leather cord.

Tanis couldn't take her gaze off him. Like Dash, he held an air of authority and danger. Of raw power that dared someone to challenge him.

Indeed, there was something about his features that reminded her of Dash. Except his eyes were a chilling blue.

Her heart sped up at the sight of him.

Dash stopped.

Tanis took a moment before she dismounted. The moment she did, Dash changed into his human form.

Only then did the stranger move. Tsking, he eyed her coldly.

"Do I even want to know what you've gone and done now, Majesty?"

Dash glanced to her, and she saw the irritation in his eyes. "I assume Halla's already told you, otherwise you wouldn't be standing there, looking like that."

"But why, Dash? Why? And I'm not talking about turning her into a human. You know better."

The crow cawed.

Dash let out a tired sigh. "Tanis, this is Ryper and Chrysis. Ryper is the annoying man. Feel free to ignore him. I do most of the time." Then he met Ryper's gaze. "And why are you here, anyway? Shouldn't you be in Licordia, guarding my throne? Annoying anyone else?"

Ryper snorted in response. "We need to talk. Alone."

"Five words that always make my sphincter clench whenever you say them."

Marthen clapped Dash on the back as he joined them. "You're really not going to like what he has to say." He stepped past Dash toward Tanis. "Come, my lady. Let them have their counsel. You and I can go explore the elfin palace. It's even more spectacular inside."

She really wanted to hear what was going on, but knew it wasn't her place. So, taking Marthen's arm, she allowed him to lead her away.

Dash watched Tanis leave before he closed the distance between him and Ryper. By Ryper's stance, he knew this was going to be bad. But there was no need in delaying it. "What happened?"

Ryper held out a folded piece of vellum to him. "I sent Ronan, Cadoc and Mischief on to Licordia with Chrys while I came here to fetch Dove."

"I'm assuming Chrys brought the note to you after she dropped them off?"

"Of course I did," she said, ruffling her feathers.

Dreading what was inside, Dash opened it and read Ronan's report. As he'd already expected, Keryna was behind his sister's death.

What he hadn't known was the fact that his kingdom had been invaded. "So, Meara has officially taken my throne and army."

Ryper screwed his face up. "At least she thinks that. But I'm sure Aderyn and Kronnel still have control of your forces.

While I don't trust Kronnel anymore than you do, Aderyn is one of us. Her troops will be standing by to fight to the death at your command."

Awesome. "How is Meara still alive? She shouldn't be able to invade my kingdom without the *apaswere* attacking her."

Ryper wrinkled his nose. "Technicality. Her brother received an invitation from you to bring his army in."

"I never issued an invitation to a centaur."

"It was a good forgery. One that passed the scrutiny of the *apaswere*. As such, Meara accepted the invitation on behalf of her brother."

That infuriated him. The whole point of writing a contract on the flesh of an *apaswere* was to ensure it was always kept. Whoever broke the contract would be hunted down and killed by one of their agents.

The only way to break the contract was to kill the *apaswere* who wore it, which was next to impossible, or to find a loophole like the one Ryper had just explained.

Dash wanted to beat someone over this. "Where's Dove?" he asked.

"Behind you."

Dash tensed at that deep, gruff tone that no one ever expected to come out of the elfin bastard nobleman. Not because he wasn't tall and rugged as hell, but because he normally didn't speak. To anyone. Getting a single word out of him often took a royal proclamation.

Two was a miracle.

Dubhdara hadn't just been screwed over by Meara and her court, he'd been shafted first by his mother and the elfin race. Mostly because his royal elfin mother had refused to name his father. That refusal had cost her everything, and her son almost as much. Both in reputation and standing as she'd been executed for her treasonous affair, and her bastard son had been relegated to being raised by his disgraced relatives who'd hated the sight of him, as they blamed him for their penury and stripped titles.

It was why Baldur had sent him to Meara as a hostage when Dash had been handed over. Dove had never forgiven his mother's husband for that, and Dash didn't blame him.

But it was good to see his old friend. Holding his arm out to Dove, he offered him a smile.

Dove took his hand and pulled him in for a brotherly hug. He pounded him so hard on the back that it took Dash's breath.

"We were getting ready to head back when Marthen told me you were here," Ryper said. "Good timing."

"I don't know about that." Dash stepped away from Dove. "I feel like I'm chasing my tail."

Ryper shook his head. "I'm thinking we were intentionally sent out to chase geese."

Dash frowned. "Meaning?"

"He thinks the wand is still in Licordia." Chrys flew to Dash's shoulder. "Ryper wants me to go and see if I can find it."

Those words hit him almost as hard as Dove's greeting. "I don't understand."

Ryper inclined his head to the parchment. "Think about it. If you wanted to buy yourself time and stay hidden until it was time to cast a deadly spell, what better way than to send your enemy off in search of something you still have?"

Dash cursed. "It was all a setup."

"That's what I'm thinking. Why else pick Pagos of all places?"

Ryper was right. "I should have thought of that."

"Your mind is on other matters, and we understand. Easy to miss things when your emotionally compromised."

Dove cleared his throat. "I'm sorry about Renata."

Dash didn't respond. There wasn't anything to say. The pain was still too raw to deal with.

It just wasn't right, and he didn't know how to cope with the loss of her, so he refused to.

For now.

"I appreciate it." It was all he could think of to say. It was so paltry, especially given everything they'd been through.

He glanced around the yard and noticed the curious onlookers who were keeping their distance while trying to figure out why the three of them were friends.

"How are you doing?" Dash asked Dove.

Dove shrugged. "Haven't killed anyone today. But there's always tomorrow."

That was probably the best he could do, and Dash was amazed at his restraint. Just as he was amazed that Dove had returned home. None of them were still sure why he'd come back, given everything the elves had done to him and his mother.

But that was the thing about Dove. He didn't share his feelings or his thoughts very often.

Chrys stretched her wings. "Anything you want me to tell the others, Sire?"

"Be careful. We'll be there as soon as we can. Until we join them, stay low."

"And tell Aderyn to stay out of my room," Ryper said petulantly.

Dash scowled. "Something I need to know?"

"Not really."

Why didn't he believe that?

Maybe because it was an unwarranted comment. There was definitely something odd between them, but he was too tired to delve into it right now, and knowing Ryper, he wouldn't elaborate even if he beat the shite out of him.

So, Dash let it go. He carefully stroked her head. "You be careful, too, Chrys."

She inclined her head to him. "And you." With that, she launched herself from his shoulder and took flight.

Dash watched her vanish into the darkness.

As soon as she was gone, Ryper draped an arm around his shoulders. "So... what about the dragon?"

"Don't you even."

Ryper tsked at him. "I thought you'd sworn to never jeopardize your wizard powers."

Dove laughed.

Dash ground his teeth over their teasing. "Both of you stop before I forget what I owe you, and I gut you where you stand."

Ryper moved away and held his hand up. "I'll say no more, Dash. But you know how hard won the truce between the dragons and unicorns has been."

Yes, he did. And they already had a war brewing with the centaurs. Last thing he needed was for another one to start with Tanis's father.

Which made him curious about something. "I have one question for you?"

Ryper arched a brow. "That is?"

"Are we sure the wanted poster is false? Or are there seven kingdoms actually rebelling against me and coming together to offer a bounty for my head? And if there are seven, which ones are they?"

Dove and Ryper exchanged a thoughtful grimace before Ryper answered. "Thirteen kingdoms. We can strike out Licordia, Tenmaru, Alarium, Pagos and Indara. That leaves eight kingdoms, with the centaurs currently sitting on your throne."

"So, what I'm hearing from you, Ryp, is that I should have been a kinder, gentler monarch."

Ryper snorted. "Not from me. What I'm thinking is we missed a few heads we should have mounted on pikes."

"Starting with Meara's."

They both turned to stare at Dove over that harsh comment.

Dove didn't even flinch. "Don't look at me like that. If the two of you had listened to me and killed the bitch when I told you to, we wouldn't have to march an army into Licordia and kill her now, would we?" He met Dash's gaze and the hatred there went all the way to Dove's soul. "This time, can I have her throat?"

Dash wanted to be reasonable. He wanted to be the king Marthen had trained him to be and not the blood son of his ruthless mother and cold-hearted father. But honestly... he craved her throat as much as Dove did. "I can't promise you that, Dove."

"Why not?"

"Because if I get to her first, I'm going to kill her."

CHAPTER 16

What are we going to do?"

Bink shushed the stupid human as he tried to think of something, anything to get them out of this. So much for having control of the situation.

He had control of nothing.

"We have to stay hidden," he whispered to Fort, forcing the human to crouch down. They were in one of the lower rooms of the palace, doing their best to stay out of sight and away from the hearing of the centaurs.

At this point, he didn't know if Keryna was alive or dead. Nor did he care. Meara had tortured her for the wand that he still had in the pouch at his side.

A part of him wanted to use it to barter with the queen. But the saner part of him knew better than to try. There was no reasoning with her. She was even more ruthless than Dash.

The one good thing about the High King was that he

didn't believe in torture. He punished those who deserved it and at times he made an example of them. But unlike the queen, he didn't relish cruelty.

She did.

Even now, Bink heard the screams of those who were begging for mercy. Begging for death.

That evil bitch enjoyed the sounds of it. She treated it like a symphony and even dined while they suffered.

How had he lost control of this so quickly? He still didn't know. He was supposed to be king. Not hiding like a rat in a sewer.

Fort was supposed to be a celebrated dragon slayer.

Now...

They would be lucky to escape with their lives and appendages.

Think, Bink. Think.

He still had the golden wand. That meant that, at the worst, he had something with which to bargain. Meara was tearing apart the palace and everyone she could in her efforts to find what he had.

That gave him an advantage.

You can't negotiate with crazy.

He knew that, too.

But the stupid human didn't. He glanced over to Fort as he considered his options.

Humans did have their uses.

"Fort... I have something you can do."

"What?"

"The queen wants what we have, right?"

He nodded.

"Let's give it to her."

Fort scratched his head. "I thought we were going to sell it and be rich."

"That's exactly what we're going to do. We're going to offer it to her and be rewarded."

Fort screwed his face up. "I don't understand."

"You're going to take your dragon skull and the spell to her. Show them to her so that she knows you're serious. I'll stay behind to keep the wand safe until we have a bargain."

Fort scratched at his nose. "I don't know, Bink. It seems like a bad idea."

But it was the only shot they had at getting out of this mess. "You have to trust me."

After a few seconds, Fort nodded. "All right. What do I need to do?"

Bink pulled out a copy of the spell and handed it over to the human. "You'll need this. Take it to the queen and make sure you repeat everything I tell you."

Meara was in a rare tantrum as she paced the floor of Dash's office. Honestly, she was homesick. She hated being in these lands. They were too...

Happy for her tastes. What was wrong with the unicorns? They really were an inferior species. All they wanted to do was sit around and write poetry and philosophy. Play music. Discuss ideas.

Respect each other. Have laws...

It was nauseating. Where were the blood sports? Criminals in need of punishment?

At least Dash's father had believed in a good round of gladiatorial games.

Dash had learned nothing from his time in her lands.

How many more unicorns would she have to kill to learn something more than what she already knew?

While the killing should make her happy, it was beginning to just piss her off. Were they all really this stupid?

How could none of them know where Renata's body was?

Or her horn?

They were all useless. Absolutely useless.

"My queen?"

She stopped pacing as Adsel came into the room. "Yes?"

"I have a human here who wants to speak with you."

A human? How novel. She hadn't run into that many of them here in the palace. Although, she'd been told there were quite a few of them in the town. "Why?"

"He says he has knowledge of the wand you seek."

Now that got her attention. "Then by all means, show him in."

She turned toward the door to watch the pathetic little wastrel enter. He had a weasel-like quality to him, which wasn't helped by his scraggly beard. She waited a moment for him to speak.

Instead, he shook so badly that she expected he might piss on the marble floor.

"Do you have a reason for being here?" she prompted.

"I... I..." He cleared his throat.

"You what?" she said testily. *Are an idiot?* That was a given, and she wasn't sure how she held the insult in.

"I am a great dragon slayer."

Meara laughed. *Him*? He was quaking in fear of her, and she was about half the size of a dragon's claw. How could he face down a dragon if she scared him this badly?

Imbecile.

Yet her laughter made his cheeks flush with color. "I know where the wand is."

That killed her laughter instantly. "You know what?"

"The wand you seek. I know where it is."

Now, she was paying attention. "How? Where?"

He swallowed audibly. "I took it from Keryna." He pulled a piece of parchment from his pocket and held it out to her. "I also have a spell you can use to kill the unicorn king."

She glanced to Adsel who quickly took the missive and read it.

"It appears to be so, my queen." He handed it to her.

Finally, she found a modicum of happiness.

Taking it from her advisor, she eagerly read over the items.

Which then eroded her joy. Seriously? Was this a joke? Or madness? "Who the hell has the skin of a flayed murderer? Virgin troll... what? This is the dumbest spell I've ever seen! Who came up with this?"

The human actually raised his hand. "I don't know who made the spell. But we have all those items."

"*We*?" she asked.

"My partner and I. We collected them."

That was beginning to lift her spirits a tad. Meara arched a brow at Adsel. "And where, pray tell, is this partner?"

"Guarding the wand or horn thing you need."

She carefully folded up the spell. "Well, we'll just have to find that partner of yours, won't we?"

"Uh..." The human began to panic as he looked around the room. He backed up and ran into Adsel. "He... he... said—"

"I don't care what he said, human. You're going to tell me everything I want to know."

CHAPTER 17

T anis lay in bed, listening to the sound of Dash's heart beating beneath her cheek. It still amazed her that he could choose to sleep as either a human or unicorn.

Or more to the point, that he trusted her enough to sleep with her in a human body. She still hadn't forgotten what he'd said about unicorns and their horns. He was vulnerable in this body. Especially while he was sound asleep.

Which made her curious where he hid his wand when he was human. She never saw any sign of it, but she knew he had to keep it nearby. For that, she gave him credit. He was talented at hiding it.

Not that she would ever use it against him. She was only curious.

Just as the elves, Dove and Ryper were about the true nature of their relationship. It'd been hard these last couple of days avoiding their personal questions as they made plans for how best to invade Dash's lands and regain his army.

Neither of them was willing to elaborate on the nature of what existed between them. Mostly because they didn't know themselves.

They really didn't discuss their relationship when they were alone.

She was too afraid to ask because she knew better. Even if he wasn't the High King, he was a unicorn. She was a dragon. Her current body was only temporary.

Once she returned to being a dragon, there would be no way for them to have any kind of relationship. At least not a physical one.

Her father would kill her if he ever found out, and there was no telling what he might do to-or demand from-Dash. Dragons were forbidden to cross species. They were barely allowed to mate outside their clans, and only then for political reasons that had to be sanctioned by their councils.

She could only imagine the scandal this would cause in Indara. A dragon princess with their unicorn High King. Her life would be the least of what they'd take.

Not that it mattered. They were leaving today to march toward Licordia where the dragon slayer was in hiding.

And where Meara sat on Dash's throne.

A sudden knock sounded on the door, startling her.

Bolting upright in her arms, Dash came awake with a curse, ready to fight.

They both laughed as they realized no one was crashing through the door to attack them.

Dash placed a kiss on her forehead then pulled a fur over

her. He grabbed another to wrap around his lean hips before he went to answer it.

Tanis reached for his tunic on the floor to pull it over to her. It was tangled with his belt and dagger. As she separated them, she noticed something odd.

The ornate black dagger that he carried. The way the early morning light caught the engraved design of it highlighted the center spiral design.

The center spiral design...

It's his wand.

She gasped in shock. Though it was hidden in the design, it was unmistakable once seen. *Very* clever. Especially since the black leather of the hilt wrapped around part of the horn to protect and disguise it. No one would see it, even though it was right there.

In plain sight.

Glancing at the door where he stood, she quickly set the dagger aside and shrugged his tunic on before he caught her inspecting it.

He'd be furious if he knew she'd discovered his weakness. Wouldn't he? Yes. Yes, he would. She was sure he would.

Act normal.

She wrinkled her nose and cursed herself silently. Why did she always do this? She knew she couldn't really act nonchalant when she was trying to. Her panic rose to a frantic level.

Distract yourself.

Like that was easy.

At least that was her thought until her gaze went to

Dash at the door in his near naked state. The fur had slipped so that the curve of one buttocks was mostly exposed to her.

Yeah... That was... very, very nice.

Smiling, she cocked her head to better appreciate the sight he made.

That definitely distracted her and took her mind off everything except how wonderful he'd tasted last night.

He closed the door, then turned back toward her, and frowned. "Are you all right?"

Heat scalded her cheeks. "I was admiring my view."

He flashed a wicked grin at her before he dropped the fur. "My ever-hungry dragon. What am I to do with you?"

She squealed as he launched himself at her and rolled across the bed so that she landed on top of him in the center of the mattress. Cupping her face, he kissed her deeply.

"Who was at the door?" she asked.

He pulled back with a groan. "An elf."

"I figured that. Care to elaborate?"

"An irritating elf."

She smirked at his humor.

"It was another update. From what they've gathered from their spies and allies, we're facing a number of mercenaries she's put together. Only a handful of her own troops —probably because she's afraid of officially violating our contract. They suspect Dythnal, Vaskalia, Ningyo and Cosaria have offered money for my head, but none of them are offering any soldiers to her, probably because they're afraid of violating our treaties. Since she has my lands and army in addition to hers, those rulers don't want to leave their territories and risk thinning their numbers for fear of her killing their commanders, and then invading their lands. Or of my regaining control and retaliating against them."

"Makes sense." The elves were helping because their lands fell between Meara's and Dash's. If the centaurs kept Dash's land, then the elves would be surrounded by her troops on both borders. It would only be a matter of time before she'd attack them and try to conquer their lands, too.

"I suppose five kingdoms against you is better than seven."

He shook his head without comment. But his expression said he was less than amused.

"Was there anything else?" she asked.

"They're planning to march within the hour."

Gasping, she started to climb off him.

He pulled her to a stop. "That's why I didn't want to tell you."

"We don't need to be the last ones out the door."

He scoffed. "I'm the High King. They can wait on me."

She gave him a droll stare.

"Can't I pretend to be selfish?"

She kissed him. "You can pretend, beast, but we both know better."

As she started to pull his tunic off, a dark shadow fell across the room, followed by a familiar deep, thrumming rhythmic sound.

Dash scowled. "Is that..."

"Dragon wings."

They both scooted from the bed and ran to the windows. Dash opened the wooden shutters.

Tanis stood frozen as she saw the last thing she'd

expected. There were several dozen dragons flying in the air over the elfin fortress.

"Do you know them?" he asked.

Yes, she did. "It's my sister, Ragna... with her elite guard."

"Is she here for you or me?"

That was a good question. "I don't know. She's never been particularly fond of me." She glanced sideways at Dash. "You, even less so."

"Beautiful. You should probably get dressed. I can't imagine any scenario where our current relationship would be met with applause from any member of your family." He immediately conjured a pair of chain mail breeches.

Tanis snorted at his wardrobe choice. "You're not meeting them as a unicorn?"

"I want as much protection between my balls and your sister as I can get at the moment." He added a few more layers of armor to his groin.

Laughing, she went to retrieve her clothes. "You know, if she is thoroughly pissed, that will only melt and scald those sensitive areas of your body. You're better off as a unicorn."

"Fuck me, you're right," he breathed before he changed into a unicorn... with leather armor covering his equine groin.

Laughing even harder, she dressed as quickly as she could. One thing about Ragna, she had no patience, and Tanis couldn't imagine what had brought her here.

It wasn't like her sister to leave home for any reason. She loved Indara. Reva would at least travel from time to time to other cities, and even other kingdoms.

Ragna seldom went more than a few leagues from their

father's palace, as she believed Esin to be the greatest city in the world, and the dragons to be the superior race above all others.

But if this was because Tanis had left home, she didn't want to keep her sister waiting. Ragna would be furious over having to come fetch her. The slightest delay would only serve to grow her anger exponentially. Something that really wasn't hard to do.

Tanis had been known to infuriate her older sister by simply entering a room.

Clearing her throat.

Being seen...

Sadly, she and Ragna had never gotten along. From the moment of Tanis's birth, Ragna had hated her and begrudged her everything.

By the time they made it to the courtyard where her sister had landed, Baldur, Tova and Hinrik were trying to calm Ragna who was having one of her more stellar tantrums.

Tanis drew up short as she realized just how big a dragon was when she wasn't in a dragon's body. Funny how her sister had seemed rather small to her in the past.

Now... she was barely the size of one of Ragna's black dew claws.

This was absolutely terrifying. No wonder most of the other species wet themselves in their presence. She suddenly had a whole new respect for Dash when he'd confronted her in that net.

Ragna reared up to tower over them. Like Davin, she had a green head and wings, with yellow accents. Her belly was a warmer gold that blended into orange scales. Tanis had always thought of them as much prettier than her own orange ones.

Her sister far more graceful in movement.

Their father had thought so, too. He'd often called Tanis clunky, and truthfully, she was in comparison.

At least that was her thought until Ragna stamped her foot and shook the ground so hard that she almost fell from the tremor it caused. Had Dash not been beside her, she probably would have fallen. Instead, she caught herself against his side.

"I know my sister's here, and I demand to see her. Where do you have her chained?"

Without thinking, Tanis pushed herself away from her unicorn, and went to her sister. "Ragna, stop."

Her sister whipped her tail.

Tanis barely ducked it in time to let it whistle over her head.

Then, Ragna would have scorched her had Dash not rushed to cover her. "Enough!" he roared.

Ragna froze at the authority in his tone. "What is this?" She studied his unicorn form, trying to figure out if he was the king or not.

Tanis straightened up so that she could face her again. "It's me, coal-breath. Would stop terrifying the natives?"

Ragna finally understood what she was saying. "Tanis? What did they do to you?"

"Nothing. I asked to be made human."

Her sister sneered as if that was the worst thing she could imagine. "Why would you do such an awful thing? Are you insane?"

"I had my reasons. What are *you* doing here?"

Ragna glanced around at the others before she tapped her claws against the ground with a thunderous tapping. "I was sent to find you and bring you home before you started a war." She made an awful face. "Not like that, though. Ugh! Have you any idea what they'll do to you if I take you home as a *human*? What were you thinking? Idiot!"

Something about this didn't seem right.

It wasn't her sister's anger or outrage. That was completely normal. Ragna was eternally furious.

No...

There was something more going on here.

"You came to fetch me with an army?" Tanis gestured at the dragons that circled above them. That was what bothered her. Ragna barely tolerated anyone. And those weren't just random guards.

They were an elite force.

And the fact that her sister was here at all. What was going on?

"After what happened to you last time, we were worried." Ragna raked a furious glare over her. "And apparently, we had every right to be. Look at what you did to yourself!"

"Should I make her human, too?"

She cast a bemused stare at Dash who spoke silently in her head. "Not the time, love," she whispered to him.

Although, to be honest, it might not be a bad idea. It would take some of the piss out of her sister. Ragna could probably use the humility.

If only.

But there was still something odd going on with all this

that didn't make sense. Ragna didn't care about her. That was a cold, harsh fact.

Neither did their father. Not really. Her timid mother might. But Tanis couldn't imagine her mother winning a fight with her family that would cause Ragna to come here with an army to fetch her. Their father would never allow such an encroachment into another king's territory.

It would breach their treaty.

The only one who would have cared to come after her would have been her brother and maybe Marla, and they would have come alone. Right now, Marla was too concerned about her hatchlings, and was too caught up in her own grief to be worried about her. She didn't blame Marla for either one of those. Marla should be more concerned about her children.

Which came back to the one mystery.

Why was her sister here? And how did she know this was where Tanis was? Who would have taken word to Ragna?

And why?

The battle gryphons...

One of them could have carried word back home that she was here. That made sense. While they might live and work here, they were still Indarian citizens, and they'd have family at home. Maybe one of the gryphons had thought to curry favor by telling her father of her location.

That made sense.

And it would explain some of Ragna's hostility. Tanis considered how she might calm Ragna down.

Really, there was only one thing she could think of. But

even it was a long shot. "We need to speak alone, Ragna. Meet me outside the gate in the outer bailey."

Dash turned to face her so that his back was to her sister. He lowered his tone so that it wouldn't reach up to Ragna's ears. "Are you sure about this?"

"I need to talk to her. Find out why she's really here. Trust me." She ruffled his ears and mane, which didn't appease him. If anything, he looked even more aggravated.

And it only made her sister all the angrier given how dragons felt about unicorns.

Swallowing hard, Tanis headed for the gate.

Ragna shot skyward then flew over to the open field of the outer bailey.

Grumbling to herself, Tanis really regretted her human body that couldn't do that in a single bound. She really missed being a dragon right now.

At least that was her thought until she vanished from where she was walking and appeared in the field next to her sister.

Dash... The very thought of him made her smile.

He was wonderfully considerate that way. Even though it cost him powers he couldn't afford to lose right now, he was more worried about her than himself.

It was why she loved him.

But those warm feelings faded the moment Ragna lowered her snout to glower at her.

Tanis didn't say a word as she realized there was a large contingency of centaurs and others in the woods surrounding them out here. Had they come with her sister?

This was no escort. It was a good-sized army.

Tanis started back toward the gate to warn them, but

Ragna cut off her path. "Why did you leave home? What were you thinking, you idiot?"

Frustrated that she couldn't get past Ragna, she growled. "That someone needed to avenge our brother and that none of you cared."

Smoke drifted out of her nostrils. "And how has that worked out for you... *human?*"

Better than her sister could ever imagine, but she wasn't about to let Ragna know anything about her relationship with Dash. "What are you really doing here? I know you don't care about me. None of you do."

No one in her family had ever bothered to hunt for her while she'd been held in captivity. It wasn't in them to do such. *If you're not dragon enough to fight off a human or unicorn, you deserve what happens to you...* So why would they be here now? With a dragon platoon and a centaur army?

This didn't make a bit of sense.

Ragna pulled back. "Are you really traveling with the High King?"

Every alert inside her went off. "Why do you ask?"

"I was sent to find him and swear fealty. Father heard about the bounty, and he doesn't want the king to think that we're one of the kingdoms putting money up for his death. Was that the unicorn I saw you with?"

That made her feel better. Given some of the things she'd heard her family say about Dash in the past, and the fact that dragons were known to have a lot of treasure, she had wondered, in spite of her assurances to Dash, if they hadn't been one of the kingdoms offering to pay that bounty.

It made her feel much better to know they weren't that treacherous, after all.

But if they weren't in league with Meara, why were there centaurs in the trees?

"How did you know where I was?" Tanis asked.

"A messenger told me."

"What messenger?"

"An ally of Father's, if you must know. Contrary to your puerile stupidity, we do have friends and allies in other kingdoms. Some of the gryphons who live here are still citizens of Indara and loyal to our kingdom."

So, she'd been right. One of the gryphons was spying on them. Wonderful.

Ragna lifted her head to peer toward the palace. "Who was the unicorn I saw inside? Is he the High King?"

She ignored the question. "Since you're here, I still need your help to reclaim Davin's skull."

Ragna made a sound of extreme disgust. "What is it with you and—"

"Just do it, Ragna! If not for our family and Davin's, then do it for your High King."

"What's he got to do with it?"

Tanis cringed as she realized what she'd let slip. She shouldn't have mentioned anything about Dash. What could she say that would shut her sister down and get her mind off him?

Perhaps a partial truth?

Or something to distract her?

Maybe the centaurs with Ragna were the rebels and not some of Meara's troops. Since her father didn't follow

281

unicorn politics, it was possible her sister didn't know that Meara was on Dash's throne.

So, Tanis went with distraction to get Ragna away from the main reason. "I won't become a dragon again, until I reclaim his skull. Those are the terms that I accepted in order to become human to find him."

Ragna made a sound of supreme disgust. "How stupid are you?"

"According to all of you, I'm the dumbest creature ever born. But I wanted to be human to take revenge on the dragon slayer who murdered Davin."

Ragna shook her head. "Can't you just kill the one who turned you human and be done with it?"

"No. Those weren't the terms."

Ragna growled. "This is ridiculous. Where's the king?"

Why did she care so much? Her insistence was beginning to wear on her nerves.

More than that, it was beginning to make her suspicious.

"What does it matter?"

Ragna turned as still as stone for several heartbeats. It was if she waited for something.

Finally, she moved. "Very well. We'll march with you to reclaim Davin's skull."

Her sudden reversal caught her off guard. Was this for real? She'd so seldom won an argument with her sister that she wasn't sure how to handle this or react.

It felt...

Weird. Unnatural.

Scary.

"You're sure?" Tanis asked.

Ragna flicked her tail in agitation. "I can't take you home in *that* body. Have you any idea what they'd do to both of us?"

She knew what they'd do to her, but Ragna had always been spared that part of their father's wrath. "Okay. Rest your troops, and I'll let the others know."

Ragna sent out the resonating dragon call to the others who were still circling above.

Once Tanis was satisfied that they were landing in the field, she headed back toward the palace to let Dash and the rest know. Which turned out to be a good thing as the landing dragons were making all the elves a bit nervous.

Not that she blamed them. They did look like an invading army.

"Are you all right?" Dash asked as soon as she was inside the inner bailey again.

"I don't know. It's not just dragons out there. I saw others hidden in the forest. Centaurs and such." Tanis couldn't explain the weird feeling she had. "I don't know if they're rebels with her, or what. But Ragna swears my father is on your side."

"You don't believe her?"

"I don't don't believe her."

He cocked his head. "That makes no sense."

"I know." She smiled at him. "Don't listen to me. I'm an idiot. Everyone thinks so. Ragna particularly."

"I don't so." Dash conjured a saddle for her.

And before she could take a step toward him, armor covered her as well.

Tanis paused. "What's this?"

"Protecting my partner."

She closed the small gap between them so that she could bury her face against his neck and hug him.

"Careful, Dragon. You do that and you'll embarrass us both."

Laughing, she kissed his neck and stepped back.

"Hey! Make way! Step back. Coming through! Move. Move. Move!"

Tanis frowned at the familiar frenetic voice that was nearing them. It wasn't until something small slammed into her and ricocheted off to land on Dash's mane where it became tangled with his hair that she saw it was a small Halla.

"Hello there." Tanis carefully pulled the hobgoblin free so that she could hover in the air by their sides.

Halla shook herself and then grew to normal size. "Where have you two been? Do you know how hard I've had to search? You vanished!"

Dash flicked his unicorn tail. "I knew you'd find us. You always do."

Halla scoffed. "Have you any idea how many want you dead, Sire?"

"Yes. Yes, I do."

"You found your hobgoblin." Marthen smiled as he joined them. "Good to see you, Halla. And just in time for battle."

"No. Wait. What?"

Dash nodded. "We're heading for Licordia."

She burst out laughing. Then she stopped. "You're serious? You do know what's happened, right?"

"Meara took my throne and put a bounty out on my life."

"You heard about all that. Good. Then you heard about her other allies, too?"

Marthen's eyes began to glow as Ryper and Dove joined them. At the same time his eyes glowed, Ryper's staff did the same.

Dash cursed as he understood what that meant. He turned human and pushed Tanis toward Ryper. "Get her out of here."

"What? Why?" Tanis asked.

Dash met her confused dark eyes. "Your sister isn't here to help."

Marthen nodded. "The dragons are siding with Meara. And those centaurs aren't rebels. They're Meara's troops."

CHAPTER 18

Marthen tried to pull Tanis away at the same time trumpets began to sound in warning.

She refused to go. "You need me, beast."

In his human body, Dash refused to listen to her. "I know how to fight a dragon, and I have your fire."

"Who better to fight them than one of their own?"

"But you're not a dragon right now. You're human, Tanis." Dash cupped her face in his hands. "Please... I don't want to watch you die. Do you understand?"

She glared at him. "I'm a warrior. Fully trained."

"I know that. This isn't about your skill. It's about my staying focused during this battle. I will lose if I know you're under fire."

"Yet you expect me to standby while you're in harm's way? How fair is that?"

Dash winced at the fury he heard in her tone. He respected that anger, just as he respected her skill. But this wasn't about either of those. "I'm not asking you to be fair, little dragon. I'm asking you for my sanity. I can't fight if I'm worried about watching you die."

Tanis ground her teeth, needing to argue with him. But the turmoil in those dark green eyes made her ache. She more than understood the pain she saw there. Because she felt it, too.

One of them had to give ground.

If she were a dragon, she would stand strong in this. But she wasn't.

He was in the form that he was used to fighting in. She wasn't. His powers were whole, and her powers weren't.

If he was more worried about her safety than his, he would die in battle. Or be severely wounded. He wouldn't be focused on those attacking him. He'd be more focused on those running at her.

Only an absolute, selfish moron wanting to die would continue to argue, and she loved him too much to do that. "Don't you dare break my heart, beast. I swear to the gods if you do, I'll have Ambrose bring you back from the dead just to torment you."

He gave her a tumultuous smile. "I know you will."

She fisted her hand in his hair and pulled him close to kiss those irresistible lips. "Remember, I don't love my sister as you do Renata. I will shed no tears for her. Do whatever you have to and use my fire to keep yourself safe. A dragon's throat glows for a few seconds before they emit fire. Slit it when it glows, and they'll die easily."

Dash turned to Marthen. "Keep her safe, wizard. Whatever it takes."

He inclined his head to Dash before he led her toward their underground shelter.

Dove and Ryper gave him a curious stare.

"Should I ask about that kiss?" Ryper asked.

"Shut up. I need to focus."

The dragons had taken to the sky again and were circling above while the elves were conjuring water to soak everything that could catch fire, including themselves.

Their elders were working spells to protect them from dragon fire.

Tova, Baldur and Hinrik met Dash in the center of the courtyard. Baldur let out a low growl. "They've trapped us here. The dragons are above, and centaurs have us surrounded. My gryphons are standing by, but we don't have enough to counter the dragons, and I'm not sure if they'll fight for us... or the dragons."

That was a good and valid fear.

Dash led the elves along with Dove and Ryper toward the parapets.

"Tanis said there were other troops with them." Dash climbed the stone steps so that they could see how many stood outside the gates.

"Looks like it's just mercenaries. At least from what we can tell." Tova was right behind him. "They've positioned fairy archers in the trees."

"And Stonemen," Hinrik added. "Not many, though. I'm thinking these are all mercs. Except for the centaurs, it doesn't look as if they're actual armies or soldiers sent by the kingdoms."

Dash agreed as he reached the parapets and saw the motley bunch of warriors who were gathering outside the gate.

What he didn't see was the queen herself.

"Who leads this assault?" Baldur shouted down to those preparing to battle them.

A centaur wearing unblemished armor rode forward with a standard bearer following three steps behind him. He wore his long brown hair loose around his shoulders, mostly because he knew he wouldn't be fighting in battle. With an impeccable mustache and short beard, his aristocracy was an affront to every creature surrounding him. They'd been paid to bleed in his stead.

Prince Ferox. Dash remembered that bastard well. Meara's eldest son and the one centaur besides Meara he'd like to gut and leave bleeding at his feet.

Flea-bitten little shit. Which was the color of his equine half. From tail to hoof to torso. Shit brown.

And it took everything Dash had not to take the bow from Tova beside him and send an arrow straight into the centaur's throat.

With the pompousness that could only come from someone who'd never been told no, Ferox made his demands. "We have no issue with Alarium, King Baldur. We just want a word with King Dash. If you'd be so kind as to inform him that we're here to speak with him. Thank you."

Baldur laughed at his request. "Princess Ragna said that she wanted to speak with her sister. I'm very confused with so much royalty visiting my humble kingdom without any warning. Wish word had been sent on ahead. I'd have prepared a feast and declared a national holiday."

"No need to put yourself out. Dash and I are old friends." He smiled coldly. "Please fetch him."

Old friends, my ass. Dash exchanged a smirk with Dove who rolled his eyes in response.

Yeah... the fury in Dove's eyes said it all.

He was having the same fantasy of ripping the centaur apart. Ferox had no idea that he was standing in front of three creatures who had spent years trading stories on how they'd end his life if they ever had the opportunity.

Dash had no idea how they were restraining themselves either. It was taking an act of supernatural strength for him. He could only imagine how difficult it was for Dove and Ryper. Especially given the fact that Ryper had the power and ability to land a blow even from this distance.

Baldur sighed heavily. "Well, Ferox, sorry you traveled all this way in vain. You just missed him. Sadly. He left last night. Again, had you sent word..."

"He's lying! I saw the king when we arrived." Ragna flew lower. "I don't see him now, but the unicorn was there earlier."

Baldur arched a brow at Dash. "How did they know you were here?" he whispered.

"That's the question, isn't it?" Dash glanced around at the group.

Someone, probably a gryphon, had sent word to his enemies that he was here.

Question was which one.

Baldur's cheeks reddened as he realized that he had a traitor inside their gates. Maybe more than one.

Someone who could be unlocking said gate for their enemies even as they were talking.

Ferox came a bit closer. "Where is King Deciel?" He looked straight at Dash.

How fun that he had no idea. Then again, it'd been a

long time since they last saw each other, and even then, Dash had only been in human form *very* rarely.

And only when Meara had tortured him into it.

While the elves present were all aware of his shape-shifting abilities and forms, not all races knew unicorns could shift. Because unicorns and centaurs were both equine races, the unicorns didn't usually fight centaurs as humans. They never had. Unicorns had considered it dishonorable. Same with dragons. Since unicorns were weaker as humans, they'd never fought them in human skin.

But when it came to fighting a race like the elves who used magick and swords against them, there were advantages to shifting from unicorn to human and back. A human body allowed them to have certain attacks they couldn't manage as a unicorn.

And even those races that knew they could shape-shift didn't necessarily know what a unicorn looked like in human form. At least not as a rule. Most unicorns kept their human features secret from most non-unicorns. Hence why the wanted poster wasn't a good likeness.

Hidden in plain sight.

Baldur held his hands up. "I'd be glad to let you in to look about if you want, prince."

Ferox snapped his fingers. Another centaur stepped out from the group to prance to the prince's side. Dash didn't recognize the older soldier. If he had to guess, he'd assume it to be an advisor or general the prince was conferring with.

Tova eyed them suspiciously. "What do you think, Sire?"

Dash shrugged. "No idea."

Ferox had the centaur next to him run at the gate. As

soon as he reached it, he flung an extra-large bag over the wall at them.

Dash winced as he saw that familiar gesture. There was only one thing that could be.

Someone's head and, judging by the size of the bag, there was more than one in it.

Rolling his eyes, Ryper sighed. "Why do they all have to do this? It's really old."

He wasn't wrong. And the only question was who those heads belonged to.

Everyone around him held their breath as Tova's son, Viggo, walked to the bloody sack and opened it.

Honestly, he expected one of the heads to be his own general, Kronnel.

It wasn't.

When Viggo pulled the head out, he was glad he'd ordered Marthen to pull Tanis away.

It was her father's. Shit. That was the last head he'd expected inside. Poor Iagan.

And so much for the treaty they'd signed. It only covered Iagan and Davin, which was probably why they'd both been murdered. Whoever did this, knew the terms of the treaty.

Ferox reared up proudly. "The centaurs and dragons stand united. We are done being ruled by unicorns. Stand with us, elves! Hand over the High King."

"Shit," Ryper said under his breath.

Halla tucked herself over by Dove where it was safer in case the elves turned on them.

Well, this was an unfortunate series of events. Dash could feel the target forming on his back like a living, breathing creature.

The elves had no reason to stand with him now. He was seriously regretting cutting down their mother tree.

Ryper and Dove stepped closer, letting him know they were willing to take an arrow if need be. Well maybe not Halla who was the size of his fist.

But even so, he was grateful for their support. Even so, the last thing he wanted was to see one of them die for him.

One by one, he exchanged glances with the three elfin leaders, waiting for them to make a move against him. Or shout an order for him to be taken.

In truth, he didn't feel right asking them to fight and die for his worthless hide. Not when they had their women and children at stake. This was their homeland. How could he ask them to make that sacrifice?

If his own brethren had allowed Meara to take his throne without a fight, then maybe he should he let her have it. It was one thing to march into his territory with an army and fight on a battlefield in defense of unicorn lands and homes. It was another to ask the elves to invite an army into their homes to have their families slaughtered.

He held his hands up.

Tova slapped them down. "Don't you dare insult us. You think for one second we're afraid of *them*? We're the children of gods. They're farm animals."

He arched a brow.

She grinned at him. "Unicorns are made of better stock."

He snorted at her mental gymnastics. "Nice save."

"Archers at the ready!" Hinrik called out. "Warriors, stand and prepare! Magicians, reinforce the wards."

At those orders, the last of the children and women ran to the underground shelters.

Baldur gave a curt nod then turned back toward Ferox. "Again, I'm the only king here." He ignored the protests of Hinrik and Tova, who were technically prince and princess, respectively. "If you insist on your stupidity, we will defend our lands. You can leave now on your hooves or be carried out on a litter later. Your choice."

Ferox was aghast "You're really willing to fight us when you're clearly outnumbered?"

"Who says we're outnumbered?" Baldur asked.

"I do," Hinrik said under his breath. "I can count." He started scraping his leg against the ground as if he were a horse.

Dash stifled a laugh.

Until he heard the command to attack. Then all hell opened up on them. The centaurs and their army ran for the gate as the dragons sprayed fire down on them.

Ryper slammed his staff against the ground. Light shot out from the crystal in all directions, to help fortify the shield.

For a few minutes, the shield held. But the dragons continued to hurl their fire.

Nothing came through. Nor did the arrows from the centaurs and fairies breach their wards.

Or the centaurs, or their mercs.

Dash scowled as he saw one small errant child running across the yard toward the tunnel.

Without thinking, he teleported to the little girl to help guide her to the tunnels that would see her safely away from the war zone.

Scooping her up in his arms, he ran her to safety. Tanis met him just inside the doorway.

She took the girl and ushered her deeper inside then turned back to face him. "I feel like I should be out there fighting with the rest of you."

He kissed her cheek. "I know. But you're human and I can't change that. Keep the others safe. They need a leader."

She nodded. "Don't get hurt."

"Don't get dead."

Tanis pulled him close.

Dash savored that one perfect moment of being held by her. But the sounds of war echoed outside in his ears. Time for them had run out.

With one last kiss, he left her to vanish into the tunnel with the others while he rushed to rejoin the elves at the parapet.

The moment their enemies broke through the shield rang out like a scream. And the instant they did, the elves used their magic to reinforce their armor. Arrows filled the sky so thickly that it darkened the light.

The dragons flew low, laying down fire to cover their soldiers as they swarmed the palace grounds.

Dash threw fire balls at them, shocking them with the intensity that was reinforced by Tanis's fire. Desperately, he wanted to change into his unicorn body to fight, but he knew better. The moment he did, they'd unify to come after him.

Then, it'd be over.

His only hope was the fact that in a human body, he blended in with the elves.

Suddenly, Viggo appeared by his right side. Tora was on his left. Tora caught a blow and drove a centaur back. "We were told to protect you, Sire."

Though he admitted they were capable, they were still children. "I can do this on my own."

But they hung tight to his side like Halla. No matter how hard he tried to break away, they were there.

Ryper came out of nowhere to take position at his back. "Why am I always saving your ass, brother?"

"I seem to recall I was the one saving you last time."

"That doesn't count."

Dash snorted. "I'm counting it."

"You're both idiots." Dove hefted his axe over his shoulder as he nudged Viggo aside. "Ragna killed her father. Who's in charge of the dragons now?"

Dash kicked back the centaur that came at him. "I assume Ragna thinks she is."

Being the eldest daughter, it made sense. But technically, Marla would be the regent until Davin's eldest son reached maturity. Which meant Marla and her children were in danger. No wonder she'd fled north to her father for protection. She must have suspected her sister-in-law was behind her husband's murder.

Poor Tanis that she'd never once considered Ragna's part in her brother's death.

"Duck!"

Dash did so without hesitation.

Ryper sent an ice blast to catch the flames that would have torched him had they reached him.

Changing into a unicorn, Ryper drew the dragons further away from his position.

"No!" Dash started after him, but Dove grabbed him.

"He's distracting them."

"They'll think he's me." While Ryper had a dark purple

horn, he was still a black unicorn. And his purple horn could appear black in certain light. Especially to idiots who weren't paying attention.

As Tanis had noted, most non unicorns wouldn't be able to tell them apart. One black unicorn would be the same as another.

It would be easy to mistake them.

"Damn it, Dove! Protect that stupid asshole!"

"I am!" He shoved Dash in the opposite direction Ryper had taken.

Never had Dash wanted to slap Dove and Ryper more than he did right then. Normally, Ryper was as reluctant to take his unicorn form as Chrys was to leave her crow body. Of all the times for him to find his inner equine, this wasn't it!

Fuck me! Ryper was going to get himself killed. Why would he do this?

My mother will kill me.

If that wasn't bad enough, he felt a sudden rush of hot air fly over him. Turning, he saw a dark shadow emerge from the tunnels where Tanis had been.

It was a huge dragon. One he'd seen in a meadow standing over him when he'd been captured in a net.

Tanis.

What the hell?

Stunned, he watched as she flew straight toward her sister and the other dragons that were fire–bombing the palace and elves...

CHAPTER 19

T anis knew she didn't have long. The spell that
Marthen had cast to make her a dragon again
would burn out quickly. But she couldn't breathe.
Couldn't think.

Her father was dead.

Pain and agony burned deep inside her, and all she could
see was her sister's smug face when they'd spoken before
the fighting began.

Ragna had done this. She'd murdered her own father
and had known what she'd done while pretending to be on
her side.

She lied to me! The fury inside her was absolute.

Even now, Tanis could see the little elfin girl Dash had
brought into the tunnels... Alys. She'd been sobbing.

"It was awful! They had a huge dragon head they threw
over wall that almost landed on me. They said the king
dragon was dead, and that the dragons and centaurs are
united against us! We're all going to die!"

The king dragon was dead. Those words kept echoing in her ears.

Ragna had killed their father. Which meant the bitch must have killed Davin, too. And for what? A fucking throne?

For power?

Tanis was sick to her stomach. How could Ragna do such a thing? Nothing was worth the life of their family. Nothing!

None of this made sense. Their father had actually loved Ragna. Had treated her with respect. He'd never said the horrible things to her sister that he'd said to Tanis, and she would never have considered killing him. She'd never even said a hateful or disrespectful word in his presence. How could Ragna be such a bitch?

She'd never understand this.

And Davin?

He'd loved Ragna. Had doted on Ragna as much as he'd doted on her and Reva. His sisters had been his world.

What is wrong with you, Ragna?

Why had she played this game with all of them? Acting like she cared? Like she'd come here to fetch Tanis home, when clearly, she had no intention of doing so?

Had she planned to kill her, too?

Or was there something else?

At least now she understood why none of it had seemed right. It hadn't been.

Ragna had come here to kill the elves and kill Dash. To take their kingdoms.

Now, all Tanis wanted from Ragna was blood and vengeance.

Flying up to the sky, she headed straight for the older

sister she'd once worshiped and thought the world of. The same sister whose throat she now wanted to claim.

Shocked to see her there, Ragna pulled back. "Tanis?"

"You... fucking bitch! How could you!" Tanis rammed straight into her side and sent her flying sideways.

Ragna righted herself, then glared at her. "What are you doing?"

Tanis spit fire at her sister. "You killed our father and brother!"

Ragna rolled, trying to catch her with her claws.

Tanis slapped her aside with her tail. "How could you?"

When her soldiers tried to assist Ragna, Tanis sprayed her hottest fire at them. "Stay out of this," she warned them as she turned a small circle. "This is between me and Ragna."

Ragna glared at her. "I thought you were human?"

"You wish!" She slapped her again with her tail, then caught her with her claws. "You killed my brother!"

Ragna twisted out of her hold. "He deserved it. He was weak."

Tanis screamed, then released a steady stream of bitter fire spray at her. It was the kind that burned to the core of whatever it touched.

Ragna ducked then caught her with a vicious blow.

Her rage was so great that she barely felt it. Instead, she wrapped her body around her sister and pulled her down to the ground where she slammed Ragna so hard that it left a crater in the earth.

Ragna groaned in pain.

Pulling her back up into the air, Tanis again rammed her

into the ground with as much force as she could muster. Given how much larger she was than Ragna, it was no small amount.

She repeated that four more times. And still she wasn't appeased. Tanis wanted to feel her sister's blood spray all over her.

When she lifted her up to do it again, Ragna screamed. "Stop!"

"Why should I?"

"You're killing me."

"Good. You deserve to die." Tanis meant those words with every fiber of her being. In that moment, nothing would please her more than to see Ragna in pieces. It was what she deserved.

If you weren't dragon enough to stop them, then you deserve what they did to you. How many times had Ragna said those cruel, vicious words to her?

Ragna had laughed over the brutality of what the humans and Brutus had done to her. Had relished in the death of their brother at the hands of a dragon slayer.

You don't want to be Ragna...

Tanis froze as that one reality sank in.

It was true. She didn't want to be the monster her sister had become. Unable to feel for others. Unable to be kind or caring.

The monster who'd killed her own brother.

Their father.

One who'd mocked her little sister for being raped.

No, she didn't want to be Ragna. Not for anything.

Instead, she flew to her sister's guard and did what she'd

never dared before. She held her head high. "I am your Crown Princess Tanis Dragomir and by all sovereign rights of my birth, I relieve my sister of her command due to her acts of treason against our beloved king and crown prince. All of you are to immediately stand down and return to Indara where you are to lock her up until the Regent Queen Marla and the Elder Council determines Princess Ragna's fate."

Tanis turned her attention to Erstl, Ragna's second-in-command. "Understood?"

He inclined his head to her. "Yes, princess."

Ragna started toward her, but Erstl caught Ragna and pushed her back. "You think this is over?" she snarled at Tanis.

"Until I get home, I do."

Growling, she struggled against Erstl. "Let me go! I command you!"

He held her fast. "Sorry, princess. I can't do that." He met Tanis's gaze, then inclined his head to her. "I'm under orders that I can't break."

Ragna continued to curse her as he hauled her away. "She's not your commander. I am!"

For once, they didn't listen to Ragna.

Tanis scowled as she saw one of the smaller dragons in their group. With purple and gold ombre scales, and a beautiful yellow tail, she was one Tanis hadn't seen in a long time. "Keegan?"

Keegan paused before she came back toward her. "Princess?"

"I didn't realize you flew with my sister."

Back in the day, Keegan had been one of Tanis's closest friends. But after her return, Keegan's father had refused to allow Keegan near her. No one wanted her taint to adhere to them by association.

Keegan nodded bashfully. "I didn't know about His Majesty. I'm so sorry."

"Are you loyal to the High King?"

Her black wings fluttered. "I'm loyal to Indara."

Tanis would accept that as a yes. "Then you'll follow my orders?"

"Of course, Highness."

"Without question?"

Keegan frowned. "I don't understand."

"I'm under a spell, Keegan. When it ends, I'll need protection. Will you give it to me?"

"Absolutely. It would be my honor to protect you, princess."

"Even if my form offends you?"

Keegan reared her head back and, in that moment, her formality slipped. "What aren't you saying to me, Tanny? I know you. What did you do?"

"Something you'll find offensive. But I need you as a sister. Stick with me, and I'll see you rewarded."

Keegan looked back over her shoulder. "I'm going to regret this, aren't I?"

"You just joined my sister in a rebellion where my father was beheaded. One where my sister killed my brother. This may be the only chance you have to save your life." And it was only because of their friendship when they were hatchlings that she was offering it to Keegan.

In spite of everything, they had been close. It wasn't Keegan's fault that she'd been too afraid to stand up to her father. Tanis wouldn't fault her for that.

Tanis held her tail up. "Sisters again?"

Tears misted in Keegan's eyes. "I've missed you." She wrapped her tail around Tanis's so that she could shake it. "And I will protect you. Even if you offend me."

Her heart pounding, Tanis hovered in the air with Keegan until they were sure the rest of the dragons were returning to Indara. Then, they turned their attention to the gryphons who'd pulled back from the battle out of confusion.

Without the dragons to lead them, they were hesitant to attack for either side.

Tanis arched a brow. "Who leads the gryphons?"

To her surprise, it wasn't one of the older gryphons. He was much younger. "I'm General Brychan. Who are we fighting for, Commander?"

Commander... there was a title Tanis had never held before. Strangely, she liked it. "Protect the High King and elves. Destroy the centaurs and their allies."

"Fair enough." He nodded. "Gryphons! Feast!"

Keegan clicked her teeth. "Never fought for an elf before. Bet they roast up nicely."

"Let's not try them out. Please."

She actually pouted. "But they look so edible."

Tanis was so glad Dash couldn't hear those words. "Roast the centaurs instead. I hear they have leaner meat."

"Oh. Why didn't you say so?" Keegan took off after the gryphons.

Scared of what she might have just unleashed, Tanis

turned her attention back to their allies below. There were bodies everywhere. So much for joking with Keegan. That sight made her sick to her stomach.

How she hated war.

And her heart remained lodged in her throat until she finally saw the one person she was looking for.

Dash. Still in human form, he was standing beside Dove, Tora and Viggo.

Relief poured through her as she headed for them.

Landing as close to them as she could, she used her tail to knock a centaur flying. "Would you care for a ride out of here, Sire?"

He actually laughed. "There's no saddle or bridle on you, Dragon."

She sighed at something she'd forgotten. "True. That does make it rather hard to ride, doesn't it?"

Turning around, she belched fire into another group of centaurs. "Is it wrong of me that I've missed being able to do this?"

Viggo pointed to another group. "Care to aim your fire that way?"

"Sure." She quickly took care of them.

"Over here!" Tora directed.

Dove rested his axe over his shoulder. "I'm feeling a little useless now that you have a dragon."

"Two of them, actually." Tanis jerked her chin toward Keegan who was on the ground, chasing after an entire group of fleeing centaurs.

Dash wiped at the sweat on his forehead. "Have to admit I'm in agreement. But I like being useless in this case."

In his unicorn form, Ryper came running and skidded to a halt beside them. "When did we get dragons?"

"Long story, but the important thing is we have them now."

Returning to his human body, Ryper winked at Tanis. "Finally, something went our way." No sooner had those words left his lips, then he cringed. "Did I just jinx us?"

"Yes," Dove and Dash said simultaneously.

As if summoned by Ryper or some spell his spoken words had woven, they heard a resonant cry over the clash of battle.

"Deciel Coeur de Noir! You bastard son of a whore! Come out from hiding behind my inferiors and face me." Ferox fought his way past a group of elves who'd found themselves in the way between the twisted centaur prince and what he foolishly thought was his prey.

Without his contingency of dragons to do his dirty work, Ferox had become desperate. The low life knew it was only a matter of time before his hired mercs turned tail and ran. That was the problem with such soldiers. They were never loyal to the cause.

Only to the coin.

And having winged, fire-breathing soldiers on your side tended to make even the most craven of creatures brave. But watching that advantage fly off in the middle of battle and abandon you to your enemies would shake the confidence of a loyal army. One that was made up of hired coin?

They weren't keen on sticking around for a bloodbath. A prince couldn't pay them if he was dead.

If Ferox didn't finish this soon, they'd abandon him even faster than the dragons had, and the prince knew it.

It was time to end this.

Dash changed forms and rode out to meet the centaur in the middle of the bailey.

Recognition caused Ferox to snarl as he locked gazes with Dash. The gleam in those dark eyes was one Dash knew intimately.

He'd seen it a thousand times before as he faced his enemies on and off battlefields. That look of dazed bloodlust and maddened fury.

He'd felt it himself more times than he could count. Putrid self-hatred. A need to prove to the world that he wasn't the shit stain everyone thought him to be. That he was done being kicked and pushed.

There was no sanity inside Ferox. He was only a maddened beast who smelled blood and wanted to tear apart the one he felt had done him wrong.

He didn't see Dash as a sentient being. Only a target that had to be destroyed.

This wasn't about honor. It was all about blood.

Ferox ran at him.

Tanis unleashed a stream of fire between them. Ferox pulled back and dodged it then shot an arrow at her.

Turning human, Dash used his powers to deflect the arrow away. The moment he did so, Ferox sneered. "That's where you were hiding. Were you really that afraid of me?"

"Don't flatter yourself, you matted up nag. I just didn't want to catch your fleas."

Dove sucked his breath in sharply. "He did not just say that."

Ryper scoffed. "Better than the dart donkey he uses for me whenever I piss him off."

Ignoring them, Tanis started forward, but before she could take more than a step, she turned human. Dove and Ryper immediately rushed to shield her.

Ferox tsked. "That explains that, doesn't it?"

"She's no concern of yours."

"You're right. It's not her head I need to take to my mother. It's yours."

Dash stood still as Ferox walked a small circle around him. "I'm giving you one chance to surrender, Ferox. This isn't your mother's arena." And he was no longer the angry colt he'd been there.

Fury no longer ruled him.

His red horn was long gone. Yes, that demon inside still salivated and still wanted to rip out the throat of this centaur or anyone dumb enough to challenge him, but Dash had learned how to cage that part of himself.

He no longer fought his demon. They now snuggled up close and cuddled.

Ferox scoffed at him. "Do you really think you're going to survive? The kingdoms are at each other's throats again. Even if you were to kill me, my mother will avenge my death. As will the sons and daughters of all those you've slaughtered for your crown. You've built your reign on blood and vengeance. Those families will not rest until you pay for your crimes."

Those words...

Dash froze as they tugged at something in his memory. Something fleeting.

He'd heard them before.

Where?

He couldn't remember, but it was there. Like a dream he could just barely recall. One that was...

Ferox ran at him.

Growling, Dash parried his sword stroke and drove him back with his powers. He wasn't about to fall to a centaur. Not today. Not ever.

He might have been bastard born, but he wasn't the inferior species.

Driving his shoulder into Ferox's stomach, he forced his enemy to give ground. Ferox tried to slice at his spine, but Dash dodged the blow and landed a blast of ice into the centaur's side.

It knocked Ferox sideways.

And before Dash could reach him, Ferox was surrounded by a bright light that held him immobile. Dash pulled up short and looked around for the source of it.

Marthen.

With his arm outstretched and palm aimed at the centaur, he held Ferox with his powers and used them to lift the centaur off his feet.

"What are you doing, Marthen?" Dash asked.

"Keeping you from killing him."

"Why would you be so cruel?"

"You know why."

Because it would begin the very thing Dash was trying to avoid. Unending war. Meara would use this as an excuse to rally the other kingdoms against him even more. He knew it.

As much as it galled him, Marthen was right, and he owed him for having the cooler head.

Hostages were power. He needed this rodent alive.

"Does he have to be returned intact?" Ryper asked.

Dove ran his thumb along the edge of his axe. "Surely, he could be a little worse for the wear?"

Marthen shook his head. "You're better than that."

Dove scoffed. "No. I'm really not."

Neither was Dash. Not deep in his soul. Or even on the surface. He wanted to beat Ferox the way that monster had torn through them when they'd been unable to fight back.

Even now, he could hear the ringing laughter of Ferox and his friends as they tortured them when they'd been children, left in the care of enemies who'd wanted them dead.

He knew that same echoing laughter rang inside Dove's and Ryper's souls just as loudly.

They all wanted justice. They salivated for it. And yet again, it would be denied them.

It was insufferable really. When would they get to have their peace?

His gaze went to Tanis, and the fear on her brow as she watched him. It wasn't fear of him being the demon he knew he could be. She was afraid *for* him because she cared. She didn't want him hurt.

That was all that mattered.

Without warning, all that inner fury evaporated. Dash stood there, stunned as it was literally sucked out of every part of his body. He'd never felt anything like it.

After all this time, he had that elusive peace that he'd been seeking the whole of his life.

His friends were alive. Tanis was unharmed. Really, did anything else matter?

This *was* a victory. Ferox was routed. The centaur soldiers had either fled or thrown down their weapons.

It was over.

They were still standing. Yes, they'd lost some of the elves, but the vast majority of them were alive and unharmed. Their homes and the palace remained intact.

It was enough.

"Put him in chains," Dash growled.

Ferox shrieked in anger. "You won't be able to hold your kingdoms. You may wear a crown, but everyone knows that you're nothing more than an unshodden, half—breed dogger!"

There was a time when those words would have driven Dash into a feral rage. Indeed, when he'd been held in Meara's court, he would have attacked like a mindless colt, intent on nothing more than driving his horn through Ferox's dead heart.

But he was no longer that same angry unicorn who'd hated his father.

The same 'corn who'd denied his birth and wanted to scream out at the universe for what it'd done to him.

He *was* the High King.

With a calm, calculated smile, Dash approached Ferox. "I had no control over where and how I started out in this world. But I am High King, and when I march my army into Licordia, and I will, your mother is going to have a very bad day."

He started to walk away, but he couldn't quite manage it.

With a glance to Ryper, he turned back toward Ferox.

"And I'd rather be an unshodden half-breed than a ridling botfly."

Ryper shook his head as Dash headed for Tanis.

"Botfly?" she asked.

"You don't want to know." Ryper laughed.

It was Dash who answered. "They're parasitic nasty things."

She made a face. "So, what's our plan now?"

"Same as before. I'm going to take back my kingdom." Only now, he had a renewed purpose and determination.

CHAPTER 20

Keegan poked at Tanis with one of her giant claws. "Does it hurt to be human?"

The question amused her. It wasn't that long ago she would have asked the same thing. "No. And it's not as bad as you'd think."

She looked skeptical. "If it's anything less than nightmarish awful, it's better than I think."

Tanis laughed. "Humans aren't any different than we are, except they take up a lot less room."

Keegan arched a brow over her words.

"I admit when I was a prisoner, I didn't feel quite so benevolent toward them. But my latest experience has given me a whole new," and much better, "perspective."

"It was a human who murdered your brother."

"A human couldn't have done it. During our fight, Ragna admitted she was the one who killed Davin." And Tanis still couldn't believe Ragna had done such an awful thing. Dragons were supposed to be better than that. Even in the darkest ages of Indara's history, she'd never heard of a family tearing itself apart.

Tearing apart others...

Naturally.

But the nest was supposed to be sacrosanct.

Keegan carefully stretched out beside her, making sure that she left room for Tanis. "Do you plan to go home once this over?"

Tanis felt like Keegan wanted her to say yes, but truthfully, she only wanted to stay with Dash. "I swore myself to King Dash's service in exchange for being allowed to seek my vengeance." She left out the part that he'd freed her. Mostly because she was hoping he wouldn't make her leave.

How are you going to stay in his lands?

The one thing Keegan's presence was bringing home to her was the fact that dragons didn't fit in their world. The elfin palace wasn't built for their size or weight. While the elves were being exceptionally kind to Keegan, it didn't change that one basic fact.

Dragons were huge.

It forced her to deal with a critical fact that she'd been trying to ignore. One she'd been doing her best to try to dismiss.

With Keegan here, she had to face it. There really was no future for Tanis and Dash.

No matter how much she loved him. No matter how much he loved her... they would never fit together.

Dragons didn't mix with others.

The barn door opened slowly. "Tanis?"

Her heart saddened by a reality she couldn't change, she

turned to find Dash hesitating. That was a new mood for him. Normally, he was so self-assured and determined.

Hesitant...

Just didn't fit.

She excused herself from Keegan.

"Is something wrong?" she asked as she drew closer to him.

"I didn't want to intrude on your time with your friend. But I wanted to let you know that we've..." His voice trailed off.

Now she was concerned. Something was really bothering him.

"You what?"

"The elves have reserved a place of honor for your father's... remains in their temple. I know your religion is very different from theirs, but their priests have agreed to preserve and care for him until you're ready to take him home and place him with your ancestors. They said that they've done their best to follow the dragon rites they know, but they're sure there are some things your priests keep secret from outsiders."

Tears gathered in her eyes. Not just because her father was gone. Because of the kindness of those actions. The thoughtfulness.

Of course, he would make sure the elves took care of her father.

If anyone knew how important that would be to her...

It was Dash.

"May I see him?"

He hesitated. "Are you sure about that?"

No. The last time she'd spoken to her father, they'd

fought about Davin. She'd demanded her father reclaim his head and her father had refused.

The irony of that wasn't lost on her.

Maybe if he'd listened to her and done as she asked, it might have saved him. Then again, she doubted it. Ragna had been set on this course.

"I'm sure." When she started for the door, Keegan rose and started after her.

Dash paused to look up at her. "What are you doing?"

"I'm Princess Tanis's Shield. My place is by her side."

He turned toward Tanis. "Shield?"

"Term for a bodyguard. Every member of the royal house is supposed to have one."

"Since the princess is here alone, it is my honor to serve as hers."

Clearing his throat, Dash looked a bit green. "*Is she going to curl up at the foot of our bed?*"

Tanis laughed at the question he asked in her head. "That would be an interesting thing, wouldn't it?"

"No. It'd be horrifying."

"What are you two discussing?" Keegan asked.

"Nothing," Tanis said quickly. "Will she fit in their temple?"

"She should. But to be sure, I could make her smaller."

"Just don't make me human." Keegan blushed as if she realized how horrible that sounded.

Tanis patted her foot. "I'm not offended. Might be if I was actually human, but I understand."

"Sorry. I didn't mean it that way." Before she finished speaking, she shrank down to just under half her size.

Keegan's eyes widened. "Oh, I don't like this. Not at all. You can put me back, right?"

Dash sucked his teeth. "Well, I think so."

Tanis smacked him playfully on the arm. "Don't tease her like that. She's scared."

He finally smiled. "Yes, Keegan, I promise I can put you right back."

She let out a relived breath so deep that it was punctuated by a cloud of smoke. "This is why I don't hang out with unicorns. They're inherently mean."

Tanis laughed. "No more so than most of your guard. And at least he won't put you to the hazard."

Keegan screwed her face up. "That was pretty terrible."

"Hazard?" Dash asked.

"A series of tasks and trials that all dragons are subjected to when they're trained for war. The more prestigious their rank and assignment, the worse the hazard."

He stopped walking to pin a concerned stare on Tanis. "You weren't put to a hazard, were you?"

His angry concern warmed her. "No. I wasn't allowed to join."

That only made him angrier. "Because of your captivity?"

It took her a second to realize just how furious he was on her behalf. She could sense his bloodlust.

Wanting to calm him, she took his hand, then tucked his arm under hers and pulled him forward. "We don't talk about that, remember? And it doesn't matter."

"It matters to me when you're not treated with the respect you deserve."

Leaning against him, she treasured those words. "So, you would rather they have beat me?"

He shook his head at her. "You know what I mean."

"I do know, and I appreciate your anger on my behalf."

Tanis fell silent as they neared the steps of the elfin temple. It was a beautiful structure made of glass and stone. Much smaller than the palace, it reminded her of a tree the way it reached up toward the sky. Murals of elves and nature were painted all around it.

Truthfully, she knew very little about their religion. She'd never really interacted with elves until the last few days. They'd been almost mythological to her. Like Stonemen and fairies. If any had ever come to Indara, she'd never seen them.

During her captivity, she'd only known the one unicorn, humans and a few other species who hadn't spent a lot of time conversing with her.

Most of the ones who'd been held for games had been oni, ogres or trolls. For the matches against them, Baracus had turned her into a dragon and then returned her to human form once it ended. Mostly because he hadn't wanted to pay to feed a dragon or find a place large enough to keep her.

At least that was what he told others.

The real truth was that he'd been terrified of her as a dragon. Because as a dragon, she had a finite amount of time when his drugs had been effective. Once they began wearing off, he'd end the match and turn her back human.

Between his drugs and spells, she'd been terrified that she'd never go free again.

What he hadn't counted on was her learning to fight as a

human. She'd spent months with the ogres who'd helped her learn sword-craft.

Baracus should have paid closer attention.

Just like her father should have.

Tanis slowed her pace as they entered the temple, and she saw the altar in a side nave where they'd placed her father's head. His head was so large that it took up almost the entire area.

Iagan had been such a fierce beast. His gray eyes piercing. It was surreal to her that she'd never see him again. Never hear his angry bellow cursing her.

Biting her lip, she approached him slowly. "At least he looks peaceful." As if her sister had killed him while he was asleep.

Dash was right behind her with a gentle hand against her back. "Is there anything we need to do for him or you?"

She shook her head. To the elves' credit, they'd done a wonderful job of cleaning and shining his scales and draping a crimson cloth over the back of his head where his neck should have been.

"Where do you think his body is?"

Keegan rippled her scales behind her—a shiver for a dragon. "Surely, she didn't disrespect it. He was her father."

That was a high crime to their race. Murder wasn't taken lightly, but to kill someone inside the family...

It carried the harshest of punishments. For this, she'd lose her sister, too.

Tanis felt her tears fall then. "I don't know. I still don't see how Ragna could do this." Her hand shaking, she reached out and touched her father's snout, remembering those times when she'd been a hatchling...

Back when he'd looked at her with love in his eyes. He would nuzzle her and hold her close. She hadn't allowed herself to think of those memories in so long. Because they were too painful. She missed the father she'd once known.

The one who'd looked at her with pride and love.

Sobs racked her.

Then Dash was there, pulling her against his hard body. Holding her close. Had he not been there, she would have fallen. But he would never allow that.

He had become her strength.

"I've got you, little dragon. Cry as much as you need to."

Those words made her cry even harder as she clung to him. How weird that she'd do so. Here she'd thought she was long past this. That she was stronger than this.

But it was for the loss of any chance she'd ever have to make amends with her father. He had died hating her, and she would never have a chance to regain his love.

His trust or respect.

Nor would he ever know that she wasn't the awful, defiled creature he'd called her. It stung on a level so deep that she couldn't catch her breath.

That was why she now hated her sister. Ragna had robbed her of any chance to have a father again.

And this weakness bothered her. Tanis wasn't the kind of dragon who cried. Even with Davin's death, her rage had been such that she hadn't allowed herself to sob like this. She'd been too determined to find the one responsible.

To punish the dragon slayer for daring to take his life.

Now...

It all coalesced inside her. All the pain and regret for the future she wouldn't have with them.

She'd give anything to hear her father's gruff voice, even if it was insulting. Or to hear Davin's laughter.

To see him teasing Marla and playing with his hatchlings.

Everything was so different now. There was no going home. She no longer even had a family.

This was even worse than when she'd been kidnapped. At least then her family had been intact.

Alive.

Now...

Davin and her father wouldn't be there. Ragna would be executed.

And Reva...

Her heart stopped as she thought of her other sister. Pulling back from Dash, she turned toward Keegan. "Did Reva have anything to do with this?"

Keegan looked a bit startled by the question. "I don't know. She was there when we were summoned to come here to meet the centaurs. But I have no idea what she participated in. You know how she and Ragna always are."

Tighter than fingers in a fist. But Ragna didn't always trust Reva, either.

Finding a new purpose, Tanis wiped at her eyes. "What were you told?"

"That there were vermin we needed to exterminate. Ragna said that we were to escort her to a meeting. We didn't question anything beyond that."

Because they taught not to question orders.

"How did Ragna know I was here?" Tanis looked at Dash.

"Probably one of the gryphons. Or another spy. They're

all over my court. Part of Ryper's job is ferreting out spies, but he doesn't find them all. They breed like rats."

Tanis nodded then turned back to look at her father's remains. Tears choked her again at the injustice of what had been dealt to him. *I know I wasn't your favorite, but...* "I will avenge you, Papa. I promise to make sure your throne is secured by our rightful heirs."

How ironic that she was the last one he'd want to hear that promise from. That knowledge made her ache all the more. He'd died disappointed in her.

But it didn't matter. She'd keep her promise regardless. While he might have let her down as a father, he'd been a fair and good king. Just as Dash was.

And at least Davin had secured their lineage. He had three sons to inherit Indara's throne. Those hatchlings had been her father's greatest treasure.

If Reva and Ragna were executed over this, Tanis would be the only one left of her father's children.

As much as she despised her sisters, and as cruel as they'd been to her, she wasn't sure if she could see them executed.

You're not a dragon. You've been tainted by the mongrels who took you.

Perhaps her father had been right, after all. She didn't have that same killer instinct inside her that he required of his dragons. She wanted what was fair.

The problem was that she was no longer sure what fair meant.

Heartbroken, she left the temple to head to...

She didn't know where. This wasn't home and these weren't her people.

I have nowhere I belong anymore.

That harsh reality slapped her so hard that for a moment, she couldn't breathe.

Her brother and father were dead. While Marla had been kind to her before, she might not be now.

At least one, if not both, of her sisters had killed Davin and her father. Marla would have every right to see Tanis banished, based on their actions. Even if Marla took mercy on her, Marla's family might demand exile or death to protect her sons.

For that matter, Tanis's extended relatives might do so, as well.

While Marla might be Queen Regent, she would be more at the mercy of their council than a full monarch. Because she wasn't descended from the blood of the Dragomirs, Marla's reign would be tightly monitored until her son, Draig, was old enough to inherit.

"Tanis?"

She couldn't speak at Keegan's question. The stark, bitter reality of what she was facing hit her.

She'd lost her brother. Her father.

Her sisters.

Her home.

Who am I now?

Everything she knew was gone.

Suddenly, Dash was there. He cupped her face in his hands as he stared down at her with those eerie eyes that practically glowed in the evening light. "You all right?"

"No," she breathed. "Without my father, I have no home."

"You have a home."

"No, Majesty. She's right. The council will most likely banish her. Even if she didn't have her past, they would do so to protect the young heir. His safety will take priority over hers."

"Then I will forbid it."

Those words touched her, but she knew it wouldn't matter.

"They will kill her to protect the heir, Majesty. No one will trust her after what her sister has done. Even if Reva had no part in it, she'll be banished, too."

Fury darkened his eyes. "Then why are *you* here?"

Keegan passed a sympathetic look to Tanis. "We were best friends once. I didn't want to leave her alone in her grief. I didn't realize that she had you."

His thumbs brushed against Tanis's cheeks. "You do have me, Dragon. Wherever I am, you'll always have a home."

But would she have to give up the last of her identity to stay with him?

Who would she be then?

Keegan was having to stay inside a barn like livestock because she didn't fit in anything other than the grand hall of the palace. Licordia would be no different. It was designed around unicorns and humans, not giant dragons.

What was she going to do?

CHAPTER 21

"Why did you save me?" Fort asked.

Bink had no real answer for that he could give the imbecile. Except one. "You're my partner, aren't you?"

Fort nodded as he did his best to follow Bink out from the dungeon where Bink had drugged the guards and released the idiot human after he'd been captured by Meara.

He handed a cloth to Fort. "There you go."

The last thing Bink wanted to confess was the real reason he was here. He didn't want the stupid weasel to rat him out. To be honest, he was amazed Fort hadn't already broken under the torture that evil bitch had put him through.

He wouldn't have suffered it for Fort. He'd have broken the first day and led them straight to Fort's whereabouts. "Why didn't you betray me?"

Fort stopped wiping the blood from his face to give him a hard stare. "You stupid? If I'd told her where you were, she'd have killed us both. Only hope I've had of surviving her was keeping my mouth shut and praying you'd rescue me."

So, he wasn't as stupid as he looked. Bink was impressed. Maybe he'd judged Fort a little prematurely.

He motioned for the human to duck as one of the queen's sentries went by. Getting into the dungeon had been relatively easy as he'd been alone.

Beautiful part about being an imp, they could shrink in size and scurry around in places centaurs didn't look. Bad thing about humans, they were locked in their annoyingly large bodies that tended to draw attention.

Bump into things.

"What are you doing?" a soft voice asked beside him.

Bink had to bite back a shriek at the unexpected voice that sounded right in his ear.

Dreama.

"Not scaring the shite out of people. Dammit, Brownie! What are you trying to do? And why aren't you where I told you to be?"

Dreama scowled at him. The size of an average human man's hand, she was pretty for a brownie. Long dark hair and eyes that glistened like dew. "Because there's a bunch of... things there already."

Bink scowled. "What do you mean?"

"I went to the hunting lodge to wait on you, like you said. But there's already a group hiding there."

Was she serious? "What kind of group?"

She shrugged. "The kind that's just waiting around. How should I know?"

He wanted to throttle her.

Why do I bother with accomplices? They were so annoying. But then again, they had their uses. Without her, he'd had no one to leave behind and send the king off in the wrong direction after they'd killed Princess Renata.

Still...

Fort had cost him the dragon skull.

Now, he had to get to the lodge and see for himself what she was talking about. See who the creatures were she was talking about.

Why they were there.

As carefully as he could, he led them through the palace grounds and out to the back garden. He was lucky that Keryna had trusted him enough to show him all the secret ways in and out of the palace.

Her reasoning then was to get him to help her assassinate the king. Until they'd learned that you couldn't just cut the throat of a black horn.

They were a special breed and required special means for execution.

Even cutting off their horn required a special blade.

And thinking of Keryna, he almost felt bad for her fate.

He still didn't know if she was alive or dead. If she had managed to survive the queen's torture, she had to be wishing herself dead. Especially if she looked anything like Fort. His face was swollen to where he barely looked human. He'd lost a few teeth, too.

Poor bugger.

Whatever Bink did, he had to make sure to stay out of Meara's hands. She was lethal in a way he'd never seen before. And here, he'd thought he'd seen them all and done most of them.

Ick! No wonder her citizens hated her the way they did.

Trying not to think about it, Bink made it to the postern gate and then allowed them to leave first. He took one last look about to make sure no one saw them, then he ducked through.

Once they were in the meadow, he led them toward the king's hunting lodge.

It'd been one of Keryna's favorite places to meet with Bink when they'd first teamed up.

One day, imp, this will all be mine!

He'd never understood her mind set over that. It was a nice lodge and all, but nowhere near as nice as the palace. And while the lodge had servants whenever the king was in residence, it'd been isolated and lonely when he wasn't there.

Not Bink's cup of tea, at all. Having been a servant to the fey folk in Sagaria as a boy, he'd hated every minute of it.

But he found having others wait on him far more befitting the imp he wanted to be.

He curled his lip as old memories haunted him. Uppity fey bitches. They thought themselves so superior. They were just as backbiting and petty as anyone he'd ever known. He had no use for them. Other than to rob them and hone his skills at turning friends into enemies.

A little lie here, a twist on the truth there...

Mortal enemies for life.

He liked it.

"I wish we had a horse," Fort complained.

Bink scoffed. "There's a palace full of centaurs. I'm sure one of them would love to give you ride right back to your cell."

"I didn't say I wanted to return. Just saying I wish we had a horse. I have been tortured for the last few days, you know? It hurts to walk."

"And what do you think I've been doing? Washing my spindles?" It'd been an absolute horror waiting to see if the imbecile would break and tell them who he was and where he was hiding.

Or worse, tell them that he had the horn they were all looking for. The stress alone had damn near killed him.

"Can't you use the wand and make us a horse?" Dreama asked.

"Why are you whining? You've got wings."

"Small wings," she groused. "It's tiring. Why do you think we like to catch rides on the backs of birds?"

Personally? He'd assumed they were lazy.

"Well, the wand can't make a horse." At least, he didn't think so.

To be honest, he wasn't exactly sure what all a golden horn *could* do. He only had a rudimentary understanding of that level of magick. What little he knew was what he'd picked up from the sidhe court where they both revered and reviled unicorn powers. It was there he'd hatched his greatest scheme.

Collect horns and sell those wands in Sagaria to the fey and wizards who lived there. They were far enough away from Licordia, that word had never reached the unicorns that he was poaching their precious body parts.

Thankfully, the fey knew that if they were caught with a wand, they'd be punished just as severely for purchasing it as he was for the illegal collecting. Because it wasn't like they didn't know the wand came from a unicorn that had been killed to collect it. Therefore, he'd never been afraid of betrayal on that front.

Granted it was a dangerous business, but one that had made him quite wealthy.

In the past, he'd kept mostly to green or purple horns. A few red ones, but those were hard to take as the bearers were fierce fighters and normally looking for someone to brawl with. White ones could fetch a good price, but not nearly as much as yellow or orange.

Then he'd seen the princess. The moment he'd laid eyes on her golden horn, he'd known it would be worth the price of a kingdom.

And that was before he realized it could be used to kill her half-brother, the king. If he possessed both a black and gold horn...

He'd be invincible. No one would ever be able to defeat him. He'd own the world and be the High King.

That was what he wanted now. He just needed to get his bearings and evade Meara and her troops.

Those were his thoughts until they reached the lodge where he'd originally planned to hide out.

At first, like Dreama, he had no idea who they were. Just an odd collection of beings lounging about for unknown reasons.

Until Aderyn walked into the room. He knew her by sight. She was one of the commanders for the High King's cavalry. A beautiful dapple-gray unicorn with stocking and a large star in the middle of her forehead that highlighted her orange horn, she was a beautiful brunette in human form.

The other he'd never seen before. A dark-skinned woman with gold eyes. A red-headed man and another man who could have passed himself off as part mountain. The last of their group was a frail woman who reminded him of the fey. But he'd lived among them long enough to know that she wasn't one of them.

She was something else.

"Elpis?"

She turned toward the mountain, and the moment she did, he saw the tiny horns on her head and realized that she was an oni. His breath caught. The oni rarely involved themselves in the affairs of any other species. They preferred their own kingdom and only left it for war.

Why would one of their breed be here?

It didn't make sense.

Holding his hand out to silence his companions, Bink crept closer, wanting to hear what was going on.

Aderyn folded her arms over her chest. "Should we send Chrys to Dash to let him know what's going on?"

The mountain scratched at his beard. "Forewarned is forearmed. He needs to know what he's walking into."

The red-headed man let out a tired sigh. "I just wish Ryper or Xaydin were here. They'd know what to do."

The mountain laughed. "They'd have already wiped out at least half of them."

"Very true." Aderyn inclined her head to them. "I'll go send Chrys off. I'm the one least likely to be noticed here."

"Leave Chrys to her nest. I'll go in her stead."

They all stared at the mountain over his offer.

"What?" he asked defensively. "I can get there quicker than she can, and evade others if need be. Y'all stay here and wait. I'll get back with news as soon as I can. Hopefully, Dash won't be far behind."

"Be careful, Ronan," Aderyn said. "We don't know what's between us and the elves."

"We're about to find out. Y'all be safe here. Keep your eyes open." Ronan turned himself into a peregrine falcon. "Someone want to open a door or window for me?"

The redhead tsked. "Should have thought of that before you changed forms, old man."

"Don't start with me, Cadoc. I'll peck out your eyes."

Laughing, Cadoc moved to a window not far from Bink and opened it.

Bink motioned his companions to crouch down lower. His heart pounding, he held his breath until Ronan vanished into the sky.

That was close. Grateful they hadn't been seen, he motioned his companions off to the woods.

"What's going on?" Dreama whispered.

"They're friends of the king."

Her eyes widened.

Fort pulled the cloth away from his still-bleeding lips. "What are we going to do?"

He wasn't sure. Part of him was tempted to let Meara know about them so that she could rid them of nuisance. But she was too unpredictable. And from what he'd seen, she was more likely to torture him and his group along with the ones in the lodge as she was to be grateful they'd reported them.

No...

There had to be some way to spin this so that he didn't get skinned.

He just didn't know how... yet.

"The king is worried about you."

Tanis sniffed back her tears as Keegan entered her room. While she was still a dragon, she was now the size of a large unicorn. That actually made her smile. "What happened to you?"

"His Majesty wanted me to check on you while he goes over plans with the elves. When I told him I didn't think I'd fit, he asked if I'd mind being pint-sized until he was free to come check on you himself."

"He is thoughtful, isn't he?"

Keegan moved to sit beside her bed. "He cares for you."

"I like to think so."

She lifted a claw and carefully turned Tanis's head until she met her gaze. "No, Tanny. He *really* cares for you. You have to know that. It's more than obvious to everyone else."

Tanis wanted to believe it. "What difference does it make? I'm a dragon."

"Do you have to become a dragon again? You seem awfully happy in your human body."

She screwed her face up. "Not really. I mean... some of it's not so bad." Kissing Dash. And other things she did with him that were exceptionally wonderful, but living as a human for the rest of her life?

Grisly.

Tanis shook her head. "Even in this body, I'm a dragon and I miss being me."

Keegan nodded in agreement. "I understand that a lot

more than I did." She held her paw and spread her claws wide. "It is weird to be something you're not used to."

"It really is."

Keegan sat back on her haunches. "I am so sorry about everything. Especially for not being there for you these last years. You shouldn't have been left alone."

"Thank you. I appreciate that."

A knock sounded on her door. Scowling, Tanis answered it to find Ryper on the other side.

"Is everything all right?" she asked.

"I was just checking on you. Wanted to make sure you didn't need anything."

Tanis frowned as she noticed something for the first time. There were eerie similarities between Ryper and Dash. Not just in the cadence of their voice, but the way they held themselves. Even the way they stood.

He'd looked and sounded so much like Dash when he'd said that, they could have been twins.

Ryper frowned at her. "Are you all right?"

"Has anyone ever told you how much you favor the High King?"

He laughed nervously. "You're messing with me, aren't you? We're nothing alike."

She remembered during the fighting another similar detail. "You're even a black unicorn... like him, aren't you?"

"We don't talk about that."

His sudden discomfort confused her. "Talk about what?"

"The unicorn part. It's not something I normally do. I only did what I did today to protect Dash. I like being a unicorn probably as much as you like being human."

That seemed odd to her. She didn't like being human

because she was a dragon. If he was a unicorn, why would that bother him? "Why?"

Ryper didn't answer her question. "You're obviously fine. I'm heading to bed and will see you in the morning when we leave." He vanished so fast that he practically teleported.

Keegan moved forward. "That was strange, right?"

"Very."

"Yay! I'm getting the hang of being around people. They're not quite as bad as we thought, are they?"

Tanis smiled. She'd forgotten all about Keegan's bad habit of ending most of her sentences in a question. When they'd been young, it'd made her insane.

"No. They're not nearly as bad as we thought. At least not the ones here." Most of them were very pleasant and thoughtful.

Like Ryper and especially Dash.

DASH LOOKED up as a shadow fell over him while he was reviewing the map on the table. On instinct, he drew his dagger and would have sliced open the intruder's throat had he not realized it was Ryper in the shadows.

"How many times have I told you not to sneak up on me?"

"Enough that I should remember, and yet I still forget." Ryper rubbed at the hairline cut Dash had accidentally given him. "Thanks for the shave."

Sighing, he sheathed his dagger. "Glad it wasn't closer."

"Me, too. Would have seriously ruined my night to be decapitated."

"How unlike you. Thought you wanted to die."

Ryper didn't respond as he moved so that he could see the map over Dash's shoulder. "Have you told Tanis about us?"

"How do you mean?"

Ryper glanced around the room. "We are alone, right?"

He nodded. "Even Dove went to bed."

Still, Ryper lowered his voice an octave and when he spoke, Dash understood why. "She commented on how much I favor you."

"At least you got the syntax correct this time."

Ryper growled at him. "Five fucking minutes. Seriously? You're only five minutes older."

"But I count every one of them."

He tossed one of the map markers at Dash who caught it and laughed. "Why do you always bring that up? Five minutes like it means anything?"

Dash shrugged. "What are brothers for if not to irritate the shite out of their siblings?"

Ryper rolled his eyes. Then he returned to his usual somber composure. "I do wish I'd told Renata. I kept thinking I'd have time. Now..."

"She loved you like family, anyway. You know that."

"Not the same as knowing we *were* family."

No, it wasn't and Dash wouldn't argue the point. Maybe they should have told her. But as Ryper had said, it'd never seemed the right time.

Neither of them had known how Renata would react, and they'd decided it wasn't worth the risk of anyone else finding out. And it was now painfully obvious that Renata had been incapable of keeping secrets. He still couldn't believe that she'd told Keryna about their horns.

And the spell to kill him.

Why, Renata? Why?

Didn't matter at this point. Other than he would have rather had his sister than a horn.

Which was why he kept Ryper's relationship to him a secret. And why he'd never told Renata the truth.

Ryper didn't want to be acknowledged as a prince.

He'd rather be castrated than have anyone bow to him or treat him like royalty. It just wasn't Ryper, and Dash had promised his brother that he'd never force it on him. He loved his brother too much to make him do anything he didn't want to do.

Dash pulled Ryper in for a rare hug and kissed the top of his head.

"What are you two doing?"

Dash pulled back to see Marthen putting a shield over the room to keep anyone from seeing into it. "You both know better! What if someone saw you?"

He shrugged nonchalantly. "No doubt it would spark a whole lot of new rumors as to why I'm not married, and why, unlike my father, I don't have bastard children running about."

And that had been the biggest problem for them. It would have been bad enough for Cratus to have had one bastard son for his throne.

Twins were a catastrophe.

And a death sentence.

So, the eldest son had been sent off to their father while

their mother had kept Ryper in her own kingdom where she could protect him.

Until the king had needed hostages.

To this day, Dash had no idea how Ryper had been sent off with others to Meara's court. But since it hadn't been a shock to Ryper when they met, he suspected his idiot brother had wanted to go there so that they could meet.

A typical Ryper thing to do.

And an uncommon one for their mother to send her child into danger. There was something to that story that Ryper didn't want to share, and though Dash wished he knew it, he was aware that no amount of threats or intimidation would loosen Ryper's tongue on the matter.

Unlike Renata, his brother kept his secrets.

And Ryper had been the only thing that had kept Dash from ripping Meara into pieces.

In spite of the hell she'd given them, he'd found his brother in her court. There, the two of them had forged a kinship far greater than blood. It was why he trusted Ryper, fully.

The only saving grace was that they weren't identical twins. Dash took after their father and Ryper their mother, right down to her ethereal blue eyes and impatience.

Until Tanis, no one had ever noticed their similarities.

Well... other than Marthen and their mother. But as their uncle who'd been present when they were born, Marthen had known they were related from the get-go.

"Why are you here, Marty?" Dash asked.

"I was coming to take one last look at the map when I happened upon you two cuddling like puppies. Your mother would be proud. Everyone else would be shocked and gossiping."

Dash ignored him. While Ryper was still close to their mother, Dash preferred to pretend she didn't exist. Mostly because he blamed her for not keeping both of them after they'd been born. His father had a wife. There was no reason to think that Cratus wouldn't eventually have had other children to inherit.

But their mother had wanted her blood on the Licordian throne, and it infuriated her that Dash refused to allow her to claim him now.

If she tried to let anyone know he was her son, he'd denounce her as a liar.

For all anyone knew, his mother had died at his birth.

And so long as Ryper didn't tell anyone they were brothers, no one could argue her case.

His only comfort was that so long as Ryper kept his silence, both her sons were as big a disappointment to her as she was to them.

But that was anger best left in the past.

Ryper nudged him. "Go to bed, Dash. You have a beautiful woman waiting for you."

That he did. For that reason only, he didn't argue. "You two should rest as well. We have a long journey ahead."

But he knew Ryper wouldn't sleep until he numbed himself.

Trying not to think about that either, he left them to find Tanis in their room upstairs.

She was already in bed, and the smile she greeted him with sent a wave of desire all the way to his rotten soul. Damn. Ryper was right. She was beautiful.

As he sat on the bed, she moved to help him pull his tunic off, then rested her hands gently on his shoulders. The softness of her touch singed him, and Dash took a moment to savor the sight of her warm and waiting for him.

Her dark brown eyes stared up at him as if he were all the things he'd ever wanted to be. In her eyes alone, he was noble. Decent. Heroic.

Not a despised king or a monster.

She made him feel like he was something more than the brutal demon who'd crawled out of Meara's cruelty.

You need to leave. He knew it. He had no business doing this with her. It made him no better than his hated father.

Ironically, that was what he'd said to himself every single time and still he couldn't resist her. He doubted if anything on this earth or beyond could get him out of this room tonight.

Because her touch healed him, and he was that selfish. She comforted his soul in a way nothing ever had.

I need her.

It was that simple and that impossible.

Tanis saw the look in his tormented eyes, and for a moment, she thought he would pull away from her and return to his planning.

Instead, he untied his laces, removed his pants, then slowly stretched out beside her. She shivered at the sight of his naked body lying beside hers.

His power and lithe grace was overwhelming. Her body ached and burned for his. And all she knew was that she wanted him. Even though this was impossible, and they had no future together.

She wanted to feel him inside her and share herself with him, to let him take whatever comfort or solace he could.

He lifted his hand to the laces of her gown and slowly opened the neck of it until she was bared to his hungry gaze. Tanis shivered at the dark, intense look on his face as he stared at her naked breasts.

She growled low in her throat as he trailed his hand over her tight, swollen nipples as if savoring the sight and feel of them before he took one into his palm and gently squeezed. She ground her teeth at the pleasurable sensation and her body melted.

Tanis wanted to claim his body too, to touch him in ways she hoped no other woman had ever touched him. She just wished she could make him see what a hero he was to her.

How much his kindness meant. How much she cherished every moment they had together.

He buried his lips against her throat, his breath branding her with heat. This was so vivid and hot. She'd learned to crave his touch in a way that scared her.

It was almost enough to make her want to be human forever.

But that was ridiculous.

Even so, she explored his body with her hands and delighted in the lean, masculine planes and dips. He was so hard and firm compared to her. His cheeks scratchy from his whiskers. And the manly scent of him sent her reeling.

Dash shook from the force of his raw emotions. She touched him on levels he'd never known existed. As he looked into those dark dragon eyes, he saw heaven itself. No woman had ever touched him like this. He'd never allowed himself such a comfort.

Never dared hope to possess it.

She was so giving to him. He drank the tenderness from her lips and tasted the goodness that was innate to her and so missing from him. She was an angel, and when he looked at her, he could almost believe in such things.

Rolling over, he pulled her on top of him so that he could cup her face in his hands and just stare into those precious dark eyes and the promises they held.

But he knew better than to believe in them. How could they ever have a future?

They weren't the same species. Look at what had happened with his own parents. Did he want to sire children who would be just as terrified and haunted as he was?

As Ryper?

It was one of the reasons he'd made sure that he never fathered children. There was no telling what they'd inherit from his mother. Naomi of the Tenmaru held powers that made Marthen appear weak and frail.

His own father had been scared of her at times. And Dash couldn't blame him. His mother was the only one alive who could give Meara a run for her money when it came to cruelty.

Those inherited powers were no doubt what had turned his horn black.

What had allowed him to survive captivity.

But he didn't want to think about that. Not while he was with Tanis.

She moved her head and kissed his open palm. The

gesture shook him. His heart pounding, he watched as she kissed her way up his arm to his lips.

Closing his eyes, he pulled her gown over her head, and relished the feel of her naked body against his.

Tanis moaned at the heat of his body under hers. Desire swept through her.

He gently rolled her over and placed himself between her legs. She felt the hairs of his legs rubbing against her inner thighs as he kissed her. Of his hard shaft resting against her thigh.

It was such a strange feeling to be so exposed to him. And yet it was so natural that they would share themselves. She reached up and ran her hands along his whiskered cheeks to bury them in his dark hair as she saw the needful hunger in his eyes.

"I am so glad you're with me, beast," she breathed.

Pain and pleasure mixed in his dark green eyes as he stared at her as if unable to believe he'd heard her. He looked as if he were dreaming and terrified of waking.

His muscles rippling beneath her hands, he pressed the tip of his shaft against her core.

Tanis held her breath in expectation.

He brushed his hand against her cheek. His gaze held hers as mutual understanding and care passed between them. It was a priceless moment of sharing.

Then he dipped his head and claimed her lips in a passionate, fiery kiss before he drove himself deep inside her body.

With every breath he took, she could feel him throbbing inside her. Feel him rigid and hard all over and in her.

Instinctively, she moved her hips, drawing him in

deeper as her muscles tightened around his shaft. He growled in response and a look of such pleasure crossed his face that it spurred her to bolder actions as she writhed beneath him.

Dash held his breath at the sight of her lying beneath him while she milked his body with hers. He held himself rigidly still even though it was killing him. He wanted her to want him, to not fear the desires of her own body.

She should take as much pleasure from this night as he did. More so, in fact. And he loved watching her discover her sexual power and bliss. If she had nothing else from him, he was glad that he'd taught her something more than fear of this.

Tanis was no longer timid with him. She was become almost feral with her desires, and nothing could please him more.

Growling at how good she felt, he thrusted himself deeper into her. They hissed in unison.

Never once in his life had he dared to hope of a night where he could be with a woman so unreservedly and know that she was with him by her own free will.

This had nothing to do with his rank or titles. She wasn't after him for his wealth.

She was here because she wanted to be.

Her red curls fanned out on either side of her face, reminding him of some beautiful fey creature who had stumbled upon him and claimed him with her magick. And she felt so good surrounding him. Surely there was no better pleasure than her being held in her arms.

She ran her hands over his chest and shoulders then brushed them through his hair.

He lowered himself to her and gathered her into his arms. Then slowly, very slowly, he began to gently rock himself between her thighs.

Tanis sighed in pleasure at the feel of him so deep, hard and strong inside her. She wrapped her arms around him and listened to his rapid breathing as he moved.

Arching her back to draw him in even deeper, she kissed his shoulder and inhaled the scent of him. He quickened his thrusts, sliding himself in and out of her, deeper and deeper. Her head spun from the sensations of his skin on hers, of his breath against her neck.

She breathed his name in his ear as she clung to him and met him stroke for stroke. Her body felt out of control. She was hot and tingly. And just as she was sure she would die from the pleasure of him, her body erupted into an ecstasy so intense that she screamed from it.

Dash ground his teeth at the sensation of her body gripping his while he kissed her deeply. Holding her tighter, he felt his own body release. With one last forceful thrust, he buried himself deep inside her and felt the waves of pleasure rippling through him as gave her a part of him he'd never given another single soul.

He lay completely still holding her for what seemed an eternity and yet it seemed to be no time at all.

"Is it always like this incredible?" she asked, her voice awed.

"Only with you."

She gave him a hard stare.

"I swear, Tanis. You can accuse me of many things, insincerity and flattery aren't two of them."

But as his senses returned, he knew he should have done anything other than make love to her.

Again.

And yet even as the thoughts whirled through his mind, he looked into her beautiful face and saw what he had waited a lifetime for.

All he had to do was find the courage to take it.

If only it was that easy. Honestly, he was terrified of the feelings inside him. Whenever he looked at her all those long-buried dreams resurfaced and made him wish for things he had no right to wish for.

Home. Family...

Love.

Love? You? You're a mongrel demonic bastard! Who'd ever want love from you? His father's cold words continued to haunt him even though he'd buried him long ago.

Sometimes dead wasn't dead enough.

Unable to breathe, he reluctantly withdrew from her, got up and dressed.

"Dash?"

The sound of her voice sliced through him. He paused at the door, torn between the need inside him to return to bed and take her into his arms and hold her forever, and the fear of her eventual rejection that made him want to bolt like a frightened colt.

For the first time in his life, he chose retreat. "I'll be back in a few minutes."

With no real direction on where to go, Dash returned to the great hall where he found Ryper alone, sitting at a table with bread and cake, drinking elfin ale.

"You do know *that,*" Dash indicated the cup of ale in Ryper's hand, "can be deadly to other species?"

Ryper actually smiled. "Hasn't killed me yet. Let's see how much I can drink before it does."

Shaking his head, Dash took the vacant seat next to his brother.

Ryper drained his cup and poured more. "Why did you come back?"

"Stupidity." Dash took an empty cup and poured it full.

Ryper grunted at him. "Well... as long as you hog it all. But don't be spreading it around. I have more than enough of it on my own. You keep the extra."

Ignoring the quip, Dash downed the ale in a single gulp, then poured another cup full.

"What a pair we make, eh?" Ryper sighed.

Dash drank this one a little more slowly. "How so?"

"Both of us tormented by our wonderful pasts."

Flinching at the thought, Dash fell silent as more memories surged. He knew the guilt and pain of his brother. Knew how much the past wore on Ryper's battered conscience. Just as it did his. "Thinking of Yutaka tonight?"

"Every night. His face haunts me whenever I try to sleep."

"I understand." Dash poured more drink. "I see the faces of all the ones we lost. They haunt me, too." He took another swig of ale as he tried not to think of all the children Meara had gleefully killed.

Ryper toyed with his cup. "At least most of those were strangers. I killed my own brother."

Dash winced at that. Yutaka had been their half-brother

courtesy of their mother's wandering lust, but he wasn't about to correct him as he knew Ryper didn't think of Yutaka as a half sibling any more than Dash thought of Renata that way.

Family was family. And they'd both lost too many of them.

Dash pushed his chair back so that he could level a glare at Ryper. "You had no choice or say in the matter. You did nothing wrong."

"I still killed him."

"It's not your fault," Dash repeated. He felt for him and would give anything to take away that guilt and pain.

Nothing ever would.

As they'd escaped from Meara's custody, Yutaka had seen the arrow aimed for Ryper. Before any of them realized they were about to be attacked, Yutaka had thrown Ryper to the ground and taken the arrow that had been meant for his older brother.

It was a sight neither of them had ever forgotten. Yutaka lying on top of Ryper as arrows landed all around them.

His battered face...

Worse? They'd been forced to leave him in a filthy puddle as rain fell over them.

Even now, he could see Yutaka in his mind, as if the event had been yesterday. The look of pain on his handsome features as he'd fallen away from Ryper.

I'll hold them back for you. Run to freedom.

Yutaka had fought to the bitter end. Had he not stayed behind to slow down their pursuers, they might not have escaped. They owed everything to his sacrifice.

Something Yutaka had definitely not learned from their heartless mother.

I'm sorry, little brother. And he was. Like Ryper, the guilt haunted him eternally.

That was why he'd been so determined and still was determined to make sure Tanis reclaimed her brother's skull. There was no worse feeling than to watch your brother die and not know what happened to the body.

For that alone, he'd wanted his father's throat.

Even though they'd just been children, they'd been thrown away like garbage. No one had expected them to survive, let alone return home.

Damn them all for their cruelty.

Ryper started to pour more ale, then tossed the goblet away and drank from the pitcher instead. "Why are you here when you have Tanis upstairs waiting for you?"

That was an easy question to answer. "Because I'm an idiot."

"Well, at least you know it."

Dash tossed a small loaf of bread at his brother. "Why don't you go to bed and sleep it off?"

"Eventually. Not drunk enough yet."

Dash would be concerned, except he knew that Ryper wouldn't get too drunk.

Neither of them dared. Their past didn't let them. They couldn't trust enough in others to be that out of control of their mental facilities.

Or their sword arms.

Especially not Dash. Even without a bounty on his head, he'd always had to guard against assassins and betrayers. Those who would love to see him dead for no other reason than he wore a crown.

And he couldn't stay here all night. They had a long

march ahead of them and probably a battle. While they could use an elfin portal to take them from here to the ruins where he'd found Renata's body, it was still going to be a long way to get to his palace.

Where he had an enemy waiting for him.

Along with a spy they had yet to find.

There was more than a good chance they'd be fighting again tomorrow.

Rising, he clapped Ryper on the back. "Get to bed soon."

"I will. Night, brother."

Dash ruffled his hair. It was rare for either of them to use that word for each other. They would use it for others, but rarely between themselves for fear of someone realizing what Tanis had.

Such knowledge could only endanger both their lives. It was the same reason why neither of them ever spoke a single word about their mother out loud.

Not even to each other.

That knowledge was lethal to both of them.

She wasn't just royalty...

Makkuro Naomi was a man-eating she-demon who lived to prey on others. Only one person had ever survived going up against her.

Their father.

Cratus's saving grace? Somehow, he'd managed to make her fall in love with him. That bizarre relationship baffled Dash to this day.

Well... perhaps not as much as it used to. Tanis was beginning to open his eyes to how his parents must have felt. To love someone even though you knew it was impossible to have them.

Maybe that was their real family curse. They could only love the ones they were destined to lose.

With a sigh, he headed back to bed where a beautiful dragon waited for him.

Along with all the fears that went with her. She was a part of him now. A vital part he didn't want to lose the way his father had lost his mother.

But it wasn't his place to ask her to stay.

What if she really is banished?

He would gladly welcome her to his home, but it would break her heart.

She was a dragon and he saw the sadness in her eyes whenever she spoke of it. Saw how much she'd enjoyed being in her real body, if only for a few minutes earlier today.

No, he had to set her free. It was the only decent thing for an indecent unicorn to do.

CHAPTER 22

Dash woke up to the sound of something pecking against his window. At first, he thought he was imagining it.

Until he heard the distinct pattern of the pecking.

Ronan.

Sliding away from Tanis so as not to awaken her, he pulled his pants on, then went to the window to push it open.

Sure enough, Ronan was there in that hawk form that he normally used whenever he had to travel fast.

"What are you doing here?" he asked. "I thought you were waiting for us in Licordia."

Ronan craned his bird neck to look inside. "You alone?"

Dash used his body to block Ronan's curious gaze so that he couldn't see Tanis who was naked in the bed except for the furs she had wrapped around her. "No. And I know that's not why you're here."

Even though he was a hawk, Ronan managed to give him an irritated smirk. It was quite impressive. "Aderyn wanted to update you."

That didn't bode well. "On?"

"Meara has heavily reinforced her army. She knows you're coming in through the elfin portal and that you have Ferox in custody."

Dash ground his teeth in aggravation. Hell of way to start the morning. Granted, he'd figured most of that was the case, but even so those plans told him something that just really stuck in his craw. "Who's her spy?"

"No idea, but they seem to know a lot about your plans."

Yes, they did. It infuriated him that the spy was able to hide so effectively among their group.

Not that they had to. Most of what Ronan told him was common knowledge. Baldur had given their plans over to his generals, who'd no doubt passed it along to their troops.

As for Ferox, everyone had seen him when they'd dragged him to his cage.

Ronan ruffled his feathers. "And not to pile shit onto you, but you do realize what happens in two more days?"

It would be time to cast the spell to trap his soul and kill him. "I do. I was trying not to think about it. Thanks for the reminder, Ro."

"Sorry, but that doesn't change the fact that we have to find Renata's wand, and all we know about it is that it's in the hands of some human's imp partner."

Dash frowned. "Human?" His ears honed right in on that single word. Was that the same human who'd killed his sister?

Ronan bobbed his bird head. "Like a fool, the human went to Meara and confessed it, thinking she'd reward him."

"I'm sure she did. Is he still alive? Or did she gut him on the spot?"

"Last our spies said, he's still screaming in her dungeon."

That gave him a degree of hope. All they had to do was get to him before Meara had him killed. "Good. I need you to pull him out and protect him until I get home."

"What about the trap?"

"I'm not going to walk into something I know exists."

Ronan bobbed his head again. "All right. I'll let everyone know the new plan. We'll get the human and wait for you at the lodge."

"Thanks, Ronan."

He winked at Dash then jumped from the ledge and flew off toward Licordia.

At least they knew where the human was now.

So long as Meara held the human and didn't cut his throat, they could get to the wand in time.

"Dash?"

He savored the sound of his name on Tanis's lips. Closing the window, he returned to bed to find her sitting up with a frown.

"Is everything all right?"

Not really, but he didn't want to worry her. "One of my men came with news."

"To the window?"

Dash grinned at her confusion. It was a weird rendezvous spot. "Ronan's a shape-shifter."

"Unicorn?"

"Not a unicorn. He came here as a falcon."

She cocked her head to study him. "Is that why you look so upset?"

Stunned at the ease with which she could read him, he arched a brow. "Pardon?"

"You look as if you've had bad porridge. Something doesn't agree with you. How bad was his news?"

He offered her a wicked grin. "I don't agree with anything that pulls me from your arms, Lady Dragon."

"I concur." Tanis crooked her finger for him.

As Dash moved toward the bed, something loud exploded outside the castle. It was so fierce that it rattled the windows and caused the floor beneath his feet to vibrate.

Tanis left the bed and grabbed her clothes. "Are we being attacked again?"

That was what it sounded like.

What it felt like.

Damn their timing for it.

Preparing for war, Dash used his powers to dress himself and her before he headed out the door and down the stairs.

More explosions sounded.

Elves ran down the hallway, shouting orders and gathering forces to head to the main courtyard.

It wasn't until Dash was outside the main door that he realized what was happening. *You've got to be kidding me...*

He cursed under his breath. If he didn't stop this quickly, there would be bloodbath.

"Stand down, Baldur!" he shouted at the elfin king. "It's not an enemy."

Baldur, Hinrik and Tova stared at him as if he'd lost his mind.

"How is this not an enemy attack?" Baldur asked.

Without warning, Ryper and Halla appeared by his side. "Is that who I—"

"Yes, it is," he said, cutting his brother off. It was exactly who Ryper thought.

Halla tsked then laughed.

"There's an army at my gate." Baldur crossed the bailey to stand in front of Dash. "Why should I stand down?"

Dash brushed his hands through his hair to smooth it. "They're on our side."

Baldur snorted in denial. "They're demons, oni... yokai! How in the Thirteen Kingdoms do you figure such beasts are on our side?"

Dash exchanged a grimace with Ryper. This was going to be an awkward explanation. And really, it was one he didn't even want to begin.

So instead, he asked Baldur the only pertinent question. "Who leads that army?"

"I do, of course." A smooth, deeply accented voice spoke from his left side.

Dash cursed at the unexpected appearance of his mother. She was so close to him that he jumped just as he normally did whenever Ryper snuck up on him. "I hate it when you do that." *Couldn't anyone in his family make some noise when they moved?*

She tsked. Which made Dash acutely aware of how many eyes were watching them.

But then Makkuro Naomi was a hard creature to miss. Taller than most females, she stood almost even in height to him and Ryper. And did so with a commanding presence that let everyone there know she wasn't just a queen.

She was a fierce, ruthless warrior who'd never been defeated in battle. Her long black hair was coiled beneath her orange and gold kabuto. What was easy to miss was the fact that the golden horns coming out from the sides of her helmet weren't decoration.

They were all hers. Along with those vibrant swirling blue eyes that appeared like a piercing summer sky with moving clouds. Because her irises were milky white, most assumed her to be blind.

That was their mistake. Ever vigilant, she was acutely aware of every heartbeat. And those eyes missed absolutely no detail no matter how small.

Even though she was dressed in armor reminiscent of a tiger's lethal body that came with a tiger skin cape, she was still the epitome of feminine grace and beauty.

As was befitting the empress of the Tenmaru—the kingdom of demons, oni, yokai and tengu. They possessed some of the strongest magick in all the world. As well as some of the most feared warriors.

When Naomi marched that army outside of her kingdom, most surrendered immediately. His father had been the rare exception. Which was why she'd resorted to trickery to defeat the unicorn race.

In the end, her plans had backfired.

Dash suspected it was a meeting of mutual lethality. His mother had met the only creature more barbaric and ruthless than she. If ever there had been two creatures who should never have spawned, it was his parents.

What the hell had the universe been thinking when it brought those two together?

Had his father not already had a wife, he was sure they would have united forces and ruled all the known realms. To this day, he had no idea how Renata's mother had survived. It would have been completely in character for either or both of his parents to murder her for their ambitions.

Yet neither had done so, and no one knew why.

"Your Majesty." Baldur bowed before her.

She didn't return the gesture. Instead, she stared at the elfin king as if he were something staining the bottom of her shoe.

Hinrik cleared his throat. "Does she not speak our language?" he asked Dash.

Naomi curled her lips. "Tell the insects that I don't speak to those beneath me."

Those words caused an eruption of activity.

Naomi held her hand up and immediately froze everyone in the bailey, except Dash, Ryper and her.

Dash let out a long sigh. "Really, Mother?"

"They annoy me, and I don't have time for their nonsense because they think they're not worthless when we know good and well that they are."

Dash shook his head. "Did you come all this way to say that?"

Lowering her hand and using her powers, she manifested his wanted poster. "Explain this to me."

A million snarky, rude retorts went through his head. But that would only serve to anger her and that never ended well for anyone. Even him. "It appears to be self-explanatory."

"Who are the seven kingdoms who dare to come at you?" she demanded. "I want the names of their rulers and the names of their children, parents, and anyone and anything they care about."

How typical of her to want to wipe out everyone her enemies cared for.

Ryper shrugged.

"We think it's a lie," Dash said. "No kingdom, other than Thassalia, has come forward to depose me."

The poster burst into flames and was carried away on the breeze. "Better be a lie. If you are deposed, it won't go well for any of the other kingdoms. My wrath will be eternal and excruciating."

He wanted to remind her of the fact that he'd been sent to Meara to be tortured as a colt but knew better than to bring that up. That had never been her idea. Rather, the brainchild of his father. And the one time he'd made the mistake of mentioning it to her, she'd used her powers to reassemble his father's corpse from his ashes just to desecrate it.

The one thing they knew about their mother...

She wasn't the most stable of creatures.

To this day, he didn't know or understand how Ryper and Yutaka had been sent to Meara.

Until his mother had lost control when he'd brought the subject up, he'd always assumed that she'd sent them as his father had with him. Too late, he'd learned Naomi didn't willingly put her children in harm's way.

That was the biggest difference between his mother and father.

When she'd sent him to his father, she'd assumed his

father would care for him. Cratus was lucky Dash had been the one who'd killed him during their fight.

Regardless of her love for him, Cratus's death at Naomi's hands would have been far more brutal had she known how he'd treated her son.

With an imperious air, Naomi swept her gaze over the ones she'd frozen. "I assume you're marching to take back your kingdom."

"Of course."

With a curt nod, she placed her hand over the hilt of her sword. "My soldiers are yours. Show us the enemy and we'll annihilate them for you."

That he had no doubt about. "Thank you. And while you're being so accommodating, could you please unfreeze the rest of my army?"

Pursing her lips, she glared at him. "Must I?"

"Please."

She held her hands out to Ryper. "Give us a hug before we do so."

Ryper stepped into her arms. "Good to see you, *Kaasan*."

She kissed his cheek and released him, then turned toward Dash. "And you."

"Rather not."

That caused her nostrils to flare. "We are your mother. Unless you wish for it to be known to all, hug us."

Emotional blackmail. Her forte.

"Fine." He gave her a very quick hug then stepped aside. "Good enough?"

"No." Reaching up, she yanked his hair. "You are ever my insolent boy. You're too much like your father." She spit on the ground. "Bastard that he was."

She stepped away from him then unfroze everyone. "Tell them that we will await you outside. When you're ready to march, let us know and we'll show you how our army travels."

That he already knew. It was a lot faster than even the elfin portals or dragon wings.

Hence why no one wanted to fight the Tenmaruns. They weren't just lethal. They were terrifying.

"Who was that?" Tanis asked as she joined them, with Halla in tow.

He glanced over his shoulder at them.

Ryper flashed an annoying grin at him. "Yes, Dash. Who *was* that?"

"Shut up." He shoved at his brother, then turned toward Tanis. "That was Naomi *Ōgimachi*. The empress or queen of Tenmaru."

Tanus frowned. "Is she an empress or queen?"

"She's whatever she wants to be," Ryper said.

Baldur joined them. "What is she doing here?"

Dash gestured toward the gate that separated them from his mother's forces. "Lending us her army."

"But why?" Baldur asked.

Ryper flashed him another annoying grin before he stepped away, laughing.

I hate you, brother. Ryper was enjoying this just a little too much.

Dash took a second to consider the best answer. "She's agreed to uphold her oath to the High King. Not to mention, she has a personal grudge against Meara." He saw the curious frown on Tanis's face, so he explained it with the truth. "Naomi's son, Yukata, was killed escaping from

Meara."

The sympathy in her eyes was so sincere that he actually felt it. "I'm so sorry."

"Not as sorry as Meara will be if Naomi gets her claws into her. I'm not sure I'll be able to stop that beat-down." Nor was he sure if he wanted to. Honestly, he'd love to see his mother give that bitch what she deserved.

Unlike him, Naomi didn't have a contract with Meara that prevented her from killing the centaur queen.

Tova joined them. "Have any of you happened to peek over the wall this morning?"

"No, why?" Dash asked.

"You should probably go see the size of the army Tenmaru has brought. Are we sure they're here to fight *for* you? 'Cause if they're not, it's going to be a bad day for anyone standing at your side."

Scowling, Dash headed for the parapets with Tanis following behind him.

He climbed up and then froze at the terrifying sight.

Shit...

Were there any soldiers left in Tenmaru?

Marthen appeared by his side then clapped him on the back. "Looks like someone wants to keep you safe, Majesty."

Dash was aghast at his mother's army. "Just don't with me, Marthen."

He laughed. "I wouldn't want to be a centaur right now."

Dash agreed, especially given what was ahead of them. "Then we better get on the march before their spy warns them, and they have time to route us."

TANIS WAS GATHERING the last of her belongings from their bedroom when she felt the air behind her stir. She turned, half-expecting it to be Dash.

Instead, the Tenmaru queen stood there in all her fierce glory. And it was glorious. The queen was absolutely stunning in her beauty.

Tanis swallowed hard. Not from fear, but there was an air about the queen that let everyone know she was not to be trifled with. Naomi's powers caused the hair on the back of Tanis's arms to stand on end. Those powers literally charged the air around them.

"Majesty," she said, curtsying. "To what do I owe this honor?"

Naomi cocked her head as she studied Tanis with those eerie blue, deep-set eyes. "You're a dragon." Not question. Just a mere statement of fact.

Even so, Tanis felt the need to confirm it. "I am."

Without another word, Naomi closed the distance between them and took a handful of her red hair. The queen wrapped her hand in it and held Tanis's hair in her fist. It wasn't painful, but it was firm. "You love him."

Tanis wasn't sure what to say. Again, it wasn't a question. The queen seemed to like to speak in short, direct sentences with her beautiful, lilting accent.

And still, the queen held her hair. "Have you any idea the nightmare of your fate?"

Tanis didn't like the sound of that, and she wasn't quite

certain what Naomi was talking about. "I don't know... what fate?"

"To love outside your species."

Sadness choked her at a reminder she didn't need. One that haunted her constantly. "Of course, I do."

Shaking her head, the queen released her finally. "You think so, but no you don't. You have no idea what you'll face. What your children will have to endure." She swept a look over Tanis that made her feel as if she were lacking something.

Then, she waved her hand. "This will not do."

Tanis was aghast. Was she insulting her? *What did I do to make her hate me?* "Beg pardon?"

Without answering, the queen snapped her fingers, and in an instant Tanis's clothes were changed to Tenmaru armor. She even had a tiger skin cape that matched the queen's.

Naomi nodded in approval. "Much better. That befits royalty."

Befuddled by the unexpected gift and why the queen would give her such, Tanis offered her a tentative smile. "Thank you, Majesty."

She inclined her head to Tanis. "No weapon of any kind will penetrate that armor. Continue to protect Deciel and there will be many more gifts for you."

Then, she vanished in a cloud of dark smoke.

Stunned over the encounter, Tanis stood there, half-expecting this to be a dream.

Why would the Tenmaru queen give her such a thing?

For that matter, why was protecting Dash important to the queen of oni and yokai?

A sudden, horrible suspicion went through her. *I better be wrong.*

But nothing else made sense.

She quickly finished packing, then went to find her errant... whatever he was. Boyfriend. Irritant. She stopped short of calling him a lover because that just didn't feel right to her. She'd thought they had a deeper connection than that. At least it felt deeper to her.

But what if he didn't feel the same?

Dash was standing beside Ryper when she found him. Ryper's gaze danced over new armor as the color faded from his face. He nudged Dash who looked at him until Ryper jerked his chin in her direction.

Only then did Dash turn toward her. He duplicated Ryper's actions of scanning her armor and paling greatly.

That only confirmed her suspicions. "Why didn't you tell me you had a relationship with the Tenmaru queen?"

Dash sputtered. "It's not something we speak of in public. Ever."

That actually angered her. "So we're... what? Cast-offs? You sleep with us and then we're ignored as if we never existed?"

Ryper burst out laughing.

Dash's expression was one of deep confusion and horror. "What?"

"She thinks..." Ryper couldn't finish the sentence as he broke off into another peal of laughter. He pounded Dash on the back.

Again, Ryper tried to speak, and still he continued to laugh.

"Stop!" Dash shoved him away from them. "Go over there and be stupid!" He pointed to a corner of the room.

Choking and laughing, Ryper actually obeyed him.

That only angered her more. "Why is this so funny?"

Dash stared at her. *"She's not an old lover of mine."* Then he curled his lip. "Why are you dressed like her?"

"She told me to protect you. If she's not an old flame who still has feelings for you, why did she give this to me? And why does she care so much about your well-being?"

Dash growled in his throat as he considered the best way to explain this. A thousand lies went through his mind, but none of them were believable.

Ironically, the most rational lie was the one Tanis had jumped to. That they were lovers. But he just couldn't make his mind go there.

Not with his *mother*...

He shivered at the very thought.

"Answer me, Dash. What is she to you?"

Ryper broke off into another round of laughter so hard that he actually slid down the wall to sit on the floor. If he didn't stop that, Dash was about to be missing another sibling.

He didn't want to answer that question, but if he didn't, his dragon was about to take a significant portion of his unicorn hide and nail it to the wall.

The last thing he wanted was for this day to start with a fight. Especially with her. They both had too much they needed to be focused on.

So, he did what he'd never done before... he let her in on his secret.

"She's my mother, Tanis."

Her jaw fell open as he sent those words to her mind. "Wait... what?"

He nodded. *"All my life. And that is not information anyone knows or needs to know."*

She gave him an irritated smirk before she cast her gaze to the hyena who continued to laugh. "Say you. Given *his*... reaction, are you telling me that he doesn't know?"

"He's my brother, as you noted earlier. That's why he's laughing. Please, don't tell anyone."

Tanis took a moment as those words echoed through her head. Not just what he was telling her. The fact that he gave her a secret he'd never given to anyone.

Other than those who knew because they knew.

Not to mention that it was a well-known fact that Dash was bastard born, but the common belief was that his mother had been a high-ranking unicorn who'd died giving birth to him.

No one had ever guessed *this*. No wonder he held the powers he did. He was half oni.

Half oni. Those words staggered her. And it explained so much about him. When he talked about an inner demon, she'd thought he was being poetic. Metaphoric.

No. In his case, it'd been literal.

"Are you all right?" Dash asked, putting his hand on her arm to help steady her.

She nodded. "I'm just trying to make sense of this. It was not what I was expecting you to say."

At least now she understood why he never spoke of his mother. Why he and Ryper were so cautious around others. Given how much the unicorns despised the Tenmaru, there was no telling how they'd react.

It was possible they'd revolt and overthrow him.

Yes, this was one hell of a secret he'd just given her. One that could destroy not only Dash, but his entire kingdom.

She stared up at him. "No one else knows?"

Dash let out a long breath before he made a face. *"Just my uncle."*

She leaned in to whisper, "What uncle?"

"Marthen."

Of course. She should have known. Now that he said it, she could see the similarities in their features. Even more in Ryper's.

"Anyone else I need to know about?" Tanis asked.

"Other secrets aren't mine to give. Please realize that I've given you something that I don't want anyone else to know about."

That made sense to her. Although if she had a mother as powerful and respected as Naomi, she'd want to shout it from the highest parapet. There were times he must feel the same.

How awful to have that fear inside. For both of them. It had to be hard to never be able to publicly claim each other as family.

That made her ache for him.

"Have no fear, Dash. I won't tell a soul."

Still laughing, Ryper rejoined them. "That is going to crack me up for a long time to come."

Dash grimaced. "You're sick."

"Yes, I am. Can you blame me given our childhood?" Ryper indicated Tanis with a nod. "I assume you told her?"

"I did."

He clapped Dash on the back. "You know, I think you're pissed about the wrong thing."

"How so?"

"We're not the ones dressed in oni armor. Apparently, the queen picked a favorite and it's not us." He squeezed Dash's shoulder. "I'm going to let that sink into your thick skull while I go find Dove."

Tanis rose up on her toes and kissed Dash's cheek. "I know that look. I often had it when my brother irritated me to the point I wanted to skin him to make a pair of shoes."

His gaze softened as he smiled. "At least I don't have to worry about you in battle any longer. She told you about the armor, correct?"

"That nothing can penetrate it. Yes."

"And the rest?"

Her stomach sank at his tone. What had Naomi withheld? "Rest what?"

Dash rolled his eyes. "I should have known she wouldn't..." He let his voice trail off before he spoke louder. "Koji say hello."

"Shh," a disembodied voice said. "Naomi-Joou told me not to say a word as it might scare her."

Tanis gasped. "Who is that?"

"Your armor is tsukumogami."

While it was sexy the way that rolled off his tongue, she was confused. "Sue... what?"

"Sue-koo-moe-gah-me. Easiest way to explain it is that your armor has a mind of its own. That's how it's able to protect you. Koji will fight with you and help you in battle."

"I can possess you, too, if you like."

"Don't." Dash's tone was filled with warning. "I seriously doubt Tanis would appreciate the experience."

"No, Tanis would not," she quickly agreed. The thought of her armor taking control of her was a bit more than she could handle at present. "But he can talk to me?"

Dash nodded. "And he hears everything you say."

Tanis wasn't sure what to think about that. Happy? Or creeped out?

She was definitely leaning more toward creeped out.

"Don't worry," Koji said. "You'll get used to me. And I won't let any harm come to you, princess. You're safer with me than anywhere else." It felt as if he literally gave her a hug over her entire body.

This was definitely going to take some getting used to.

Along with the fact that Dash was part oni. Granted, dragons didn't know much about them other than to avoid them. She'd never fought against one personally, but from the stories she'd heard, no one wanted to. During the worst of the Warlord Age, the Tenmaru had been on the verge of taking over every kingdom.

Only three had remained independent. Licordia. Indara. Pagos.

All the others had fallen to the Tenmaru armies. No one had ever understood how it was that Cratus had been able to negotiate with Naomi to keep her from invading Licordia. Or more than that, to allow him to be crowned High King of all Thirteen Kingdoms when she'd been the one who'd conquered most of them.

Now Tanis understood. His mother had never ceded her power to Cratus. She'd stepped down knowing that one day her son would be High King in Cratus's place.

Tanis also knew why Dash had kept it secret. The Licordians would never trust a king with demonic blood in him. They'd be terrified that he'd allow his mother to occupy their lands.

As for the other kingdoms, they were liable to unite against him to defeat him for fear of Licordia uniting with Naomi and invading them all again.

Everyone was suspicious and hate-filled when it came to the Tenmaru.

Although, given the size of the army his mother had brought to Alarium to fight with the unicorn king, attacking Dash seemed like the worst idea ever imagined.

Indeed, Tanis would say that his mother had very strong feelings for her son, and intended to protect him no matter what.

Keegan came out of the barn to join them. "Morning, Majesty..." She tilted her head to Tanis. "Princess."

Tanis smiled at her. "Good morning. I see you've regained your size."

"And if feels wonderful." Keegan stretched out her wings and flapped them.

Which knocked down three passersby.

Keegan blushed and quickly tucked them in. "Sorry! So sorry."

Tanis laughed until a loud scream rent the sky above them.

Eyes wide, she looked up to see a milky-white, iridescent, giant bird flying over their heads. One that had the body of a man.

This one she knew without asking. *Karura*. The devourer of dragons. Her stomach sank at the sight of the boogey creature her mother had used to frighten her with when she'd been small.

Keegan ducked her head down, and as funny as it was sad, tried to hide herself beside the much smaller Dash. "What is *that* doing here?"

Dash shrugged. "He's Naomi's best friend, Kyran. She's never gone to battle without him."

Tanis put her hand on Dash's arm to steady herself. "I don't like Kyran. Not at all."

"Neither do I," Keegan said quickly.

"It's all right, dragons. Kyran doesn't kill indiscriminately. He won't harm you."

He said that, but her fear didn't have ears, and neither did Keegan's. All of her people had been taught to run from the Karura.

The only good news... no centaur would be able to stand against *that*. It was said that their fire burned hotter than any dragon's. Hence why they were heralded as the destroyer of dragons.

Dash cupped Tanis's chin in his palm until she met his gaze. "No harm will come to you. Just breathe, dragon. You're safe."

"What about me?" Keegan asked.

"You, too. I promise, Kyran won't go after you. I had the discussion with Naomi, and she's sworn to me that all of our troops will be safe from hers."

While Tanis believed him, it was still hard to get past that terrifying sight of a monster she was brought up fearing.

Tova walked past them and scoffed at their embrace.

"Just kiss her for the gods' sakes, and let's get on with this ride."

Tanis laughed at Tova's surly tone and unexpected comment.

Giving her a smile, Dash kissed her quickly, then turned into a unicorn.

Tanis pulled herself up into the saddle as Halla rushed past them to join Ryper. Dash waited for her to get situated before he headed to the main gate where the others waited on horseback.

Wings sprang out of Ryper's back so that he could fly beside them in his human body with Halla by his side. Impressive. And it made her wonder if Dash had the same ability to have wings in his human body, too.

Maybe I don't know all their secrets.

It appeared they had many more than she could even guess at. Not that it mattered. They were heading to war with Keegan right behind her. That was what she needed to focus on.

Her heart pounded as she saw the huge glistening portal that Naomi had created for them. It made a mockery of the smaller elfin portals many used that often appeared as shrines to their gods.

Though she'd seen those portals, she'd never been through one. As a dragon, she was far too large.

This portal, however, was huge enough to accommodate the Karura and Keegan traveling through it side-by-side. Not that she would recommend the two of them trying to do such a thing.

Still...

It appeared as a giant mirror, except that it didn't reflect.

Rather it showed the green, wooded lands on the other side where they were heading.

Licordia.

She turned around to look at their numbers. They were an odd assembly for an army. Elves, oni, demons, yokai, a hobgoblin, a dragon, and a unicorn who held her heart.

She ran her hand through Dash's silken mane. Leaning over his neck, she whispered her one and only secret in his ear. "Before our battle, beast, there's something I want you to know... I love you, Deciel Coeur de Noir. And I'm praying for your safety."

CHAPTER 23

Dash stumbled as Tanis's words reached his ears. Had he heard them correctly? Honestly, he wasn't sure. "What?"

She leaned over his neck again and gave him a fierce hug with her entire body. "I love you, my beast. Should anything happen to either of us today, I wanted you to know *my* secret, as the last thing I want is to die without having told you."

Tanis gasped as Dash literally disintegrated from beneath her. She started to fall into the dark shadow only to have it wrap around her and pull her against the rock-hard body she'd come to know so well.

Before she could speak, he gave her a kiss so fierce that it left her breathless. Hot and cold. It was demanding and carried with it an unbelievable passion.

Everything faded away as she breathed him in and felt his strength enveloping her entire body.

At least until Dove cleared his throat to get their attention. "Anyone happen to notice an army going by? War coming? Any of this sound familiar?"

Dash pulled away from her lips to give him a stern glower. "Must you?"

"Must I annoy you? Yes. Battle..." He pointed over Tanis's shoulder. "That way. You might want to join us since we are actually fighting for *your* kingdom, High King Hard-head."

Ryper flew back toward them. He opened his mouth to speak only to have Dash hold his hand up to silence him.

"*You,* go. I don't want to hear it," Dash said in a voice that brooked no argument. "We'll be along right behind you."

Rolling their eyes, the two of them, along with Halla, drifted off into the army.

Dash cupped her face and smiled down at her. "Wish you'd told me sooner, Dragon."

"Sorry. I've never had good timing in anything."

His eyes burning her with their tenderness, he shook his head. "Not true. You are perfect in every way." He returned to being a unicorn.

Tanis was aghast as she found herself back in the saddle. How did he do that?

"And for the record, Dragon. I love you, too." With those words spoken, he flew through the portal and landed them next to a beautiful manor hall.

Tanis barely had time to take everything in as her head reeled from his declaration.

Dash loved her. While a part of her had suspected as much, it was different hearing it from his lips. That made it more permanent. More real.

He loved her. That knowledge had her heart soaring. How

could this even be possible? She'd headed out on her journey to find her brother's killer.

And she'd found the last thing she'd ever expected to have.

Someone who loved her.

How could this be?

She'd been hated for so long that the thought of anyone loving her was as alien a concept as Karura and Keegan becoming best friends.

It just didn't seem right.

Amazed, she savored the sensation of Dash carrying her up a small rise toward a manor house that sat on the hill as if it owned it. Regal. Polished, it was a great thing of beauty.

But that wasn't what she was focused on. She wanted to talk in private with Dash. There were so many things she wanted to ask him.

Tell him.

Please let us have that time later...

As Dash started for the house, a crow flew at them. "They've been taken, Sire."

Dash froze as he heard Chrysis's words. "What?"

"Meara's centaurs struck just after Ronan left to find you. They took the Outlaws hostage."

He was baffled by her words. How could this have happened? The Outlaws were natural born warriors. Every one of them.

Even outnumbered, they should have escaped. Especially Elpis. As an oni, she couldn't be held unless she wanted to.

"What of Ronan?"

"He returned after they were taken. Once I told him

what happened, he went after them so he could gather intel for you. He's in the trees around your palace, watching and waiting to give you a report."

"And Meara?" he asked.

"She has her army gathered at the elfin portal to wait for you to come through it."

Well at least Meara hadn't learned of their new plan. Small comfort that, but it was a comfort, nonetheless. And he'd gladly take it.

Dash glanced around at their troops and considered the best way to handle this. It was hard to attack when he didn't know where his friends had been taken.

No, where his family had been taken. The Outlaws were the closest thing to a family he'd ever known. He couldn't put them in danger, even though he knew they could take care of themselves. The last thing he wanted was to give an order that cost one of them their lives. Especially not after losing Renata.

"Ryper?" he called for his brother who immediately flew to his side then tucked his wings in.

"You want me to secure the Outlaws?" Ryper asked.

That was why his brother was so valuable to him. He knew his thoughts without Dash having to voice them. "Take some of Naomi's army with you. No need in doing something that dangerous without backup."

Ryper inclined his head to him before he manifested his staff and walked toward their mother to ask about taking those soldiers.

Dash considered his options. It would be a forty-minute march for the elves to reach the portal. His mother's soldiers could get there in seconds. Long before one of Meara's spies could reach her.

Divide and conquer.

"Commanders?" He summoned the elves to him as Tanis slid from his back and he transformed to his human body.

Dash met Baldur's curious stare as Hinrik, Tova, the twins and their other leaders joined him. But his first comment wasn't to Baldur. "Tanis, I want you, Keegan and the elves to march to my palace and secure it."

She arched one vibrant red brow. "Where are you going?"

"I need to lead the others through a portal to route Meara."

Tanis opened her mouth to protest.

Dash laid a tender finger against her beautiful lips. "I need you to secure my palace. Last I heard, your brother's killer is there. You have an oath to fulfill, and I have a queen to kill."

The concern in her dark eyes warmed him. "I would rather guard your back."

"And I have no one else I can trust to secure my throne and hold it."

Tanis froze as she heard Dash's words in her head. But surely, she wasn't the only one he trusted. "What of Dove?"

"He'll go with you to protect you and show you the back road to the palace."

"Who'll protect *you*?" she insisted.

He glanced over to his mother. "Naomi isn't going to risk a centaur being crowned High Queen or King. She hates them more than I do."

Nice way of publicly hedging while speaking an absolute truth. He was a politician. And a damn good one.

She narrowed her gaze. "Fine. I better see you at the palace."

"You will. Promise."

She pulled him against her and took a moment to savor their embrace, while praying it wasn't the last one they'd share. "Don't break my heart, beast," she whispered in his ear.

Dove kicked his horse forward as Dash pulled away to join his mother. "Don't worry, Tanis. He might be a unicorn, but he has nine lives."

She laughed at the thought. "Thank you, Dove."

"My pleasure."

Viggo rode to her side. "It'd be my honor to share my horse with you, princess." He held his arm down for her.

Smiling, she took his hand and allowed him to pull her up behind him. "Thank you, Viggo."

"You're very welcome. Besides, my mother would have my arse if I let anything happen to you or the High King."

"Well, we can't have that." Smiling, Tanis held on to him as he kicked his horse forward to follow after Dove.

And if she had any doubts about her feelings for Dash, this quelled them. While Viggo was also exceptionally handsome, it was like riding with her brother. She felt none of the electricity or desire Dash caused every time he came near her.

The difference was remarkable.

You better stay safe, beast. Having found Dash, she couldn't bear the thoughts of returning to her solitary life.

She had no idea how they'd manage this relationship going forward, but she was determined to try.

D ASH PAUSED beside his mother who was riding a huge okuri inu—yokai wolf. Bigger than even a bear, it made his mother look tiny on its back.

"I thought the okuri inu were escorts."

She gave him a peeved stare. "He is escorting me. Straight to battle, or are we wasting time?"

"We're going for Meara. Can you have your dragon conceal himself?"

"He's not a dragon... he's a dragon-eater."

Dash shook his head. "Whatever he is, he's large enough to give them warning and time to attack."

Naomi whistled to the Karura. He instantly vanished, yet Dash knew Kyran was still there. He could feel the thrumming breeze caused by Kyran's wings.

"Thank you."

Naomi inclined her head to him. "Lead us to victory, my precious king." She pulled the reins for her okuri inu and turned it toward the elfin gate and the portal she'd created for their larger members.

One by one, all the members of her army vanished. This was why his father had been determined to wipe the Tenmaruns out. They were almost impossible to battle. If you weren't one of them, you couldn't see them coming.

Dash didn't have that problem. Being part oni, he had no trouble seeing them as moving wisps.

In all honesty, he was grateful that Tanis wasn't with them. While he knew her armor would protect her, he really didn't want to see her in battle.

Especially not after her confession.

Trying not to think about that or how much he really did love her, too, he ducked through his mother's portal and came out with his mother's troops near the ruins where he'd found Renata's body.

It was hard to believe so little time had passed. In some ways, it seemed an eternity.

Right now, it was a blink and that blink hit him hard. He could see the image of his sister lying dead in the grass. Feel his grief over her loss anew.

Don't think about it.

He needed to focus on the battle and not his emotions.

As much as he'd loved his sister, he loved Tanis even more. This fight was for her. To make sure she had a safe place where no enemy could touch her. Where no dragon could ever again make her feel like she was unworthy when she was the noblest creature he'd ever had the honor of knowing.

She was his heart, and he would make sure no one ever again hurt her.

As they neared the centaur army, Dash stopped.

"*Why do you hesitate,* waga ko?" His mother's voice was loud and clear in his head.

He jerked his chin at their enemies. "*Take Meara hostage. Do not kill her.*"

His mother gave him a fierce scowl. "*Why ever not?*"

"*Because I want to torture her.*"

"Oh. Why didn't you say so?"The proud smile on her

face sent a chill down his spine. There was the evil mother he knew so well.

The world had no idea how lucky it was that his father had been married when the two of them met. Though to be honest, he was surprised neither of his parents had murdered Renata's mother just to get her out of their way.

He really did wonder how Shalia had escaped that death sentence.

Not that it mattered.

Right now, the only thing of importance was the army that had yet to detect them.

Dash met his mother's gaze. "They're your troops, *Gosei no kimi*—" Sovereign lady. "You call it."

She didn't hesitate. Her order for battle rang out. The oni rushed forward to attack.

Turning into a unicorn, Dash ran straight for Meara as she and her troops turned around in a panicked frenzy to battle them.

Decades worth of pent-up fury drove his hooves into the ground and carried him quickly toward his sole target. He wanted to bathe in Meara's blood. To let her know the fear and horror that she'd mercilessly meted out to him and his brethren.

Over and over, he saw the faces of the young hostages who'd died from her beatings and abuse.

Saw Yutaka. The guilt, grief and anger inside him demanded blood vengeance.

Meara would pay for it.

One of her human soldiers rode out to cut him off. Dash was having none of that. He turned human to slash at the first one who reached him, then blasted the second one with a fireball Tanis would have been proud of.

He cut through them with little effort. Returning to his unicorn body, he leapt over the third one.

Meara drove back the oni she was fighting just as Dash reached her.

He lowered his head, intending to skewer her with his horn just enough to wound her.

His unicorn horn caught her shoulder at the same time he felt something hot pierce his side. Thinking it was a dagger or sword, he started to laugh until he realized what she had in her hand.

Renata's wand.

Dash went down hard. Everything around him began to swim. He couldn't focus his gaze. Unimaginable pain tore through him as he lay on his side and looked up at the cold bitch he hated most.

Hers was the last face he wanted to see. Meara had haunted him enough.

Closing his eyes, he conjured an image of Tanis. His only regret was that he would break her heart, after all.

Please forgive me, my dragon.

NAOMI FELT the pain in her side and knew in an instant that her son had been stabbed.

Not by regular means.

That damn horn from that whiny little bitch she should have strangled at birth. *Damn you, Cratus!*

Why had she allowed him to talk her into mercy?

Unmitigated rage tore through her as she flew from the back of her mount and made her way through the air to her son. If she lost her baby to them...

She'd bring them back to life to torment them for eternity!

Meara looked up at her approach and paled. With a shriek of terror, she ran into the crowd.

The only thing that saved the centaur from her wrath was the sight of Dash lying on the ground, bleeding. Naomi lowered herself to him so that she could pull his unicorn head into her lap. He was barely breathing.

"Kyran!" She summoned her second-in-command.

In the form of a man, he appeared instantly at her side, then paled as he saw the condition Dash was in. *"Gosei no kimi?"*

"Kill them all, except for their leader. I want Meara alive!" She would enjoy making her suffer and if Dash died, Meara would pray for death, too. "And find that damn wand!"

For now, she had to attend to her son, and Marthen better know some spell to save Dash's life.

Otherwise, she'd be mourning her brother, too.

CHAPTER 24

Tanis and her group slowed as they neared Clovenshire Castle, the legendary home of the High King of the Thirteen Kingdoms. Made of stone, it was breathtaking and ominous against the mountain range behind it and the massive glistening lake to the right. Perfectly situated so that only one road led to it. A road that could be easily fortified against an invading army.

"Let me go on ahead," Chrysis said. "I'll be back with a report from Ronan."

Tanis nodded even though she had a strange feeling. "Something's not right."

Viggo turned in the saddle to look at her over his shoulder. "What do you mean?"

"Do you not feel it? Something's off." She had a sick feeling in her stomach that she couldn't explain.

After a few minutes, Chrysis returned with what she assumed was Ronan flying right behind her in the shape of a hawk.

Turning human, Ronan approached them. Tanis's eyes widened at the size of the man. Here she'd thought Dash was tall, but this one was at least a head taller with muscular broad shoulders. His dark brown hair held gold highlights and fell to his shoulders. There was something almost regal about his presence that was mitigated by his lethality.

And his features...

He was devastatingly handsome, with a rugged jaw line a set of dimples that flashed when he grinned at them.

"We've taken the palace," he announced proudly.

She gaped at his news. "What? How?"

He shrugged nonchalantly. "They didn't leave that many behind. What they did leave..." He grinned even wider. "Well, they were no match for our group. Poor things had no idea what they were in for when they brought the lions into their den."

Tanis glanced around at her group. "Should we head toward the portal to give the High King backup?"

Baldur rode to her side. "Let's secure the palace. This is the High King's seat of power. We need to make sure Meara doesn't circle back and retake it."

That made sense. And Dash had charged her with securing it for him. Tanis nodded. "We'll follow your lead, Sire."

He inclined his head, then ordered the others to follow him inside.

Ronan walked beside her as he they headed for Dash's home. "Are you all right, princess?"

"I have a bad feeling."

"There's nothing here. That, I can definitely assure you. We killed a few, and the rest are being held in the dungeon."

That made her feel a little better.

As did the presence of Keegan flying overhead. If anyone came toward them, she'd be able to see it for miles.

Still, Tanis couldn't shake her unease.

As they drew nearer Dash's home, Tanis was awed by the large, dark gray stones that climbed toward the sky. It was a mammoth fortress that spread out into a perfect square. Each corner was anchored by a tall square tower.

She expected that square and those towers to be the castle, until they rode through the gate. Inside was a spectacular manor house nestled against the far wall. It was as elegant as the outside was intimidating. No wonder Licordia was given such deference.

"It's beautiful."

Ronan nodded. "Indeed. Dash's ancestors built it over three hundred years ago to hold back those who wanted to invade and tear the unicorns down. There was a time, not that long ago, when the last of the unicorn race held only this area and were driven almost to extinction."

That was terrifying to think about.

And thankfully, the center part inside the gate had an exceptionally large field that allowed Keegan to land.

Sliding off the horse, Tanis headed for the main building.

Inside was even more illustrious. The stone walls were covered with elaborate tapestries, banners and weapons. She could just imagine Dash walking through here as both a unicorn and human. The whole place was as commanding and fierce as he was.

"Excuse me? What is all this?" An older man rushed through the hall, as if he, alone, was going to drive them out. Irritated and stern, he glared at all of them.

Ronan stepped around her. "It's all right, Kronnel. Dash sent them on ahead to secure the palace for him."

"I don't like this. Not at all."

"You never like anything, you old warhorse," Halla quipped. "And you need to be finding a servant to prepare a room for Princess Tanis."

As Tanis started past one of the rooms on her left, she paused. The door was ajar and inside...

No. It couldn't be.

Without saying a word to the others, she headed for the door and pushed it wider. Then she froze as she saw exactly what she thought she'd seen.

There, on a large, dark mahogany table lay her brother's skull. It was really here, as if fulfilling Dash's promise to her that he'd return it.

Tears filled her eyes. For a moment, she thought her legs might buckle. But somehow, she found the strength to walk toward the table.

Granted, this could be any dragon skull and it could have been here for years. She really had no way of knowing. But she didn't think Dash would be the type to keep a trophy like this. Especially since it wasn't on display. It merely rested out in the open.

Kronnel started toward her, but Ronan and Halla cut him off.

"Where did the skull come from?" Tanis asked.

Ronan approached her slowly. "It's your brother's. The

one who killed him was taken into Meara's custody. He turned it over to her, trying to keep her from killing him."

That succeeded in freeing her tears. Choking on a sob, she ran to the table so that she could place her hand on the spindly ridges at the top of his skull. Even now, she could see Davin as he'd been. His glorious scales gleaming in the light as he moved gracefully.

Davin laughing at her before he chided her over something ridiculous she'd done. He had such a rich, jolly laugh. Just hearing it made others happy.

She laid her head on top of his snout, wishing more than anything that she could see him one more time. Tell him, just once, exactly how much he'd meant to her and how much she loved him. "I'm so sorry, Davin."

Meaningless words that didn't even come close to soothing her or easing the agony in her heart.

At least I know where you are now.

Finally. She just wished Dash was here with her to see that she had what had meant the most to her then.

And with that thought came a wave of fury. Not at Dash, but at how they'd met. The nightmare of that afternoon in the meadow.

Her own desperation.

Most importantly, her quest that had started all this. "Where's the dragon slayer?"

"He escaped."

Those words only made her rage burn higher. "He what?"

Ronan winced. "Someone broke him out of the dungeon."

She glared at Ronan. How could that be? "I have to find him."

Determined to search every corner of the kingdom, she headed for the door.

But no sooner had she entered the hallway than a loud commotion sounded.

She had no idea what it was until the main doors flew open of their own volition and a whirlwind whipped through the hall, tearing at tapestries and weaponry, sending both of them flying. One moment she was in the hallway, and in the next she was carried away to a room somewhere else in the palace.

By the time everything stopped spinning and she could catch her bearings, she was in a dark bedroom. The crown above the bed and lavish furniture told her that it must belong to Dash.

Why am I here?

She turned around slowly, then saw Dash lying in the large bed in his unicorn form.

Joy filled her. Until she took a step closer, and his mother materialized beside him. Tears streaked down Naomi's face.

In that moment, Tanis knew exactly what had caused her awful feeling all morning.

Dash was near death.

"What happened?" she asked, choking on her own tears.

"That bitch had Renata's horn. She stabbed him with it."

Even more confused, Tanis didn't understand why Naomi was crying. "He'll be fine. He can heal himself."

"Not against a golden horn, he can't. He will be in agony until the wound kills him."

No. Tanis refused to believe those words. "What?"

Sobbing, Naomi couldn't answer.

Ryper materialized beside Tanis. He stared at Dash as if he'd never seen him before. Even so, the grief in his blue eyes was searing.

Tanis struggled to breathe. "Tell me this is a jest."

He shook his head. "This is his one weakness. A gold wand can kill any unicorn."

Even though she knew that, she shook her head in denial. "No. No! He will awaken."

Determined to prove them wrong, she went to the bed so that she could sit beside him and pick Dash's head up. "Listen to me, beast, you will wake up. Do you hear me?"

He didn't move.

A surge of raw, unmitigated agony tore through her. "Wake up, Dash! I can't lose you, too. Do you understand? You promised me! Wake up, damn you! Wake. Up!"

Then the sobs came. They were so horrific that she couldn't breathe. All she could do was lay her head down on his neck and cry.

It couldn't end like this. It couldn't. He was the High King. The baddest, meanest asshole ever born.

And his mother was the queen of the damned. How could he be defeated by something as small as his sister's stupid horn?

There had to be something one of them could do. Some magical trick or secret. Lifting her head, she looked at each of them in turn. "Don't you have anything to help him? Do something!"

"There's nothing they can do, Dragon."

Tanis gasped as she heard Dash's voice. Not from the unicorn she was holding, but from behind her. Turning

401

around on the bed, she saw a shimmery image of Dash, less than two feet away.

"Dash?"

"Only in spirit." He jerked his chin at his body. "I'm stuck there."

"Are you in pain?"

He didn't answer, which told her that it must be excruciating. "I'm sorry, Dragon. I promised I wouldn't leave you. I didn't mean to."

She turned back toward Ryper. "What is the lore of the golden horn?"

He frowned as if he didn't understand why she was asking. "It's the most powerful of all."

"Can it heal?"

The grief instantly left Ryper's gaze. "Well... yes, it can."

That renewed her hope. "Then her wand can undo this, yes?"

Ryper looked to his mother who had stopped crying. "We need that horn. What happened to it?"

"Bring me that centaur bitch! Tell Kyran I need the horn." Naomi's yokai armor left her at those words and headed for the door while Naomi remained in the room, dressed in a tunic and pants.

"Meara still has the horn?" Tanis asked Naomi.

His mother nodded.

That was all she needed. She turned to Ryper. "Where's Marthen?"

"Outside."

"Take me to him. Please."

Dash followed them. "What are you planning, Dragon?"

In short, to throttle a centaur herself. "I'm going to get

your sister's wand." And most likely shove it someplace that would make Meara regret ever coming after Dash.

He tried to pull her to a stop, but his hand went right through her body. Dash cursed.

For once, Tanis was going to get her way.

When they left the palace, she saw Dove speaking with Marthen. They both turned toward her with a frown.

Marthen's scowl deepened as he saw Dash's ghostly spirit trailing behind her.

"Make me a dragon again," she said without preamble.

Marthen cut a nervous stare toward Dash. "May I ask why?"

"I need to be intimidating." Tanis held her arms up to show him her body. "Something I'm definitely not as a human." If she were a dragon, however, she'd be able to back the centaur queen down and kill her if need be.

The oni might have a dragon-eating species... the centaurs didn't.

Marthen cocked his head as if he heard something.

Tanis glanced to Ryper to see if this was normal. The expression on Ryper's face said that it wasn't.

"What is it?" Ryper asked.

The words had barely left his lips before a dark-skinned human woman came toward them with a man she was holding by the scruff of his neck. Tanis had no idea who she or the nasty man was, but the woman carried herself as a veteran warrior.

She threw the man forward to land at Ryper's feet. "This maggot is begging to see a queen or king."

While Tanis wouldn't have called him a maggot per se, there was something creepy about the man with greasy hair and an unkempt beard. Tanis actually wanted to step away from him for his stench.

Until he pulled something out of the folds of his tattered cape, and she saw what it was.

A golden unicorn horn.

Renata's.

"Is one of you in charge?" he asked.

Before anyone could speak, Tanis had him on the ground and had wrenched the horn from his hand. "How did you get this?"

Ryper picked her up and removed her foot from the man's throat. "He can't answer if you kill him."

She wanted to fight Ryper's fierce hold but knew better than to try. "Put me down, Ryper. I mean it."

"I would obey her, were I you," Shadow Dash said. "She had me on my arse a few times."

Ryper only hesitated for a moment before he set her back on her feet. "Sorry."

Tanis went for the man again. He'd pushed himself up but was still coughing and wheezing.

Before she could reach him, the maggot moved to hide behind Dove.

Dove arched a brow. "I'm not going to protect you from her. So, you might want to come out and answer her questions."

"Is she going to hit me again?"

"Probably. If you don't step out from behind him and answer my questions, I definitely will."

He came around Dove cautiously. "My partner took it back from the queen."

"When?" Tanis asked.

"After she stabbed the High King and the Oni queen vanished with him. Queen Meara was laughing and distracted, bragging on how she was going to take the throne. While she wasn't looking, Bink grabbed it from the ground, and ran off with it. He handed it to me and told me to hold onto it until he came back."

Tanis frowned. "Why did he steal the horn from her?"

He shrugged. "She double crossed us. Seemed only fair we take back what's ours."

This time, it was Ryper who grabbed him up and shook him like a dog with a rag toy. "You killed my sister for that wand, you son of a bitch! It was *never* yours!"

Utter silence descended as everyone present heard Ryper's furious declaration over his relationship with Renata.

Even Dove looked at the Shadow Dash behind her and mouthed the words, *he's your brother?*

Too late, Ryper realized what he'd said. "Um..."

Tanis clapped him on the shoulder. "See how easy it is to slip up when you want to plant your foot in his guts?"

Ryper winced. He set the man down, then yanked the horn from his grasp. "This was *never* yours!"

The man had the good sense to look contrite. "I'm sorry. It weren't my idea. I was just doing what Bink told me to."

"Bink?" Tanis asked. "Your partner?"

"The imp I fell in with. We been collecting things for a bit now. Such as—"

Realizing this was the dragon slayer she'd been after, Tanis cut his words off as she ran right into him and tackled him to the ground. "You rotten piece of..."

Instead of Ryper, it was Dove who pulled her off him. "Everyone calm down."

"He helped kill my brother!"

Eyes wide, the smelly human held his hands up and shook his head. "Whoa, whoa, whoa... I don't kill nobody."

Tanis snorted. "You're not the one who's been bragging he's a great dragon slayer?"

"I don't kill nobody," he repeated. "But I did take credit for some folks I didn't kill." Realizing that he'd just confessed to being a fraud, he glanced around at everyone present. He cursed under his breath, then he raked his hand through his greasy hair. "I didn't slay a dragon. Bink made a deal with another dragon that we'd take the head and help her spread a lie so that none of the other dragons would know she killed him. She said that she couldn't let the dragons know she'd done the killing."

Ragna... But she had to be absolutely sure. "What dragon?"

"I don't remember her name. Rena. Reba..."

No... Shock filled her as she realized Reva hadn't been an accomplice to Ragna. She had actually done the deed herself. "Reva?"

"Yeah, that was her name. Reva."

Tanis staggered from the full weight of that news. While she'd suspected Reva had followed along with Ragna's plans as she always did, she'd never once thought that Reva would have done the actual killing.

Not of Davin.

How could you, Reva?

Stay focused...

Right now, they needed to get information from this... vermin.

He pulled a piece of paper from his pocket and held it out for her. "If it helps, Bink didn't give the centaur queen the right spell to kill the king, either. He was afraid she'd double cross him, so he double crossed her. This is the right spell to kill the High King. It's yours if you spare me life."

Before she had a chance to reach for it, Naomi came out of nowhere and seized it.

She read over it, then handed it to Marthen. "Is this right, or is he lying?"

Tanis ignored them. "Where are your accomplices?"

He shrugged. "Don't know. Bink gave me the wand to hold when the queen started to run him down... it was horrible. I hid to where they couldn't find me. As soon as they were gone, I came here through the elf portal."

Dove arched a brow. "And you thought you'd be safer with us?"

"I brung the wand and spell for the High King. Isn't there a reward for it?"

Ryper went for him again, but Dove held the human while Ronan grabbed Ryper.

"Stop it!" Ronan snapped at Ryper as he held him in one giant fist. "Think of your brother. We need the wand."

That finally succeeded in calming him.

Shadow Dash glared at the human. "Lock him in the dungeon for now."

"No! Not again!" Fort whined.

Marthen moved toward them and held the parchment out to Naomi. "There's something not right about this spell."

Dove hesitated with Fort.

"What does that mean?" Tanis asked.

"These aren't the right items to kill him."

Ryper pulled out Renata's wand, then paled. "This isn't a golden wand, either." He held his hand up for them to see the gold that had come off in his palm. "It's a fake."

Tanis's stomach shrank at the sight. "It's a white horn." Hopefully one taken from a dead unicorn and not an innocent child.

The human paled. "He double crossed me?"

Dove smirked. "You're surprised?"

His eyes darkened with fury. "He's after the king's horn. Said it was more powerful and for me to distract you while he cut it from the king's head."

That news hit Tanis like a slap.

Dear gods! She turned toward the Shadow Dash, but he was gone. Terror consumed her as she ran back through the palace to Dash's bedroom.

As soon as she reached it, she threw open the doors.

To her complete horror, there was an imp on the bed, sawing through Dash's horn with a dagger.

"No!" She ran at the grimy little varmint. "Get away from him."

The imp turned on her with a hiss. "You want to fight?" He motioned her to come at him as he held his dagger out toward her.

Tanis backed up...

Until she remembered the armor she was wearing. With a fierce roar, she ran at him. He slashed at her arm, but her armor caught the weapon and kept it.

Gasping, he tried to run, but she wasn't having any of

that. She caught him and was planning to toss him on the ground. Instead, he flipped up and the spindles on his head slashed her across the face.

She hissed in pain.

He pulled out Renata's horn and plunged it deep into her shoulder. Unlike his dagger, it penetrated her armor. Koji screamed in pain.

Honestly, she felt like crying out, too, as her shoulder throbbed.

But there was no way she was going to allow this creature to leave this room with that wand. Not when it meant so much to Dash.

The imp twirled it in his hand. "What's the matter? Afraid of an imp?" He lunged at her.

Tanis caught his wrist and stepped into arms, using her weight to knock him off balance. The two of them went crashing to the floor. With both hands on his wrist, she made sure to keep him from stabbing her again while she wrestled him for that wand.

The wretched bastard wrapped his other hand in her hair, jerked her head back and bit her in the neck.

Furious, she headed butted him as she twisted his hand and finally wrenched the wand loose.

The moment she did, he shrank in size and ran toward the window.

Turning into a hawk, Ronan scooped him up with his claws. The imp immediately grew large, causing Ronan to fall.

Slippery little bastard. Tanis slid across the room, knocking him off his feet. With no other weapon, she stabbed him with Renata's horn.

The moment she did, he burst into a thousand cinders.

Whoa! Was that what would have happened to her had she not been wearing enchanted armor?

The thought was terrifying.

But she didn't have time to think about it as she heard Naomi gasp. Her heart pounding, she returned to the bed to see the blood flowing from the wound the imp had made on Dash's horn by trying to remove it.

"No, no, no," she breathed. Tanis had to find a way to heal him.

She looked across the room to where Marthen and Ryper stood. "I know this stupid wand can do something. Don't tell me it can't." Tears blinded her.

Desperate, Tanis glanced to the ceiling. "Renata? If you can hear me, Dash said that some of you is still in this wand. If it's true, help me save him. Please."

As if it could hear her, the wand heated up in her hand and began to glow.

Unsure of what to do, Tanis held it next to Dash's horn on his forehead.

At first nothing happened.

Then, the color of his black horn began to fade to white.

Naomi shook her head. "He's dying."

Tanis refused to believe that. "What?"

Ryper swallowed hard before he spoke. "When they're still attached to our bodies, our horns return to white as we die. It's why poachers have to cut our horns off while we're alive."

"Which also kills a unicorn," Halla said with a sob.

Her heart pounded as she realized that Ryper was right. Dash's horn was losing all its color. It was already gray.

"Do something!" she demanded of Marthen.

"I know of nothing to do. Only Renata or a black horn can access the magick of her wand."

Sobbing even harder, Tanis crawled up on the bed beside Dash. She couldn't lose him. Not like this. "Damn it, beast! You are not leaving me. Do you hear? You're not going to die! I forbid it! I don't want to be alone anymore."

Don't leave me. Please.

She didn't have anyone else.

She didn't belong anywhere else.

I don't want to be with anyone, but you. Ever.

More tears fell until she was blinded from them. Still holding the wand, she wiped at them, then curled herself around Dash's body and touched the horrid gash on his horn.

"Please stay with me, beast." The moment she whispered those words, sparks flew from Renata's wand and drifted over him.

Stunned, Tanis held her breath as the color began to fade from Renata's horn to mix with Dash's. Black and gold swirled and danced along his spiral until his horn darkened.

Then, the most miraculous thing of all happened...

The inside of his horn was its original ebony, but the outer ridges were now a shimmering gold, as was the tip.

"What the hell?" Ryper stepped forward.

An instant later, Dash opened his eyes as Renata's wand turned snow white in Tanis's hand.

Unsure of what had happened, Tanis sat there completely frozen.

Halla flew to their side. "Sire... Your horn. It's two colors."

"What?" Dash asked.

Marthen manifested a mirror and stepped forward with it to show Dash. "Your horn is now black and gold. Has anyone ever seen or heard of this?"

Everyone in the room shook their head. Dash changed into his human form so that he could hold his wand in his hand and examine it. He ran his hand reverently over the golden edge of the spiral. "Dragon tears," he whispered.

Tanis scowled. "What?"

Laughing, he cupped her cheek in his hand. "We all forgot about the magical power of dragon tears. There's nothing stronger than a dragon's love."

"But I'm not a dragon."

Brushing her hair back from her cheek, he smiled at her. "Your body may be human, but you still have the heart and soul of a dragon." He rubbed his cheek against hers. "Your precious tears saved me, Dragon."

Laughing, she wrapped her arms around him. "Don't you ever die on me again, beast!"

Dash pulled back to look at the group in his room. "Would the lot of you give us a few minutes alone?"

Halla crossed her arms over her chest. "I'm thinking you two need a chaperone."

Dash narrowed an evil glare at her. "Don't make me pull your wings off, goblin."

Halla turned herself into a regular-sized human so that she could hug Dash. "I'm glad you're here to threaten me again, Sire."

One by one, they filed out of the room.

Dash wiped the tears from her face, then held his hand

up so that he could stare at the moisture on his skin. "I hate that I made you cry."

"If it really saved your life, I'm glad that you did."

His expression turned soft and loving as he stared at her in awe. "What are we going to do, Dragon?"

"How do you mean?"

"Our pact... for you to return to your body, you have to kill the one who murdered your brother."

Not the human dragon slayer she'd made the pact to kill. Her sister.

Tanis felt the color drain from her face. She was going to have to kill Reva in order to become a dragon again. That was something she'd never planned on or thought about when she'd made that deal with Dash.

Davin's killer was supposed to be a human she hated. Not an older sister she loved.

What have I done?

But as she looked up into those clear, green eyes, she realized that being a dragon would mean never staring into those eyes again. Never snuggling with him or sitting in his lap as she was currently doing.

"What's wrong, Dragon?"

"Did you mean what you said to me?"

"I never say anything I don't mean."

She reached up to playfully tug at his hair. "Maybe being human isn't so bad, then... I've kind of gotten used to it."

He smiled a smile that warmed her all the way to her toes.

Until she thought of something else. Then, she went completely cold as her happiness evaporated. He would need a unicorn bride.

"What's wrong?"

"N-nothing." She started to get off the bed.

Dash pulled her back into his arms. "I know you, Dragon. What demons are in your head now?"

She licked her lips as she faced a horrible fact. "I no longer have any place that I belong."

He gave her a stern glower. "You're exactly where you belong. But I won't force you to stay with me. That's not my decision. It's yours. If you are sure you won't miss being a dragon..."

"But what would I be here?" His mistress? The very thought made her sick. She couldn't bear the reality that he would have to marry and have children.

With someone else.

Swallowing the pain, she met his gaze levelly. "You never did answer that question, Dash."

His frown deepened. "What do you think I'm offering you?"

"I can't stay here and watch you marry someone else, beast. It would kill me."

His mouth began to work like a fish dragged from its watery nest. "Why would you ever think I'd ask that of you?"

"Then what?"

"Marry me, silly dragon. There's no one else I'd ever have as my queen."

For a full minute, she couldn't move or breathe. Was he serious? "Really?"

"Of course. I love you, Tanis. I told you that."

"Really?" she repeated.

Laughing, he pulled her against him and gave her a kiss so hot that it stole her breath. "Yes, Dragon. Marry me."

"Would you say yes already, Highness? The two of you are making me seasick... and nauseated for another reason."

Tanis covered her face as she remembered that her armor was sentient. "Yes," she said from behind her hands.

Dash gently lowered her hands so that he could rub his nose against hers. "One day, my precious queen, I hope you'll value yourself as much as I value you." Then, to her greatest shock, he held up his wand and turned it into a beautiful charm. He manifested a bracelet for her.

"In our kingdom, whenever unicorns are in love, they exchange their wands with their beloved as a sign of ultimate trust." He held the bracelet up for her to see it. "Of course, my father never allowed anyone else to hold his. But I'm not my father." He fastened the bracelet around her wrist.

Tanis couldn't believe her eyes. He trusted her completely.

And in that moment, she realized how much she trusted him in return. How funny that she'd met him while seeking death and instead, he'd given her life.

A life she'd never dreamed of having. It was miraculous and amazing.

A dragon and a unicorn.

Even if she never took her dragon body again, she could live in absolute ecstasy.

And all because she'd dared something the old Tanis would never have done. She went after her future and found it.

All she needed now was the courage to see it through.

"I love you, Deciel Coeur de Noir." Black heart, demon and unicorn.

"And I love you, Tanis Dragomir. Now and forever. No one will ever hurt you again."

She knew that was true because for the first time in her life, she had a real, proven champion.

Tears of joy filled her as she realized something. Her first champion, Davin, had led her to Dash. Even in death, her brother had kept her safe.

It might sound silly, but she felt as if Davin was watching and approving.

For the first time, she had a future in the sunlight. Not one of solitude and hiding. And she was going to embrace it with both hands, no matter how scary it might seem.

CHAPTER 25

Dash, Tanis, Halla, and Ryper stood in the room where Ryper had preserved Renata's body.

His heart broken, Dash knelt by her side. "I'd hoped to have enough of her essence left to talk to her one more time."

Tanis placed a gentle hand on his shoulder. "I'm sure she knew how much you loved her."

"I still can't get over our fight. The things I said that I didn't mean."

Ryper moved to the other side of Dash. "Have you tried to use your horn?"

"What?"

"It's gold and black. No one knows the powers you hold now. Use your wand to see if you can summon her."

Ryper was right. His wand should have powers from both colors. Not to mention the fact that Dash wasn't completely a unicorn. He was part oni. He might have the ability to summon her essence.

Tanis carefully pulled Dash's horn charm off her bracelet and handed it to him.

Using his powers, he enlarged the wand to its full size. "Here goes nothing."

Tanis bit her lip as Dash's eyes began to glow. More than that, sparks flew from the horn in much the way they'd done when he made her human.

At first, she thought nothing would happen. But as the sparks went to a shadow, she realized that it had taken the shape of a young woman.

Renata's spirit slowly manifested there.

Her breath caught at how beautiful she was with long black hair like Dash's.

Regal and poised, Renata looked around as if in a daze. "Dash? Ryper?"

"Hey, dart donkey," Dash said affectionately in a trembling voice. "I've missed you."

A sad smile tugged at the edges of her lips. "I'm so sorry, Dash. I was stupid not to listen to your warnings. I knew you weren't cruel, and I am sorry for that, too."

"No... you were being you, and I shouldn't have yelled at you for it. I'm the one who's sorry."

Her gaze went to his wand and her brows drew together sharply. "What did you do to your horn?"

"I broke it."

She shook her head. "That's not broken. You've changed. And it looks like it confused your wand."

Dash chuckled. "You said I was always confusing."

"You were. An awful mixture of 'kill them all' and 'protect everyone.'" Then, her gaze went to Ryper. "I love you, too, brother. I'm sorry I never told you that I knew you were Dash's twin."

Ryper's jaw went slack. "How?"

"How can anyone not know? You two are just alike. My mother told me that Dash had a twin that his mother kept with her in her kingdom. She was worried that one day you'd come here and steal my father's affection from me. When I was little, I assumed you were identical... until the day you finally came home with Dash. I knew instantly you were the one from Tenmaru."

"I wish I'd known that you knew."

"Don't regret it, big brother. Neither of you." Her gaze went to Halla. "Or you, my dearest friend. I should have listened to you, too."

"I wish I'd known you were leaving that night. I would have told Dash and saved you."

Renata shook her head. "Regret nothing," she repeated. "I made my choice. I'm just sorry that it hurt all of you."

Then, she met Tanis's gaze. "At least I get to meet you. I just wish we could have been sisters. Please take care of my brothers for me, Tanis. They need someone to watch over them and keep them from being stupid."

Tanis laughed at that, until she realized something. "How do you know my name?"

Renata smiled. "I will always be with my family. Even though you don't see me, I'm never far away." And with that, she blew them a kiss and vanished.

Tears filled her eyes. "You were right, Dash. She is gentle and sweet."

Ryper wiped at his eyes. "Not all the time. Trust me, she

had her moments that would test the patience of the gods. But, yeah. She was precious."

Dash moved to the left side of Renata's body while Ryper stood on the right. "Are we ready to send her off to her Sweet Meadow?"

Ryper nodded.

Biting her lip, Tanis knew the Sweet Meadow was the unicorn paradise realm that they all hoped to go to after they died.

Halla came over to her and held her hand while the two of them used their powers to disintegrate her body and return its essence to the universe.

Their funereal custom was so different from what she was used to. Dragons held feasts for days before they carried the body of their loved one to the catacombs where they would rest with their ancestors. It was imperative for dragons to remain intact for eternity.

The thought of cremation was terrifying to her people.

Which was why she still needed to return Davin's skull to Marla.

But this, they needed to take care of first. The last thing a unicorn wanted was for a trophy hunter to use any part of their remains for a spell.

As they left the room, they were greeted by Naomi and the elves who had yet to return home.

Mostly because Naomi wanted to secure Dash's throne while they went to Indara. And since the elves didn't know she was his mother, they didn't trust her not to usurp it in Dash's absence.

So here they all remained.

While they now knew that Ryper was Dash's brother, no one knew who their mother was.

Naomi inclined her head to them. "It's done?"

They nodded.

Dash put his arm around Tanis's shoulders. "We're going to take care of the dragon slayer and then we'll head to Indara. We shouldn't be gone long."

Baldur flashed a grin at Dash. "Not saying or wishing for anything bad to happen to you, Sire. But if... say it did. Who is heir?"

Dash snorted at his question. "Ryper."

All the color faded from Baldur's face as he stepped back. "Seriously?"

Ryper grinned. "Good. I always wanted to be king." He turned around and winked at Dash. "I think my first law will be to torture elves."

Dove smirked at him. "Not funny."

Ryper gave him a droll stare. "You don't count, Dove. Besides, you're only half elf."

"So they tell me," Dove said drily. "On both accounts."

Ignoring them, Dash pulled Tanis down the hallway that led to the dungeon where the dragon slayer had been imprisoned.

It was a cold, dank place. Tanis placed her hand to her nose to help blot out some of the stench. She'd ask Dash what that smell was, but she didn't really want to know.

As they rounded a corner, Dash froze mid step.

"Something wrong?"

He didn't say a word as he went to one of the cells to look inside it. "Keryna?"

Filthy and ragged, with bruises all over her, she ran to the bars. "Majesty? Have you come to free me?"

Dash didn't say a word, but by the furious tic in his jaw, Tanis knew he had no intention of freeing her.

Murdering her, maybe. Letting her go...

Never.

Without a word, Dash turned sharply and led Tanis to the cell where the human named Fort was being kept.

Fort looked as hopeful as Keryna. "Majesty! You're alive!"

"No thanks to you."

That took the joy out of his grimy face. "Am I to be executed?"

Dash looked at her. "His fate is in your hands, my love. Whatever you want, I grant."

Tanis had spent so much time wanting his life that she'd almost allowed it to destroy hers.

But as she stared at the awful wretch she wanted to hate, she actually felt sorry for him. According to what he'd told them, his brownie partner Dreama had abandoned him. Bink was dead.

Fort was alone.

As much trouble as he'd caused, he wasn't the one who'd killed Davin. Hurting him wouldn't accomplish anything. After all, he was an arrogant braggart tool.

He wasn't worth the price of dung. And after this, she'd never again think of him.

"I thought I wouldn't be able to live so long as he had life in his bones. Now..." She sighed heavily. "I realize how insignificant he is. Let him go free."

Dash's jaw went slack.

"But not in Licordia," she added. "He should be set free in Thassalia."

"No!" Fort gasped. "They'll kill me!"

They might. But that wasn't her problem or her concern.

Dash kissed her hand. "My queen has spoken." He waved his wand and used his powers to transport Fort to Meara's court where she had fled to after her battle.

Meara thought herself safe, but she wasn't.

Not by a long shot.

Her days were numbered, she just didn't know it.

Then, Dash turned to face her. "Will you do me a favor, Tanis? Please return upstairs and send Ryper down here."

A bad feeling went through her as she suspected why he wanted Ryper in the dungeon. "Do you want me to return with him?"

"Please don't."

Oh yeah. She was right. He had something awful planned for Keryna.

But he had his reasons, and she wasn't going to interfere. She kissed him on his cheek and headed for the stairs.

While Dash had come a long way from the beast she'd first met, he still had a long way to go.

Yet in this, she wouldn't judge him, nor would she begrudge him his vengeance.

So, she returned upstairs and found Ryper. "Dash needs you in the dungeon."

He actually paled. "Why?"

"For something I think you'll enjoy."

Ryper appeared skeptical, but he went to join his brother anyway.

While Tanis waited for them, she saw her mother-in-law heading toward her.

That intense look on her face and in her stormy blue eyes sent a shiver down her spine. "Is something wrong, Majesty?"

Naomi smiled and her eyes instantly turned friendly. "No. But I do want to give you a gift." She handed her a small wooden box.

Engraved in gold and heavily carved, it was exquisite. She was honored to have such a beautiful gift.

"Thank you, Majesty."

She tsked. "Open the box, silly girl."

Tanis lifted the lid to find a small vial of yellow liquid inside. "What's this?"

Naomi looked over her shoulder at her brother. "Something we came up with for you."

"It's a wedding present." Marthen smiled.

That made her a bit more nervous. "What do I do with it?"

"Drink it." Naomi removed the top from it and handed it to her.

Tanis hesitated. While she trusted Dash implicitly, she wasn't so sure about the rest of his family. Could this be poison? She had no way of knowing.

But the last thing she wanted to do was insult them.

They looked expectant. Not dangerous. Maybe it would fine...

With a deep breath for courage, she lifted it to her lips and quickly drank it down. Bitter and nasty, it made her grimace in distaste. "Bleh!"

Laughing, Naomi took the vial from her hand and returned it to the box.

"May I ask what it is I just drank?" Tanis had barely finished those words before her stomach began to rumble and cramp. Suddenly, she felt sick.

Terribly sick.

What did they do to me?

Eyes wide, she ran for the door to the courtyard outside. She was going to vomit. She knew it.

Tanis barely made it through the doors before she ...

Belched?

Yeah, that was it. She belched.

Then an instant later, she was huge. No... not huge. She was a dragon!

Tears misted her eyes as she looked down on the palace and made sure to lift her tail so as not to hurt anyone or destroy anything.

She was a dragon! Joy spread through her.

Until...

Reality sank into her with a vicious bite. If she were a dragon, she couldn't have Dash.

No. No. No! Panic consumed her as she realized in that moment that she didn't want this. Not at the cost of losing him.

"Breathe, Tanis," Naomi said from the ground. "Close your eyes and wish to be human again."

What? Why?

Not quite sure about that, she did as the queen suggested. And an instant later, she was again in her human body.

Shocked to the core of her soul, she lifted her arms up

and saw the same blue kirtle she'd been wearing before she became a dragon.

Naomi rubbed her on the back. "Just as a unicorn can change, so can you. That is our wedding gift."

Wait... were they saying what she thought they were? "I'm a shape-shifter?"

Marthen smiled at her. "Sort of. It's the same magick that originally changed the unicorns. We found the spell for it in an old archive. You can only be a dragon or a human. But the choice of form is completely yours to make from this day forward."

She hugged him and then Naomi. "Thank you both so much!"

Naomi smoothed her hair. "As I told you, take care of Deciel for me and you will have many gifts. But I should warn you of one thing."

"That is?"

"Be careful shifting while pregnant. You don't want to harm your baby."

"I'm not pregnant."

"Not yet." Marthen grinned. "But I know a future where you will be."

She couldn't wait.

Tanis was still thanking them when Dash and Ryper joined them.

There was a steely somberness to both of them that was a bit unsettling.

"Are you ready to return to Indara?" Dash asked.

Maybe. In his current mood, she wasn't so sure. "I think so."

He assumed his unicorn form, complete with an ornate saddle and reins that were designed for her comfort.

Ryper lifted her up and set her in the saddle.

She didn't miss the sight of a blood smear on his hand. Nor the look of satisfaction in his eyes.

"We'll be back as soon as we can," Dash said.

Ryper inclined his head to him. "I'll hold down your rebellions until your return."

Dash sighed. "Thanks."

The group stepped back so that Dash could take flight and head for her former home.

Once they were alone, Tanis leaned over his neck. "Should I ask about Keryna?"

"Probably not. Suffice it to say, she won't be manipulating anyone else for the rest of eternity."

"Fair enough." She couldn't blame him at all. Had Fort been responsible for Davin's death, he would have probably met the same fate.

No... he would have met a worse one.

And neither of them spoke again until they reached the foothills of the Pyrigian Lands that weren't too far from Licordia. Keegan was waiting for them there when Dash landed beside her.

"I thought the two of you were right behind me?"

Tanis dismounted. "Sorry. Something came up." She moved away from Dash before she resumed her dragon body.

Dash stepped back and eyed her. "Someone kept a secret."

"Not really. Naomi and Marthen gave this to me while I was waiting on you and Ryper."

"Ah."

She took her brother's skull from Keegan, then let out a war cry.

Within a few minutes, Marla's father's soldiers had them surrounded.

"What are you doing here?" the commander of the group asked as they walked a threatening circle around them.

"I am Princess Tanis Dragomir—"

Dash cleared his throat, reminding her that she was no longer a princess.

"And High Queen Tanis Coeur de Noir of Licordia. I have brought a gift for the Regent Queen of Indara."

It was only then that Marla pushed her way through the men, and she realized her sister-in-law had flown in with the group. "Tanis? Is that really you?"

She nodded as soon as she saw her, then she held out her front paws so that Marla could see Davin's skull. "I promised I'd return him to you and your children." Then, Tanis turned toward Keegan who held her father's skull. "As well as my father's head that was brutally taken."

Gasping, Marla drew up short. "So, it's true. They really did kill the king."

Tanis nodded. "Reva was the one who killed Davin. Ragna killed our father."

Marla's gaze went to Dash then back to her. "And are you here to challenge me for my crown?"

Tanis shook her head. "I have my own to look after, and I intend to return there immediately. I only came to fulfill my promise to you."

Marla took Davin's skull and cradled it to her chest. The

gratitude in her eyes was searing. "You are always welcome here, Tanis. My kingdom is your home should you ever need it."

"Thank you. But all I want is for you to swear fealty to my husband."

"Husband?" Marla looked around at the dragons.

Dash cleared his throat to get her attention.

Marla gasped. "Forgive me, Sire. I didn't see you there."

"All good. I'm just glad no one stepped on me."

Smiling at that, Tanis returned to her human body. "I wish you well, sister. I know you'll see justice done in the name of my father and brother." But she didn't want to witness it. For better or worse, Reva and Ragna were her sisters.

And while she should hate them for what they'd done, she didn't. Had it not been for them, she would never have met her unicorn.

Marla bowed to Dash. "The Indarians are forever loyal, Your Majesty."

"Thank you, Your Highness."

Marla smiled at Tanis. "Be happy, little sister. May the gods grant you a home full of hatchlings."

"Thank you, Marla. May the gods smile on you and keep you in their safety."

And with that, Dash took them home.

THEY DIDN'T TALK MUCH, and luckily, it wasn't that long a journey. But it was a beautiful one as they went over the

Windy Crossing waters that separated Indara from Licordia.

When Tanis had been a young hatchling, she'd dreamed of flying over this area where it was forbidden because it was a shared border with Licordia, and her father had always feared the unicorns breaking their truce.

The winds here were said to make a dragon's wings stronger.

She'd never once imagined she'd be making the journey while riding on someone else. But that was okay. She didn't mind in the least.

In fact, Dash made everything better.

And once they were home, Ryper actually pouted. "I feel robbed. I didn't even get to rough up a single elf while you were gone. They all behaved."

"You'll get over it. Besides, I'm sure someone could incite a riot from Tova or her children."

Ryper laughed. "Where's Chrys? She's good at that."

Dash shook his head. "Don't disturb her quite yet."

"Why?"

"We're not finished, brother."

Ryper's expression turned serious. "Meara."

Dash nodded. "For now, she thinks her kingdom protects her."

The fire returned to Ryper's gaze. "Are you telling us that we finally get to skin a centaur?"

"Long time coming. But yes. We're going to skin a centaur. I need Chrys and Ronan to find Xaydin. It's time to break a contract."

CHAPTER 26

THREE WEEKS LATER

Ronan entered the Vaskalian tavern that sat on the border with Sagaria. Vaskalia was the home kingdom of trolls, ogres and giants. Sagaria was ruled by a sidhe court.

The Wounded Whelp tavern was set with one half of its building in Sagaria and the other half in Vaskalia. Their border ran right through the center of it. As a result, it was a haven for both kingdoms and for other creatures who were passing by.

Of all the places in the Thirteen Kingdoms for Xaydin to have taken up residence, it had to be this one.

A filthy hole in the mud, with some of deadliest patrons imaginable.

Of course, Xaydin would be renting here.

Why would Ronan expect anything else from a former crown prince whose father had been murdered?

And he saw his target the minute he lowered his hood.

In the farthest corner, with his back to the wall. Xaydin was impossible to miss. His jet-black hair held a bluish tint in the dim light, and it matched the ornate leather armor he wore. Those stern well-chiseled features usually caused any woman, and some men, to gravitate toward him and lose their senses.

Until they realized that he didn't have much of a sense of humor nor did he ever want company.

At least not the company of strangers.

And the instant he looked up and saw Ronan, his eyes turned vibrant red.

"What do you want, Ro?"

No preamble. All business. That was Xaydin.

"Something you're going to enjoy."

Xaydin scoffed. "That is a mighty small list and conversation isn't on it."

Ronan laughed as he sat down across from him. "I know. But Dash has a favor to ask."

Xaydin drained his cup then sat back and crossed his arms over his chest. "I'm listening."

"He has an *apaswere* he wants you to kill."

One jet-black eyebrow shot north. "Now I'm really listening."

"Dash wants to go after Meara. He needs you to execute the *apaswere* with their treaty on it."

A slow, evil smile spread across his face. "Done."

"Don't you need any more information?"

Xaydin shook his head. "Killing *apaswere* is what I live for. It's at the top of my very short fun list." And with that, he stood up, tossed coins on the table and headed for the door.

"Is that it?"

Xaydin turned around at the door and lifted the hood of his black cloak. "I'll send him the head once I finish."

EPILOGUE

Meara paced her office as she tried to think of what to do. She'd gambled and lost.

And they'd be coming for her.

Not just Dash, but all of the survivors of her first attempt to take Licordia.

Damn.

But first, she had to find the *apaswere* demon who held her treaty with Dash. So long as that demon lived, Dash couldn't enter her lands with an army or without an invitation from her.

If she knew that bastard, and she did, Dash would have already sent out his assassins to kill the demon and end their treaty.

Granted, it was almost impossible to kill one.

But it wasn't *completely* impossible.

With the skills and abilities of those remnants he called allies, she had no doubt that one of them could kill an *apaswere*.

Her only hope was to locate it and hold it here, out of Dash's reach.

Her spies were looking. So far nothing.

A knock sounded on her door.

"Enter."

As expected, it was Adsel. But he didn't appear pleased.

"What's wrong?"

"There are no more reports from our spies. We think they might have been found and killed."

"Then send more," she snapped.

"Yes, my queen." He hesitated in the doorway.

"Is there anything else?"

"The general was asking about Ferox. Are we planning to try and rescue him?"

Meara scoffed at the thought. "He failed me. Let him rot with the unicorns."

"Very good, my queen." He started for the door.

"Wait, Adsel."

He immediately paused. "Yes?"

"Send a hired assassin after Ferox. The last thing I want is for them to get information from him."

Adsel's eyes widened at the ferocity of her command, but he had the wisdom to keep his opinion to himself. "Yes, my queen."

Meara didn't care what he thought of her. His job was to serve.

As for her son...

She felt a degree of sadness, but it was overridden by her disappointment. Ferox had known better than to fail.

He had six brothers who were all chomping to take his

place. Now it was time for them to show her if they were worthy of her throne.

TANIS LAY in bed with Dash while the dawning light threw shadows on their walls. They'd received word yesterday that her sisters had been executed.

It still hurt. But mostly because of the betrayal.

She'd never understand how they could have turned on the parent and brother who'd loved them so much. None of it made sense.

"What are you thinking, my queen?"

She forced down her morbid thoughts to smile at him. "I was wondering about our children. If they'll be dragons or unicorns or both."

"No telling. Ryper and I are half oni and we don't have horns."

"You have one," she reminded him.

He laughed, then pulled her hand down to a certain part of his anatomy. "Two whenever you're near me."

She rolled her eyes at his jest while she cupped him and watched the pleasure she gave him play across those handsome features.

A sudden tapping on the window interrupted them.

Dash growled as he realized it was either Ronan or Chrys. "That just put me in a foul mood."

She laughed at his awful pun.

Getting up from the bed, he manifested a robe and went to the window to find Ronan there. "What?"

"Sorry for interrupting."

"No, you're not."

He didn't know how Ronan managed it in his hawk form, but he actually grinned. "No, I'm not. Mostly because I'm freezing my bird sac off while you're lounging around in comfort."

"I am your king, you know?"

"I know. But I'm too valuable for you to kill... for now."

Dash let out an irritated sigh. "Is there a point to your visit?"

"There is. I found Xaydin."

That filled him with more joy than it should have. "Is he after the *apaswere*?"

"He is, indeed. I've never seen him giddy before. It actually scared me."

"Yeah. He's not a fan."

"Any idea why?"

Dash shrugged. "Killing them is his calling."

Ronan shivered. "Anyway, he said he'd send the head to you once he found and executed the right *apaswere*."

"Good. Thank you, Ronan."

"My pleasure." He started away, then paused. "By the way, I came across an old man while I was tracking down Xaydin."

"And?"

"Told me to tell you 'thank you' for making him human."

Stunned, Dash stared at him. "What?"

"His name was Thomas Drake. Said he'd made a deal with you back when he was a gryphon, and you tried to talk him out of it. He wanted you to know that he had no regrets."

Huh. That was the last thing Dash had ever expected to hear. For reasons unknown, it did make him feel good to know that Drake wasn't out there, holding a grudge.

"Let me know if you need anything." This time, Ronan took off.

Still amazed, Dash turned to find Tanis standing a few feet away.

"Was Thomas Drake the man you made a human?"

"He was."

That made her smile. Until she looked out the window. "So, you're going to war with Meara?"

"We're all going to war with Meara. But that's not what I want to think about right now." He reached out for Tanis.

She caught his wrist in her hand. "Before you make that decision, there's something you should know."

His heart skipped a beat at the warning note in her voice. "What?"

She led his hand to her stomach. "I'm pregnant."

Joy tore through him. "Are you sure?"

She nodded. "Your mother confirmed it."

He couldn't believe it.

Pregnant.

"Then I have an even greater reason to secure the kingdoms."

"Just remember, Dash, I don't want to raise our child alone. The baby will need a father."

"And I'll be the best father who ever lived."

Tanis smiled at those words. He meant them. And if he was half as wonderful at being a father as he was a husband, their child would be beyond lucky.

He pulled her into his arms and hugged her close. "I will restore peace, Dragon."

She had no doubt of him or their future.

Peace.

Happiness.

Family.

She was going to make sure of it.

Also by Sherrilyn Kenyon
(Listed in Correct Reading Order)

Myths & Outlaws

House of Fire and Magic

Nick Chronicles

Infinity

Invincible

Infamous

Inferno

Illusion

Instinct

Invision

Intensity

Shadows of Fire

Sabotage

Last Christmas

Savage

Simi

The League

Born of Night

Born of Fire

Born of Ice

ABOUT THE AUTHOR

Defying all odds is what #1 New York Times and international bestselling author Sherrilyn Kenyon does best. Rising from extreme poverty as a child that culminated in being a homeless mother with an infant, she has become one of the most popular and influential authors in the world (in both adult and young adult fiction), with dedicated legions of fans known as  Paladins—thousands of whom proudly sport tattoos from her numerous genre-defying series.

Since her first book debuted in 1993 while she was still in college, she has placed more than 80 novels on the New York Times list in all formats and genres, including manga and graphic novels, and has more than 70 million books in print worldwide. Her current series include: Dark-Hunters®, Chronicles of Nick®, Deadman's Cross™, Black Hat Society™, Nevermore™, Silent Swans™, Lords of Avalon® and, The League®.

Over the years, her Lords of Avalon® novels have been

adapted by Marvel, and her Dark-Hunters® and Chronicles of Nick® are New York Times bestselling manga and comics and are #1 bestselling adult coloring books.

Join her and her Paladins online at QueenofAllShadows.com and www.facebook.com/mysherrilyn.

Printed in the USA
CPSIA information can be obtained
at www.ICGtesting.com
LVHW090850230924
791853LV00005B/97/J